EIGHT TALES FROM THE MAJOR PHASE

BOOKS BY HENRY JAMES
IN NORTON PAPERBACK

*The Ambassadors
*The American
Eight Tales from the Major Phase
"In the Cage" and Others
*The Portrait of a Lady
*The Turn of the Screw
*The Wings of the Dove

*A Norton Critical Edition

EIGHT TALES FROM THE MAJOR PHASE:
IN THE CAGE & OTHERS

Henry James

EDITED, AND WITH AN INTRODUCTION

BY MORTON DAUWEN ZABEL

W · W · NORTON & COMPANY

New York · London

W. W. Norton & Company, Inc.
500 Fifth Avenue, New York, N.Y. 10110
www.wwnorton.com

W. W. Norton & Company Ltd.
Castle House, 75/76 Wells Street, London W1T 3QT

ISBN 0-393-00286-1

567890

CONTENTS

INTRODUCTION

In the Cage, the short novel that lends its title to this collection of eight tales of Henry James's high maturity, has always been one of his most fascinating works among a large number of his devotees. Most of them would probably not hesitate to rank it with *Daisy Miller*, "The Aspern Papers," "The Lesson of the Master," "The Turn of the Screw," and "The Beast in the Jungle" as one of his masterpieces of the *nouvelle* kind—"the beautiful and blest *nouvelle*" which he cultivated with special enthusiasm and raised to its first point of mastery in English fiction. Certainly the tale gave him an occasion to exercise the "controlled and guarded acceptance," the "perfect economic mastery," he always felt as a challenge in the form: another opportunity in which "the general sense of the expansive, the explosive principle in [his] material" could be "adroitly allowed to flush and colour and animate the disputed value, but with its other appetites and treacheries, its characteristic space-hunger and space-cunning, kept down." Yet this brilliant story has been oddly neglected by readers and publishers—and by the general reader, we may suppose, for the simple reason that for fifty years James's American publishers have failed to restore it to print. Not even the excited acclaim of his art during the past two decades has prompted a revival of it. In any tracing of James's later career and powers, however, *In the Cage* joins with the other searching books he produced in rapid succession in the second half of the 1890s—*The Other House, The Spoils of Poynton, What Maisie Knew,* "The Turn of the Screw," *The Awkward Age*—to mark the steps by which, now that he had put behind him the five-year misadventure of his efforts to become a successful writer of plays, he initiated the final and triumphant phase of his genius.

Written in the earlier months of 1898 and never serialized in a magazine—James gives no account of its origin or evolution in his surviving *Notebooks*—the tale was first published as a book in London on August 8 of that year and in America on September 26 by Herbert S. Stone and Company, the remarkable Chicago firm which, begun in 1893 as Stone and Kimball, quickly became the leading sponsor of *avant-garde* writing in the United States and with its pioneer "little magazine," *The Chap-Book,* did so much to exhibit the new international activity in literature to American readers. In London, James had recently appeared among the *avant-garde* writers of *The Yellow Book.* Now, during his two years' enlistment under Stone's imprint, he joined company with such then unknown or little-known writers as Ibsen, Shaw, Yeats, George Moore, Wells, Santayana, Max Beerbohm, Maeterlinck, Verlaine and the Symbolists, and the new school of American realists—Hamlin Garland, Harold Frederic, Robert Herrick—to give Chicago its first proud moment in the vanguard of modern writing. (Another was to come in 1912 when Harriet Monroe's *Poetry,* Lindsay, Sandburg, Masters, Sherwood Anderson, and their midwestern colleagues made the city what Mencken was to call, in a much-boasted accolade, "the literary capital of the United States.") *What Maisie Knew* had been serialized in *The Chap-Book* and then published as a book by Stone in 1897. *In the Cage* followed it the next year.[1] When the firm was dissolved in 1905 its booklist was bought by Fox, Duffield and Company of New York, by whom a second issue of *In the Cage* was printed from the

[1] For an excellent account of this firm and James's part in it see *A History of Stone and Kimball and Herbert S. Stone and Company* by Sidney Kramer (Chicago: Norman W. Forgue and University of Chicago Press, 1940).

original plates in 1906. Then, except for its inclusion in the
New York Edition of James's *Novels and Tales* published
by Scribners in 1907–9 (simultaneously in London by
Macmillan), the story dropped out of sight in America.
(Its fate in England was to prove similarly curious. It
formed one of the small volumes in Martin Secker's edition
of James's *Tales* in 1915–16, of which some copies were
imported in America by LeRoy Phillips of Boston; it reappeared in the thirty-five-volume set that Percy Lubbock
made of James's fiction for Macmillan in 1921–23; but since
then it has remained unpublished in London as well.) Its
present reappearance in America after the lapse of half a
century gives occasion to rediscover its charm and artistry,
and to say something about its value and significance
among James's works.

I

James, it perhaps goes without saying, achieved his
greatest strength and powers as an artist in fiction in the
twenty-one novels of varying length and success he wrote
during his lifetime, from the crude beginnings of *Watch
and Ward* in 1871 and the awkward but unmistakable
force of *Roderick Hudson* in 1875, to the unfinished drafts
of *The Sense of the Past* and *The Ivory Tower* that appeared in 1917 after his death. But during almost five
decades he continuously exercised his skill and vision, in
their fullest range of insight and invention, in the shorter
narrative forms. Between the first of his stories thus far recovered, "A Tragedy of Error" in 1864, and the five tales
of his last collection, *The Finer Grain* in 1910, he wrote
some hundred and eleven of these—short stories, long
stories, short novels, *nouvelles*. If we refer his larger powers
to his novels, there is no necessity of limiting his subtlety
or richness of art to these, for they are fully as evident in
his shorter works. And it is in the tales perhaps even more
than in his novels that the scope and diversity of his moral
drama are apparent, as well as his developing resources as
a craftsman and inventor. They give us not only the ground
and reach of his imagination; they serve equally as matrix

or seedbed of the major novels themselves. All his themes appear in them—his "international subject," his drama of the rival worlds of Europe and America, his studies of writers and artists, his criticism of manners and society, his essays in fantasy and the "ghostly," his exploration of character and morality, his analysis of the present and his sense of the past. The reader of James soon discovers one of his most engrossing pursuits to be the tracing and threading of these themes, in all their complex ramifications and relationships, as they appear in this great body of tales. And one of the discoveries he soon makes is that repeatedly, throughout his half century of fiction writing, James brought to concise or crystallized expression the problems that taxed his mind—gave focal or epigrammatic form to the moral themes and dramatic motifs that most deeply engaged his imagination.

The greater masters of fiction often show a habit of doing this. At certain points in their labors they seem to feel the need of reducing to their essence, of bringing to concentrated definition, the subjects that lie at the heart of their work. Flaubert did so in the *Trois Contes*—in "Un Coeur simple," in which he condensed the theme of bourgeois tragedy or delusion that gave him the larger dramas of *Madame Bovary, L'Éducation sentimentale,* and *Bouvard et Pécuchet;* in "La Légende de Saint Julien l'Hospitalier," where the saint's legend permitted him to crystallize the theme of temptation, passion, and sacrifice that had yielded *La Tentation de Saint Antoine;* in "Hérodias," where the biblical drama of Salome and St. John enabled him to reduce to its essence the barbaric lust of *Salammbô.* The three tales become in effect epigrams on the three domains of Flaubert's imagination. Thomas Mann showed a like tendency. "Tonio Kröger" is an epitomized version of the fate of the artist in a bourgeois society that had already given him *Buddenbrooks* at the outset of his career; "Tristan" is a concise anticipation of what was to become the immense dialectical drama of *The Magic Mountain;* "Death in Venice" is a vignette of the tragedy of genius that extends from *Buddenbrooks* to the Joseph epic and *Dr. Faustus;* certain other tales—"The 'Bajazzo,'" "Disorder

and Early Sorrow," "Mario and the Magician," *The Trans-
posed Heads, The Holy Sinner*—act as further points of
punctuation or axiomatic summary in Mann's career. Con-
rad brought his moral and dramatic ideas to similar moments of definition in at least five tales whose titles themselves define his cardinal motifs—"Youth," "Heart of
Darkness," "Typhoon," "The Secret Sharer," *The Shadow-
Line*. Kafka's central symbols are defined as much by titles
like "The Burrow," "The Giant Mole," and "Metamorpho-
sis" as by *The Castle* and *The Trial*.[2] The symbolic impulse in modern fiction has, it is true, worked in an opposite
direction; it has encouraged the ambition to achieve a total
or inclusive subject—*War and Peace, A la Recherche du
Temps perdu, La Condition humaine*. But when that impulse seeks the focus of metaphor or concrete symbolism
we get another order of title. We get *The Magic Mountain, The Castle, Les Faux-Monnayeurs,* or *Ulysses*—des-
ignations that contribute key emblems to the language,
radical metaphors to thought, and so become modes of
comprehending the life which the art of fiction seeks, as
by its deepest instinctive passion, to embody or illuminate.

Henry James had the luck or genius to come upon such
themes and titles a dozen times during his half century of
authorship. Certain of his novels have given classic terms
or clues to the evaluation of modern experience, revealed
in titles which, like proverbs, epitomize a historic situation
or moral challenge: *The American, The Awkward Age,
The Ambassadors, The Sense of the Past,* and notably the
four of biblical origin—*The Sacred Fount, The Wings of*

---

[2] Examples could be carried further: Dickens in "The Haunted
Man," "A Christmas Carol," "The Battle of Life"; Tolstoy in
"Youth," "The Landlord's Morning," "The Death of Ivan Ily-
itch"; Kipling in "The Man Who Was," "The Man Who Would
be King," "The Mark of the Beast," "At the End of the Passage,"
"The Wish House"; Lawrence in "England, My England," "Sun,"
"The Woman Who Rode Away," "The Virgin and the Gypsy,"
The Man Who Died; Hemingway in "Big Two-Hearted River,"
"Cat in the Rain," "A Clean Well-Lighted Place," "Old Man at
the Bridge," "The Snows of Kilimanjaro"; Gide in *L'Immoraliste*
and *La Porte étroite;* Faulkner in "Barn Burning," "Death
Drag," "Turnabout," "The Bear," etc.

the Dove, The Golden Bowl, The Ivory Tower. His shorter tales show the same motif-stating instinct. He made the name of Daisy Miller a figure of speech for the generation that first puzzled over the problem of American innocence; the adjective of "An International Episode" pointed explicitly to a central test in modern culture. But with even greater ingenuity James frequently hit upon themes and titles that were to become part of the vocabulary of social, moral, or aesthetic criticism: thus "The Passionate Pilgrim," "The Lesson of the Master," "The Real Thing," "The Figure in the Carpet," "The Altar of the Dead," "The Turn of the Screw," "The Great Good Place," "The Beast in the Jungle." *In the Cage* is a notable case of such clue-defining precision. Once we have read the story it names, once we seize the key the phrase puts in our hands, we realize how here again James defined one of the focal ideas of his life-work. It is a theme that ramifies his social and moral drama in many directions. In varying degrees it is evident in the seven tales that accompany *In the Cage* in the present volume.

II

The "germ" that gave James his story—for here we find him putting into characteristic practice one of his cardinal axioms: that "odd law" which "somehow always makes the minimum of valid suggestion serve the man of imagination better than the maximum"—was gathered, like that of *The Princess Casamassima*, during his "attentive exploration of London" and from "the habit and the interest of walking the streets." There, his "eyes greatly open" and his "mind curious," he responded to the "mystic solicitation, the urgent appeal," of the "meanings and revelations" in "the thick jungle" of "the great grey Babylon." In those days of the 1890s before the spread of the telephone system, the telegram was a means of quick communication in large cities, and a common feature of the London streets was the local postal-telegraph office, usually installed in a convenient grocer's shop—"the small local office of one's immediate neighbourhood, scene of the transaction of so much of one's daily business, haunt of one's needs and one's duties, of one's labours and one's patiences, almost of one's rewards and one's disappointments, one's joys and one's sorrows." Such shops had for an explorer like James "so much of London to give out, so much of its huge perpetual story to tell, that any momentary wait there seemed to take place in a strong social draught, the stiffest possible breeze of the human comedy." It was in such a shop, "in Mayfair or in Kensington"—so he tells us in his preface to Volume XI of the New York Edition—that the "spark" of his tale was kindled by the "wonderment" of his "speculation" about the "confined and cramped and yet considerably tutored young officials of either sex" who were "made so free, intellectually, of a range of experience otherwise quite closed to them." His inveterate speculation became "an amusement, or an obsession," in "that deepest abyss of all the wonderments that break out for the student of great cities." And it was thus that his "young woman," the "caged telegraphist," assumed the character of "a proper little monument" in the vast and complex social scene surrounding her obscure citadel—became one more opportunity for James to put into operation his insatiable "critical impulse." ("To criticise is to appreciate, to appropriate, to take intellectual possession, to establish in fine a relation with the criticised thing and make it one's own.") She struck him as a "focus of divination" and the key to her secret drama as "simply the girl's 'subjective' adventure—that of her quite definitely winged intelligence; just as the catastrophe, just as the solution, depend[ed] on her winged wit."

How accurately James's clue fastened itself on his mind is immediately evident in the aphoristic concision of the brilliant opening sentences with which his tale begins and by which he establishes at a stroke his scene and subject:

It had occurred to her early that in her position—that of a young person spending, in framed and wired confinement, the life of a guinea-pig or a magpie—she should know a great many persons without their recognising the acquaintance. That made it an emotion the more lively—

*though singularly rare and always, even then, with oppor-
tunity still very much smothered—to see any one come in
whom she knew outside, as she called it, any one who could
add anything to the meanness of her function. Her function was to sit there with two young men—the other telegraphist and the counter-clerk; to mind the "sounder," which
was always going, to dole out stamps and postal-orders,
weigh letters, answer stupid questions, give difficult change
and, more than anything else, count words as numberless
as the sands of the sea, the words of the telegrams thrust,
from morning to night, through the gap left in the high
lattice, across the encumbered shelf that her forearm ached
with rubbing.*

Thus he situates the humblest heroine of all his tales
—there in her "frail structure of wood and wire," in "the
duskiest corner of a shop pervaded not a little, in winter,
by the poison of perpetual gas, and at all times by the
presence of hams, cheese, dried fish, soap, varnish, paraffin, and other solids and fluids that she came to know perfectly by their smells without consenting to know them by
their names." Yet obscure though her life and work are in
the vast scene of London, she is granted her shy fragment
of destiny. She too is to become one of those "frail vessels"
—to apply to her a phrase of George Eliot's that James always admired—in whom is "borne onward through the
ages the treasure of human affection." She will join James's
more splendid heroines in having her "inadequacy eked
out with comic relief and underplots . . . when not with
murders and battles and the great mutations of the world,"
and thus in "figuring as the main props of [his] theme."

"*Elle avait eu, comme une autre, son histoire d'amour.*"
Like Flaubert's household drudge Félicité in "Un Coeur
simple," of whom one seems to catch an echo here, James's
telegraphist has her suitor. He is Mr. Mudge, once her co-
worker in the Mayfair shop but now removed "to a higher
sphere—to a more commanding position, that is, though
to a much lower neighbourhood," to which he wants her
transferred so that, "dangled before her every minute of
the day, he should see her, as he called it, 'hourly.'" And

behind her lies the harsh tragedy of her impoverished family—"the worries of the early times of their great misery, her own, her mother's and her elder sister's—the last of whom had succumbed to all but absolute want when, as conscious and incredulous ladies, suddenly bereft, betrayed, overwhelmed, they had slipped faster and faster down the steep slope at the bottom of which she alone had rebounded." The girl has thus far resisted Mr. Mudge's importunities. She is not ready to quit her cage in Mayfair, where the rumor of a great social world surrounds her and in whose stir she senses a summons. And it is out of that world that the one moment of thrilling adventure in her deprived life comes to her.

"The amusements of captives are full of a desperate contrivance." Early in Chapter III we are given this hint of the girl's plight. And as in higher and nobler instances of classic drama, her moment of fate, when it reaches her, proves to combine a stroke of chance with a prepared intention. Into the shop to send their telegrams come two persons who belong to the high aristocratic life of London—Lady Bradeen and Captain Everard. Some half-guessed, discreetly masked relationship exists between them—illicit love apparently, though it may be a more desperate collusion, some conspiracy of passion that presently threatens social disgrace and scandalous consequences.

What the danger is we never know, any more than the girl does—any more than James himself professes to know. (One of his friends in the '90s, André Raffalovich, remembered "once teasing" James "to know what the Olympian young man in *In the Cage* had done wrong. He swore he did not know, he would rather not know."[3] Captain Everard's peril, whatever ingenuity we may give to deciphering it, is one of the many secrets that remain masked in James's fictions.) From her cage the girl projects her hungry curiosity, her covert desire to identify her obscure fate with the lovers' brilliant but hazardous lives. Gradually she feels something more. Like so many of James's captives she

[3] The anecdote is given in Forrest Reid's *Private Road* (London, 1940); it is quoted in Simon Nowell-Smith's *The Legend of the Master* (London, 1948), p. 122.

finds herself caught in an obsession. Everard's reckless gal-
lantry appears to touch her own bleak plight. He too, she
sees, "almost under peril of life," is also "clenched in a situation." It becomes "more and more between them that if
he might convey to her he was free, with all the impossible locked away into a closed chapter, her own case might
become different for her, she might understand him and
meet him and listen." But—"he could convey nothing of the
sort, and he only fidgeted and floundered in his want of
power." The handsome cavalier is as helpless in the snare
of his intrigue as she is in her caged and baffled yearning.
Her desire to share or relieve his danger, her mute hope
of coming to his rescue, possesses her days. And at length
her chance is given her.

A telegram, apparently incriminating, has gone astray.
She alone, with her tenacious memory of every word the
lovers have exchanged in their messages, can recover the
words that will save them from disaster. When crisis comes
she recalls the words infallibly. She delivers the pair from
danger—delivers them, at the same time, from her sharing
of their secret and so prepares the day when Lady Bradeen,
her husband dying, will claim her reluctant lover in marriage. The girl remembers his "supplicating eyes and a fever
in his blood"; remembers the moment when danger almost
brought him to a point of intimate communication with her;
treasures her triumph of "having on her side, hard and pedantic, helped by some miracle," and "with her impossible condition, only answered him, yet supplicating back,
through the bars of the cage." But once she has rescued
him from his desperation, Everard simply walks out of the
shop and out of her life. "And without another look, without a word of thanks, without time for anything or anybody, he turned on them the broad back of his great stature, straightened his triumphant shoulders and strode out
of the place."

At the end, hearing from her friend Mrs. Jordan that the
Captain will soon marry the widowed Lady Bradeen, "our
young lady" goes off into the London fog. "Presently, after
a few sightless turns," she comes out on the Paddington
canal. "Distinguishing vaguely what the low parapet en-

closed she stopped close to it and stood a while very intently, but perhaps still sightlessly, looking down on it. A policeman, while she remained, strolled past her; then, going his way a little further and half lost in the atmosphere, paused and watched her. But she was quite unaware—she was full of her thoughts. . . ."

What are they? Knowing her as we now do, we know they turn to the bleakness her life must resume, to the dull marriage with Mr. Mudge that awaits her, to the future to which poverty and privation condemn her—"the vivid reflexion of her own dreams and delusions and her own return to reality." Like Catherine Sloper at the end of *Washington Square* she too must sit down to her fate "—for life, as it were." Like Isabel Archer at the end of *The Portrait of a Lady,* though she may look "all about her" and listen "a little," she now knows "where to turn": "there [is] a very straight path." Like Maggie Verver at the end of *The Golden Bowl* she stands "in the cool twilight and [takes] in, all about her, where it lurked, her reason for what she had done" and "how, to her soul, all the while, it had been for the sake of this end."

She stands, like these other heroines of James in their hours of defeat or secret triumph, face to face with a recognition. It is, true enough, a recognition of her obscurity and surrender, of what bleak disillusionment has overtaken her "dreams and delusions"; yet it is something more. Her cruel experience of reality, whatever it brings of sacrifice or a diminishment of her faith in life, also brings what the foredoomed *peripeteia* must always compel—what one of the perceptive students of this subject in James has called "the extension and refinement of consciousness, of that intelligence which, in Santayana's words, is 'the highest form of vitality.' "[4] Of that illumination, the ultimate goal in James's moral faith, the little telegraphist can finally boast

[4] L. C. Knights, "Henry James and the Trapped Spectator," in *Explorations* (London, 1946), pp. 155–69; here 168. The only other recent discussion of any length of *In the Cage* is that of Albert C. Friend, "A Forgotten Story of Henry James," *The South Atlantic Quarterly,* Vol. LIII, pp. 100–108 (January, 1954).

her share. She joins the other heroes and heroines of the
Jamesian drama—Christopher Newman, Catherine Sloper,
Isabel Archer, Hyacinth Robinson, Maisie, Fleda Vetch,
Strether, Milly Theale, Maggie Verver—who, caught, caged,
or pinioned in situations that bring them to defeat, tragedy,
or a liberating disillusionment, snatch from the baffling
odds or denials of experience the only reward which the
life condemned to limitation and reality permits. It is to
this final comfort—a strength or access of character—that
the "sense of exclusion from experience" must come at last:
to a capture of the trophy of the spirit's "vitality" and self-
knowledge, the "qualities making for life."

III

In the Cage thus provides an essential key to the reading of James, even if it must at once be conceded that no
single clue—whether it be the international theme, the
American fate, the antagonisms of life and art, appearance
and reality, privilege and privation, innocence and experience—suffices of itself in the full experience of his art, where
ideas or conflicts so intricately intermesh and the moral debate is so complex and continuous. The story was written
out of James's observation of the humble life of hardship
and privation; it joins with *The Princess Casamassima* and
"The Bench of Desolation" in showing his study of a realm
of life he is usually charged with leaving unexplored. "The
Altar of the Dead" also touches that way of experience in
the obscure destiny of its heroine; so does "Brooksmith";
and they touch it with searching compassion. The other
stories in this book treat of more familiar Jamesian terri-
tory. Four of them—"The Author of Beltraffio," "The Figure in the Carpet," "Broken Wings," "The Great Good
Place"—concern the vocation and claims of art that were
James's most intimate experience and to which, early and
late, he turned repeatedly in his novels and tales. Another,
"The Jolly Corner," the next to last story James published,
is his culminating treatment of the conflict which Europe
and America had imposed on the Americans of his generation and whose test he felt to be a moral imperative in his

own career. But whatever the ostensible subject of these tales; however for convenience we may define, classify, or categorize them, they are all stories that hinge on the test of spiritual or moral truth and the inescapable proof it imposes on character. That test is basic to whatever external or superficial drama the tales may show. The clue provided by *In the Cage* helps to bring it into focus, under whatever guise or conditions it may manifest itself.

The men or women the tales present all arrive at a point of life when the reality to which, consciously or not, their fate or nature has committed them closes down—makes clear or final their responsibility to its demands; seizes or cages them in a destiny that at last declares itself as the body of their fate, the truth from which there is neither release nor reprieve. For it is a fundamental condition of James's drama—one, it may be said, that has often figured mistakenly or under distortion in the popular conception of his work—that it hinges on a contradiction, an implicit paradox. That drama appears to deal with the life of privilege or luxury, with the ardors of liberty and possibility, with freedom of choice or will and the social or personal amenity which makes such freedom operative: with, in other words, the great nineteenth-century aspiration toward self-reliance, self-fulfillment, moral emancipation. This is the larger *donnée* of James's lifework. It came to him as part of his personal inheritance: the wealth and station of his family in America, his father's moral and religious liberalism, the response and access to opportunity in his American generation, the sense of capacity that was fully as native to the air of James's world as it was to that of Emerson, Thoreau, and Whitman. Yet against these privileges there works, secretly or unsuspected, an opposing law—a law of limitation, of necessity and sacrifice; a law, as he himself defined it, of exclusion.

The great spectacle that presented itself to James's generation when they looked out, in America or Europe, on "history as a still-felt past and a complacently personal future, at society, manners, types, characters, possibilities and prodigies and mysteries of fifty sorts"; when they felt the "sense of glory" to offer "ever so many things at once, not only beauty and art and supreme design, but history and fame and power, the world in fine raised to the richest and noblest expression," was to be subjected, when the demands of moral realism began to assert themselves, to the check of a severe reproof, a chastening denial. To what curtailment of confidence in his own nature James's sense of this law may be referred can never be certain. To what refusals his character compelled him must perhaps always remain a matter for speculation. How far his instinct of estrangement or otherness dictated his recognition becomes only occasionally apparent in his utterances—as when, on one occasion late in life, he asserted that he was possessed by "the imagination of disaster" and saw "life indeed as ferocious and sinister." But there is no mistaking the workings of the rule in his tales.

It operates as the discipline of art in *Roderick Hudson* and all the tales of artists and writers that followed it. It asserts itself as a reversal of pride or expectation in *The American, The Portrait of a Lady,* and thus onward to *The Ambassadors, The Golden Bowl,* and *The Ivory Tower.* It acts repeatedly as a reproof to moral arrogance or as a corrective to the assumptions of an untested optimism. It acts continuously in certain forms of experience that James applied insistently to the characters of his drama—the experience of treachery for one, which stalks his people intently and seems to single out those who have given most of generous expectancy and confidence to life; the tragedy of failure in love or of responding to love which comes of the deceiving workings of an idealized conception of the self or the personal fate; the experience of a self-deception that is rooted in the cautions of egotism or selfishness; the pathos of innocence preyed upon by corruption or depravity. It appears at its most implacable in the discovery that one's fate is finally wholly one's own; that it is determined less by outward circumstance or delusion than by character; that neither wealth nor art nor even intelligence can be taken as refuges from its claims; and that liberation of spirit can be achieved only at the cost of acceptance, recognition, and the expiation which reality imposes on those who have challenged or denied its authority.

These are, to be sure, ancient modes of tragedy or tragic affirmation. But the force they assume in James's work comes of the unstinted ardor of his sensitivity to life, his excited response to its promises, his faith in the creative capacities of will and mind, the aspiration to "glory" he confers on his men and women. Few Americans of his time surpassed him in this sense of enthusiasm. It never deserted him personally: he could boast to the end of his "inexhaustible sensibility." And it is the very reach of their opportunities, the zeal of their expectation, that gives the measure of tragic and moral validity to his characters when reality descends on them. Then, from the trap or commitment of their personal fate, they become agents of the value life assumes when its limits declare themselves. The consequences vary. They do not necessarily insure a triumph, however secret or elusive. They do not always bring acceptance or vindication. What they bring inevitably is a vision, if perhaps only a glimpse, of the truth that liberates: the sense that while such truth, like sorrow, "wears us, uses us," we "wear it and use it in return; and it is blind, whereas we after a manner see."[5]

IV

It is not to be argued here that the stories in this volume are tales of caged characters, captive consciences, trapped spectators, and nothing else. Each has its "subject," social, moral, psychological, as the case may be; each refers to principles of conduct, choice, and responsibility which bring it into relationship with James's larger judgment of experience and values. But none of them would be seriously misread if the clue or criterion of *In the Cage* were applied. For it soon becomes evident that James's central moral situation appears in one form or another in each of them; that they are all, in fact, tales of the crisis of dilemma, isolation, or decision to which the necessity of moral choice brings a man, so defining the restrictive necessity in

[5] From a letter—one of the greatest James ever wrote and a radical statement of his personal morality—to Grace Norton, July 28, 1883: *Letters of Henry James* (1920), Vol. I, pp. 100–2.

his personal fate and imposing on him the test of recognition or acceptance.

"The fictive hero successfully appeals to us only as an eminent instance," James said in opening the prefaces to his lifework, "of our own conscious kind." And in another preface he defined "the most general state of one's most exposed and assaulted figures" as a "state of bewilderment . . . the condition of a humble heart, a bowed head, a patient wonder, a suspended judgment, before the 'awful will' and the mysterious decrees of Providence."[6] He laid emphasis on the fact that "the whole thing comes to depend on the *quality* of bewilderment characteristic of one's creature." The "exhibitional charm" he ascribes to his "salient characters" derives from their exposure or vulnerability to that bewilderment: from what they show of a "great capacity for life" doomed to "fall somehow into some abysmal trap" or into those "sad places at which the hand of generosity has been cautioned and stayed." Though the fate that brings them to "such straits" is of a kind to "*stifle* the sacred spark" and bring on the "shrinking hour"; though it repeatedly betrays "so much spent intensity" and "so much baffled calculation" to "negative adventure" or to "an absolutely blank reverse or starved residuum" of what life once promised, it is through the disappointment which enforces in "the weak agent," "blinded seeker," or "captured spirit" an enhancement of his "sense of experience" that he must seize the reward his "shrunken or blighted fortunes" offer him. Only then will his drama show what increasingly became a major issue with James: the "operative irony" which "implies and projects the possible other case, the case rich and edifying where the actuality is pretentious and vain."

James's prefaces, letters, and journals are continuous in these hints of a central preoccupation. The irony he postulates as constitutional to experience may work now as comedy, now as tragedy. The point is that it works per-

[6] Quotations here that are not taken directly from the tales themselves are from James's discussion of them in his prefaces and *Notebooks*. See the bibliographical note at the end of this book.

sistently; and that it almost invariably hinges on the conflict of capacity with deprivation, privilege with denial, freedom with restriction, which forms the axis or leverage of his essential drama.

Thus Mark Ambient, the author of "Beltraffio." His genius has brought him to greatness in his art. The passionate young pilgrim who comes to pay him homage from America sees in his achievement a supreme "example of beauty of execution and 'intimate' importance of theme." His art is complete, "triumphant," "the most complete presentation that had yet been made of the gospel of art," a "kind of aesthetic warcry." He evidently embodies an ideal James wrote down for himself in his notebooks: "To live *in* the world of creation—to get into it and stay in it—to frequent it and haunt it—to *think* intensely and fruitfully —to woo combinations and inspirations into being by a depth and continuity of attention and meditation—this is the only thing." His life appears to be an equivalent triumph of charm and amenity: "there was genius in his house too"—it is "a palace of art, on a slightly reduced scale," it is "the dearest haunt of the old English *genius loci.*" His wife, his child, his garden, pictures, books, all carry the stamp of an achieved perfection: "it was not the picture, the poem, the fictive page, that seemed to me a copy; these things were the originals, and the life of a happy and distinguished people was fashioned in their image." But it soon becomes apparent that Ambient's triumph is severely hedged.

His "love of beauty, of art, the aesthetic view of life," is despised by his "narrow, cold, Calvinistic wife, a rigid moralist." The issue between the pair is their child, whom she determines to save for "morality and religion, in order to expiate, as it were, the countenance that the family have given to godless ideas in the literary career of the father." The contest is deadly and it is closed. When he formulated the tale in his notebooks, James feared it would prove "very probably too gruesome—the catastrophe too unnatural." Yet he drives the catastrophe to its logical limits. It is not only an agent of expiation that the child becomes; it becomes a sacrifice. When its mother has allowed it to die rather than expose it to the "well of corruption" she believes her husband's mind and art to be, Ambient finds that his art has cost him his dearest possession; that his tragedy exemplifies what Rilke was to express in a bitter aphorism that employs the image of a prison: "In fortune art is an embellishment of life; in misfortune it becomes an iron door."[7]

It proves to be such also in "Brooksmith," where the issue is tragic, in "Broken Wings," where it is bitter with disillusionment, in "The Figure in the Carpet," where it produces a parable of enigma, and in "The Great Good Place," where it ends in surrender and conciliation. Brooksmith, the immaculate butler, has made himself a kind of artist during his long service to Oliver Offord, and "in recall of Stendhal's inveterate motto, [has] caught a glimpse, all untimely, of 'la beauté parfaite,'" as embodied in the house and life of his master—the "delightful society," rare talk, perfection of comfort and order. When his master dies and the house with him, the servant, "formed by nature, as unluckily happened, to enjoy this privilege to the utmost," suffers a "deprivation of everything." His loss becomes a "bitterness in [his] cup"; he enacts what the editors of the Notebooks call "a dilemma that constantly fascinated James—the dilemma of the highly sensitive intelligence frustrated and starved by the lack of fit material and a proper environment for its development." A "poor lost spirit," he succumbs to "the measured maximum of the fatal experience." "He had indeed been spoiled," says the narrator; "he knew I really couldn't help him, and that I knew he knew I couldn't." He sinks in station; disappears; dies at last, apparently a suicide.

Here the outcome is unrelieved. In "Broken Wings" it is lit with fortitude and resolution. Stuart Straith and Mrs Harvey, both artists, have had their years of success; have been taken on as ornaments of rich houses where, like Neil Paraday in "The Death of the Lion," they have become "gallant victims" of social condescension and vanity. But when they fall from public favor it is "the grim realities

[7] "Die Kunst ist im Glück eine Zier; im Unglück eine eiserne Tür."

of shrunken 'custom'" they must face, "the felt chill of a lower professional temperature." Then they must at last share a recognition of what has formerly kept them apart. "Sad companions," they must look "each other, with their identities of pluck and despair, a little hard in the face"; must "confess each to the other, relievingly, what they kept from every one else"; must acknowledge themselves in "confessions, *aveux*, tragic surrenders to the truth," and know themselves brought, "for some consolatory purpose, together." "Everything costs that one does for the rich," says Mrs. Harvey. "Let us at least be beaten together!" says Straith. "And now to work!" they both conclude "in sweetness as well as sadness."

They are permitted at length to share the secret that finally faces them, where Brooksmith took his into silence and Ambient was condemned to live with his in the solitude of his art. All four of the stories thus far considered have dealt with secret or barely communicable destinies: compacts with fate that impose a solitary commitment. Going on to the remaining four, we get an increasing sense of James's own share in such a commitment, his own pact with the fate to which his art and vocation compelled him, until at last, in "The Jolly Corner," his avowal becomes all but explicit. That the life in art enforces such a dedication, that it pledges its votary to a secret that eludes his powers of communication, was clearly a living—and an increasingly urgent—presentiment to him. The "bewilderment" he specified as "characteristic" of "one's creature" became a cognate of the consciousness he set up as an imperative of the active, self-realizing mind.

"The Figure in the Carpet" is perhaps his most celebrated parable of the dilemma. James's notes on the tale insist on "secrecy" as its central clue. Hugh Vereker's art contains a "very beautiful and valuable, very interesting and remunerative *secret*." "They don't *know* his work who don't know, who haven't felt, or guessed, or perceived, this interior thought—this special *beauty*." His devotees, while "admiring," are driven almost to desperation—"inquisitive, sympathetic, mystified, sceptical"—in the clutch of their curiosity, "worriment," "wonderment," "torment." They are almost led to supposing Vereker "mad" in his concealment of the essential thread of his work—not its "esoteric meaning," as the newspapers say, but its *"only* meaning," the "very soul and core of the work." They become "quite possessed with their search," "devoured with curiosity," enslaved to "a strange mystifying uncomfortable delicacy." The fable becomes one of the most sheerly ingenious James ever devised, "spent intensity" and "baffled calculation" working at an extravagant pitch, and with the obsession of "the intended sense" ending in bafflement and "the issue of the affair" becoming "whether the very secret of perception hasn't been lost." James admitted that he was concerned here to exhibit "a small group of well-meaning persons engaged in a test." The test becomes the crux of the tale. It produces the ultimate case of the "caged consciousness" caught not only in a human riddle but in an aesthetic one—a virtual paradigm of James's notion of the creative mystery. It also becomes one of his ironic parables of the critical necessity—of that "responsive reach of critical perception" which Vereker "is destined never to waylay with success" in a public prone to an "odd numbness of the general sensibility," a "marked collective mistrust of anything like close or analytic appreciation."

In "The Altar of the Dead" the ground of obsession shifts from art to personal emotion, from an aesthetic secret to a human secret or prepossession become ingrown, all-consuming, morbid. The first paragraph of the story emphasizes pointedly the grip on Stransom of his lost love Mary Antrim's death, whose anniversary he keeps every year. "It would be more to the point perhaps to say that this occasion kept *him:* it kept him at least effectually from doing anything else. It took hold of him again and again with a hand of which time had softened but never loosened the touch." His dedication grows and deepens in him until it becomes a dedication to all the dead Stransom has ever lost. It becomes, as James phrased it in his notebook, a "worship of the Dead"—"the only religion he has," his private mode of expiating the oblivion of the "forgotten," the "unhonoured, neglected, shoved out of sight," and the "rudeness, the coldness, that surrounds their memory—the want of

place made for them in the life of the survivors." It is because "the essence of his religion is really to make and to
keep such a place" that Stransom, otherwise an unbeliever,
engages to dedicate and maintain an altar for his dead in
"a temple of the old persuasion," a Catholic church in a
"great grey suburb of London" where candles are set, increasing in numbers as the years take toll, to the memory
of every friend and person he has lost. To all, that is, but
one. For Acton Hague, the hero of his youth, "the only
man with whom he had ever been intimate, the friend,
almost adored, of his University years, the subject, later, of
his passionate loyalty," at whose hands Stransom had suffered a betrayal which had cut his soul to the quick and
apparently maimed his faith in life, "no flame could ever
rise on any altar of his."

James said in his preface to "The Altar of the Dead"
that "the idea embodied in this composition must . . . have
never been so absent from [his] view as to call for an organised search." "It was 'there'—it had always, or from ever
so far back, been there." It "went back for its full intensity,
no doubt, neither to a definite moment nor to a particular
shock" but to an "old, deep-seated conception that had long
awaited its opportunity," "amusedly biding its time." The
idea derives, of course, from one of the deepest prepposses-
sions of James's emotional and aesthetic life—that "sense of
the past" in which he sensed not only a luxury of the spirit
but a profound peril. And while he argues that "the sense
of the state of the dead is but part of the sense of the state
of the living," it is significant that in the New York Edition
he paired "The Altar of the Dead" with "The Beast in the
Jungle," that other tale of a "poor sensitive gentleman" who
becomes the victim of a "conviction, lodged in his brain,
part and parcel of his imagination from far back," which
estranges him from life, and who meets his doom in a hor-
rified recognition that he is "the man of his time, *the* man,
to whom nothing on earth was to have happened." John
Marcher becomes the victim of his idealized conception of
his personal fate. Stransom falls prey to his idealized conception of the dead. Both of them are victims of a fear,
contempt, or distrust of life that deprives them of the will

to affirm or engage themselves in it. As Marcher misses
the love that May Bartram offers him, so Stransom finds
himself baffled and confounded in his effort to respond to
the appeal of the woman he discovers to be a fellow wor-
shiper at his private altar—the woman Acton Hague had
wronged by a greater betrayal than Stransom suffered but
who has learned to pardon Hague and honor the memory
of what he once gave her life. The missing of life through
pride, the fear of life through a deceiving vanity, the desperate effort to come to terms with life when will or energy
is spent or rendered impotent by self-delusion: this was the
theme—tragic obverse in James's work of the companion
theme of the passion for experience, consciousness, "the
sense of having lived"—which by his own admission had engaged his mind "from ever so far back," and which gave
him, in these two tales, two of his subtlest parables of the
"blinded seeker" whose blindness, however nobly inflicted,
is the darkest prison to which the spirit may be condemned.

George Dane, in "The Great Good Place," is trapped not
by privation, ignorance, or failure, but by success. James,
we are bound to feel, was himself deeply involved in the
subjects of "The Figure in the Carpet" and "The Altar of
the Dead." In "The Great Good Place" his participation
asserts itself as even more intimate—so intimate, apparently,
that it led him to refrain from comment on the story in his
prefaces. Though he admits that the tale "embodies a calculated effect," he says no more than that "any gloss or
comment would be a tactless challenge."

Its hero is an author so beset by the claims, demands,
and distractions of his calling; so beset, further, by his in-
curable avidity for life and art, his sense of unachieved purpose and unrecognized intention, that his ruling passion becomes a desire for "respite," "escape." The tale soon resorts
to an imagery of imprisonment, of Gulliver-like impotence
in captivity:

*There was no footing on which a man who had ever
liked life—liked it at any rate as he had—could now escape
it. He must reap as he had sown. It was a thing of meshes;
he had simply gone to sleep under the net and had simply*

waked up there. The net was too fine; the cords crossed
each other at spots too near together, making at each a
little tight hard knot that tired fingers were this morning
too limp and too tender to touch.

To this image James, in a brief foreshadowing of the story
in an early notebook, adds another: the image of a releasing
dream—"a deep sleep in which he dreams he *has* had his
respite." We are moving now toward the realm of hallucination, and toward James's most elaborate excursion into
it in *The Sense of the Past,* with "The Altar of the Dead,"
"The Beast in the Jungle," and "The Jolly Corner" marking
three of many stations on the way. We soon enter Dane's
dream.

What Dane finds himself transported to is not a mind-
less freedom from the career that is baffling him, but an
asylum—"some great abode of an Order, some mild Monte
Cassino, some Grande Chartreuse more accessible." He
knows "he had really never anywhere beheld anything at
once so calculated and so generous." He has achieved a
haven where the will is at last in abeyance, the clamor of
achievement arrested, the claims of distraction silenced.
And what James himself has arrived at is of course not "the
vulgar daydream of a rich bourgeois intellectual" which
some critics have accused him of writing here but—W. H.
Auden's comment is undoubtedly the sound one—a kind of
"religious parable."[8] It is less a "social utopia" he depicts
than "a spiritual state which is achievable by the individual": where, as the Brother says to Dane in the story,
"every man must arrive by himself and on his own feet."
"We must have first got here as we can, and we meet after
long journeys by complicated ways." When Dane asks
"Where is it?" the Brother replies "I shouldn't be surprised
if it were much nearer than one ever suspected." "Nearer
'town,' do you mean?" "Nearer everything—nearer every
one." Nearer, that is, to reality: to "life with all its rage," to
"the vague unrest of the need for action," to distraction, vulgarity, frustration, without all of which, as Auden puts it,

8 In his "Introduction" to James's *The American Scene* (New
York: Charles Scribner's Sons, 1946), p. xxii.

the dedicated spirit "would never understand by contrast
the nature of the Good Place nor desire it with sufficient
desperation to stand a chance of arriving." Success and ambition can bring their own kind of deprivation. Dane's vision of abnegation has permitted the withdrawal from rage
that ensures sanity, and the only return to reality that
enables the spirit to recover itself "refreshed and reconsecrated."

Of "The Jolly Corner" James said no more in his preface
than that his motive was to produce "an analysis of some
one of the conceivably rarest and intensest grounds for an
'unnatural' anxiety, a *malaise* so incongruous and discord-
ant, in the given prosaic prosperous conditions, as almost
to be compromising." And in his *Notebooks,* drafting his
plan for *The Sense of the Past,* he allowed that "The Jolly
Corner" was likewise the story of a "secret"—"that is within
the hero's breast"—and that its "most intimate idea" hinged
on "his turning the tables on a 'ghost,'" a "visiting or
haunting apparition otherwise qualified to appall *him;*
and thereby winning a sort of victory by the appearance,
and the evidence, that this personage or presence was
more overwhelmingly affected by him than he by *it.*" The
story became, however, something more complex than this
hint allows.

Spencer Brydon is another man beset—like Dane, like
Stransom—by a "particular wanton bewilderment." He has
lived for himself—lived for years in a Europe that has
spared him the tumult of American life and given him, as
he thinks, freedom for pleasure and self-fulfillment. He
now returns after more than thirty years to the New York
of his youth, where everything he encounters has the aspect of "so many set traps for displeasure." The trap most
expressly laid for him is his old childhood home on lower
Fifth Avenue. Around that house his "exasperated consciousness" revolves; the life he rejected insists on being ap-
peased; "a real test for him" lurks in it. What he had put
behind him is his old unmastered self, the past he has believed fully rejected, the "American fate" with which he
has never come to terms. They have haunted him for years
and now he determines to stalk them down. Yet when he

tries to do so he finds his other self turning on him and challenging him—"the fanged or the antlered animal brought at last to bay." In Brydon's contest with "his *alter ego*" the pursued becomes the pursuer, the haunter the haunted.[9] The trap has narrowed down to something even more intimate than Dane's baffled distraction. It has become the snare of Brydon's personal obsession, uneasy memory, unresolved conscience, unconfronted fate. His "concentrated conscious combat" thus engages him at the closest possible quarters. He stiffens his will against evading it. "The *question* springs" at him like another beast in the jungle: "wasn't he now in *most* intimate presence of some inconceivable occult activity?"

On the night Brydon returns to the empty house to lay his ghost at last, he finds himself in turn stalked by the specter. "It gloomed, it loomed, it was something, it was somebody, the prodigy of a personal presence." But when it finally faces him he is less shocked by its ravaged ugliness, "evil, odious, blatant, vulgar," than by "an irony." "Such an identity fitted his at *no* point, made its alternative monstrous": "that meaning at least, while he gaped, it offered him; for he could but gape at his other self in this other anguish, gape as a proof that *he*, standing there for the achieved, the enjoyed, the triumphant life, couldn't be faced in his triumph." Yet he faints on seeing it. Was the ghost that eluded him in the upper rooms of the house the ghost of the unlived and irrecoverable life he might have had at home, and the mutilated specter he confronts on descending to the street door a revelation of his actual self, maimed by evasion and selfishness, a stalking vision of the existence he has never fulfilled?[10]

[9] For the background and significance of this tale, and of the whole range of the supernatural theme in James, see Leon Edel's admirable collection of *The Ghostly Tales of Henry James*, with its excellent biographical and critical interpretations (New Brunswick: Rutgers University Press, 1948).

[10] The maimed ghost in "The Jolly Corner" has been taken by almost all interpreters to be the specter of the mutilation Brydon's life would have suffered had he remained in America. But this view has never fully accounted for the complicated ambiguity of the haunter and haunted, pursued and pursuer, in the

When Brydon recovers from his shock it is with the sensation of having been brought back from "the uttermost end of an interminable grey passage," of feeling that his confrontation has "brought him to knowledge"—"to knowledge—yes, this was the beauty of his state." But that knowledge remains illusory until he hears from Alice Staverton, the woman who has known him from youth and who has waited patiently for his return (her role compares closely with that of the woman in "The Altar of the Dead" or of May Bartram in "The Beast in the Jungle"), that she has known the other self, the "awful beast," all the time; that she "*could* have liked him": "he was no horror. I had accepted him." She has been, throughout the years, prepared to love Brydon not only for what he could have been but for what he is. His reconciliation comes less from what he has learned of himself than from what he discovers Alice never needed to learn. He is released from self-regard for life and love at last. "The Jolly Corner"—whose key words have from the first emphasized the "alter ego" "confronted" and "brought at last to bay"—ends with a confrontation Brydon's most desperate needs and ruses had never been able to anticipate. His recognition has broken open the cell of his self-deception and delivered him from "his poor ruined sight" into the light of a knowledge Alice can now share with him.

The issue here has been to define a central subject in James's art as eight of his most finished tales in the last twenty-five years of his career as a writer of fiction present it. That it was a subject profoundly involved in his moral vision, his sense of the claims of experience and knowledge, his lifelong concern with the tests of consciousness and selfhood, becomes apparent as soon as we pass from these

story, or for the apparent and puzzling presence of *two* ghosts— the one that eludes Brydon in the upper rooms of the house and the one that finally confronts him below near the street door. Floyd Stovall, in his recent analysis of the tale, argues that the mutilated specter is the apparition of Brydon's selfish life "as he lived during his European years," not the self he missed becoming by leaving America. ("Henry James's 'The Jolly Corner,'" *Nineteenth-Century Fiction*, Vol. XII, pp. 72–84, June, 1957.)

particular tales to the many others that surround and connect with them, and notably to the novels in which the theme of the captive consciousness takes on the larger proportions of social and moral drama. And it is obvious that this theme is intimately allied with what is perhaps James's major concern as a dramatic artist—the "point of view" which he saw as an imperative of his craft and by means of which the structure and informing intelligence of a tale becomes focused in a center of consciousness—a center never so assertive as when some condition of isolation, moral captivity, or psychic obsession defines and imposes it on mind or emotion. The subject will not, of course, always appear with equal emphasis in James's work. It will often relax into comedy, satire, studies of manners and morals, of a different sort. But that it is focal and essential, a lifelong preoccupation and an almost obsessional claim in his drama, is beyond mistaking.

When he came to write the greatest and most deeply felt of his tragedies in *The Wings of the Dove*, the theme taxed James in its profoundest personal reverberations. That tragedy is one of a caged captive pre-eminently: of Milly Theale, "early stricken and doomed, condemned to die under short respite, while also enamoured of the world," whose desperate "impulse" it becomes "to wrest from her shrinking hour still as much of the fruit of life as possible." It was of her fate that James wrote one of the most acute sentences in his prefaces: "The process of life gives way fighting, and often may so shine out on the lost ground as in no other connexion." The statement echoes back into James's art almost to his beginnings in fiction—to Strether in *The Ambassadors* who comes "at last . . . really to face his doom" through having been "primed with a moral scheme of the most approved pattern which was yet framed to break down on any approach to vivid facts"; to Hyacinth Robinson in *The Princess Casamassima*, "jealous of all the ease of life of which he tastes so little, and bitten, under this exasperation, with an aggressive, vindictive, destructive social faith," only to find himself "most acquainted with destiny in the form of a lively inward revolution"; to Christopher Newman in *The American,*

"stricken, smarting, sore" under the treachery he has suffered, only to "hold his revenge and cherish it and feel its
sweetness, and then in the very act of forcing it home . . .
sacrifice it in disgust"; to Isabel Archer in *The Portrait of
a Lady*, another innocent betrayed, keeping vigil "by her
dying fire, far into the night, under the spell of recognitions on which she finds the last sharpness suddenly wait."
The echo strikes from one of James's primary and profoundest convictions. It sounds in some of its most characteristic and eloquent suggestions in the tales in this
book. *In the Cage* gave him an occasion to express it in
an axiomatic form which no reader who wishes to trace its
workings in the great, complex, and splendid panorama of
James's drama will wish to miss or, once he has read the
story, fail to remember.

                                    Morton Dauwen Zabel

THE AUTHOR OF
BELTRAFFIO

I

Much as I wished to see him I had kept my letter of introduction three weeks in my pocket-book. I was nervous and timid about meeting him—conscious of youth and ignorance, convinced that he was tormented by strangers, and especially by my country-people, and not exempt from the suspicion that he had the irritability as well as the dignity of genius. Moreover, the pleasure, if it should occur —for I could scarcely believe it was near at hand—would be so great that I wished to think of it in advance, to feel it there against my breast, not to mix it with satisfactions more superficial and usual. In the little game of new sensations that I was playing with my ingenuous mind I wished to keep my visit to the author of "Beltraffio" as a trump-card. It was three years after the publication of that fascinating work, which I had read over five times and which now, with my riper judgement, I admire on the whole as much as ever. This will give you about the date of my first visit—of any duration—to England; for you will not have forgotten the commotion, I may even say the scandal, produced by Mark Ambient's masterpiece. It was the most complete presentation that had yet been made of the gos-

pel of art; it was a kind of aesthetic war-cry. People had
endeavoured to sail nearer to "truth" in the cut of their
sleeves and the shape of their sideboards; but there had
not as yet been, among English novels, such an example
of beauty of execution and "intimate" importance of theme.
Nothing had been done in that line from the point of view
of art for art. That served me as a fond formula, I may
mention, when I was twenty-five; how much it still serves
I won't take upon myself to say—especially as the discern-
ing reader will be able to judge for himself. I had been
in England, briefly, a twelvemonth before the time to
which I began by alluding, and had then learned that Mr.
Ambient was in distant lands—was making a considerable
tour in the East; so that there was nothing to do but to
keep my letter till I should be in London again. It was of
little use to me to hear that his wife had not left England
and was, with her little boy, their only child, spending the
period of her husband's absence—a good many months—at
a small place they had down in Surrey. They had a house
in London, but actually in the occupation of other persons.
All this I had picked up, and also that Mrs. Ambient was
charming—my friend the American poet, from whom I had
my introduction, had never seen her, his relations with the
great man confined to the exchange of letters; but she
wasn't, after all, though she had lived so near the rose, the
author of "Beltraffio," and I didn't go down into Surrey to
call on her. I went to the Continent, spent the following
winter in Italy and returned to London in May. My visit
to Italy had opened my eyes to a good many things, but
to nothing more than the beauty of certain pages in the
works of Mark Ambient. I carried his productions about
in my trunk—they are not, as you know, very numerous,
but he had preluded to "Beltraffio" by some exquisite things
—and I used to read them over in the evening at the inn. I
used profoundly to reason that the man who drew those
characters and wrote that style understood what he saw
and knew what he was doing. This is my sole ground for
mentioning my winter in Italy. He had been there much
in former years—he was saturated with what painters call
the "feeling" of that classic land. He expressed the charm

of the old hill-cities of Tuscany, the look of certain lonely grass-grown places which, in the past, had echoed with life; he understood the great artists, he understood the spirit of the Renaissance; he understood everything. The scene of one of his earlier novels was laid in Rome, the scene of another in Florence, and I had moved through these cities in company with the figures he set so firmly on their feet. This is why I was now so much happier even than before in the prospect of making his acquaintance.

At last, when I had dallied with my privilege long enough, I dispatched to him the missive of the American poet. He had already gone out of town; he shrank from the rigour of the London "season," and it was his habit to migrate on the first of June. Moreover I had heard he was this year hard at work on a new book, into which some of his impressions of the East were to be wrought, so that he desired nothing so much as quiet days. That knowledge, however, didn't prevent me—*cet âge est sans pitié*—from sending with my friend's letter a note of my own, in which I asked his leave to come down and see him for an hour or two on some day to be named by himself. My proposal was accompanied with a very frank expression of my sentiments, and the effect of the entire appeal was to elicit from the great man the kindest possible invitation. He would be delighted to see me, especially if I should turn up on the following Saturday and would remain till the Monday morning. We would take a walk over the Surrey commons, and I could tell him all about the other great man, the one in America. He indicated to me the best train, and it may be imagined whether on the Saturday afternoon I was punctual at Waterloo. He carried his benevolence to the point of coming to meet me at the little station at which I was to alight, and my heart beat very fast as I saw his handsome face, surmounted with a soft wide-awake and which I knew by a photograph long since enshrined on my mantel-shelf, scanning the carriage-windows as the train rolled up. He recognised me as infallibly as I had recognised himself; he appeared to know by instinct how a young American of critical pretensions, rash youth, would look when much divided between eagerness and modesty.

He took me by the hand and smiled at me and said: "You must be—a—*you*, I think!" and asked if I should mind going on foot to his house, which would take but a few minutes. I remember feeling it a piece of extraordinary affability that he should give directions about the conveyance of my bag; I remember feeling altogether very happy and rosy, in fact quite transported, when he laid his hand on my shoulder as we came out of the station.

I surveyed him, askance, as we walked together; I had already, I had indeed instantly, seen him as all delightful. His face is so well known that I needn't describe it; he looked to me at once an English gentleman and a man of genius, and I thought that a happy combination. There was a brush of the Bohemian in his fineness; you would easily have guessed his belonging to the artist guild. He was addicted to velvet jackets, to cigarettes, to loose shirt-collars, to looking a little dishevelled. His features, which were firm but not perfectly regular, are fairly enough represented in his portraits; but no portrait I have seen gives any idea of his expression. There were innumerable things in it, and they chased each other in and out of his face. I have seen people who were grave and gay in quick alternation; but Mark Ambient was grave and gay at one and the same moment. There were other strange oppositions and contradictions in his slightly faded and fatigued countenance. He affected me somehow as at once fresh and stale, at once anxious and indifferent. He had evidently had an active past, which inspired one with curiosity; yet what was that compared to his obvious future? He was just enough above middle height to be spoken of as tall, and rather lean and long in the flank. He had the friendliest frankest manner possible, and yet I could see it cost him something. It cost him small spasms of the self-consciousness that is an Englishman's last and dearest treasure—the thing he pays his way through life by sacrificing small pieces of even as the gallant but moneyless adventurer in "Quentin Durward" broke off links of his brave gold chain. He had been thirty-eight years old at the time "Beltraffio" was published. He asked me about his friend in America, about the length of my stay in England, about the last news in London and the people I had seen there; and I remember looking for the signs of genius in the very form of his questions and thinking I found it. I liked his voice as if I were somehow myself having the use of it.

There was genius in his house too I thought when we got there; there was imagination in the carpets and curtains, in the pictures and books, in the garden behind it, where certain old brown walls were muffled in creepers that appeared to me to have been copied from a masterpiece of one of the pre-Raphaelites. That was the way many things struck me at that time, in England—as reproductions of something that existed primarily in art or literature. It was not the picture, the poem, the fictive page, that seemed to me a copy; these things were the originals, and the life of happy and distinguished people was fashioned in their image. Mark Ambient called his house a cottage, and I saw afterwards he was right; for if it hadn't been a cottage it must have been a villa, and a villa, in England at least, was not a place in which one could fancy him at home. But it was, to my vision, a cottage glorified and translated; it was a palace of art, on a slightly reduced scale—and might besides have been the dearest haunt of the old English *genius loci*. It nestled under a cluster of magnificent beeches, it had little creaking lattices that opened out of, or into, pendent mats of ivy, and gables, and old red tiles, as well as a general aspect of being painted in water-colours and inhabited by people whose lives would go on in chapters and volumes. The lawn seemed to me of extraordinary extent, the garden-walls of incalculable height, the whole air of the place delightfully still, private, proper to itself. "My wife must be somewhere about," Mark Ambient said as we went in. "We shall find her perhaps—we've about an hour before dinner. She may be in the garden. I'll show you my little place."

We passed through the house and into the grounds, as I should have called them, which extended into the rear. They covered scarce three or four acres, but, like the house, were very old and crooked and full of traces of long habitation, with inequalities of level and little flights of steps —mossy and cracked were these—which connected the different parts with each other. The limits of the place, cleverly dissimulated, were muffled in the great verdurous screens. They formed, as I remember, a thick loose curtain at the further end, in one of the folds of which, as it were, we presently made out from afar a little group. "Ah there she is!" said Mark Ambient; "and she has got the boy." He noted that last fact in a slightly different tone from any in which he yet had spoken. I wasn't fully aware of this at the time, but it lingered in my ear and I afterwards understood it.

"Is it your son?" I inquired, feeling the question not to be brilliant.

"Yes, my only child. He's always in his mother's pocket. She coddles him too much." It came back to me afterwards too—the sound of these critical words. They weren't petulant; they expressed rather a sudden coldness, a mechanical submission. We went a few steps further, and then he stopped short and called the boy, beckoning to him repeatedly.

"Dolcino, come and see your daddy!" There was something in the way he stood still and waited that made me think he did it for a purpose. Mrs. Ambient had her arm round the child's waist, and he was leaning against her knee; but though he moved at his father's call she gave no sign of releasing him. A lady, apparently a neighbour, was seated near her, and before them was a garden-table on which a tea-service had been placed.

Mark Ambient called again, and Dolcino struggled in the maternal embrace; but, too tightly held, he after two or three fruitless efforts jerked about and buried his head deep in his mother's lap. There was a certain awkwardness in the scene; I thought it odd Mrs. Ambient should pay so little attention to her husband. But I wouldn't for the world have betrayed my thought and, to conceal it, I began loudly to rejoice in the prospect of our having tea in the garden. "Ah she won't let him come!" said my host with a sigh; and we went our way till we reached the two ladies. He mentioned my name to his wife, and I noticed that he addressed her as "My dear," very genially, without a trace of resentment at her detention of the child. The quickness of the transition made me vaguely ask myself if he were perchance henpecked—a shocking surmise which I instantly dismissed. Mrs. Ambient was quite such a wife as I should have expected him to have; slim and fair, with a long neck and pretty eyes and an air of good breeding. She shone with a certain coldness and practised in intercourse a certain bland detachment, but she was clothed in gentleness as in one of those vaporous redundant scarves that muffle the heroines of Gainsborough and Romney. She had also a vague air of race, justified by my afterwards learning that she was "connected with the aristocracy." I have seen poets married to women of whom it was difficult to conceive that they should gratify the poetic fancy—women with dull faces and glutinous minds, who were none the less, however, excellent wives. But there was no obvious disparity in Mark Ambient's union. My hostess—so far as she could be called so—delicate and quiet, in a white dress, with her beautiful child at her side, was worthy of the author of a work so distinguished as "Beltraffio." Round her neck she wore a black velvet ribbon, of which the long ends, tied behind, hung down her back, and to which, in front, was attached a miniature portrait of her little boy. Her smooth shining hair was confined in a net. She gave me an adequate greeting and Dolcino—I thought this small name of endearment delightful—took advantage of her getting up to slip away from her and go to his father, who seized him in silence and held him high for a long moment, kissing him several times.

I had lost no time in observing that the child, not more than seven years old, was extraordinarily beautiful. He had the face of an angel—the eyes, the hair, the smile of innocence, the more than mortal bloom. There was something that deeply touched, that almost alarmed, in his beauty, composed, one would have said, of elements too fine and pure for the breath of this world. When I spoke to him and he came and held out his hand and smiled at me I felt a sudden strange pity for him—quite as if he had been an orphan or a changeling or stamped with some social stigma. It was impossible to be in fact more exempt from these misfortunes, and yet, as one kissed him, it was hard to keep from murmuring all tenderly "Poor little devil!" though why one should have applied this epithet to a living cherub is more than I can say. Afterwards indeed I knew a trifle better; I grasped the truth of his being too fair to live, wondering at the same time that his parents shouldn't have guessed it and have been in proportionate grief and despair. For myself I had no doubt of his evanescence, having already more than once caught in the fact the particular infant charm that's as good as a death-warrant.

The lady who had been sitting with Mrs. Ambient was a jolly ruddy personage in velveteen and limp feathers, whom I guessed to be the vicar's wife—our hostess didn't introduce me—and who immediately began to talk to Ambient about chrysanthemums. This was a safe subject, and yet there was a certain surprise for me in seeing the author of "Beltraffio" even in such superficial communion with the Church of England. His writings implied so much detachment from that institution, expressed a view of life so profane, as it were, so independent and so little likely in general to be thought edifying, that I should have expected to find him an object of horror to vicars and their ladies—of horror repaid on his own part by any amount of effortless derision. This proved how little I knew as yet of the English people and their extraordinary talent for keeping up their forms, as well as of some of the mysteries of Mark Ambient's hearth and home. I found afterwards that he had, in his study, between nervous laughs and free cigar-puffs, some wonderful comparisons for his clerical neighbours; but meanwhile the chrysanthemums were a source of harmony, as he and the vicaress were equally attached to them, and I was surprised at the knowledge they exhibited of this interesting plant. The lady's visit, however, had presumably been long, and she presently rose for departure and kissed Mrs. Ambient. Mark started to walk with her to the gate of the grounds, holding Dolcino by the hand.

"Stay with me, darling," Mrs. Ambient said to the boy, who had surrendered himself to his father.

Mark paid no attention to the summons, but Dolcino

turned and looked at her in shy appeal. "Can't I go with papa?"

"Not when I ask you to stay with me."

"But please don't ask me, mamma," said the child in his small clear new voice.

"I must ask you when I want you. Come to me, dearest." And Mrs. Ambient, who had seated herself again, held out her long slender slightly too osseous hands.

Her husband stopped, his back turned to her, but without releasing the child. He was still talking to the vicaress, but this good lady, I think, had lost the thread of her attention. She looked at Mrs. Ambient and at Dolcino, and then looked at me, smiling in a highly amused cheerful manner and almost to a grimace.

"Papa," said the child, "mamma wants me not to go with you."

"He's very tired—he has run about all day. He ought to be quiet till he goes to bed. Otherwise he won't sleep." These declarations fell successively and very distinctly from Mrs. Ambient's lips.

Her husband, still without turning round, bent over the boy and looked at him in silence. The vicaress gave a genial irrelevant laugh and observed that he was a precious little pet. "Let him choose," said Mark Ambient. "My dear little boy, will you go with me or will you stay with your mother?"

"Oh it's a shame!" cried the vicar's lady with increased hilarity.

"Papa, I don't think I can choose," the child answered, making his voice very low and confidential. "But I've been a great deal with mamma to-day," he then added.

"And very little with papa! My dear fellow, I think you *have* chosen!" On which Mark Ambient walked off with his son, accompanied by re-echoing but inarticulate comments from my fellow-visitor.

His wife had seated herself again, and her fixed eyes, bent on the ground, expressed for a few moments so much mute agitation that anything I could think of to say would be but a false note. Yet she none the less quickly recovered herself, to express the sufficiently civil hope that I didn't mind having had to walk from the station. I reassured her on this point, and she went on: "We've got a thing that might have gone for you, but my husband wouldn't order it." After which and another longish pause, broken only by my plea that the pleasure of a walk with our friend would have been quite what I would have chosen, she found for reply: "I believe the Americans walk very little."

"Yes, we always run," I laughingly allowed.

She looked at me seriously, yet with an absence in her pretty eyes. "I suppose your distances are so great."

"Yes, but we break our marches! I can't tell you the pleasure to me of finding myself here," I added. "I've the greatest admiration for Mr. Ambient."

"He'll like that. He likes being admired."

"He must have a very happy life then. He has many worshippers."

"Oh yes, I've seen some of them," she dropped, looking away, very far from me, rather as if such a vision were before her at the moment. It seemed to indicate, her tone, that the sight was scarcely edifying, and I guessed her quickly enough to be in no great intellectual sympathy with the author of "Beltraffio." I thought the fact strange, but somehow, in the glow of my own enthusiasm, didn't think it important: it only made me wish rather to emphasise that homage.

"For me, you know," I returned—doubtless with a due suffisance—"he's quite the greatest of living writers."

"Of course I can't judge. Of course he's very clever," she said with a patient cheer.

"He's nothing less than supreme, Mrs. Ambient! There are pages in each of his books of a perfection classing them with the greatest things. Accordingly for me to see him in this familiar way, in his habit as he lives, and apparently to find the man as delightful as the artist—well, I can't tell you how much too good to be true it seems and how great a privilege I think it." I knew I was gushing, but I couldn't help it, and what I said was a good deal less than what I felt. I was by no means sure I should dare to say even so much as this to the master himself, and there was a kind of rapture in speaking it out to his wife which was not affected by the fact that, as a wife, she appeared peculiar. She listened to me with her face grave again and her lips a little compressed, listened as if in no doubt, of course, that her husband was remarkable, but as if at the same time she had heard it frequently enough and couldn't treat it as stirring news. There was even in her manner a suggestion that I was so young as to expose myself to being called forward—an imputation and a word I had always loathed; as well as a hinted reminder that people usually got over their early extravagance. "I assure you that for me this is a red-letter day," I added.

She didn't take this up, but after a pause, looking round her, said abruptly and a trifle dryly: "We're very much afraid about the fruit this year."

My eyes wandered to the mossy mottled garden-walls, where plum-trees and pears, flattened and fastened upon the rusty bricks, looked like crucified figures with many arms. "Doesn't it promise well?"

"No, the trees look very dull. We had such late frosts."

Then there was another pause. She addressed her attention to the opposite end of the grounds, kept it for her husband's return with the child. "Is Mr. Ambient fond of gardening?" it occurred to me to ask, irresistibly impelled as I felt myself, moreover, to bring the conversation constantly back to him.

"He's very fond of plums," said his wife.

"Ah well then I hope your crop will be better than you fear. It's a lovely old place," I continued. "The whole impression's that of certain places he has described. Your house is like one of his pictures."

She seemed a bit frigidly amused at my glow. "It's a pleasant little place. There are hundreds like it."

"Oh it has his *tone*," I laughed, but sounding my epithet and insisting on my point the more sharply that my companion appeared to see in my appreciation of her simple establishment a mark of mean experience.

It was clear I insisted too much. "His tone?" she repeated with a harder look at me and a slightly heightened colour.

"Surely he has a tone, Mrs. Ambient."

"Oh yes, he has indeed! But I don't in the least consider that I'm living in one of his books at all. I shouldn't care for that in the least," she went on with a smile that had in some degree the effect of converting her really sharp protest into an insincere joke. "I'm afraid I'm not very literary. And I'm not artistic," she stated.

"I'm very sure you're not ignorant, not stupid," I ventured to reply, with the accompaniment of feeling immediately afterwards that I had been both familiar and patronising. My only consolation was in the sense that she had begun it, had fairly dragged me into it. She had thrust forward her limitations.

"Well, whatever I am I'm very different from my husband. If you like him you won't like me. You needn't say anything. Your liking me isn't in the least necessary!"

"Don't defy me!" I could but honourably make answer.

She looked as if she hadn't heard me, which was the best thing she could do; and we sat some time without further speech. Mrs. Ambient had evidently the enviable English quality of being able to be mute without unrest. But at last she spoke—she asked me if there seemed many people in town. I gave her what satisfaction I could on this point, and we talked a little of London and of some of its characteristics at that time of the year. At the end of this I came back irrepressibly to Mark.

"Doesn't he like to be there now? I suppose he doesn't find the proper quiet for his work. I should think his things had been written for the most part in a very still place. They suggest a great stillness following on a kind of tumult. Don't you think so?" I laboured on. "I suppose London's a tremendous place to collect impressions, but a refuge like this, in the country, must be better for working them up. Does he get many of his impressions in London, should you say?" I proceeded from point to point in this malign inquiry simply because my hostess, who probably thought me an odious chattering person, gave me time; for when I paused —I've not represented my pauses—she simply continued to let her eyes wander while her long fair fingers played with the medallion on her neck. When I stopped altogether, however, she was obliged to say something, and what she said was that she hadn't the least idea where her husband got his impressions. This made me think her, for a moment, positively disagreeable; delicate and proper and rather aristocratically fine as she sat there. But I must either have lost that view a moment later or been goaded by it to further aggression, for I remember asking her if our great man were in a good vein of work and when we might look for the appearance of the book on which he was engaged. I've every reason now to know that she found me insufferable.

She gave a strange small laugh as she said: "I'm afraid you think I know much more about my husband's work than I do. I haven't the least idea what he's doing," she then added in a slightly different, that is a more explanatory, tone and as if from a glimpse of the enormity of her confession. "I don't read what he writes."

She didn't succeed, and wouldn't even had she tried much harder, in making this seem to me anything less than monstrous. I stared at her and I think I blushed. "Don't you admire his genius? Don't you admire 'Beltraffio'?"

She waited, and I wondered what she could possibly say. She didn't speak, I could see, the first words that rose to her lips; she repeated what she had said a few minutes before. "Oh of course he's very clever!" And with this she got up; our two absentees had reappeared.

II

Mrs. Ambient left me and went to meet them; she stopped and had a few words with her husband that I didn't hear and that ended in her taking the child by the hand and returning with him to the house. Her husband joined me in a moment, looking, I thought, the least bit conscious and constrained, and said that if I would come in with him he would show me my room. In looking back upon these first moments of my visit I find it important to avoid the error of appearing to have at all fully measured his situation from the first or made out the signs of things mastered only afterwards. This later knowledge throws a backward light and makes me forget that, at least on the

occasion of my present reference—I mean that first afternoon—Mark Ambient struck me as only enviable. Allowing
for this he must yet have failed of much expression as we
walked back to the house, though I remember well the answer he made to a remark of mine on his small son.

"That's an extraordinary little boy of yours. I've never
seen such a child."

"Why," he asked while we went, "do you call him
extraordinary?"

"He's so beautiful, so fascinating. He's like some perfect
little work of art."

He turned quickly in the passage, grasping my arm. "Oh
don't call him that, or you'll—you'll—!" But in his hesitation
he broke off suddenly, laughing at my surprise. Immediately afterwards, however, he added: "You'll make his little
future very difficult."

I declared that I wouldn't for the world take any liberties
with his little future—it seemed to me to hang by threads
of such delicacy. I should only be highly interested in
watching it.

"You Americans are very keen," he commented on this.
"You notice more things than we do."

"Ah if you want visitors who aren't struck with you," I
cried, "you shouldn't have asked me down here!"

He showed me my room, a little bower of chintz, with
open windows where the light was green, and before he
left me said irrelevantly: "As for my small son, you know,
we shall probably kill him between us before we've done
with him!" And he made this assertion as if he really believed it, without any appearance of jest, his fine nearsighted expressive eyes looking straight into mine.

"Do you mean by spoiling him?"

"No, by fighting for him!"

"You had better give him to me to keep for you," I said.
"Let me remove the apple of discord!"

It was my extravagance of course, but he had the air
of being perfectly serious. "It would be quite the best thing
we could do. I should be all ready to do it."

"I'm greatly obliged to you for your confidence."

But he lingered with his hands in his pockets. I felt as

if within a few moments I had, morally speaking, taken several steps nearer to him. He looked weary, just as he faced me then, looked preoccupied and as if there were something one might do for him. I was terribly conscious of the limits of my young ability, but I wondered what such a service might be, feeling at bottom nevertheless that the only thing I could do for him was to like him. I suppose he guessed this and was grateful for what was in my mind, since he went on presently: "I haven't the advantage of being an American, but I also notice a little, and I've an idea that"—here he smiled and laid his hand on my shoulder —"even counting out your nationality you're not destitute of intelligence. I've only known you half an hour, but—!" For which again he pulled up. "You're very young after all."

"But you may treat me as if I could understand you!" I said; and before he left me to dress for dinner he had virtually given me a promise that he would.

When I went down into the drawing-room—I was very punctual—I found that neither my hostess nor my host had appeared. A lady rose from a sofa, however, and inclined her head as I rather surprisedly gazed at her. "I dare say you don't know me," she said with the modern laugh. "I'm Mark Ambient's sister." Whereupon I shook hands with her, saluting her very low. Her laugh was modern—by which I mean that it consisted of the vocal agitation serving between people who meet in drawing-rooms as the solvent of social disparities, the medium of transitions; but her appearance was—what shall I call it?—medieval. She was pale and angular, her long thin face was inhabited by sad dark eyes and her black hair intertwined with golden fillets and curious clasps. She wore a faded velvet robe which clung to her when she moved and was "cut," as to the neck and sleeves, like the garments of old Italians. She suggested a symbolic picture, something akin even to Dürer's Melancholia, and was so perfect an image of a type which I, in my ignorance, supposed to be extinct, that while she rose before me I was almost as much startled as if I had seen a ghost. I afterwards concluded that Miss Ambient wasn't incapable of deriving pleasure from this weird effect, and I now believe that reflexion concerned in her having sunk

again to her seat with her long lean but not ungraceful
arms locked together in an archaic manner on her knees
and her mournful eyes addressing me a message of intentness which foreshadowed what I was subsequently to
suffer. She was a singular fatuous artificial creature, and I
was never more than half to penetrate her motives and
mysteries. Of one thing I'm sure at least: that they were
considerably less insuperable than her appearance announced. Miss Ambient was a restless romantic disappointed spinster, consumed with the love of Michael-Angel-
esque attitudes and mystical robes; but I'm now convinced
she hadn't in her nature those depths of unutterable
thought which, when you first knew her, seemed to look
out from her eyes and to prompt her complicated gestures.
Those features in especial had a misleading eloquence; they
lingered on you with a far-off dimness, an air of obstructed
sympathy, which was certainly not always a key to the
spirit of their owner; so that, of a truth, a young lady could
scarce have been so dejected and disillusioned without having committed a crime for which she was consumed with
remorse, or having parted with a hope that she couldn't
sanely have entertained. She had, I believe, the usual allowance of rather vain motives: she wished to be looked at,
she wished to be married, she wished to be thought
original.

It costs me a pang to speak in this irreverent manner of
one of Ambient's name, but I shall have still less gracious
things to say before I've finished my anecdote, and moreover—I confess it—I owe the young lady a bit of a grudge.
Putting aside the curious cast of her face she had no natural
aptitude for an artistic development, had little real intelligence. But her affectations rubbed off on her brother's
renown, and as there were plenty of people who darkly dis-
approved of him they could easily point to his sister as a
person formed by his influence. It was quite possible to regard her as a warning, and she had almost compromised
him with the world at large. He was the original and she
the inevitable imitation. I suppose him scarce aware of the
impression she mainly produced, beyond having a general
idea that she made up very well as a Rossetti; he was used

to her and was sorry for her, wishing she would marry and observing how she didn't. Doubtless I take her too seriously, for she did me no harm, though I'm bound to allow that I can only half-account for her. She wasn't so mystical as she looked, but was a strange indirect uncomfortable embarrassing woman. My story gives the reader at best so very small a knot to untie that I needn't hope to excite his curiosity by delaying to remark that Mrs. Ambient hated her sister-in-law. This I learned but later on, when other matters came to my knowledge. I mention it, however, at once, for I shall perhaps not seem to count too much on having beguiled him if I say he must promptly have guessed it. Mrs. Ambient, a person of conscience, put the best face on her kinswoman, who spent a month with her twice a year; but it took no great insight to recognise the very different personal paste of the two ladies, and that the usual feminine hypocrisies would cost them on either side much more than the usual effort. Mrs. Ambient, smooth-haired, thin-lipped, perpetually fresh, must have regarded her crumpled and dishevelled visitor as an equivocal joke; she herself so the opposite of a Rossetti, she herself a Reynolds or a Lawrence, with no more far-fetched note in her composition than a cold ladylike candour and a well-starched muslin dress.

It was in a garment and with an expression of this kind that she made her entrance after I had exchanged a few words with Miss Ambient. Her husband presently followed her and, there being no other company, we went to dinner. The impressions I received at that repast are present to me still. The elements of oddity in the air hovered, as it were, without descending—to any immediate check of my delight. This came mainly of course from Ambient's talk, the easiest and richest I had ever heard. I mayn't say to-day whether he laid himself out to dazzle a rather juvenile pilgrim from over the sea; but that matters little—it seemed so natural to him to shine. His spoken wit or wisdom, or whatever, had thus a charm almost beyond his written; that is if the high finish of his printed prose be really, as some people have maintained, a fault. There was such a kindness in him, however, that I've no doubt it gave him ideas for me, or about me, to see me sit as open-mouthed as I now figure myself. Not so the two ladies, who not only were very nearly dumb from beginning to end of the meal, but who hadn't even the air of being struck with such an exhibition of fancy and taste. Mrs. Ambient, detached, and inscrutable, met neither my eye nor her husband's: she attended to her dinner, watched her servants, arranged the puckers in her dress, exchanged at wide intervals a remark with her sister-in-law and, while she slowly rubbed her lean white hands between the courses, looked out of the window at the first signs of evening—the long June day allowing us to dine without candles. Miss Ambient appeared to give little direct heed to anything said by her brother; but on the other hand she was much engaged in watching its effect upon me. Her "die-away" pupils continued to attach themselves to my countenance, and it was only her air of belonging to another century that kept them from being importunate. She seemed to look at me across the ages, and the interval of time diminished for me the inconvenience. It was as if she knew in a general way that he must be talking very well, but she herself was so at home among such allusions that she had no need to pick them up and was at liberty to see what would become of the exposure of a candid young American to a high aesthetic temperature.

The temperature was aesthetic certainly, but it was less so than I could have desired, for I failed of any great success in making our friend abound about himself. I tried to put him on the ground of his own genius, but he slipped through my fingers every time and shifted the saddle to one or other of his contemporaries. He talked about Balzac and Browning, about what was being done in foreign countries, about his recent tour in the East and the extraordinary forms of life to be observed in that part of the world. I felt he had reasons for holding off from a direct profession of literary faith, a full consistency or sincerity, and therefore dealt instead with certain social topics, treating them with extraordinary humour and with a due play of that power of ironic evocation in which his books abound. He had a deal to say about London as London appears to the observer who has the courage of some of his conclusions during the high-pressure time—from April to July—of its gregarious life. He flashed his faculty of playing with the caught image and liberating the wistful idea over the whole scheme of manners or conception of intercourse of his compatriots, among whom there were evidently not a few types for which he had little love. London in short was grotesque to him, and he made capital sport of it; his only allusion that I can remember to his own work was his saying that he meant some day to do an immense and general, a kind of epic, social satire. Miss Ambient's perpetual gaze seemed to put to me: "Do you perceive how artistic, how very strange and interesting, we are? Frankly now is it possible to be *more* artistic, *more* strange and interesting, than this? You surely won't deny that we're remarkable." I was irritated by her use of the plural pronoun, for she had no right to pair herself with her brother; and moreover, of course, I couldn't see my way to—at all genially—include Mrs. Ambient. Yet there was no doubt they were, taken together, unprecedented enough, and, with all allowances, I had never been left, or condemned, to draw so many rich inferences.

After the ladies had retired my host took me into his study to smoke, where I appealingly brought him round, or so tried, to some disclosure of fond ideals. I was bent on proving I was worthy to listen to him, on repaying him for what he had said to me before dinner, by showing him how perfectly I understood. He liked to talk; he liked to defend his convictions and his honour (not that I attacked them); he liked a little perhaps—it was a pardonable weakness—to bewilder the youthful mind even while wishing to win it over. My ingenuous sympathy received at any rate a shock from three or four of his professions—he made me occasionally gasp and stare. He couldn't help forgetting, or rather couldn't know, how little, in another and dryer clime, I had ever sat in the school in which he was master; and he promoted me as at a jump to a sense of its penetralia. My trepidations, however, were delightful; they were just what I had hoped for, and their only fault was that they passed away too quickly; since I found that for the main points I was essentially, I was quite constitutionally, on

Mark Ambient's "side." This was the taken stand of the artist to whom every manifestation of human energy was a thrilling spectacle and who felt for ever the desire to resolve his experience of life into a literary form. On that high head of the passion for form—the attempt at perfection, the quest for which was to his mind the real search for the holy grail—he said the most interesting, the most inspiring things. He mixed with them a thousand illustrations from his own life, from other lives he had known, from history and fiction, and above all from the annals of the time that was dear to him beyond all periods, the Italian cinquecento. It came to me thus that in his books he had uttered but half his thought, and that what he had kept back—from motives I deplored when I made them out later—was the finer, and braver part. It was his fate to make a great many still more "prepared" people than me not inconsiderably wince; but there was no grain of bravado in his ripest things (I've always maintained it, though often contradicted), and at bottom the poor fellow, disinterested to his finger-tips and regarding imperfection not only as an aesthetic but quite also as a social crime, had an extreme dread of scandal. There are critics who regret that having gone so far he didn't go further; but I regret nothing—putting aside two or three of the motives I just mentioned—since he arrived at a noble rarity and I don't see how you can go beyond that. The hours I spent in his study—this first one and the few that followed it; they were not after all so numerous—seem to glow, as I look back on them, with a tone that is partly that of the brown old room, rich, under the shaded candle-light where we sat and smoked, with the dusky delicate bindings of valuable books; partly that of his voice, of which I still catch the echo, charged with the fancies and figures that came at his command. When we went back to the drawing-room we found Miss Ambient alone in possession and prompt to mention that her sister-in-law had a quarter of an hour before been called by the nurse to see the child, who appeared rather unwell—a little feverish.

"Feverish! how in the world comes he to be feverish?" Ambient asked. "He was perfectly right this afternoon."

"Beatrice says you walked him about too much—you almost killed him."

"Beatrice must be very happy—she has an opportunity to triumph!" said my friend with a bright bitterness which was all I could have wished it.

"Surely not if the child's ill," I ventured to remark by way of pleading for Mrs. Ambient.

"My dear fellow, you aren't married—you don't know the nature of wives!" my host returned with spirit.

I tried to match it. "Possibly not; but I know the nature of mothers."

"Beatrice is perfect as a mother," sighed Miss Ambient quite tremendously and with her fingers interlaced on her embroidered knees.

"I shall go up and see my boy," her brother went on. "Do you suppose he's asleep?"

"Beatrice won't let you see him, dear"—as to which our young lady looked at me, though addressing our companion.

"Do you call that being perfect as a mother?" Ambient asked.

"Yes, from her point of view."

"Damn her point of view!" cried the author of "Beltraffio." And he left the room; after which we heard him ascend the stairs.

I sat there for some ten minutes with Miss Ambient, and we naturally had some exchange of remarks, which began, I think, by my asking her what the point of view of her sister-in-law could be.

"Oh it's so very odd. But we're so very odd altogether. Don't you find us awfully unlike others of our class?—which indeed mostly, in England, is awful. We've lived so much abroad. I adore 'abroad.' Have you people like us in America?"

"You're not all alike, you interesting three—or, counting Dolcino, four—surely, surely; so that I don't think I understand your question. We've no one like your brother—I may go so far as that."

"You've probably more persons like his wife," Miss Ambient desolately smiled.

"I can tell you that better when you've told me about her point of view."

"Oh yes—oh yes. Well," said my entertainer, "she doesn't like his ideas. She doesn't like them for the child. She thinks them undesirable."

Being quite fresh from the contemplation of some of Mark Ambient's *arcana* I was particularly in a position to appreciate this announcement. But the effect of it was to make me, after staring a moment, burst into laughter which I instantly checked when I remembered the indisposed child above and the possibility of parents nervously or fussily anxious.

"What has that infant to do with ideas?" I asked. "Surely he can't tell one from another. Has he read his father's novels?"

"He's very precocious and very sensitive, and his mother thinks she can't begin to guard him too early." Miss Ambient's head drooped a little to one side and her eyes fixed themselves on futurity. Then of a sudden came a strange alteration; her face lighted to an effect more joyless than any gloom, to that indeed of a conscious insincere grimace, and she added: "When one has children what one writes becomes a great responsibility."

"Children are terrible critics," I prosaically answered. "I'm really glad I haven't any."

"Do you also write then? And in the same style as my brother? And do you like that style? And do people appreciate it in America? I don't write, but I think I feel." To these and various other inquiries and observations my young lady treated me till we heard her brother's step in the hall again and Mark Ambient reappeared. He was so flushed and grave that I supposed he had seen something symptomatic in the condition of his child. His sister apparently had another idea; she gazed at him from afar—as if he had been a burning ship on the horizon—and simply murmured "Poor old Mark!"

"I hope you're not anxious," I as promptly pronounced.

"No, but I'm disappointed. She won't let me in. She has locked the door, and I'm afraid to make a noise." I dare say there might have been a touch of the ridiculous in such a confession, but I liked my new friend so much that it took nothing for me from his dignity. "She tells me—from behind the door—that she'll let me know if he's worse."

"It's very good of her," said Miss Ambient with a hollow sound.

I had exchanged a glance with Mark in which it's possible he read that my pity for him was untinged with contempt, though I scarce know why he should have cared; and as his sister soon afterward got up and took her bedroom candlestick he proposed we should go back to his study. We sat there till after midnight; he put himself into his slippers and an old velvet jacket, he lighted an ancient pipe, but he talked considerably less than before. There were longish pauses in our communion, but they only made me feel we had advanced in intimacy. They helped me further to understand my friend's personal situation and to imagine it by no means the happiest possible. When his face was quiet it was vaguely troubled, showing, to my increase of interest—if that was all that was wanted!—that for him too life was the same struggle it had been for so many another man of genius. At last I prepared to leave him, and then, to my ineffable joy, he gave me some sheets of his forthcoming book—which, though unfinished, he had indulged in the luxury, so dear to writers of deliberation, of having "set up," from chapter to chapter, as he advanced. These early pages, the *prémices*, in the language of letters, of that new fruit of his imagination, I should take to my room and look over at my leisure. I was in the act of leaving him when the door of the study noiselessly opened and Mrs. Ambient stood before us. She observed us a moment, her candle in her hand, and then said to her husband that as she supposed he hadn't gone to bed she had come down to let him know Dolcino was more quiet and would probably be better in the morning. Mark Ambient made no reply; he simply slipped past her in the doorway, as if for fear she might seize him in his passage, and bounded upstairs to judge for himself of his child's condition. She looked so frankly discomfited that I for a moment believed her about to give him chase. But she resigned herself with a sigh and her eyes turned, ruefully and without a ray, to

the lamplit room where various books at which I had been
looking were pulled out of their places on the shelves and
the fumes of tobacco hung in midair. I bade her good-night
and then, without intention, by a kind of fatality, a perversity that had already made me address her overmuch on
that question of her husband's powers, I alluded to the precious proof-sheets with which Ambient had entrusted me
and which I nursed there under my arm. "They're the opening chapters of his new book," I said. "Fancy my satisfaction at being allowed to carry them to my room!"

She turned away, leaving me to take my candlestick from
the table in the hall; but before we separated, thinking it
apparently a good occasion to let her know once for all—
since I was beginning, it would seem, to be quite "thick"
with my host—that there was no fitness in my appealing to
her for sympathy in such a case; before we separated, I
say, she remarked to me with her quick fine well-bred inveterate curtness: "I dare say you attribute to me ideas
I haven't got. I don't take that sort of interest in my husband's proof-sheets. I consider his writings most objectionable!"

III

I had an odd colloquy the next morning with Miss
Ambient, whom I found strolling in the garden before
breakfast. The whole place looked as fresh and trim, amid
the twitter of the birds, as if, an hour before, the house-
maids had been turned into it with their dust-pans and
feather-brushes. I almost hesitated to light a cigarette and
was doubly startled when, in the act of doing so, I suddenly
saw the sister of my host, who had, at the best, something
of the weirdness of an apparition, stand before me. She
might have been posing for her photograph. Her sad-col-
oured robe arranged itself in serpentine folds at her feet;
her hands locked themselves listlessly together in front; her
chin rested on a cinque-cento ruff. The first thing I did after
bidding her good-morning was to ask her for news of her
little nephew—to express the hope she had heard he was
better. She was able to gratify this trust—she spoke as if we

might expect to see him during the day. We walked through the shrubberies together and she gave me further light on her brother's household, which offered me an opportunity to repeat to her what his wife had so startled and distressed me with the night before. *Was* it the sorry truth that she thought his productions objectionable?

"She doesn't usually come out with that so soon!" Miss Ambient returned in answer to my breathlessness.

"Poor lady," I pleaded, "she saw I'm a fanatic."

"Yes, she won't like you for that. But you mustn't mind, if the rest of us like you! Beatrice thinks a work of art ought to have a 'purpose.' But she's a charming woman—don't you think her charming? I find in her quite the grand air."

"She's very beautiful," I produced with an effort; while I reflected that though it was apparently true that Mark Ambient was mismated it was also perceptible that his sister was perfidious. She assured me her brother and his wife had no other difference but this one—that she thought his writings immoral and his influence pernicious. It was a fixed idea; she was afraid of these things for the child. I answered that it was in all conscience enough, the trifle of a woman's regarding her husband's mind as a well of corruption, and she seemed much struck with the novelty of my remark. "But there hasn't been any of the sort of trouble that there so often is among married people," she said. "I suppose you can judge for yourself that Beatrice isn't at all —well, whatever they call it when a woman kicks over! And poor Mark doesn't make love to other people either. You might think he would, but I assure you he doesn't. All the same of course, from her point of view, you know, she has a dread of my brother's influence on the child—on the formation of his character, his 'ideals,' poor little brat, his principles. It's as if it were a subtle poison or a contagion—something that would rub off on his tender sensibility when his father kisses him or holds him on his knee. If she could she'd prevent Mark from even so much as touching him. Every one knows it—visitors see it for themselves; so there's no harm in my telling you. Isn't it excessively odd? It comes from Beatrice's being so religious and so tremendously moral—so *à cheval* on fifty thousand *riguardi*. And then of course we mustn't forget," my companion added, a little unexpectedly, to this polyglot proposition, "that some of Mark's ideas are—well, really—rather impossible, don't you know?"

I reflected as we went into the house, where we found Ambient unfolding *The Observer* at the breakfast-table, that none of them were probably quite so "impossible, don't you know?" as his sister. Mrs. Ambient, a little "the worse," as was mentioned, for her ministrations, during the night, to Dolcino, didn't appear at breakfast. Her husband described her, however, as hoping to go to church. I afterwards learnt that she did go, but nothing naturally was less on the cards than that we should accompany her. It was while the church-bell droned near at hand that the author of "Beltraffio" led me forth for the ramble he had spoken of in his note. I shall attempt here no record of where we went or of what we saw. We kept to the fields and copses and commons, and breathed the same sweet air as the nibbling donkeys and the browsing sheep, whose woolliness seemed to me, in those early days of acquaintance with English objects, but part of the general texture of the small dense landscape, which looked as if the harvest were gathered by the shears and with all nature bleating and braying for the violence. Everything was full of expression for Mark Ambient's visitor—from the big bandy-legged geese whose whiteness was a "note" amid all the tones of green as they wandered beside a neat little oval pool, the foreground of a thatched and whitewashed inn, with a grassy approach and a pictorial sign—from these humble wayside animals to the crests of high woods which let a gable or a pinnacle peep here and there and looked even at a distance like trees of good company, conscious of an individual profile. I admired the hedge-rows, I plucked the faint-hued heather, and I was for ever stopping to say how charming I thought the threadlike footpaths across the fields, which wandered in a diagonal of finer grain from one smooth stile to another. Mark Ambient was abundantly good-natured and was as much struck, dear man, with some of my observations as I was with the literary allusions of the landscape. We sat and smoked on stiles, broaching paradoxes in the decent

English air; we took short cuts across a park or two where the bracken was deep and my companion nodded to the old woman at the gate; we skirted rank coverts which rustled here and there as we passed, and we stretched ourselves at last on a heathery hillside where if the sun wasn't too hot neither was the earth too cold, and where the country lay beneath us in a rich blue mist. Of course I had already told him what I thought of his new novel, having the previous night read every word of the opening chapters before I went to bed.

"I'm not without hope of being able to make it decent enough," he said as I went back to the subject while we turned up our heels to the sky. "At least the people who dislike my stuff—and there are plenty of them, I believe—will dislike this thing (if it does turn out well) most." This was the first time I had heard him allude to the people who couldn't read him—a class so generally conceived to sit heavy on the consciousness of the man of letters. A being organised for literature as Mark Ambient was must certainly have had the normal proportion of sensitiveness, or irritability; the artistic *ego*, capable in some cases of such monstrous development, must have been in his composition sufficiently erect and active. I won't therefore go so far as to say that he never thought of his detractors or that he had any illusions with regard to the number of his admirers —he could never so far have deceived himself as to believe he was popular, but I at least then judged (and had occasion to be sure later on) that stupidity ruffled him visibly but little, that he had an air of thinking it quite natural he should leave many simple folk, tasting of him, as simple as ever he found them, and that he very seldom talked about the newspapers, which, by the way, were always even abnormally vulgar about him. Of course he may have thought them over—the newspapers—night and day; the only point I make is that he didn't show it; while at the same time he didn't strike one as a man actively on his guard. I may add that, touching his hope of making the work on which he was then engaged the best of his books, it was only partly carried out. That place belongs incontestably to "Beltraffio," in spite of the beauty of certain parts of its successor. I quite believe, however, that he had at the moment of which I speak no sense of having declined; he was in love with his idea, which was indeed magnificent, and though for him, as I suppose for every sane artist, the act of execution had in it as much torment as joy, he saw his result grow like the crescent of the young moon and promise to fill the disk. "I want to be truer than I've ever been," he said, settling himself on his back with his hands clasped behind his head; "I want to give the impression of life itself. No, you may say what you will, I've always arranged things too much, always smoothed them down and rounded them off and tucked them in—done everything to them that life doesn't do. I've been a slave to the old superstitions."

"You a slave, my dear Mark Ambient? You've the freest imagination of our day!"

"All the more shame to me to have done some of the things I have! The reconciliation of the two women in 'Natalina,' for instance, which could never really have taken place. That sort of thing's ignoble—I blush when I think of it! This new affair must be a golden vessel, filled with the purest distillation of the actual; and oh how it worries me, the shaping of the vase, the hammering of the metal! I have to hammer it so fine, so smooth; I don't do more than an inch or two a day. And all the while I have to be so careful not to let a drop of the liquor escape! When I see the kind of things Life herself, the brazen hussy, does, I despair of ever catching her peculiar trick. She has an impudence, Life! If one risked a fiftieth part of the effects she risks! It takes ever so long to believe it. You don't know yet, my dear youth. It isn't till one has been watching her some forty years that one finds out half of what she's up to! Therefore one's earlier things must inevitably contain a mass of rot. And with what one sees, on one side, with its tongue in its cheek, defying one to be real enough, and on the other the *bonnes gens* rolling up their eyes at one's cynicism, the situation has elements of the ludicrous which the poor reproducer himself is doubtless in a position to appreciate better than any one else. Of course one mustn't worry about the *bonnes gens*," Mark Ambient went on while my thoughts reverted to his ladylike wife as interpreted by his remarkable sister.

"To sink your shaft deep and polish the plate through which people look into it—that's what your work consists of," I remember ingeniously observing.

"Ah polishing one's plate—that's the torment of execution!" he exclaimed, jerking himself up and sitting forward. "The effort to arrive at a surface, if you think anything of that decent sort necessary—some people don't, happily for them! My dear fellow, if you could see the surface I dream of as compared with the one with which I've to content myself. Life's really too short for art—one hasn't time to make one's shell ideally hard. Firm and bright, firm and bright is very well to say—the devilish thing has a way sometimes of being bright, and even of being hard, as mere tough frozen pudding is hard, without being firm. When I rap it with my knuckles it doesn't give the right sound. There are horrible sandy stretches where I've taken the wrong turn because I couldn't for the life of me find the right. If you knew what a dunce I am sometimes! Such things figure to me now base pimples and ulcers on the brow of beauty!"

"They're very bad, very bad," I said as gravely as I could.

"Very bad? They're the highest social offence I know; it ought—it absolutely ought; I'm quite serious—to be capital. If I knew I should be publicly thrashed else I'd manage to find the true word. The people who can't—some of them don't so much as know it when they see it—would shut their inkstands, and we shouldn't be deluged by this flood of rubbish!"

I shall not attempt to repeat everything that passed between us, nor to explain just how it was that, every moment I spent in his company, Mark Ambient revealed to me more and more the consistency of his creative spirit, the spirit in him that felt all life as plastic material. I could but envy him the force of that passion, and it was at any rate through the receipt of this impression that by the time we returned I had gained the sense of intimacy with him that I have noted. Before we got up for the homeward stretch he alluded to his wife's having once—or perhaps more than once—asked him whether he should like Dolcino to read "Beltraffio." He must have been unaware at the moment of all that this conveyed to me—as well doubtless of my extreme curiosity to hear what he had replied. He had said how much he hoped Dolcino would read *all* his works—when he was twenty; he should like him to know what his father had done. Before twenty it would be useless; he wouldn't understand them.

"And meanwhile do you propose to hide them—to lock them up in a drawer?" Mrs. Ambient had proceeded.

"Oh no—we must simply tell him they're not intended for small boys. If you bring him up properly after that he won't touch them."

To this Mrs. Ambient had made answer that it might be very awkward when he was about fifteen, say; and I asked her husband if it were his opinion in general, then, that young people shouldn't read novels.

"Good ones—certainly not!" said my companion. I suppose I had had other views, for I remember saying that for myself I wasn't sure it was bad for them if the novels were "good" to the right intensity of goodness. "Bad for *them,* I don't say so much!" my companion returned. "But very bad, I'm afraid, for the poor dear old novel itself." That oblique accidental allusion to his wife's attitude was followed by a greater breadth of reference as we walked home. "The difference between us is simply the opposition between two distinct ways of looking at the world, which have never succeeded in getting on together, or in making any kind of common household, since the beginning of time. They've borne all sorts of names, and my wife would tell you it's the difference between Christian and Pagan. I may be a pagan, but I don't like the name; it sounds sectarian. She thinks me at any rate no better than an ancient Greek. It's the difference between making the most of life and making the least, so that you'll get another better one in some other time and place. Will it be a sin to make the most of that one too, I wonder; and shall we have to be bribed off in the future state as well as in the present? Perhaps I care too much for beauty—I don't know, I doubt if a poor devil *can;* I delight in it, I adore it, I think of it continually, I try to produce it, to reproduce it. My wife holds that we shouldn't cultivate or enjoy it without extraordinary precautions and reserves. She's always afraid of it, always on her guard. I don't know what it can ever have done to her, what grudge it owes her or what resentment rides. And she's so pretty, too, herself! Don't you think she's lovely? She was at any rate when we married. At that time I wasn't aware of that difference I speak of—I thought it all came to the same thing: in the end, as they say. Well, perhaps it will in the end. I don't know what the end will be. Moreover, I care for seeing things as they are; that's the way I try to show them in any professed picture. But you mustn't talk to Mrs. Ambient about things as they are. She has a moral dread of things as they are."

"She's afraid of them for Dolcino," I said: surprised a moment afterward at being in a position—thanks to Miss Ambient—to be so explanatory; and surprised even now that Mark shouldn't have shown visibly that he wondered what the deuce I knew about it. But he didn't; he simply declared with a tenderness that touched me: "Ah nothing shall ever hurt *him!*"

He told me more about his wife before we arrived at the gate of home, and if he be judged to have aired overmuch his grievance I'm afraid I must admit that he had some of the foibles as well as the gifts of the artistic temperament; adding, however, instantly that hitherto, to the best of my belief, he had rarely let this particular cat out of the bag. "She thinks me immoral—that's the long and short of it," he said as we paused outside a moment and his hand rested on one of the bars of his gate; while his conscious expressive perceptive eyes—the eyes of a foreigner, I had begun to account them, much more than of the usual Englishman —viewing me now evidently as quite a familiar friend, took part in the declaration. "It's very strange when one thinks it all over, and there's a grand comicality in it that I should like to bring out. She's a very nice woman, extraordinarily well-behaved, upright and clever and with a tremendous lot of good sense about a good many matters. Yet her conception of a novel—she has explained it to me once or twice, and she doesn't do it badly as exposition—is a thing so false that it makes me blush. It's a thing so hollow, so dishonest, so lying, in which life is so blinked and blinded, so dodged and disfigured, that it makes my ears burn. It's two different ways of looking at the whole affair," he repeated, pushing open the gate. "And they're irreconcilable!" he added with a sigh. We went forward to the house, but on the walk, halfway to the door, he stopped and said to me: "If you're going into this kind of thing there's a fact you should know beforehand; it may save you some disappointment. There's a hatred of art, there's a hatred of literature—I mean of the genuine kinds. Oh the shams—*those* they'll swallow by the bucket!" I looked up at the charming house, with its genial colour and crookedness, and I answered with a smile that those evil passions might exist, but that I should never have expected to find them there. "Ah it doesn't matter after all," he a bit nervously laughed; which I was glad to hear, for I was reproaching myself with having worked him up.

If I had it soon passed off, for at luncheon he was delightful; strangely delightful considering that the difference between himself and his wife was, as he had said, irreconcilable. He had the art, by his manner, by his smile, by his natural amenity, of reducing the importance of it in the common concerns of life; and Mrs. Ambient, I must add, lent herself to this transaction with a very good grace. I watched her at table for further illustrations of that fixed idea of which Miss Ambient had spoken to me; for in the light of the united revelations of her sister-in-law and her husband she had come to seem to me almost a sinister personage. Yet the signs of a sombre fanaticism were not more immediately striking in her than before; it was only after a while that her air of incorruptible conformity, her tapering monosyllabic correctness, began to affect me as in themselves a cold thin flame. Certainly, at first, she resembled a woman with as few passions as possible; but if she had a passion at all it would indeed be that of Philistinism. She might have been (for there are guardian-spirits, I suppose, of all great principles) the very angel of the pink of propriety—putting the pink for a principle, though I'd rather put some dismal cold blue. Mark Ambient, apparently, ten years before, had simply and quite inevitably taken her for an angel, without asking himself of what. He had been right in calling my attention to her beauty. In looking for some explanation of his original surrender to her I saw more than before that she was, physically speaking, a wonderfully cultivated human plant—that he might well have owed her a brief poetic inspiration. It was impossible to be more propped and pencilled, more delicately tinted and petalled.

If I had had it in my heart to think my host a little of a hypocrite for appearing to forget at table everything he had said to me in our walk, I should instantly have cancelled such a judgement on reflecting that the good news his wife was able to give him about their little boy was ground enough for any optimistic reaction. It may have come partly too from a certain compunction at having breathed to me at all harshly on the cool fair lady who sat there—a desire to prove himself not after all so mismated. Dolcino continued to be much better, and it had been promised him he should come downstairs after his dinner. As soon as we had risen from our own meal Mark slipped away, evidently for the purpose of going to his child; and no sooner had I observed this than I became aware his wife had simultaneously vanished. It happened that Miss Ambient and I, both at the same moment, saw the tail of her dress whisk out of a doorway; an incident that led the young lady to smile at me as if I now knew all the secrets of the Ambients. I passed with her into the garden and we sat down on a dear old bench that rested against the west wall of the house. It was a perfect spot for the middle period of a Sunday in June, and its felicity seemed to come partly from an antique sun-dial which, rising in front of us and forming the centre of a small intricate parterre, measured the moments ever so slowly and made them safe for leisure and talk. The garden bloomed in the suffused afternoon, the tall beeches stood still for an example, and, behind and above us, a rose-tree of many seasons, clinging to the faded grain of the brick, expressed the whole character of the scene in a familiar exquisite smell. It struck me as a place to offer genius every favour and sanction—not to bristle with challenges and checks. Miss Ambient asked me if I had enjoyed my walk with her brother and whether we had talked of many things.

"Well, of most things," I freely allowed, though I remembered we hadn't talked of Miss Ambient.

"And don't you think some of his theories are very peculiar?"

"Oh I guess I agree with them all." I was very particular, for Miss Ambient's entertainment, to guess.

"Do you think art's everything?" she put to me in a moment.

"In art, of course I do!"

"And do you think beauty's everything?"

"Everything's a big word, which I think we should use as little as possible. But how can we not want beauty?"

"Ah there you are!" she sighed, though I didn't quite know what she meant by it. "Of course it's difficult for a woman to judge how far to go," she went on. "I adore everything that gives a charm to life. I'm intensely sensitive to form. But sometimes I draw back—don't you see what I mean?—I don't quite see where I shall be landed. I only want to be quiet, after all," Miss Ambient continued as if she had long been baffled of this modest desire. "And one must be good, at any rate, must not one?" she pursued with a dubious quaver—an intimation apparently that what I might say one way or the other would settle it for her. It was difficult for me to be very original in reply, and I'm afraid I repaid her confidence with an unblushing platitude. I remember moreover attaching to it an inquiry, equally destitute of freshness and still more wanting perhaps in tact, as to whether she didn't mean to go to church, since that was an obvious way of being good. She made answer that she had performed this duty in the morning, and that for her, of Sunday afternoons, supreme virtue consisted in answering the week's letters. Then suddenly and without transition she brought out: "It's quite a mistake about Dolcino's being better. I've seen him and he's not at all right."

I wondered, and somehow I think I scarcely believed. "Surely his mother would know, wouldn't she?"

She appeared for a moment to be counting the leaves on one of the great beeches. "As regards most matters one can easily say what, in a given situation, my sister-in-law will, or would, do. But in the present case there are strange elements at work."

"Strange elements? Do you mean in the constitution of the child?"

"No, I mean in my sister-in-law's feelings."

"Elements of affection of course; elements of anxiety," I concurred. "But why do you call them strange?"

She repeated my words. "Elements of affection, elements of anxiety. She's very anxious."

Miss Ambient put me indescribably ill at ease; she almost scared me, and I wished she would go and write her letters. "His father will have seen him now," I said, "and if he's not satisfied he will send for the doctor."

"The doctor ought to have been here this morning," she promptly returned. "He lives only two miles away."

I reflected that all this was very possibly but a part of the general tragedy of Miss Ambient's view of things; yet I asked her why she hadn't urged that view on her sister-in-law. She answered me with a smile of extraordinary significance and observed that I must have very little idea of her "peculiar" relations with Beatrice; but I must do her the justice that she re-enforced this a little by the plea that any distinguishable alarm of Mark's was ground enough for a difference of his wife's. He was always nervous about the child, and as they were predestined by nature to take opposite views, the only thing for the mother was to cultivate a false optimism. In Mark's absence and that of his betrayed fear she would have been less easy. I remembered what he had said to me about their dealings with their son—that between them they'd probably put an end to him; but I didn't repeat this to Miss Ambient: the less so that just then her brother emerged from the house, carrying the boy in his arms. Close behind him moved his wife, grave and pale; the little sick face was turned over Ambient's shoulder and toward the mother. We rose to receive the group, and as they came near us Dolcino twisted himself about. His enchanting eyes showed me a smile of recognition, in which, for the moment, I should have taken a due degree of comfort. Miss Ambient, however, received another impression, and I make haste to say that her quick sensibility, which visibly went out to the child, argues that in spite of her affectations she might have been of some human use. "It won't do at all—it won't do at all," she said to me under her breath. "I shall speak to Mark about the Doctor."

Her small nephew was rather white, but the main difference I saw in him was that he was even more beautiful than the day before. He had been dressed in his festal garments—a velvet suit and a crimson sash—and he looked like a little invalid prince too young to know condescension and smiling familiarly on his subjects.

"Put him down, Mark, he's not a bit at his ease," Mrs. Ambient said.

"Should you like to stand on your feet, my boy?" his father asked.

He made a motion that quickly responded. "Oh, yes; I'm remarkably well."

Mark placed him on the ground; he had shining pointed shoes with enormous bows. "Are you happy now, Mr. Ambient?"

"Oh yes, I'm particularly happy," Dolcino replied. But the words were scarce out of his mouth when his mother caught him up and, in a moment, holding him on her knees, took her place on the bench where Miss Ambient and I had been sitting. This young lady said something to her brother, in consequence of which the two wandered away into the garden together.

IV

I remained with Mrs. Ambient, but as a servant had brought out a couple of chairs I wasn't obliged to seat myself beside her. Our conversation failed of ease, and I, for my part, felt there would be a shade of hypocrisy in my now trying to make myself agreeable to the partner of my friend's existence. I didn't dislike her—I rather admired her; but I was aware that I differed from her inexpressibly. Then I suspected, what I afterwards definitely knew and have

already intimated, that the poor lady felt small taste for
her husband's so undisguised disciple; and this of course
was not encouraging. She thought me an obtrusive and
designing, even perhaps a depraved, young man whom a
perverse Providence had dropped upon their quiet lawn to
flatter his worst tendencies. She did me the honour to say
to Miss Ambient, who repeated the speech, that she didn't
know when she had seen their companion take such a fancy
to a visitor; and she measured apparently my evil influence
by Mark's appreciation of my society. I had a consciousness,
not oppressive but quite sufficient, of all this; though I
must say that if it chilled my flow of small-talk it yet didn't
prevent my thinking the beautiful mother and beautiful
child, interlaced there against their background of roses, a
picture such as I doubtless shouldn't soon see again. I was
free, I supposed, to go into the house and write letters, to
sit in the drawing-room, to repair to my own apartment and
take a nap; but the only use I·made of my freedom was to
linger still in my chair and say to myself that the light
hand of Sir Joshua might have painted Mark Ambient's
wife and son. I found myself looking perpetually at the latter small mortal, who looked constantly back at me, and
that was enough to detain me. With these vaguely-amused
eyes he smiled, and I felt it an absolute impossibility to
abandon a child with such an expression. His attention
never strayed; it attached itself to my face as if among all
the small incipient things of his nature throbbed a desire
to say something to me. If I could have taken him on my
own knee he perhaps would have managed to say it;
but it would have been a critical matter to ask his mother
to give him up, and it has remained a constant regret for
me that on that strange Sunday afternoon I didn't even for
a moment hold Dolcino in my arms. He had said he felt
remarkably well and was especially happy; but though
peace may have been with him as he pillowed his charming
head on his mother's breast, dropping his little crimson silk
legs from her lap, I somehow didn't think security was. He
made no attempt to walk about; he was content to swing
his legs softly and strike one as languid and angelic.

Mark returned to us with his sister; and Miss Ambient,

repeating her mention of the claims of her correspondence, passed into the house. Mark came and stood in front of his wife, looking down at the child, who immediately took hold of his hand and kept it while he stayed. "I think Mackintosh ought to see him," he said; "I think I'll walk over and fetch him."

"That's Gwendolen's idea, I suppose," Mrs. Ambient replied very sweetly.

"It's not such an out-of-the-way idea when one's child's ill," he returned.

"I'm not ill, papa; I'm much better now," sounded in the boy's silver pipe.

"Is that the truth, or are you only saying it to be agreeable? You've a great idea of being agreeable, you know."

The child seemed to meditate on this distinction, this imputation, for a moment; then his exaggerated eyes, which had wandered, caught my own as I watched him. "Do *you* think me agreeable?" he inquired with the candour of his age and with a look that made his father turn round to me laughing and ask, without saying it, "Isn't he adorable?"

"Then why don't you hop about, if you feel so lusty?" Ambient went on while his son swung his hand.

"Because mamma's holding me close!"

"Oh yes; I know how mamma holds you when I come near!" cried Mark with a grimace at his wife.

She turned her charming eyes up to him without deprecation or concession. "You can go for Mackintosh if you like. I think myself it would be better. You ought to drive."

"She says that to get me away," he put to me with a gaiety that I thought a little false; after which he started for the Doctor's.

I remained there with Mrs. Ambient, though even our exchange of twaddle had run very thin. The boy's little fixed white face seemed, as before, to plead with me to stay, and after a while it produced still another effect, a very curious one, which I shall find it difficult to express. Of course I expose myself to the charge of an attempt to justify by a strained logic after the fact a step which may have been on my part but the fruit of a native want of discretion; and indeed the traceable consequences of that perversity were too lamentable to leave me any desire to trifle with the question. All I can say is that I acted in perfect good faith and that Dolcino's friendly little gaze gradually kindled the spark of my inspiration. What helped it to glow were the other influences—the silent suggestive garden-nook, the perfect opportunity (if it was not an opportunity for that it was an opportunity for nothing) and the plea I speak of, which issued from the child's eyes and seemed to make him say: "The mother who bore me and who presses me here to her bosom—sympathetic little organism that I am—has really the kind of sensibility she has been represented to you as lacking, if you only look for it patiently and respectfully. How is it conceivable she shouldn't have it? How is it possible that I should have so much of it—for I'm quite full of it, dear strange gentleman —if it weren't also in some degree in her? I'm my great father's child, but I'm also my beautiful mother's, and I'm sorry for the difference between them!" So it shaped itself before me, the vision of reconciling Mrs. Ambient with her husband, of putting an end to their ugly difference. The project was absurd of course, for had I not had his word for it—spoken with all the bitterness of experience —that the gulf dividing them was well-nigh bottomless? Nevertheless, a quarter of an hour after Mark had left us, I observed to my hostess that I couldn't get over what she had told me the night before about her thinking her husband's compositions "objectionable." I had been so very sorry to hear it, had thought of it constantly and wondered whether it mightn't be possible to make her change her mind. She gave me a great cold stare, meant apparently as an admonition to me to mind my business. I wish I had taken this mute counsel, but I didn't take it. I went on to remark that it seemed an immense pity so much that was interesting should be lost on her.

"Nothing's lost upon me," she said in a tone that didn't make the contradiction less. "I know they're very interesting."

"Don't you like papa's books?" Dolcino asked, addressing his mother but still looking at me. Then he added to me: "Won't you read them to me, American gentleman?"

"I'd rather tell you some stories of my own," I said. "I know some that are awfully good."

"When will you tell them? To-morrow?"

"To-morrow with pleasure, if that suits you."

His mother took this in silence. Her husband, during our walk, had asked me to remain another day; my promise to her son was an implication that I had consented, and it wasn't possible the news could please her. This ought doubtless to have made me more careful as to what I said next, but all I can plead is that it didn't. I soon mentioned that just after leaving her the evening before, and after hearing her apply to her husband's writings the epithet already quoted, I had on going up to my room sat down to the perusal of those sheets of his new book that he had been so good as to lend me. I had sat entranced till nearly three in the morning—I had read them twice over. "You say you haven't looked at them. I think it's such a pity you shouldn't. Do let me beg you to take them up. They're so very remarkable. I'm sure they'll convert you. They place him in—really—such a dazzling light. All that's best in him is there. I've no doubt it's a great liberty, my saying all this; but pardon me, and *do* read them!"

"Do read them, mamma!" the boy again sweetly shrilled. "Do read them!"

She bent her head and closed his lips with a kiss. "Of course I know he has worked immensely over them," she said; after which she made no remark, but attached her eyes thoughtfully to the ground. The tone of these last words was such as to leave me no spirit for further pressure, and after hinting at a fear that her husband mightn't have caught the Doctor I got up and took a turn about the grounds. When I came back ten minutes later she was still in her place watching her boy, who had fallen asleep in her lap. As I drew near she put her finger to her lips and a short time afterwards rose, holding him; it being now best, she said, that she should take him upstairs. I offered to carry him and opened my arms for the purpose; but she thanked me and turned away with the child still in her embrace, his head on her shoulder. "I'm very strong," was her last word as she passed into the house, her slim flexible figure bent backward with the filial weight. So I never laid a longing hand on Dolcino.

I betook myself to Ambient's study, delighted to have a quiet hour to look over his books by myself. The windows were open to the garden; the sunny stillness, the mild light of the English summer, filled the room without quite chasing away the rich dusky tone that was a part of its charm and that abode in the serried shelves where old morocco exhaled the fragrance of curious learning, as well as in the brighter intervals where prints and medals and miniatures were suspended on a surface of faded stuff. The place had both colour and quiet; I thought it a perfect room for work and went so far as to say to myself that, if it were mine to sit and scribble in, there was no knowing but I might learn to write as well as the author of "Beltraffio." This distinguished man still didn't reappear, and I rummaged freely among his treasures. At last I took down a book that detained me a while and seated myself in a fine old leather chair by the window to turn it over. I had been occupied in this way for half an hour—a good part of the afternoon had waned—when I became conscious of another presence in the room and, looking up from my quarto, saw that Mrs. Ambient, having pushed open the door quite again in the same noiseless way marking or disguising her entrance the night before, had advanced across the threshold. On seeing me she stopped; she had not, I think, expected to find me. But her hesitation was only of a moment; she came straight to her husband's writing-table as if she were looking for something. I got up and asked her if I could help her. She glanced about an instant and then put her hand upon a roll of papers which I recognised, as I had placed it on that spot at the early hour of my descent from my room.

"Is this the new book?" she asked, holding it up.

"The very sheets," I smiled; "with precious annotations."

"I mean to take your advice"—and she tucked the little bundle under her arm. I congratulated her cordially and ventured to make of my triumph, as I presumed to call it, a subject of pleasantry. But she was perfectly grave and turned away from me, as she had presented herself, with-

out relaxing her rigour; after which I settled down to my
quarto aga: with the reflexion that Mrs. Ambient was
truly an eccentric. My triumph, too, suddenly seemed to
me rather vain. A woman who couldn't unbend at a moment exquisitely indicated would never understand Mark
Ambient. He came back to us at last in person, having
brought the Doctor with him. "He was away from home,"
Mark said, "and I went after him to where he was supposed to be. He had left the place, and I followed him to
two or three others, which accounts for my delay." He was
now with Mrs. Ambient, looking at the child, and was to
see Mark again before leaving the house. My host noticed
at the end of two minutes that the proof-sheets of his new
book had been removed from the table; and when I told
him, in reply to his question as to what I knew about them,
that Mrs. Ambient had carried them off to read he turned
almost pale with surprise. "What has suddenly made her
so curious?" he cried; and I was obliged to tell him that
I was at the bottom of the mystery. I had had it on my
conscience to assure her that she really ought to know of
what her husband was capable. "Of what I'm capable?
Elle ne s'en doute que trop!" said Ambient with a laugh;
but he took my meddling very good-naturedly and contented himself with adding that he was really much afraid
she would burn up the sheets, his emendations and all, of
which latter he had no duplicate. The Doctor paid a long
visit in the nursery, and before he came down I retired to
my own quarters, where I remained till dinner-time. On
entering the drawing-room at this hour I found Miss Ambient in possession, as she had been the evening before.

"I was right about Dolcino," she said, as soon as she
saw me, with an air of triumph that struck me as the climax of perversity. "He's really very ill."

"Very ill! Why when I last saw him, at four o'clock, he
was in fairly good form."

"There has been a change for the worse, very sudden
and rapid, and when the Doctor got here he found diphtheritic symptoms. He ought to have been called, as I knew,
in the morning, and the child oughtn't to have been brought
into the garden."

"My dear lady, he was very happy there," I protested with horror.

"He would be very happy anywhere. I've no doubt he's very happy now, with his poor little temperature—!" She dropped her voice as her brother came in, and Mark let us know that as a matter of course Mrs. Ambient wouldn't appear. It was true the boy had developed diphtheritic symptoms, but he was quiet for the present and his mother earnestly watching him. She was a perfect nurse, Mark said, and Mackintosh would come back at ten. Our dinner wasn't very gay—with my host worried and absent; and his sister annoyed me by her constant tacit assumption, conveyed in the very way she nibbled her bread and sipped her wine, of having "told me so." I had had no disposition to deny anything she might have told me, and I couldn't see that her satisfaction in being justified by the event relieved her little nephew's condition. The truth is that, as the sequel was to prove, Miss Ambient had some of the qualities of the sibyl and had therefore perhaps a right to the sibylline contortions. Her brother was so preoccupied that I felt my presence an indiscretion and was sorry I had promised to remain over the morrow. I put it to Mark that clearly I had best leave them in the morning; to which he replied that, on the contrary, if he was to pass the next days in the fidgets my company would distract his attention. The fidgets had already begun for him, poor fellow; and as we sat in his study with our cigars after dinner he wandered to the door whenever he heard the sound of the Doctor's wheels. Miss Ambient, who shared this apartment with us, gave me at such moments significant glances; she had before rejoining us gone upstairs to ask about the child. His mother and his nurse gave a fair report, but Miss Ambient found his fever high and his symptoms very grave. The Doctor came at ten o'clock, and I went to bed after hearing from Mark that he saw no present cause for alarm. He had made every provision for the night and was to return early in the morning.

I quitted my room as eight struck the next day and when I came downstairs saw, through the open door of the house, Mrs. Ambient standing at the front gate of the grounds in colloquy with Mackintosh. She wore a white dressing-gown, but her shining hair was carefully tucked away in its net, and in the morning freshness, after a night of watching, she looked as much "the type of the lady" as her sister-in-law had described her. Her appearance, I suppose, ought to have reassured me; but I was still nervous and uneasy, so that I shrank from meeting her with the necessary challenge. None the less, however, was I impatient to learn how the new day found him; and as Mrs. Ambient hadn't seen me I passed into the grounds by a roundabout way and, stopping at a further gate, hailed the Doctor just as he was driving off. Mrs. Ambient had returned to the house before he got into his cart.

"Pardon me, but as a friend of the family I should like very much to hear about the little boy."

The stout sharp circumspect man looked at me from head to foot and then said: "I'm sorry to say I haven't seen him."

"Haven't seen him?"

"Mrs. Ambient came down to meet me as I alighted, and told me he was sleeping so soundly, after a restless night, that she didn't wish him disturbed. I assured her I wouldn't disturb him, but she said he was quite safe now and she could look after him herself."

"Thank you very much. Are you coming back?"

"No sir; I'll be hanged if I come back!" cried the honest practitioner in high resentment. And the horse started as he settled beside his man.

I wandered back into the garden, and five minutes later Miss Ambient came forth from the house to greet me. She explained that breakfast wouldn't be served for some time and that she desired a moment herself with the Doctor. I let her know that the good vexed man had come and departed, and I repeated to her what he had told me about his dismissal. This made Miss Ambient very serious, very serious indeed, and she sank into a bench, with dilated eyes, hugging her elbows with crossed arms. She indulged in many strange signs, she confessed herself immensely distressed, and she finally told me what her own last news of her nephew had been. She had sat up very late—after me, after Mark—and before going to bed had knocked at the door of the child's room, opened to her by the nurse. This good woman had admitted her and she had found him quiet, but flushed and "unnatural," with his mother sitting by his bed. "She held his hand in one of hers," said Miss Ambient, "and in the other—what do you think?—the proof-sheets of Mark's new book! She was reading them there intently: did you ever hear of anything so extraordinary? Such a very odd time to be reading an author whom she never could abide!" In her agitation Miss Ambient was guilty of this vulgarism of speech, and I was so impressed by her narrative that only in recalling her words later did I notice the lapse. Mrs. Ambient had looked up from her reading with her finger on her lips—I recognised the ges-ture she had addressed me in the afternoon—and, though the nurse was about to go to rest, had not encouraged her sister-in-law to relieve her of any part of her vigil. But cer-tainly at that time the boy's state was far from reassuring —his poor little breathing so painful; and what change could have taken place in him in those few hours that would justify Beatrice in denying Mackintosh access? This was the moral of Miss Ambient's anecdote, the moral for herself at least. The moral for me, rather, was that it *was* a very singular time for Mrs. Ambient to be going into a novelist she had never appreciated and who had simply happened to be recommended to her by a young Ameri-can she disliked. I thought of her sitting there in the sick-chamber in the still hours of the night and after the nurse had left her, turning and turning those pages of genius and wrestling with their magical influence.

I must be sparing of the minor facts and the later emo-tions of this sojourn—it lasted but a few hours longer—and devote but three words to my subsequent relations with Ambient. They lasted five years—till his death—and were full of interest, of satisfaction and, I may add, of sadness. The main thing to be said of these years is that I had a secret from him which I guarded to the end. I believe he never suspected it, though of this I'm not absolutely sure. If he had so much as an inkling the line he had taken, the line of absolute negation of the matter to himself, shows

an immense effort of the will. I may at last lay bare my secret, giving it for what it is worth; now that the main suf-
ferer has gone, that he has begun to be alluded to as one
of the famous early dead and that his wife has ceased to
survive him; now too that Miss Ambient, whom I also saw
at intervals during the time that followed, has, with her
embroideries and her attitudes, her necromantic glances
and strange intuitions, retired to a Sisterhood, where, as I
am told, she is deeply immured and quite lost to the world.

Mark came in to breakfast after this lady and I had for
some time been seated there. He shook hands with me in
silence, kissed my companion, opened his letters and newspapers and pretended to drink his coffee. But I took these
movements for mechanical and was little surprised when
he suddenly pushed away everything that was before him
and, with his head in his hands and his elbows on the table,
sat staring strangely at the cloth.

"What's the matter, *caro fratello mio?*" Miss Ambient
quavered, peeping from behind the urn.

He answered nothing, but got up with a certain violence
and strode to the window. We rose to our feet, his relative
and I, by a common impulse, exchanging a glance of some
alarm; and he continued to stare into the garden. "In heav-
en's name what has got possession of Beatrice?" he cried
at last, turning round on us a ravaged face. He looked from
one of us to the other—the appeal was addressed to us alike.

Miss Ambient gave a shrug. "My poor Mark, Beatrice is
always—Beatrice!"

"She has locked herself up with the boy—bolted and
barred the door. She refuses to let me come near him!" he
went on.

"She refused to let Mackintosh see him an hour ago!"
Miss Ambient promptly returned.

"Refused to let Mackintosh see him? By heaven I'll smash
in the door!" And Mark brought his fist down upon the
sideboard, which he had now approached, so that all the
breakfast-service rang.

I begged Miss Ambient to go up and try to have speech
of her sister-in-law, and I drew Mark out into the garden.

"You're exceedingly nervous, and Mrs. Ambient's probably right," I there undertook to plead. "Women know; women should be supreme in such a situation. Trust a mother—a devoted mother, my dear friend!" With such words as these I tried to soothe and comfort him, and, marvellous to relate, I succeeded, with the help of many cigarettes, in making him walk about the garden and talk, or suffer me at least to do so for near an hour. When about that time had elapsed his sister reappeared, reaching us rapidly and with a convulsed face while she held her hand to her heart.

"Go for the Doctor, Mark—go for the Doctor this moment!"

"Is he dying? Has she killed him?" my poor friend cried, flinging away his cigarette.

"I don't know what she has done! But she's frightened, and now she wants the Doctor."

"He told me he'd be hanged if he came back!" I felt myself obliged to mention.

"Precisely—therefore Mark himself must go for him, and not a messenger. You must see him and tell him it's to save your child. The trap has been ordered—it's ready."

"To save him? I'll save him, please God!" Ambient cried, bounding with his great strides across the lawn.

As soon as he had gone I felt I ought to have volunteered in his place, and I said as much to Miss Ambient; but she checked me by grasping my arm while we heard the wheels of the dog-cart rattle away from the gate. "He's off—he's off—and now I can think! To get him away—while I think —while I think!"

"While you think of what, Miss Ambient?"

"Of the unspeakable thing that has happened under this roof!"

Her manner was habitually that of such a prophetess of ill that I at first allowed for some great extravagance. But I looked at her hard, and the next thing felt myself turn white. "Dolcino *is* dying then—he's dead?"

"It's too late to save him. His mother has let him die! I tell you that because you're sympathetic, because you've imagination," Miss Ambient was good enough to add, interrupting my expression of horror. "That's why you had the idea of making her read Mark's new book!"

"What has that to do with it? I don't understand you. Your accusation's monstrous."

"I see it all—I'm not stupid," she went on, heedless of my emphasis. "It was the book that finished her—it was that decided her!"

"Decided her? Do you mean she has murdered her child?" I demanded, trembling at my own words.

"She sacrificed him; she determined to do nothing to make him live. Why else did she lock herself in, why else did she turn away the Doctor? The book gave her a horror; she determined to rescue him—to prevent him from ever being touched. He had a crisis at two o'clock in the morning. I know that from the nurse, who had left her then, but whom, for a short time, she called back. The darling got much worse, but she insisted on the nurse's going back to bed, and after that she was alone with him for hours."

I listened with a dread that stayed my credence, while she stood there with her tearless glare. "Do you pretend then she has no pity, that she's cruel and insane?"

"She held him in her arms, she pressed him to her breast, not to see him; but she gave him no remedies; she did nothing the Doctor ordered. Everything's there untouched. She has had the honesty not even to throw the drugs away!"

I dropped upon the nearest bench, overcome with my dismay—quite as much at Miss Ambient's horrible insistence and distinctness as at the monstrous meaning of her words. Yet they came amazingly straight, and if they did have a sense I saw myself too woefully figure in it. Had I been then a proximate cause—? "You're a very strange woman and you say incredible things," I could only reply.

She had one of her tragic headshakes. "You think it necessary to protest, but you're really quite ready to believe me. You've received an impression of my sister-in-law— you've guessed of what she's capable."

I don't feel bound to say what concession on this score I made to Miss Ambient, who went on to relate to me that within the last half-hour Beatrice had had a revulsion, that she was tremendously frightened at what she had done; that her fright itself betrayed her; and that she would now give heaven and earth to save the child. "Let us hope she will!" I said, looking at my watch and trying to time poor Ambient; whereupon my companion repeated all portentously "Let us hope so!" When I asked her if she herself could do nothing, and whether she oughtn't to be with her sister-in-law, she replied: "You had better go and judge! She's like a wounded tigress!"

I never saw Mrs. Ambient till six months after this, and therefore can't pretend to have verified the comparison. At the latter period she was again the type of the perfect lady. "She'll treat him better after this," I remember her sister-in-law's saying in response to some quick outburst, on my part, of compassion for her brother. Though I had been in the house but thirty-six hours this young lady had treated me with extraordinary confidence, and there was therefore a certain demand I might, as such an intimate, make of her. I extracted from her a pledge that she'd never say to her brother what she had just said to me, that she'd let him form his own theory of his wife's conduct. She agreed with me that there was misery enough in the house without her contributing a new anguish, and that Mrs. Ambient's proceedings might be explained, to her husband's mind, by the extravagance of a jealous devotion. Poor Mark came back with the Doctor much sooner than we could have hoped, but we knew five minutes afterwards that it was all too late. His sole, his adored little son was more exquisitely beautiful in death than he had been in life. Mrs. Ambient's grief was frantic; she lost her head and said strange things. As for Mark's—but I won't speak of that. *Basta, basta,* as he used to say. Miss Ambient kept her secret—I've already had occasion to say that she had her good points—but it rankled in her conscience like a guilty participation and, I imagine, had something to do with her ultimately retiring from the world. And, apropos of consciences, the reader is now in a position to judge of my compunction for my effort to convert my cold hostess. I ought to mention that the death of her child in some degree converted her. When the new book came out (it was long delayed) she read it over as a whole, and her husband told me that during the few supreme weeks before her death—she failed rapidly after losing her son, sank into a consumption and faded away at Mentone—she even dipped into the black "Beltraffio."

[1884]

BROOKSMITH

We are scattered now, the friends of the late Mr. Oliver
Offord; but whenever we chance to meet I think we are
conscious of a certain esoteric respect for each other. "Yes,
you too have been in Arcadia," we seem not too grumpily
to allow. When I pass the house in Mansfield Street I remember that Arcadia was there. I don't know who has it
now, and don't want to know; it's enough to be so sure that
if I should ring the bell there would be no such luck for
me as that Brooksmith should open the door. Mr. Offord,
the most agreeable, the most attaching of bachelors, was
a retired diplomatist, living on his pension and on something of his own over and above; a good deal confined, by
his infirmities, to his fireside and delighted to be found there
any afternoon in the year, from five o'clock on, by such
visitors as Brooksmith allowed to come up. Brooksmith was
his butler and his most intimate friend, to whom we all
stood, or I should say sat, in the same relation in which
the subject of the sovereign finds himself to the prime minister. By having been for years, in foreign lands, the most
delightful Englishman any one had ever known, Mr. Offord had in my opinion rendered signal service to his country. But I suppose he had been too much liked—liked even
by those who didn't like *it*—so that as people of that sort
never get titles or dotations for the horrid things they've

not done, his principal reward was simply that we went to see him.

Oh we went perpetually, and it was not our fault if he was not overwhelmed with this particular honour. Any visitor who came once came again; to come merely once was a slight nobody, I'm sure, had ever put upon him. His circle therefore was essentially composed of habitués, who were habitués for each other as well as for him, as those of a happy salon should be. I remember vividly every element of the place, down to the intensely Londonish look of the grey opposite houses, in the gap of the white curtains of the high windows, and the exact spot where, on a particular afternoon, I put down my tea-cup for Brooksmith, lingering an instant, to gather it up as if he were plucking a flower. Mr. Offord's drawing-room was indeed Brooksmith's garden, his pruned and tended human parterre, and if we all flourished there and grew well in our places it was largely owing to his supervision.

Many persons have heard much, though most have doubtless seen little, of the famous institution of the salon, and many are born to the depression of knowing that this finest flower of social life refuses to bloom where the English tongue is spoken. The explanation is usually that our women have not the skill to cultivate it—the art to direct through a smiling land, between suggestive shores, a sinuous stream of talk. My affectionate, my pious memory of Mr. Offord contradicts this induction only, I fear, more insidiously to confirm it. The sallow and slightly smoked drawing-room in which he spent so large a portion of the last years of his life certainly deserved the distinguished name; but on the other hand it couldn't be said at all to owe its stamp to any intervention throwing into relief the fact that there was no Mrs. Offord. The dear man had indeed, at the most, been capable of one of those sacrifices to which women are deemed peculiarly apt: he had recognised—under the influence, in some degree, it is true, of physical infirmity—that if you wish people to find you at home you must manage not to be out. He had in short accepted the truth which many dabblers in the social art are slow to learn, that you must really, as they say, take a line, and that the only way as yet discovered of being at home is to stay at home. Finally his own fireside had become a summary of his habits. Why should he ever have left it?—since this would have been leaving what was notoriously pleasantest in London, the compact charmed cluster (thinning away indeed into casual couples) round the fine old last-century chimney-piece which, with the exception of the remarkable collection of miniatures, was the best thing the place contained. Mr. Offord wasn't rich; he had nothing but his pension and the use for life of the somewhat superannuated house.

When I'm reminded by some opposed discomfort of the present hour how perfectly we were all handled there, I ask myself once more what had been the secret of such perfection. One had taken it for granted at the time, for anything that is supremely good produces more acceptance than surprise. I felt we were all happy, but I didn't consider how our happiness was managed. And yet there were questions to be asked, questions that strike me as singularly obvious now that there's nobody to answer them. Mr. Offord had solved the insoluble; he had, without feminine help—save in the sense that ladies were dying to come to him and that he saved the lives of several—established a salon; but I might have guessed that there was a method in his madness, a law in his success. He hadn't hit it off by a mere fluke. There was an art in it all, and how was the art so hidden? Who indeed if it came to that was the occult artist? Launching this enquiry the other day I had already got hold of the tail of my reply. I was helped by the very wonder of some of the conditions that came back to me—those that used to seem as natural as sunshine in a fine climate.

How was it for instance that we never were a crowd, never either too many or too few, always the right people *with* the right people—there must really have been no wrong people at all—always coming and going, never sticking fast nor overstaying, yet never popping in or out with an indecorous familiarity? How was it that we all sat where we wanted and moved when we wanted and met whom we wanted and escaped whom we wanted; joining, accord-

ing to the accident of inclination, the general circle or falling in with a single talker on a convenient sofa? Why were
all the sofas so convenient, the accidents so happy, the talk-
ers so ready, the listeners so willing, the subjects presented
to you in a rotation as quickly foreordained as the courses
at dinner? A dearth of topics would have been as unheard
of as a lapse in the service. These speculations couldn't fail
to lead me to the fundamental truth that Brooksmith had
been somehow at the bottom of the mystery. If he hadn't
established the salon at least he had carried it on. Brooksmith in short was the artist!

We felt this covertly at the time, without formulating
it, and were conscious, as an ordered and prosperous community, of his evenhanded justice, all untainted with
flunkeyism. He had none of that vulgarity—his touch was
infinitely fine. The delicacy of it was clear to me on the
first occasion my eyes rested, as they were so often to rest
again, on the domestic revealed, in the turbid light of the
street, by the opening of the house-door. I saw on the spot
that though he had plenty of school he carried it without
arrogance—he had remained articulate and human. L'École
Anglaise Mr. Offord used laughingly to call him when, later
on, it happened more than once that we had some conversation about him. But I remember accusing Mr. Offord
of not doing him quite ideal justice. That he wasn't one
of the giants of the school, however, was admitted by my
old friend, who really understood him perfectly and was
devoted to him, as I shall show; which doubtless poor
Brooksmith had himself felt, to his cost, when his value in
the market was originally determined. The utility of his
class in general is estimated by the foot and the inch, and
poor Brooksmith had only about five feet three to put into
circulation. He acknowledged the inadequacy of this provision, and I'm sure was penetrated with the everlasting fitness of the relation between service and stature. If *he* had
been Mr. Offord he certainly would have found Brooksmith
wanting, and indeed the laxity of his employer on this score
was one of many things he had had to condone and to
which he had at last indulgently adapted himself.

I remember the old man's saying to me: "Oh my serv-

ants, if they can live with me a fortnight they can live with
me for ever. But it's the first fortnight that tries 'em." It
was in the first fortnight for instance that Brooksmith had
had to learn that he was exposed to being addressed as
"my dear fellow" and "my poor child." Strange and deep
must such a probation have been to him, and he doubtless
emerged from it tempered and purified. This was written to
a certain extent in his appearance; in his spare brisk little
person, in his cloistered white face and extraordinarily
polished hair, which told of responsibility, looked as if it
were kept up to the same high standard as the plate; in
his small clear anxious eyes, even in the permitted, though
not exactly encouraged, tuft on his chin. "He thinks me
rather mad, but I've broken him in, and now he likes the
place, he likes the company," said the old man. I embraced
this fully after I had become aware that Brooksmith's main
characteristic was a deep and shy refinement, though I remember I was rather puzzled when, on another occasion,
Mr. Offord remarked: "What he likes is the talk—mingling
in the conversation." I was conscious I had never seen
Brooksmith permit himself this freedom, but I guessed in
a moment that what Mr. Offord alluded to was a participation more intense than any speech could have represented
—that of being perpetually present on a hundred legitimate
pretexts, errands, necessities, and breathing the very atmosphere of criticism, the famous criticism of life. "Quite an
education, sir, isn't it, sir?" he said to me one day at the
foot of the stairs when he was letting me out; and I've always remembered the words and the tone as the first sign
of the quickening drama of poor Brooksmith's fate. It was
indeed an education, but to what was this sensitive young
man of thirty-five, of the servile class, being educated?

Practically and inevitably, for the time, to companion-
ship, to the perpetual, the even exaggerated reference and
appeal of a person brought to dependence by his time of
life and his infirmities and always addicted moreover—this
was the exaggeration—to the art of giving you pleasure by
letting you do things for him. There were certain things
Mr. Offord was capable of pretending he liked you to do
even when he didn't—this, I mean, if he thought *you* liked

them. If it happened that you didn't either—which was rare, yet might be—of course there were cross-purposes; but Brooksmith was there to prevent their going very far. This was precisely the way he acted as moderator; he averted misunderstandings or cleared them up. He had been capable, strange as it may appear, of acquiring for this purpose an insight into the French tongue, which was often used at Mr. Offord's; for besides being habitual to most of the foreigners, and they were many, who haunted the place or arrived with letters—letters often requiring a little worried consideration, of which Brooksmith always had cognisance —it had really become the primary language of the master of the house. I don't know if all the *malentendus* were in French, but almost all the explanations were, and this didn't a bit prevent Brooksmith's following them. I know Mr. Offord used to read passages to him from Montaigne and Saint-Simon, for he read perpetually when alone—when *they* were alone, that is—and Brooksmith was always about. Perhaps you'll say no wonder Mr. Offord's butler regarded him as "rather mad." However, if I'm not sure what he thought about Montaigne I'm convinced he admired Saint-Simon. A certain feeling for letters must have rubbed off on him from the mere handling of his master's books, which he was always carrying to and fro and putting back in their places.

I often noticed that if an anecdote or a quotation, much more a lively discussion, was going forward, he would, if busy with the fire or the curtains, the lamp or the tea, find a pretext for remaining in the room till the point should be reached. If his purpose was to catch it you weren't discreet, you were in fact scarce human, to call him off, and I shall never forget a look, a hard stony stare—I caught it in its passage—which, one day when there were a good many people in the room, he fastened upon the footman who was helping him in the service and who, in an undertone, had asked him some irrelevant question. It was the only manifestation of harshness I ever observed on Brooksmith's part, and I at first wondered what was the matter. Then I became conscious that Mr. Offord was relating a very curious anecdote, never before perhaps made so public, and imparted to the narrator by an eye-witness of the fact, bearing on Lord Byron's life in Italy. Nothing would induce me to reproduce it here, but Brooksmith had been in danger of losing it. If I ever should venture to reproduce it I shall feel how much I lose in not having my fellow auditor to refer to.

The first day Mr. Offord's door was closed was therefore a dark date in contemporary history. It was raining hard and my umbrella was wet, but Brooksmith received it from me exactly as if this were a preliminary for going upstairs. I observed however that instead of putting it away he held it poised and trickling over the rug, and I then became aware that he was looking at me with deep acknowledging eyes—his air of universal responsibility. I immediately understood—there was scarce need of question and answer as they passed between us. When I took in that our good friend had given up as never before, though only for the occasion, I exclaimed dolefully: "What a difference it will make—and to how many people!"

"I shall be one of them, sir!" said Brooksmith; and that was the beginning of the end.

Mr. Offord came down again, but the spell was broken, the great sign being that the conversation was for the first time not directed. It wandered and stumbled, a little frightened, like a lost child—it had let go the nurse's hand. "The worst of it is that now we shall talk about my health—*c'est la fin de tout*," Mr. Offord said when he reappeared; and then I recognised what a note of change that would be—for he had never tolerated anything so provincial. We "ran" to each other's health as little as to the daily weather. The talk became ours, in a word—not his; and as ours, even when *he* talked, it could only be inferior. In this form it was a distress to Brooksmith, whose attention now wandered from it altogether: he had so much closer a vision of his master's intimate conditions than our superficialities represented. There were better hours, and he was more in and out of the room, but I could see he was conscious of the decline, almost of the collapse, of our great institution. He seemed to wish to take counsel with me about it, to feel responsible for its going on in some form or other. When for the second period—the first had lasted several days—he had to tell me that his employer didn't receive, I half-expected to hear him say after a moment "Do you think I ought to, sir, in his place?"—as he might have asked me, with the return of autumn, if I thought he had better light the drawing-room fire.

He had a resigned philosophic sense of what his guests —our guests, as I came to regard them in our colloquies— would expect. His feeling was that he wouldn't absolutely have approved of himself as a substitute for Mr. Offord; but he was so saturated with the religion of habit that he would have made, for our friends, the necessary sacrifice to the divinity. He would take them on a little further and till they could look about them. I think I saw him also mentally confronted with the opportunity to deal—for once in his life—with some of his own dumb preferences, his limitations of sympathy, *weeding* a little in prospect and returning to a purer tradition. It was not unknown to me that he considered that toward the end of our host's career a certain laxity of selection had crept in.

At last it came to be the case that we all found the closed door more often than the open one; but even when it was closed Brooksmith managed a crack for me to squeeze through; so that practically I never turned away without having paid a visit. The difference simply came to be that the visit was to Brooksmith. It took place in the hall, at the familiar foot of the stairs, and we didn't sit down, at least Brooksmith didn't; moreover it was devoted wholly to one topic and always had the air of being already over— beginning, so to say, at the end. But it was always interesting—it always gave me something to think about. It's true that the subject of my meditation was ever the same—ever "It's all very well, but what *will* become of Brooksmith?" Even my private answer to this question left me still unsatisfied. No doubt Mr. Offord would provide for him, but *what* would he provide?—that was the great point. He couldn't provide society; and society had become a necessity of Brooksmith's nature. I must add that he never showed a symptom of what I may call sordid solicitude— anxiety on his own account. He was rather livid and intensely grave, as befitted a man before whose eyes the "shade of that which once was great" was passing away. He had the solemnity of a person winding up, under depressing circumstances, a long-established and celebrated business; he was a kind of social executor or liquidator. But his manner seemed to testify exclusively to the uncertainty of *our* future. I couldn't in those days have afforded it—I lived in two rooms in Jermyn Street and didn't "keep a man"; but even if my income had permitted I shouldn't have ventured to say to Brooksmith (emulating Mr. Offord) "My dear fellow, I'll take you on." The whole tone of our intercourse was so much more an implication that it was *I* who should now want a lift. Indeed there was a tacit assurance in Brooksmith's whole attitude that he should have me on his mind.

One of the most assiduous members of our circle had been Lady Kenyon, and I remember his telling me one day that her ladyship had in spite of her own infirmities, lately much aggravated, been in person to inquire. In answer to this I remarked that she would feel it more than any one. Brooksmith had a pause before saying in a certain tone— there's no reproducing some of his tones—"I'll go and see her." I went to see her myself and learned he had waited on her; but when I said to her, in the form of a joke but with a core of earnest, that when all was over some of us ought to combine, to club together, and set Brooksmith up on his own account, she replied a trifle disappointingly: "Do you mean in a public-house?" I looked at her in a way that I think Brooksmith himself would have approved, and then I answered: "Yes, the Offord Arms." What I had meant of course was that for the love of art itself we ought to look to it that such a peculiar faculty and so much acquired experience shouldn't be wasted. I really think that if we had caused a few black-edged cards to be struck off and circulated—"Mr. Brooksmith will continue to receive on the old premises from four to seven; business carried on as usual during the alterations"—the greater number of us would have rallied.

Several times he took me upstairs—always by his own proposal—and our dear old friend, in bed (in a curious flowered and brocaded casaque which made him, especially as his head was tied up in a handkerchief to match, look, to my imagination, like the dying Voltaire) held for ten minutes a sadly shrunken little salon. I felt indeed each time as if I were attending the last *coucher* of some social sovereign. He was royally whimsical about his sufferings and not at all concerned—quite as if the Constitution provided for the case—about his successor. He glided over *our* sufferings charmingly, and none of his jokes—it was a gallant abstention, some of them would have been so easy—were at our expense. Now and again, I confess, there was one at Brooksmith's, but so pathetically sociable as to make the excellent man look at me in a way that seemed to say: "Do exchange a glance with me, or I shan't be able to stand it." What he wasn't able to stand was not what Mr. Offord said about him, but what he wasn't able to say in return. His idea of conversation for himself was giving you the convenience of speaking to him; and when he went to "see" Lady Kenyon for instance it was to carry her the tribute of his receptive silence. Where would the speech of his betters have been if proper service had been a manifestation of sound? In that case the fundamental difference would have had to be shown by *their* dumbness, and many of them, poor things, were dumb enough without that provision. Brooksmith took an unfailing interest in the preservation of the fundamental difference; it was the thing he had most on his conscience.

What had become of it however when Mr. Offord passed away like any inferior person—was relegated to eternal stillness after the manner of a butler above-stairs. His aspect on the event—for the several successive days—may be imagined, and the multiplication by funereal observance of the things he didn't say. When everything was over—it was late the same day—I knocked at the door of the house of mourning as I so often had done before. I could never call on Mr. Offord again, but I had come literally to call on Brooksmith. I wanted to ask him if there was anything I could do for him, tainted with vagueness as this enquiry could only be. My presumptuous dream of taking him into my own service had died away: my service wasn't worth his being taken into. My offer could only be to help him to find another place, and yet there was an indelicacy, as it were, in taking for granted that his thoughts would immediately be fixed on another. I had a hope that he would be able to give his life a different form—though certainly not the form, the frequent result of such bereavements, of his setting up a little shop. That would have been dreadful; for I should have wished to forward any enterprise he might embark in, yet how could I have brought myself to go and pay him shillings and take back coppers over a counter? My visit then was simply an intended compliment. He took it as such, gratefully and with all the tact in the world. He knew I really couldn't help him and that I knew he knew I couldn't; but we discussed the situation—with a good deal of elegant generality—at the foot of the stairs, in the hall already dismantled, where I had so often discussed other situations with him. The executors were in possession, as was still more apparent when he made me pass for a few minutes into the dining-room, where various objects were muffled up for removal.

Two definite facts, however, he had to communicate; one being that he was to leave the house for ever that night (servants, for some mysterious reason, seem always to depart by night), and the other—he mentioned it only at the last and with hesitation—that he was already aware his late master had left him a legacy of eighty pounds. "I'm very glad," I said, and Brooksmith was of the same mind: "It was so like him to think of me." This was all that passed between us on the subject, and I know nothing of his judgement of Mr. Offord's memento. Eighty pounds are always eighty pounds, and no one has ever left *me* an equal sum; but, all the same, for Brooksmith, I was disappointed. I don't know what I had expected, but it was almost a shock. Eighty pounds might stock a small shop—a *very* small shop; but, I repeat, I couldn't bear to think of that. I asked my friend if he had been able to save a little, and he replied: "No, sir; I've had to do things." I didn't enquire what things they might have been; they were his own affair, and I took his word for them as assentingly as if he had had the greatness of an ancient house to keep up; especially as there was

something in his manner that seemed to convey a prospect
of further sacrifice.

"I shall have to turn round a bit, sir—I shall have to look
about me," he said; and then he added indulgently, mag-
nanimously: "If you should happen to hear of anything for
me—"

I couldn't let him finish; this was, in its essence, too much
in the really grand manner. It would be a help to my getting him off my mind to be able to pretend I *could* find
the right place, and that help he wished to give me, for
it was doubtless painful to him to see me in so false a position. I interposed with a few words to the effect of how
well aware I was that wherever he should go, whatever
he should do, he would miss our old friend terribly—miss
him even more than I should, having been with him so
much more. This led him to make the speech that has remained with me as the very text of the whole episode.

"Oh sir, it's sad for *you*, very sad indeed, and for a great
many gentlemen and ladies; that it is, sir. But for me, sir,
it is, if I may say so, still graver even than that: it's just
the loss of something that was everything. For me, sir," he
went on with rising tears, "he was just *all*, if you know
what I mean, sir. You have others, sir, I dare say—not that
I would have you understand me to speak of them as in
any way tantamount. But you have the pleasures of society, sir; if it's only in talking about him, sir, as I dare
say you do freely—for all his blest memory has to fear from
it—with gentlemen and ladies who have had the same honour. That's not for me, sir, and I've to keep my associations to myself. Mr. Offord was *my* society, and now, you
see, I just haven't any. You go back to conversation, sir,
after all, and I go back to my place," Brooksmith stammered, without exaggerated irony or dramatic bitterness,
but with a flat unstudied veracity and his hand on the knob
of the street-door. He turned it to let me out and then he
added: "I just go downstairs, sir, again, and I stay there."

"My poor child," I replied in my emotion, quite as Mr.
Offord used to speak, "my dear fellow, leave it to me: *we'll*
look after you, we'll all do something for you."

"Ah if you could give me some one *like* him! But there

ain't two such in the world," Brooksmith said as we parted.

He had given me his address—the place where he would be to be heard of. For a long time I had no occasion to make use of the information: he proved on trial so very difficult a case. The people who knew him and had known Mr. Offord didn't want to take him, and yet I couldn't bear to try to thrust him among strangers—strangers to his past when not to his present. I spoke to many of our old friends about him and found them all governed by the odd mixture of feelings of which I myself was conscious—as well as disposed, further, to entertain a suspicion that he was "spoiled," with which I then would have nothing to do. In plain terms a certain embarrassment, a sensible awkwardness when they thought of it, attached to the idea of using him as a menial: they had met him so often in society. Many of them would have asked him, and did ask him, or rather did ask me to ask him, to come and see them; but a mere visiting-list was not what I wanted for him. He was too short for people who were very particular; nevertheless I heard of an opening in a diplomatic household which led me to write him a note, though I was looking much less for something grand than for something human. Five days later I heard from him. The secretary's wife had decided, after keeping him waiting till then, that she couldn't take a servant out of a house in which there hadn't been a lady. The note had a P.S.: "It's a good job there wasn't, sir, such a lady as some."

A week later he came to see me and told me he was "suited," committed to some highly respectable people— they were something quite immense in the City—who lived on the Bayswater side of the Park. "I dare say it will be rather poor, sir," he admitted; "but I've seen the fireworks, haven't I, sir?—it can't be fireworks *every* night. After Mansfield Street there ain't much choice." There was a certain amount, however, it seemed; for the following year, calling one day on a country cousin, a lady of a certain age who was spending a fortnight in town with some friends of her own, a family unknown to me and resident in Chester Square, the door of the house was opened, to my surprise and gratification, by Brooksmith in person. When I came out I had some conversation with him from which I gathered that he had found the large City people too dull for endurance, and I guessed, though he didn't say it, that he had found them vulgar as well. I don't know what judgement he would have passed on his actual patrons if my relative hadn't been their friend; but in view of that connexion he abstained from comment.

None was necessary, however, for before the lady in question brought her visit to a close they honoured me with an invitation to dinner, which I accepted. There was a largeish party on the occasion, but I confess I thought of Brooksmith rather more than of the seated company. They required no depth of attention—they were all referable to usual irredeemable inevitable types. It was the world of cheerful commonplace and conscious gentility and prosperous density, a full-fed material insular world, a world of hideous florid plate and ponderous order and thin conversation. There wasn't a word said about Byron, or even about a minor bard then much in view. Nothing would have induced me to look at Brooksmith in the course of the repast, and I felt sure that not even my overturning the wine would have induced him to meet my eye. We were in intellectual sympathy—we felt, as regards each other, a degree of social responsibility. In short we had been in Arcadia together, and we had both come to *this!* No wonder we were ashamed to be confronted. When he had helped on my overcoat, as I was going away, we parted, for the first time since the earliest days of Mansfield Street, in silence. I thought he looked lean and wasted, and I guessed that his new place wasn't more "human" than his previous one. There was plenty of beef and beer, but there was no reciprocity. The question for him to have asked before accepting the position wouldn't have been "How many footmen are kept?" but "How much imagination?"

The next time I went to the house—I confess it wasn't very soon—I encountered his successor, a personage who evidently enjoyed the good fortune of never having quitted his natural level. Could any be higher? he seemed to ask —over the heads of three footmen and even of some visitors. He made me feel as if Brooksmith were dead; but I didn't dare to enquire—I couldn't have borne his "I haven't the least idea, sir." I dispatched a note to the address that worthy had given me after Mr. Offord's death, but I received no answer. Six months later however I was favoured with a visit from an elderly dreary dingy person who introduced herself to me as Mr. Brooksmith's aunt and from whom I learned that he was out of place and out of health and had allowed her to come and say to me that if I could spare half an hour to look in at him he would take it as a rare honour.

I went the next day—his messenger had given me a new address—and found my friend lodged in a short sordid street in Marylebone, one of those corners of London that wear the last expression of sickly meanness. The room into which I was shown was above the small establishment of a dyer and cleaner who had inflated kid gloves and discoloured shawls in his shop-front. There was a great deal of grimy infant life up and down the place, and there was a hot moist smell within, as of the "boiling" of dirty linen. Brooksmith sat with a blanket over his legs at a clean little window where, from behind stiff bluish-white curtains, he could look across at a huckster's and a tinsmith's and a small greasy public-house. He had passed through an illness and was convalescent, and his mother, as well as his aunt, was in attendance on him. I liked the nearer relative, who was bland and intensely humble, but I had my doubts of the remoter, whom I connected perhaps unjustly with the opposite public-house—she seemed somehow greasy with the same grease—and whose furtive eye followed every movement of my hand as if to see if it weren't going into my pocket. It didn't take this direction—I couldn't, unsolicited, put myself at that sort of ease with Brooksmith. Several times the door of the room opened and mysterious old women peeped in and shuffled back again. I don't know who they were; poor Brooksmith seemed encompassed with vague prying beery females.

He was vague himself, and evidently weak, and much embarrassed, and not an allusion was made between us to Mansfield Street. The vision of the salon of which he had

been an ornament hovered before me however, by contrast, sufficiently. He assured me he was really getting better, and his mother remarked that he would come round
if he could only get his spirits up. The aunt echoed this
opinion, and I became more sure that in her own case she
knew where to go for such a purpose. I'm afraid I was
rather weak with my old friend, for I neglected the opportunity, so exceptionally good, to rebuke the levity
which had led him to throw up honourable positions—fine
stiff steady berths in Bayswater and Belgravia, with morning prayers, as I knew, attached to one of them. Very likely
his reasons had been profane and sentimental; he didn't
want morning prayers, he wanted to be somebody's dear
fellow; but I couldn't be the person to rebuke him. He shuffled these episodes out of sight—I saw he had no wish to
discuss them. I noted further, strangely enough, that it
would probably be a questionable pleasure for him to see
me again: he doubted now even of my power to condone
his aberrations. He didn't wish to have to explain; and his
behaviour was likely in future to need explanation. When
I bade him farewell he looked at me a moment with eyes
that said everything: "How can I talk about those exquisite years in this place, before these people, with the old
women poking their heads in? It was very good of you to
come to see me; it wasn't my idea—*she* brought you. We've
said everything; it's over; you'll lose all patience with me,
and I'd rather you shouldn't see the rest." I sent him some
money in a letter the next day, but I saw the rest only in
the light of a barren sequel.

A whole year after my visit to him I became aware once,
in dining out, that Brooksmith was one of the several servants who hovered behind our chairs. He hadn't opened the
door of the house to me, nor had I recognised him in the
array of retainers in the hall. This time I tried to catch his
eye, but he never gave me a chance, and when he handed
me a dish I could only be careful to thank him audibly.
Indeed I partook of two *entrées* of which I had my doubts,
subsequently converted into certainties, in order not to snub
him. He looked well enough in health, but much older, and
wore in an exceptionally marked degree the glazed and ex-

pressionless mask of the British domestic *de race*. I saw
with dismay that if I hadn't known him I should have taken
him, on the showing of his countenance, for an extravagant illustration of irresponsive servile gloom. I said to myself that he had become a reactionary, gone over to the
Philistines, thrown himself into religion, the religion of his
"place," like a foreign lady *sur le retour*. I divined moreover that he was only engaged for the evening—he had
become a mere waiter, had joined the band of the white-
waistcoated who "go out." There was something pathetic
in this fact—it was a terrible vulgarisation of Brooksmith.
It was the mercenary prose of butlerhood; he had given
up the struggle for the poetry. If reciprocity was what he
had missed where was the reciprocity now? Only in the
bottoms of the wine-glasses and the five shillings—or whatever they get—clapped into his hand by the permanent
man. However, I supposed he had taken up a precarious
branch of his profession because it after all sent him less
downstairs. His relations with London society were more
superficial, but they were of course more various. As I went
away on this occasion I looked out for him eagerly among
the four or five attendants whose perpendicular persons,
fluting the walls of London passages, are supposed to lu-
bricate the process of departure; but he was not on duty.
I asked one of the others if he were not in the house, and
received the prompt answer: "Just left, sir. Anything I can
do for you, sir?" I wanted to say "Please give him my kind
regards"; but I abstained—I didn't want to compromise
him; and I never came across him again.

Often and often, in dining out, I looked for him, sometimes accepting invitations on purpose to multiply the
chances of my meeting him. But always in vain; so that
as I met many other members of the casual class over and
over again I at last adopted the theory that he always pro-
cured a list of expected guests beforehand and kept away
from the banquets which he thus learned I was to grace. At
last I gave up hope, and one day at the end of three years
I received another visit from his aunt. She was drearier and
dingier, almost squalid, and she was in great tribulation
and want. Her sister, Mrs. Brooksmith, had been dead a

year, and three months later her nephew had disappeared.
He had always looked after her a bit—since her troubles;
I never knew what her troubles had been—and now she
hadn't so much as a petticoat to pawn. She had also a niece,
to whom she had been everything before her troubles, but
the niece had treated her most shameful. These were details; the great and romantic fact was Brooksmith's final
evasion of his fate. He had gone out to wait one evening
as usual, in a white waistcoat she had done up for him with
her own hands—being due at a large party up Kensington
way. But he had never come home again and had never
arrived at the large party, nor at any party that any one
could make out. No trace of him had come to light—no
gleam of the white waistcoat had pierced the obscurity of
his doom. This news was a sharp shock to me, for I had
my ideas about his real destination. His aged relative had
promptly, as she said, guessed the worst. Somehow and
somewhere he had got out of the way altogether, and now
I trust that, with characteristic deliberation, he is changing
the plates of the immortal gods. As my depressing visitant
also said, he never *had* got his spirits up. I was fortunately
able to dismiss her with her own somewhat improved. But
the dim ghost of poor Brooksmith is one of those that I
see. He had indeed been spoiled.

[1891]

THE ALTAR OF
THE DEAD

I

He had a mortal dislike, poor Stransom, to lean anniversaries, and loved them still less when they made a pretence of a figure. Celebrations and suppressions were equally painful to him, and but one of the former found a place in his life. He had kept each year in his own fashion the date of Mary Antrim's death. It would be more to the point perhaps to say that this occasion kept *him:* it kept him at least effectually from doing anything else. It took hold of him again and again with a hand of which time had softened but never loosened the touch. He waked to his feast of memory as consciously as he would have waked to his marriage-morn. Marriage had had of old but too little to say to the matter: for the girl who was to have been his bride there had been no bridal embrace. She had died of a malignant fever after the wedding-day had been fixed, and he had lost before fairly tasting it an affection that promised to fill his life to the brim.

Of that benediction, however, it would have been false to say this life could really be emptied: it was still ruled by a pale ghost, still ordered by a sovereign presence. He had not been a man of numerous passions, and even in all these years no sense had grown stronger with him than the sense of being bereft. He had needed no priest and no altar to make him for ever widowed. He had done many things in the world—he had done almost all but one: he had never, never forgotten. He had tried to put into his existence whatever else might take up room in it, but had failed to make it more than a house of which the mistress was eternally absent. She was most absent of all on the recurrent December day that his tenacity set apart. He had no arranged observance of it, but his nerves made it all their own. They drove him forth without mercy, and the goal of his pilgrimage was far. She had been buried in a London suburb, a part then of Nature's breast, but which he had seen lose one after another every feature of freshness. It was in truth during the moments he stood there that his eyes beheld the place least. They looked at another image, they opened to another light. Was it a credible future? Was it an incredible past? Whatever the answer it was an immense escape from the actual.

It's true that if there weren't other dates than this there were other memories; and by the time George Stransom was fifty-five such memories had greatly multiplied. There were other ghosts in his life than the ghost of Mary Antrim. He had perhaps not had more losses than most men, but he had counted his losses more; he hadn't seen death more closely, but had in a manner felt it more deeply. He had formed little by little the habit of numbering his Dead: it had come to him early in life that there was something one had to do for them. They were there in their simplified intensified essence, their conscious absence and expressive patience, as personally there as if they had only been stricken dumb. When all sense of them failed, all sound of them ceased, it was as if their purgatory were really still on earth; they asked so little that they got, poor things, even less, and died again, died every day, of the hard usage of life. They had no organised service, no reserved place, no honour, no shelter, no safety. Even ungenerous people provided for the living, but even those who were called most generous did nothing for the others. So on George Stransom's part had grown up with the years a resolve that he at least would do something, do it, that is, for his own —would perform the great charity without reproach. Every man *had* his own, and every man had, to meet this charity, the ample resources of the soul.

It was doubtless the voice of Mary Antrim that spoke for them best; as the years at any rate went by he found himself in regular communion with these postponed pensioners, those whom indeed he always called in his thoughts the Others. He spared them the moments, he organised the charity. Quite how it had risen he probably never could have told you, but what came to pass was that an altar, such as was after all within everybody's compass, lighted with perpetual candles and dedicated to these secret rites, reared itself in his spiritual spaces. He had wondered of old, in some embarrassment, whether he had a religion; being very sure, and not a little content, that he hadn't at all events the religion some of the people he had known wanted him to have. Gradually this question was straightened out for him: it became clear to him that the religion instilled by his earliest consciousness had been simply the religion of the Dead. It suited his inclination, it satisfied his spirit, it gave employment to his piety. It answered his love of great offices, of a solemn and splendid ritual; for no shrine could be more bedecked and no ceremonial more stately than those to which his worship was attached. He had no imagination about these things but that they were accessible to any who should feel the need of them. The poorest could build such temples of the spirit—could make them blaze with candles and smoke with incense, make them flush with pictures and flowers. The cost, in the common phrase, of keeping them up fell wholly on the generous heart.

II

He had this year, on the eve of his anniversary, as happened, an emotion not unconnected with that range of feeling. Walking home at the close of a busy day he was arrested in the London street by the particular effect of a shop-front that lighted the dull brown air with its mercenary grin and before which several persons were gathered. It was the window of a jeweller whose diamonds and sapphires seemed to laugh, in flashes like high notes of sound, with the mere joy of knowing how much more they were "worth" than most of the dingy pedestrians staring at them from the other side of the pane. Stransom lingered long enough to suspend, in a vision, a string of pearls about the white neck of Mary Antrim, and then was kept an instant longer by the sound of a voice he knew. Next him was a mumbling old woman, and beyond the old woman a gentleman with a lady on his arm. It was from him, from Paul Creston, the voice had proceeded: he was talking with the lady of some precious object in the window. Stransom had no sooner recognised him than the old woman turned away; but just with this growth of opportunity came a felt strangeness that stayed him in the very act of laying his hand on his friend's arm. It lasted but the instant, only that space sufficed for the flash of a wild question. Was *not* Mrs. Creston dead?—the ambiguity met him there in the short drop of her husband's voice, the drop conjugal, if it ever was, and in the way the two figures leaned to each other. Creston, making a step to look at something else, came nearer, glanced at him, started and exclaimed—behaviour the effect of which was at first only to leave Stransom staring, staring back across the months at the different face, the wholly other face, the poor man had shown him last, the blurred ravaged mask bent over the open grave by which they had stood together. That son of affliction wasn't in mourning now; he detached his arm from his companion's to grasp the hand of the older friend. He coloured as well as smiled in the strong light of the shop when Stransom raised a tentative hat to the lady. Stransom had just time to see she was pretty before he found himself gaping at a fact more portentous. "My dear fellow, let me make you acquainted with my wife."

Creston had blushed and stammered over it, but in half a minute, at the rate we live in polite society, it had practically become, for our friend, the mere memory of a shock. They stood there and laughed and talked; Stransom had instantly whisked the shock out of the way, to keep it for private consumption. He felt himself grimace, he heard himself exaggerate the proper, but was conscious of turning not a little faint. That new woman, that hired performer Mrs. Creston? Mrs. Creston had been more living for him than any woman but one. This lady had a face that shone as publicly as the jeweller's window, and in the happy candour with which she wore her monstrous character was an effect of gross immodesty. The character of Paul Creston's wife thus attributed to her was monstrous for reasons Stransom could judge his friend to know perfectly that he knew. The happy pair had just arrived from America, and Stransom hadn't needed to be told this to guess the nationality of the lady. Somehow it deepened the foolish air that her husband's confused cordiality was unable to conceal. Stransom recalled that he had heard of poor Creston's having, while his bereavement was still fresh, crossed the sea for what people in such predicaments call a little change. He had found little change indeed, he had brought the little change back; it was the little change that stood there and that, do what he would, he couldn't, while he showed those high front teeth of his, look other than a conscious ass about. They were going into the shop, Mrs. Creston said, and she begged Mr. Stransom to come with them and help to decide. He thanked her, opening his watch and pleading an engagement for which he was already late, and they parted while she shrieked into the fog "Mind now you come to see me right away!" Creston had had the delicacy not to suggest that, and Stransom hoped it hurt him somewhere to hear her scream it to all the echoes.

He felt quite determined, as he walked away, never in his life to go near her. She was perhaps a human being, but Creston oughtn't to have shown her without precautions, oughtn't indeed to have shown her at all. His precautions should have been those of a forger or a murderer, and the people at home would never have mentioned extradition. This was a wife for foreign service or purely external use; a decent consideration would have spared her the injury of comparisons. Such was the first flush of George Stransom's reaction; but as he sat alone that night—there were particular hours he always passed alone—the harshness dropped from it and left only the pity. *He* could spend an evening with Kate Creston, if the man to whom she had given everything couldn't. He had known her twenty years, and she was the only woman for whom he might perhaps have been unfaithful. She was all cleverness and sympathy and charm; her house had been the very easiest in all the world and her friendship the very firmest. Without accidents he had loved her, without accidents every one had loved her: she had made the passions about her as regular as the moon makes the tides. She had been also of course far too good for her husband, but he never suspected it, and in nothing had she been more admirable than in the exquisite art with which she tried to keep every one else (keeping Creston was no trouble) from finding it out. Here was a man to whom she had devoted her life and for whom she had given it up—dying to bring into the world a child of his bed; and she had had only to submit to her fate to have, ere the grass was green on her grave, no more existence for him than a domestic servant he had replaced. The frivolity, the indecency of it made Stransom's eyes fill; and he had that evening a sturdy sense that he alone, in a world without delicacy, had a right to hold up his head. While he smoked, after dinner, he had a book in his lap, but he had no eyes for his page: his eyes, in the swarming void of things, seemed to have caught Kate Creston's, and it was into their sad silences he looked. It was to him her sentient spirit had turned, knowing it to be of her he would think. He thought for a long time of how the closed eyes of dead women could still live—how they could open again, in a quiet lamplit room, long after they had looked their last. They had looks that survived—had them as great poets had quoted lines.

The newspaper lay by his chair—the thing that came in the afternoon and the servants thought one wanted; without sense for what was in it he had mechanically unfolded and then dropped it. Before he went to bed he took it up, and this time, at the top of a paragraph, he was caught by five words that made him start. He stood staring, before the fire, at the "Death of Sir Acton Hague, K.C.B.," the man who ten years earlier had been the nearest of his

friends and whose deposition from this eminence had practically left it without an occupant. He had seen him after
their rupture, but hadn't now seen him for years. Standing
there before the fire he turned cold as he read what had
befallen him. Promoted a short time previous to the gov-
ernorship of the Westward Islands, Acton Hague had died,
in the bleak honour of this exile, of an illness consequent
on the bite of a poisonous snake. His career was compressed
by the newspaper into a dozen lines, the perusal of which
excited on George Stransom's part no warmer feeling than
one of relief at the absence of any mention of their quarrel,
an incident accidentally tainted at the time, thanks to their
joint immersion in large affairs, with a horrible publicity.
Public indeed was the wrong Stransom had, to his own
sense, suffered, the insult he had blankly taken from the
only man with whom he had ever been intimate; the friend,
almost adored, of his University years, the subject, later,
of his passionate loyalty: so public that he had never spoken
of it to a human creature, so public that he had completely
overlooked it. It had made the difference for him that
friendship too was all over, but it had only made just that
one. The shock of interests had been private, intensely so;
but the action taken by Hague had been in the face of
men. Today it all seemed to have occurred merely to the
end that George Stransom should think of him as "Hague"
and measure exactly how much he himself could resemble
a stone. He went cold, suddenly and horribly cold, to bed.

III

The next day, in the afternoon, in the great grey suburb, he knew his long walk had tired him. In the dreadful cemetery alone he had been on his feet an hour. Instinctively, coming back, they had taken him a devious
course, and it was a desert in which no circling cabman
hovered over possible prey. He paused on a corner and
measured the dreariness; then he made out through the
gathered dusk that he was in one of those tracts of London which are less gloomy by night than by day, because,
in the former case, of the civil gift of light. By day there

was nothing, but by night there were lamps, and George Stransom was in a mood that made lamps good in themselves. It wasn't that they could show him anything, it was only that they could burn clear. To his surprise, however, after a while, they did show him something: the arch of a high doorway approached by a low terrace of steps, in the depth of which—it formed a dim vestibule—the raising of a curtain at the moment he passed gave him a glimpse of an avenue of gloom with a glow of tapers at the end. He stopped and looked up, recognising the place as a church. The thought quickly came to him that since he was tired he might rest there; so that after a moment he had in turn pushed up the leathern curtain and gone in. It was a temple of the old persuasion, and there had evidently been a function—perhaps a service for the dead; the high altar was still a blaze of candles. This was an exhibition he always liked, and he dropped into a seat with relief. More than it had ever yet come home to him it struck him as good there should be churches.

This one was almost empty and the other altars were dim; a verger shuffled about, an old woman coughed, but it seemed to Stransom there was hospitality in the thick sweet air. Was it only the savour of the incense or was it something of larger intention? He had at any rate quitted the great grey suburb and come nearer to the warm centre. He presently ceased to feel intrusive, gaining at last even a sense of community with the only worshipper in his neighbourhood, the sombre presence of a woman, in mourning unrelieved, whose back was all he could see of her and who had sunk deep into prayer at no great distance from him. He wished he could sink, like her, to the very bottom, be as motionless, as rapt in prostration. After a few moments he shifted his seat; it was almost indelicate to be so aware of her. But Stransom subsequently quite lost himself, floating away on the sea of light. If occasions like this had been more frequent in his life he would have had more present the great original type, set up in myriad temples, of the unapproachable shrine he had erected in his mind. That shrine had begun in vague likeness to church pomps, but the echo had ended by growing more distinct than the

sound. The sound now rang out, the type blazed at him
with all its fires and with a mystery of radiance in which
endless meanings could glow. The thing became as he sat
there his appropriate altar and each starry candle an appropriate vow. He numbered them, named them, grouped
them—it was the silent roll-call of his Dead. They made together a brightness vast and intense, a brightness in which
the mere chapel of his thoughts grew so dim that as it faded
away he asked himself if he shouldn't find his real comfort
in some material act, some outward worship.

This idea took possession of him while, at a distance,
the black-robed lady continued prostrate; he was quietly
thrilled with his conception, which at last brought him to
his feet in the sudden excitement of a plan. He wandered
softly through the aisles, pausing in the different chapels,
all save one applied to a special devotion. It was in this
clear recess, lampless and unapplied, that he stood longest
—the length of time it took him fully to grasp the conception of gilding it with his bounty. He should snatch it from
no other rites and associate it with nothing profane; he
would simply take it as it should be given up to him and
make it a masterpiece of splendour and a mountain of fire.
Tended sacredly all the year, with the sanctifying church
round it, it would always be ready for his offices. There
would be difficulties, but from the first they presented
themselves only as difficulties surmounted. Even for a person so little affiliated the thing would be a matter of arrangement. He saw it all in advance, and how bright in
especial the place would become to him in the intermissions of toil and the dusk of afternoons; how rich in assurance at all times, but especially in the indifferent world.
Before withdrawing he drew nearer again to the spot
where he had first sat down, and in the movement he met
the lady whom he had seen praying and who was now on
her way to the door. She passed him quickly, and he had
only a glimpse of her pale face and her unconscious, almost sightless eyes. For that instant she looked faded and
handsome.

This was the origin of the rites more public, yet certainly
esoteric, that he at last found himself able to establish. It

took a long time, it took a year, and both the process and the result would have been—for any who knew—a vivid picture of his good faith. No one did know, in fact—no one but the bland ecclesiastics whose acquaintance he had promptly sought, whose objections he had softly over-ridden, whose curiosity and sympathy he had artfully charmed, whose assent to his eccentric munificence he had eventually won, and who had asked for concessions in exchange for indulgences. Stransom had of course at an early stage of his enquiry been referred to the Bishop, and the Bishop had been delightfully human, the Bishop had been almost amused. Success was within sight, at any rate, from the moment the attitude of those whom it concerned became liberal in response to liberality. The altar and the sacred shell that half-encircled it, consecrated to an osten-sible and customary worship, were to be splendidly main-tained; all that Stransom reserved to himself was the num-ber of his lights and the free enjoyment of his intention. When the intention had taken complete effect the enjoy-ment became even greater than he had ventured to hope. He liked to think of this effect when far from it, liked to convince himself of it yet again when near. He was not often indeed so near as that a visit to it hadn't perforce something of the patience of a pilgrimage; but the time he gave to his devotion came to seem to him more a con-tribution to his other interests than a betrayal of them. Even a loaded life might be easier when one had added a new necessity to it.

How much easier was probably never guessed by those who simply knew there were hours when he disappeared and for many of whom there was a vulgar reading of what they used to call his plunges. These plunges were into depths quieter than the deep sea-caves, and the habit had at the end of a year or two become the one it would have cost him most to relinquish. Now they had really, his Dead, something that was indefeasibly theirs; and he liked to think that they might in cases be the Dead of others, as well as that the Dead of others might be invoked there under the protection of what he had done. Whoever bent a knee on the carpet he had laid down appeared to him to act in the spirit of his intention. Each of his lights had a name for him, and from time to time a new light was kindled. This was what he had fundamentally agreed for, that there should always be room for them all. What those who passed or lingered saw was simply the most resplendent of the altars called suddenly into vivid usefulness, with a quiet elderly man, for whom it evidently had a fascination, often seated there in a maze or a doze; but half the satisfaction of the spot for this mysterious and fitful worshipper was that he found the years of his life there, and the ties, the affections, the struggles, the submissions, the conquests, if there had been such, a record of that adventurous journey in which the beginnings and the endings of human relations are the lettered mile-stones. He had in general little taste for the past as a part of his own history; at other times and in other places it mostly seemed to him pitiful to consider and impossible to repair; but on these occasions he accepted it with something of that positive gladness with which one adjusts one's self to an ache that begins to succumb to treatment. To the treatment of time the malady of life begins at a given moment to succumb; and these were doubtless the hours at which that truth most came home to him. The day was written for him there on which he had first become acquainted with death, and the successive phases of the acquaintance were marked each with a flame.

The flames were gathering thick at present, for Stransom had entered that dark defile of our earthly descent in which some one dies every day. It was only yesterday that Kate Creston had flashed out her white fire; yet already there were younger stars ablaze on the tips of the tapers. Various persons in whom his interest had not been intense drew closer to him by entering this company. He went over it, head by head, till he felt like the shepherd of a huddled flock, with all a shepherd's vision of differences imperceptible. He knew his candles apart, up to the colour of the flame, and would still have known them had their positions all been changed. To other imaginations they might stand for other things—that they should stand for something to be hushed before was all he desired; but he was intensely conscious of the personal note of each and of the distinguishable way it contributed to the concert. There were hours at which he almost caught himself wishing that certain of his friends would now die, that he might establish with them in this manner a connexion more charming than, as it happened, it was possible to enjoy with them in life. In regard to those from whom one was separated by the long curves of the globe such a connexion could only be an improvement: it brought them instantly within reach. Of course there were gaps in the constellation, for Stransom knew he could only pretend to act for his own, and it wasn't every figure passing before his eyes into the great obscure that was entitled to a memorial. There was a strange sanctification in death, but some characters were more sanctified by being forgotten than by being remembered. The greatest blank in the shining page was the memory of Acton Hague, of which he inveterately tried to rid himself. For Acton Hague no flame could ever rise on any altar of his.

IV

Every year, the day he walked back from the great graveyard, he went to church as he had done the day his idea was born. It was on this occasion, as it happened, after a year had passed, that he began to observe his altar to be haunted by a worshipper at least as frequent as himself. Others of the faithful, and in the rest of the church, came and went, appealing sometimes, when they disappeared, to a vague or to a particular recognition; but this unfailing presence was always to be observed when he arrived and still in possession when he departed. He was surprised, the first time, at the promptitude with which it assumed an identity for him—the identity of the lady whom two years before, on his anniversary, he had seen so intensely bowed, and of whose tragic face he had had so flitting a vision. Given the time that had passed, his recollection of her was fresh enough to make him wonder. Of himself she had of course no impression, or rather had had none at first: the time came when her manner of transacting her business suggested her having gradually guessed his call to be of the same order. She used his altar for her own purpose—he could only hope that, sad and solitary as she always struck him, she used it for her own Dead. There were interruptions, infidelities, all on his part, calls to other associations and duties; but as the months went on he found her whenever he returned, and he ended by taking pleasure in the thought that he had given her almost the contentment he had given himself. They worshipped side by side so often that there were moments when he wished he might be sure, so straight did their prospect stretch away of growing old together in their rites. She was younger than he, but she looked as if her Dead were at least as numerous as his candles. She had no colour, no sound, no fault, and another of the things about which he had made up his mind was that she had no fortune. Always black-robed, she must have had a succession of sorrows. People weren't poor, after all, whom so many losses could overtake; they were positively rich when they had had so much to give up. But the air of this devoted and indifferent woman, who always made, in any attitude, a beautiful accidental line, conveyed somehow to Stransom that she had known more kinds of trouble than one.

He had a great love of music and little time for the joy of it; but occasionally, when workaday noises were muffled by Saturday afternoons, it used to come back to him that there were glories. There were moreover friends who reminded him of this and side by side with whom he found himself sitting out concerts. On one of these winter evenings, in Saint James's Hall, he became aware after he had seated himself that the lady he had so often seen at church was in the place next him and was evidently alone, as he also this time happened to be. She was at first too absorbed in the consideration of the programme to heed him, but when she at last glanced at him he took advantage of the movement to speak to her, greeting her with the remark that he felt as if he already knew her. She smiled as she said "Oh yes, I recognise you"; yet in spite of this admission of long acquaintance it was the first he had seen of her smile. The effect of it was suddenly to contribute more to that acquaintance than all the previous meetings had done. He hadn't "taken in," he said to himself, that she was so pretty. Later, that evening—it was while he rolled along in a hansom on his way to dine out—he added that he hadn't taken in that she was so interesting. The next morning in the midst of his work he quite suddenly and irrelevantly reflected that his impression of her, beginning so far back, was like a winding river that had at last reached the sea.

His work in fact was blurred a little all that day by the sense of what had now passed between them. It wasn't much, but it had just made the difference. They had listened together to Beethoven and Schumann; they had talked in the pauses, and at the end, when at the door, to which they moved together, he had asked her if he could help her in the matter of getting away. She had thanked him and put up her umbrella, slipping into the crowd without an allusion to their meeting yet again and leaving him to remember at leisure that not a word had been exchanged about the usual scene of that coincidence. This omission struck him now as natural and then again as perverse. She mightn't in the least have allowed his warrant for speaking to her, and yet if she hadn't he would have judged her an underbred woman. It was odd that when nothing had really ever brought them together he should have been able successfully to assume they were in a manner old friends— that this negative quantity was somehow more than they could express. His success, it was true, had been qualified by her quick escape, so that there grew up in him an absurd desire to put it to some better test. Save in so far as some other poor chance might help him, such a test could be only to meet her afresh at church. Left to himself he would have gone to church the very next afternoon, just for the curiosity of seeing if he should find her there. But he wasn't left to himself, a fact he discovered quite at the last, after he had virtually made up his mind to go. The influence that kept him away really revealed to him how little to himself his Dead *ever* left him. He went only for *them*—for nothing else in the world.

The force of this revulsion kept him away ten days: he hated to connect the place with anything but his offices or to give a glimpse of the curiosity that had been on the point of moving him. It was absurd to weave a tangle about a matter so simple as a custom of devotion that might with ease have been daily or hourly; yet the tangle got itself woven. He was sorry, he was disappointed: it was as if a long happy spell had been broken and he had lost a familiar security. At the last, however, he asked himself if he was to stay away for ever from the fear of this muddle about motives. After an interval neither longer nor shorter than usual he re-entered the church with a clear conviction that he should scarcely heed the presence or the absence of the lady of the concert. This indifference didn't prevent his at once noting that for the only time since he had first seen her she wasn't on the spot. He had now no scruple about giving her time to arrive, but she didn't arrive, and when he went away still missing her he was profanely and consentingly sorry. If her absence made the tangle more intricate, that was all her own doing. By the end of another year it was very intricate indeed; but by that time he didn't in the least care, and it was only his cultivated consciousness that had given him scruples. Three times in three months he had gone to church without finding her, and he felt he hadn't needed these occasions to show him his suspense had dropped. Yet it was, incongruously, not indifference, but a refinement of delicacy that had kept him from asking the sacristan, who would of course immediately have recognised his description of her, whether she had been seen at other hours. His delicacy had kept him from asking any question about her at any time, and it was exactly the same virtue that had left him so free to be decently civil to her at the concert.

This happy advantage now served him anew, enabling him when she finally met his eyes—it was after a fourth trial—to predetermine quite fixedly his awaiting her retreat. He joined her in the street as soon as she had moved, asking her if he might accompany her a certain distance. With her placid permission he went as far as a house in the neighbourhood at which she had business: she let him know it was not where she lived. She lived, as she said, in a mere slum, with an old aunt, a person in connexion with whom she spoke of the engrossment of humdrum duties and regular occupations. She wasn't, the mourning niece, in her first youth, and her vanished freshness had left something behind that, for Stransom, represented the proof it had been tragically sacrificed. Whatever she gave him the assurance of she gave without references. She might have been a divorced duchess—she might have been an old maid who taught the harp.

V

They fell at last into the way of walking together almost every time they met, though for a long time still they never met but at church. He couldn't ask her to come and see him, and as if she hadn't a proper place to receive him she never invited her friend. As much as himself she knew the world of London, but from an undiscussed instinct of privacy they haunted the region not mapped on the social chart. On the return she always made him leave her at the same corner. She looked with him, as a pretext for a pause, at the depressed things in suburban shop-fronts; and there was never a word he had said to her that she hadn't beautifully understood. For long ages he never knew her name, any more than she had ever pronounced his own; but it was not their names that mattered, it was only their perfect practice and their common need.

These things made their whole relation so impersonal that they hadn't the rules or reasons people found in ordinary friendships. They didn't care for the things it was supposed necessary to care for in the intercourse of the world. They ended one day—they never knew which of them expressed it first—by throwing out the idea that they didn't care for each other. Over this idea they grew quite intimate; they rallied to it in a way that marked a fresh start in their confidence. If to feel deeply together about certain things wholly distinct from themselves didn't constitute a safety, where was safety to be looked for? Not lightly nor often, not without occasion nor without emotion, any more than in any other reference by serious people to a mystery of their faith; but when something had happened to warm,

as it were, the air for it, they came as near as they could
come to calling their Dead by name. They felt it was coming very near to utter their thought at all. The word "they"
expressed enough; it limited the mention, it had a dignity
of its own, and if, in their talk, you had heard our friends
use it, you might have taken them for a pair of pagans of
old alluding decently to the domesticated gods. They never
knew—at least Stransom never knew—how they had learned
to be sure about each other. If it had been with each a
question of what the other was there for, the certitude had
come in some fine way of its own. Any faith, after all, has
the instinct of propagation, and it was as natural as it was
beautiful that they should have taken pleasure on the spot
in the imagination of a following. If the following was for
each but a following of one it had proved in the event sufficient. Her debt, however, of course, was much greater
than his, because while she had only given him a worshipper he had given her a splendid temple. Once she said she
pitied him for the length of his list—she had counted his
candles almost as often as himself—and this made him wonder what could have been the length of hers. He had wondered before at the coincidence of their losses, especially
as from time to time a new candle was set up. On some
occasion some accident led him to express this curiosity,
and she answered as if in surprise that he hadn't already
understood. "Oh for me, you know, the more there are the
better—there could never be too many. I should like hundreds and hundreds—I should like thousands; I should like
a great mountain of light."

Then of course in a flash he understood. "Your Dead are
only One?"

She hung back at this as never yet. "Only One," she answered, colouring as if now he knew her guarded secret.
It really made him feel he knew less than before, so difficult was it for him to reconstitute a life in which a single
experience had so belittled all others. His own life, round
its central hollow, had been packed close enough. After
this she appeared to have regretted her confession, though
at the moment she spoke there had been pride in her very
embarrassment. She declared to him that his own was the

larger, the dearer possession—the portion one would have chosen if one had been able to choose; she assured him she could perfectly imagine some of the echoes with which his silences were peopled. He knew she couldn't: one's relation to what one had loved and hated had been a relation too distinct from the relations of others. But this didn't affect the fact that they were growing old together in their piety. She was a feature of that piety, but even at the ripe stage of acquaintance in which they occasionally arranged to meet at a concert or to go together to an exhibition she was not a feature of anything else. The most that happened was that his worship became paramount. Friend by friend dropped away till at last there were more emblems on his altar than houses left him to enter. She was more than any other the friend who remained, but she was unknown to all the rest. Once when she had discovered, as they called it, a new star, she used the expression that the chapel at last was full.

"Oh no," Stransom replied, "there's a great thing wanting for that! The chapel will never be full till a candle is set up before which all the others will pale. It will be the tallest candle of all."

Her mild wonder rested on him. "What candle do you mean?"

"I mean, dear lady, my own."

He had learned after a long time that she earned money by her pen, writing under a pseudonym she never disclosed in magazines he never saw. She knew too well what he couldn't read and what she couldn't write, and she taught him to cultivate indifference with a success that did much for their good relations. Her invisible industry was a convenience to him; it helped his contented thought of her, the thought that rested in the dignity of her proud obscure life, her little remunerated art and her little impenetrable home. Lost, with her decayed relative, in her dim suburban world, she came to the surface for him in distant places. She was really the priestess of his altar, and whenever he quitted England he committed it to her keeping. She proved to him afresh that women have more of the spirit of religion than men; he felt his fidelity pale and faint in com-

parison with hers. He often said to her that since he had
so little time to live he rejoiced in her having so much; so
glad was he to think she would guard the temple when
he should have been called. He had a great plan for that,
which of course he told her too, a bequest of money to
keep it up in undiminished state. Of the administration of
this fund he would appoint her superintendent, and if the
spirit should move her she might kindle a taper even for
him.

"And who will kindle one even for me?" she then seriously asked.

VI

She was always in mourning, yet the day he came
back from the longest absence he had yet made her appearance immediately told him she had lately had a bereavement. They met on this occasion as she was leaving the
church, so that postponing his own entrance he instantly
offered to turn round and walk away with her. She considered, then she said: "Go in now, but come and see me
in an hour." He knew the small vista of her street, closed
at the end and as dreary as an empty pocket, where the
pairs of shabby little houses, semi-detached but indissolubly
united, were like married couples on bad terms. Often,
however, as he had gone to the beginning he had never
gone beyond. Her aunt was dead—that he immediately
guessed, as well as that it made a difference; but when she
had for the first time mentioned her number he found himself, on her leaving him, not a little agitated by this sudden
liberality. She wasn't a person with whom, after all, one
got on so very fast: it had taken him months and months
to learn her name, years and years to learn her address. If
she had looked, on this reunion, so much older to him, how
in the world did he look to her? She had reached the period
of life he had long since reached, when, after separations,
the marked clock-face of the friend we meet announces the
hour we have tried to forget. He couldn't have said what
he expected as, at the end of his waiting, he turned the
corner where for years he had always paused; simply not

to pause was a sufficient cause for emotion. It was an event, somehow; and in all their long acquaintance there had never been an event. This one grew larger when, five minutes later, in the faint elegance of her little drawing-room, she quavered out a greeting that showed the measure she took of it. He had a strange sense of having come for something in particular; strange because literally there was nothing particular between them, nothing save that they were at one on their great point, which had long ago become a magnificent matter of course. It was true that after she had said "You can always come now, you know," the thing he was there for seemed already to have happened. He asked her if it was the death of her aunt that made the difference; to which she replied: "She never knew I knew you. I wished her not to." The beautiful clearness of her candour—her faded beauty was like a summer twilight—disconnected the words from any image of deceit. They might have struck him as the record of a deep dissimulation, but she had always given him a sense of noble reasons. The vanished aunt was present, as he looked about him, in the small complacencies of the room, the beaded velvet and the fluted moreen; and though, as we know, he had the worship of the Dead, he found himself not definitely regretting this lady. If she wasn't in his long list, however, she was in her niece's short one, and Stransom presently observed to the latter that now at least, in the place they haunted together, she would have another object of devotion.

"Yes, I shall have another. She was very kind to me. It's that that's the difference."

He judged, wondering a good deal before he made any motion to leave her, that the difference would somehow be very great and would consist of still other things than her having let him come in. It rather chilled him, for they had been happy together as they were. He extracted from her at any rate an intimation that she should now have means less limited, that her aunt's tiny fortune had come to her, so that there was henceforth only one to consume what had formerly been made to suffice for two. This was a joy to Stransom, because it had hitherto been equally impossible for him either to offer her presents or contentedly to stay his hand. It was too ugly to be at her side that way, abounding himself and yet not able to overflow—a demonstration that would have been signally a false note. Even her better situation too seemed only to draw out in a sense the loneliness of her future. It would merely help her to live more and more for their small ceremonial, and this at a time when he himself had begun wearily to feel that, having set it in motion, he might depart. When they had sat a while in the pale parlour she got up—"This isn't *my* room: let us go into mine." They had only to cross the narrow hall, as he found, to pass quite into another air. When she had closed the door of the second room, as she called it, he felt at last in real possession of her. The place had the flush of life—it was expressive; its dark red walls were articulate with memories and relics. These were simple things—photographs and water-colours, scraps of writing framed and ghosts of flowers embalmed; but a moment sufficed to show him they had a common meaning. It was here she had lived and worked, and she had already told him she would make no change of scene. He read the reference in the objects about her—the general one to places and times; but after a minute he distinguished among them a small portrait of a gentleman. At a distance and without their glasses his eyes were only so caught by it as to feel a vague curiosity. Presently this impulse carried him nearer, and in another moment he was staring at the picture in stupefaction and with the sense that some sound had broken from him. He was further conscious that he showed his companion a white face when he turned round on her gasping: "Acton Hague!"

She matched his great wonder. "Did you know him?"

"He was the friend of all my youth—of my early manhood. And *you* knew him?"

She coloured at this and for a moment her answer failed; her eyes embraced everything in the place, and a strange irony reached her lips as she echoed: "Knew him?"

Then Stransom understood, while the room heaved like the cabin of a ship, that its whole contents cried out with him, that it was a museum in his honour, that all her later years had been addressed to him and that the shrine he himself had reared had been passionately converted to this

use. It was all for Acton Hague that she had kneeled every
day at his altar. What need had there been for a consecrated
candle when he was present in the whole array? The revelation so smote our friend in the face that he dropped into a
seat and sat silent. He had quickly felt her shaken by the
force of his shock, but as she sank on the sofa beside him
and laid her hand on his arm he knew almost as soon
that she mightn't resent it as much as she'd have liked.

VII

He learned in that instant two things: one being that
even in so long a time she had gathered no knowledge of
his great intimacy and his great quarrel; the other that in
spite of this ignorance, strangely enough, she supplied on
the spot a reason for his stupor. "How extraordinary," he
presently exclaimed, "that we should never have known!"

She gave a wan smile which seemed to Stransom stranger
even than the fact itself. "I never, never spoke of him."

He looked again about the room. "Why then, if your
life had been so full of him?"

"Mayn't I put you that question as well? Hadn't your
life also been full of him?"

"Any one's, every one's life who had the wonderful experience of knowing him. I never spoke of him," Stransom
added in a moment, "because he did me—years ago—an unforgettable wrong." She was silent, and with the full effect
of his presence all about them it almost startled her guest
to hear no protest escape her. She accepted his words; he
turned his eyes to her again to see in what manner she accepted them. It was with rising tears and a rare sweetness
in the movement of putting out her hand to take his own.
Nothing more wonderful had ever appeared to him than, in
that little chamber of remembrance and homage, to see her
convey with such exquisite mildness that as from Acton
Hague any injury was credible. The clock ticked in the
stillness—Hague had probably given it to her—and while
he let her hold his hand with a tenderness that was almost
an assumption of responsibility for his old pain as well as

his new, Stransom after a minute broke out: "Good God, how he must have used *you!*"

She dropped his hand at this, got up and, moving across the room, made straight a small picture to which, on examining it, he had given a slight push. Then turning round on him with her pale gaiety recovered, "I've forgiven him!" she declared.

"I know what you've done," said Stransom; "I know what you've done for years." For a moment they looked at each other through it all with their long community of service in their eyes. This short passage made, to his sense, for the woman before him, an immense, an absolutely naked confession; which was presently, suddenly blushing red and changing her place again, what she appeared to learn he perceived in it. He got up and "How you must have loved him!" he cried.

"Women aren't like men. They can love even where they've suffered."

"Women are wonderful," said Stransom. "But I assure you I've forgiven him too."

"If I had known of anything so strange I wouldn't have brought you here."

"So that we might have gone on in our ignorance to the last?"

"What do you call the last?" she asked, smiling still.

At this he could smile back at her. "You'll see—when it comes."

She thought of that. "This is better perhaps; but as we were—it was good."

He put her the question. "Did it never happen that he spoke of me?"

Considering more intently she made no answer, and he then knew he should have been adequately answered by her asking how often he himself had spoken of their terrible friend. Suddenly a brighter light broke in her face and an excited idea sprang to her lips in the appeal: "You *have* forgiven him?"

"How, if I hadn't, could I linger here?"

She visibly winced at the deep but unintended irony of

this; but even while she did so she panted quickly: "Then in the lights on your altar—?"

"There's never a light for Acton Hague!"

She stared with a dreadful fall. "But if he's one of your Dead?"

"He's one of the world's, if you like—he's one of yours. But he's not one of mine. Mine are only the Dead who died possessed of me. They're mine in death because they were mine in life."

"*He* was yours in life then, even if for a while he ceased to be. If you forgave him you went back to him. Those whom we've once loved—"

"Are those who can hurt us most," Stransom broke in.

"Ah it's not true—you've *not* forgiven him!" she wailed with a passion that startled him.

He looked at her as never yet. "What was it he did to you?"

"Everything!" Then abruptly she put out her hand in farewell. "Good-bye."

He turned as cold as he had turned that night he read the man's death. "You mean that we meet no more?"

"Not as we've met—not *there!*"

He stood aghast at this snap of their great bond, at the renouncement that rang out in the word she so expressively sounded. "But what's changed—for you?"

She waited in all the sharpness of a trouble that for the first time since he had known her made her splendidly stern. "How can you understand now when you didn't understand before?"

"I didn't understand before only because I didn't know. Now that I know, I see what I've been living with for years," Stransom went on very gently.

She looked at him with a larger allowance, doing this gentleness justice. "How can I then, on this new knowledge of my own, ask you to continue to live with it?"

"I set up my altar, with its multiplied meanings," Stransom began; but she quickly interrupted him.

"You set up your altar, and when I wanted one most I found it magnificently ready. I used it with the gratitude I've always shown you, for I knew it from of old to be dedicated to Death. I told you long ago that my Dead weren't many. Yours were, but all you had done for them was none too much for *my* worship! You had placed a great light for Each—I gathered them together for One!"

"We had simply different intentions," he returned. "That, as you say, I perfectly knew, and I don't see why your intention shouldn't still sustain you."

"That's because you're generous—you can imagine and think. But the spell's broken."

It seemed to poor Stransom, in spite of his resistance, that it really was, and the prospect stretched grey and void before him. All he could say, however, was: "I hope you'll try before you give up."

"If I had known you had ever known him I should have taken for granted he had his candle," she presently answered. "What's changed, as you say, is that on making the discovery I find he never has had it. That makes *my* attitude"—she paused as thinking how to express it, then said simply—"all wrong."

"Come once again," he pleaded.

"Will you give him his candle?" she asked.

He waited, but only because it would sound ungracious; not because of a doubt of his feeling. "I can't do that!" he declared at last.

"Then good-bye." And she gave him her hand again.

He had got his dismissal; besides which, in the agitation of everything that had opened out to him, he felt the need to recover himself as he could only do in solitude. Yet he lingered—lingered to see if she had no compromise to express, no attenuation to propose. But he only met her great lamenting eyes, in which indeed he read that she was as sorry for him as for any one else. This made him say: "At least, in any case, I may see you here."

"Oh yes, come if you like. But I don't think it will do."

He looked round the room once more, knowing how little he was sure it would do. He felt also stricken and more and more cold, and his chill was like an ague in which he had to make an effort not to shake. Then he made doleful reply: "I must try on my side—if you can't try on yours." She came out with him to the hall and into the doorway, and here he put her the question he held he could least answer from his own wit. "Why have you never let me come before?"

"Because my aunt would have seen you, and I should have had to tell her how I came to know you."

"And what would have been the objection to that?"

"It would have entailed other explanations; there would at any rate have been that danger."

"Surely she knew you went every day to church," Stransom objected.

"She didn't know what I went for."

"Of me then she never even heard?"

"You'll think I was deceitful. But I didn't need to be!"

He was now on the lower door-step, and his hostess held the door half-closed behind him. Through what remained of the opening he saw her framed face. He made a supreme appeal. "What *did* he do to you?"

"It would have come out—*she* would have told you. That fear at my heart—that was my reason!" And she closed the door, shutting him out.

VIII

He had ruthlessly abandoned her—that of course was what he had done. Stransom made it all out in solitude, at leisure, fitting the unmatched pieces gradually together and dealing one by one with a hundred obscure points. She had known Hague only after her present friend's relations with him had wholly terminated; obviously indeed a good while after; and it was natural enough that of his previous life she should have ascertained only what he had judged good to communicate. There were passages it was quite conceivable that even in moments of the tenderest expansion he should have withheld. Of many facts in the career of a man so in the eye of the world there was of course a common knowledge; but this lady lived apart from public affairs, and the only time perfectly clear to her would have been the time following the dawn of her own drama. A man in her place would have "looked up" the past—would even have consulted old newspapers. It remained remarkable indeed that in her long contact with the partner of her retrospect no accident had lighted a train; but there was no arguing about that; the accident had in fact come: it had simply been that security had prevailed. She had taken what Hague had given her, and her blankness in respect of his other connexions was only a touch in the picture of that plasticity Stransom had supreme reason to know so great a master could have been trusted to produce.

This picture was for a while all our friend saw; he caught his breath again and again as it came over him that the woman with whom he had had for years so fine a point of contact was a woman whom Acton Hague, of all men in the world, had more or less fashioned. Such as she sat there today she was ineffaceably stamped with him. Beneficent, blameless as Stransom held her, he couldn't rid himself of the sense that he had been, as who should say, swindled. She had imposed upon him hugely, though she had known it as little as he. All this later past came back to him as a time grotesquely misspent. Such at least were his first re-flexions; after a while he found himself more divided and only, as the end of it, more troubled. He imagined, recalled, reconstituted, figured out for himself the truth she had re-fused to give him; the effect of which was to make her seem to him only more saturated with her fate. He felt her spirit, through the whole strangeness, finer than his own to the very degree in which she might have been, in which she certainly had been, more wronged. A woman, when wronged, was always more wronged than a man, and there were conditions when the least she could have got off with was more than the most he could have to bear. He was sure this rare creature wouldn't have got off with the least. He was awestruck at the thought of such a surrender—such a prostration. Moulded indeed she had been by power-ful hands, to have converted her injury into an exaltation so sublime. The fellow had only had to die for everything that was ugly in him to be washed out in a torrent. It was vain to try to guess what had taken place, but nothing could be clearer than that she had ended by accusing herself. She absolved him at every point, she adored her very wounds. The passion by which he had profited had rushed back after its ebb, and now the tide of tenderness, arrested for ever at flood, was too deep even to fathom. Stransom sincerely considered that he had forgiven him; but how little he had achieved the miracle that she had achieved! His forgiveness was silence, but hers was mere unuttered sound. The light she had demanded for his altar would have broken his silence with a blare; whereas all the lights in the church were for her too great a hush.

She had been right about the difference—she had spoken the truth about the change: Stransom was soon to know himself as perversely but sharply jealous. *His* tide had ebbed, not flowed; if he had "forgiven" Acton Hague, that forgiveness was a motive with a broken spring. The very fact of her appeal for a material sign, a sign that should make her dead lover equal there with the others, presented the concession to her friend as too handsome for the case. He had never thought of himself as hard, but an exorbitant article might easily render him so. He moved round and round this one, but only in widening circles—the more he looked at it the less acceptable it seemed. At the same time he had no illusion about the effect of his refusal; he perfectly saw how it would make for a rupture. He left her alone a week, but when at last he again called this conviction was cruelly confirmed. In the interval he had kept away from the church, and he needed no fresh assurance from her to know she hadn't entered it. The change was complete enough: it had broken up her life. Indeed it had broken up his, for all the fires of his shrine seemed to him suddenly to have been quenched. A great indifference fell upon him, the weight of which was in itself a pain; and he never knew what his devotion had been for him till in that shock it ceased like a dropped watch. Neither did he know with how large a confidence he had counted on the final service that had now failed: the mortal deception was that in this abandonment the whole future gave way.

These days of her absence proved to him of what she was capable; all the more that he never dreamed she was vindictive or even resentful. It was not in anger she had forsaken him; it was in simple submission to hard reality, to the stern logic of life. This came home to him when he sat with her again in the room in which her late aunt's conversation lingered like the tone of a cracked piano. She tried to make him forget how much they were estranged, but in the very presence of what they had given up it was impossible not to be sorry for her. He had taken from her so much more than she had taken from him. He argued with her again, told her she could now have the altar to herself; but she only shook her head with pleading sadness, begging him not to waste his breath on the impossible, the extinct. Couldn't he see that in relation to her private need the rites he had established were practically an elaborate exclusion? She regretted nothing that had happened; it had all been right so long as she didn't know, and it was only that now she knew too much and that from the moment their eyes were open they would simply have to conform. It had doubtless been happiness enough for them to go on together so long. She was gentle, grateful, resigned; but this was only the form of a deep immoveability. He saw he should never more cross the threshold of the second room, and he felt how much this alone would make a stranger of him and give a conscious stiffness to his visits. He would have hated to plunge again into that well of reminders, but he enjoyed quite as little the vacant alternative.

After he had been with her three or four times it struck him that to have come at last into her house had had the horrid effect of diminishing their intimacy. He had known her better, had liked her in greater freedom, when they merely walked together or kneeled together. Now they only pretended; before they had been nobly sincere. They began to try their walks again, but it proved a lame imitation, for these things, from the first, beginning or ending, had been connected with their visits to the church. They had either strolled away as they came out or gone in to rest on the return. Stransom, besides, now faltered; he couldn't walk as of old. The omission made everything false; it was a dire mutilation of their lives. Our friend was frank and monotonous, making no mystery of his remonstrance and no secret of his predicament. Her response, whatever it was, always came to the same thing—an implied invitation to him to judge, if he spoke of predicaments, of how much comfort she had in hers. For him indeed was no comfort even in complaint, since every allusion to what had befallen them but made the author of their trouble more present. Acton Hague was between them—that was the essence of the matter, and never so much between them as when they were face to face. Then Stransom, while still wanting to banish him, had the strangest sense of striving for an ease that would involve having accepted him. Deeply disconcerted by what he knew, he was still worse tormented by really not knowing. Perfectly aware that it would have been horribly vulgar to abuse his old friend or to tell his companion the story of their quarrel, it yet vexed him that her depth of reserve should give him no opening and should have the effect of a magnanimity greater even than his own.

He challenged himself, denounced himself, asked himself if he were in love with her that he should care so much what adventures she had had. He had never for a moment allowed he was in love with her; therefore nothing could have surprised him more than to discover he was jealous. What but jealousy could give a man that sore contentious wish for the detail of what would make him suffer? Well enough he knew indeed that he should never have it from the only person who today could give it to him. She let him press her with his sombre eyes, only smiling at him with an exquisite mercy and breathing equally little the word that would expose her secret and the word that would appear to deny his literal right to bitterness. She told nothing, she judged nothing; she accepted everything but the possibility of her return to the old symbols. Stransom divined that for her too they had been vividly individual, had stood for particular hours or particular attributes—particular links in her chain. He made it clear to himself, as he believed, that his difficulty lay in the fact that the very nature of the plea for his faithless friend constituted a prohibition; that it happened to have come from *her* was precisely the vice that attached to it. To the voice of impersonal generosity he felt sure he would have listened; he would have deferred to an advocate who, speaking from abstract justice, knowing of his denial without having known Hague, should have had the imagination to say: "Ah remember only the best of him; pity him; provide for him." To provide

for him on the very ground of having discovered another
of his turpitudes was not to pity but to glorify him. The
more Stransom thought the more he made out that whatever this relation of Hague's it could only have been a
deception more or less finely practised. Where had it come
into the life that all men saw? Why had one never heard
of it if it had had the frankness of honourable things?
Stransom knew enough of his other ties, of his obligations
and appearances, not to say enough of his general character, to be sure there had been some infamy. In one way
or another this creature had been coldly sacrificed. That
was why at the last as well as the first he must still leave
him out and out.

IX

And yet this was no solution, especially after he had
talked again to his friend of all it had been his plan she
should finally do for him. He had talked in the other days,
and she had responded with a frankness qualified only by
a courteous reluctance, a reluctance that touched him, to
linger on the question of his death. She had then practically
accepted the charge, suffered him to feel he could depend
upon her to be the eventual guardian of his shrine; and it
was in the name of what had so passed between them that
he appealed to her not to forsake him in his age. She listened at present with shining coldness and all her habitual
forbearance to insist on her terms; her deprecation was even
still tenderer, for it expressed the compassion of her own
sense that he was abandoned. Her terms, however, remained the same, and scarcely the less audible for not being
uttered; though he was sure that secretly even more than
he she felt bereft of the satisfaction his solemn trust was to
have provided her. They both missed the rich future, but
she missed it most, because after all it was to have been
entirely hers; and it was her acceptance of the loss that gave
him the full measure of her preference for the thought of
Acton Hague over any other thought whatever. He had
humour enough to laugh rather grimly when he said to
himself: "Why the deuce does she like him so much more

than she likes me?"—the reasons being really so conceivable. But even his faculty of analysis left the irritation standing, and this irritation proved perhaps the greatest misfortune that had ever overtaken him. There had been nothing yet that made him so much want to give up. He had of course by this time well reached the age of renouncement; but it had not hitherto been vivid to him that it was time to give up everything.

Practically, at the end of six months, he had renounced the friendship once so charming and comforting. His privation had two faces, and the face it had turned to him on the occasion of his last attempt to cultivate that friendship was the one he could look at least. This was the privation he inflicted; the other was the privation he bore. The conditions she never phrased he used to murmur to himself in solitude: "One more, one more—only just one." Certainly he was going down; he often felt it when he caught himself, over his work, staring at vacancy and giving voice to that inanity. There was proof enough besides in his being so weak and so ill. His irritation took the form of melancholy, and his melancholy that of the conviction that his health had quite failed. His altar moreover had ceased to exist; his chapel, in his dreams, was a great dark cavern. All the lights had gone out—all his Dead had died again. He couldn't exactly see at first how it had been in the power of his late companion to extinguish them, since it was neither for her nor by her that they had been called into being. Then he understood that it was essentially in his own soul the revival had taken place, and that in the air of this soul they were now unable to breathe. The candles might mechanically burn, but each of them had lost its lustre. The church had become a void; it was his presence, her presence, their common presence, that had made the indispensable medium. If anything was wrong everything was—her silence spoiled the tune.

Then when three months were gone he felt so lonely that he went back; reflecting that as they had been his best society for years his Dead perhaps wouldn't let him forsake them without doing something more for him. They stood there, as he had left them, in their tall radiance, the bright cluster that had already made him, on occasions when he was willing to compare small things with great, liken them to a group of sea-lights on the edge of the ocean of life. It was a relief to him, after a while, as he sat there, to feel they had still a virtue. He was more and more easily tired, and he always drove now; the action of his heart was weak and gave him none of the reassurance conferred by the action of his fancy. None the less he returned yet again, returned several times, and finally, during six months, haunted the place with a renewal of frequency and a strain of impatience. In winter the church was unwarmed and exposure to cold forbidden him, but the glow of his shrine was an influence in which he could almost bask. He sat and wondered to what he had reduced his absent associate and what she now did with the hours of her absence. There were other churches, there were other altars, there were other candles; in one way or another her piety would still operate; he couldn't absolutely have deprived her of her rites. So he argued, but without contentment; for he well enough knew there was no other such rare semblance of the mountain of light she had once mentioned to him as the satisfaction of her need. As this semblance again gradually grew great to him and his pious practice more regular, he found a sharper and sharper pang in the imagination of her darkness; for never so much as in these weeks had his rites been real, never had his gathered company seemed so to respond and even to invite. He lost himself in the large lustre, which was more and more what he had from the first wished it to be—as dazzling as the vision of heaven in the mind of a child. He wandered in the fields of light; he passed, among the tall tapers, from tier to tier, from fire to fire, from name to name, from the white intensity of one clear emblem, of one saved soul, to another. It was in the quiet sense of having saved his souls that his deep strange instinct rejoiced. This was no dim theological rescue, no boon of a contingent world; they were saved better than faith or works could save them, saved for the warm world they had shrunk from dying to, for actuality, for continuity, for the certainty of human remembrance.

By this time he had survived all his friends; the last

straight flame was three years old, there was no one to add
to the list. Over and over he called his roll, and it appeared
to him compact and complete. Where should he put in another, where, if there were no other objection, would it
stand in its place in the rank? He reflected, with a want of
sincerity of which he was quite conscious, that it would be
difficult to determine that place. More and more, besides,
face to face with his little legion, reading over endless histories, handling the empty shells and playing with the
silence—more and more he could see that he had never introduced an alien. He had had his great compassions, his
indulgences—there were cases in which they had been immense; but what had his devotion after all been if it hadn't
been at bottom a respect? He was, however, himself surprised at his stiffness; by the end of the winter the responsibility of it was what was uppermost in his thoughts. The
refrain had grown old to them, that plea for just one more.
There came a day when, for simple exhaustion, if symmetry
should demand just one he was ready so far to meet symmetry. Symmetry was harmony, and the idea of harmony
began to haunt him; he said to himself that harmony was
of course everything. He took, in fancy, his composition to
pieces, redistributing it into other lines, making other juxta-
positions and contrasts. He shifted this and that candle, he
made the spaces different, he effaced the disfigurement of
a possible gap. There were subtle and complex relations,
a scheme of cross-reference, and moments in which he
seemed to catch a glimpse of the void so sensible to the
woman who wandered in exile or sat where he had seen
her with the portrait of Acton Hague. Finally, in this way,
he arrived at a conception of the total, the ideal, which
left a clear opportunity for just another figure. "Just one
more—to round it off; just one more, just one," continued
to hum in his head. There was a strange confusion in the
thought, for he felt the day to be near when he too should
be one of the Others. What in this event would the Others
matter to him, since they only mattered to the living? Even
as one of the Dead what would his altar matter to him,
since his particular dream of keeping it up had melted
away? What had harmony to do with the case if his lights

were all to be quenched? What he had hoped for was an instituted thing. He might perpetuate it on some other pretext, but his special meaning would have dropped. This meaning was to have lasted with the life of the one other person who understood it.

In March he had an illness during which he spent a fortnight in bed, and when he revived a little he was told of two things that had happened. One was that a lady whose name was not known to the servants (she left none) had been three times to ask about him; the other was that in his sleep and on an occasion when his mind evidently wandered he was heard to murmur again and again: "Just one more—just one." As soon as he found himself able to go out, and before the doctor in attendance had pronounced him so, he drove to see the lady who had come to ask about him. She was not at home; but this gave him the opportunity, before his strength should fail again, to take his way to the church. He entered it alone; he had declined, in a happy manner he possessed of being able to decline effectively, the company of his servant or of a nurse. He knew now perfectly what these good people thought; they had discovered his clandestine connexion, the magnet that had drawn him for so many years, and doubtless attached a significance of their own to the odd words they had repeated to him. The nameless lady was the clandestine connexion—a fact nothing could have made clearer than his indecent haste to rejoin her. He sank on his knees before his altar while his head fell over on his hands. His weakness, his life's weariness overtook him. It seemed to him he had come for the great surrender. At first he asked himself how he should get away; then, with the failing belief in the power, the very desire to move gradually left him. He had come, as he always came, to lose himself; the fields of light were still there to stray in; only this time, in straying, he would never come back. He had given himself to his Dead, and it was good: this time his Dead would keep him. He couldn't rise from his knees; he believed he should never rise again; all he could do was to lift his face and fix his eyes on his lights. They looked unusually, strangely splendid, but the one that always drew him most had an un-

precedented lustre. It was the central voice of the choir, the
glowing heart of the brightness, and on this occasion it
seemed to expand, to spread great wings of flame. The
whole altar flared—dazzling and blinding; but the source
of the vast radiance burned clearer than the rest, gathering
itself into form, and the form was human beauty and human charity, was the far-off face of Mary Antrim. She
smiled at him from the glory of heaven—she brought the
glory down with her to take him. He bowed his head in
submission and at the same moment another wave rolled
over him. Was it the quickening of joy to pain? In the midst
of his joy at any rate he felt his buried face grow hot as
with some communicated knowledge that had the force of
a reproach. It suddenly made him contrast that very rapture with the bliss he had refused to another. This breath
of the passion immortal was all that other had asked; the
descent of Mary Antrim opened his spirit with a great com-
punctious throb for the descent of Acton Hague. It was as
if Stransom had read what her eyes said to him.

After a moment he looked round in a despair that made
him feel as if the source of life were ebbing. The church
had been empty—he was alone; but he wanted to have
something done, to make a last appeal. This idea gave him
strength for an effort; he rose to his feet with a movement
that made him turn, supporting himself by the back of a
bench. Behind him was a prostrate figure, a figure he had
seen before; a woman in deep mourning, bowed in grief or
in prayer. He had seen her in other days—the first time of his
entrance there, and he now slightly wavered, looking at her
again till she seemed aware he had noticed her. She raised
her head and met his eyes: the partner of his long worship
had come back. She looked across at him an instant with
a face wondering and scared; he saw he had made her
afraid. Then quickly rising she came straight to him with
both hands out.

"Then you *could* come? God sent you!" he murmured
with a happy smile.

"You're very ill—you shouldn't be here," she urged in anxious reply.

"God sent me too, I think. I was ill when I came, but

the sight of you does wonders." He held her hands, which steadied and quickened him. "I've something to tell you."

"Don't tell me!" she tenderly pleaded; "let me tell you. This afternoon, by a miracle, the sweetest of miracles, the sense of our difference left me. I was out—I was near, thinking, wandering alone, when, on the spot, something changed in my heart. It's my confession—there it is. To come back, to come back on the instant—the idea gave me wings. It was as if I suddenly saw something—as if it all became possible. I could come for what you yourself came for: that was enough. So here I am. It's not for my own—that's over. But I'm here for *them*." And breathless, infinitely relieved by her low precipitate explanation, she looked with eyes that reflected all its splendour at the magnificence of their altar.

"They're here for you," Stransom said, "they're present tonight as they've never been. They speak for you—don't you see?—in a passion of light; they sing out like a choir of angels. Don't you hear what they say?—they offer the very thing you asked of me."

"Don't talk of it—don't think of it; forget it!" She spoke in hushed supplication, and while the alarm deepened in her eyes she disengaged one of her hands and passed an arm round him to support him better, to help him to sink into a seat.

He let himself go, resting on her; he dropped upon the bench and she fell on her knees beside him, his own arm round her shoulder. So he remained an instant, staring up at his shrine. "They say there's a gap in the array—they say it's not full, complete. Just one more," he went on, softly —"isn't that what you wanted? Yes, one more, one more."

"Ah no more—no more!" she wailed, as with a quick new horror of it, under her breath.

"Yes, one more," he repeated, simply; "just one!" And with this his head dropped on her shoulder; she felt that in his weakness he had fainted. But alone with him in the dusky church a great dread was on her of what might still happen, for his face had the whiteness of death.

[1895]

THE FIGURE IN
THE CARPET

I

I had done a few things and earned a few pence—I had
perhaps even had time to begin to think I was finer than
was perceived by the patronising; but when I take the little
measure of my course (a fidgety habit, for it's none of the
longest yet) I count my real start from the evening George
Corvick, breathless and worried, came in to ask me a service. He had done more things than I, and earned more
pence, though there were chances for cleverness I thought
he sometimes missed. I could only, however, that evening
declare to him that he never missed one for kindness. There
was almost rapture in hearing it proposed to me to prepare
for *The Middle*, the organ of our lucubrations, so called
from the position in the week of its day of appearance, an
article for which he had made himself responsible and of
which, tied up with a stout string, he laid on my table the
subject. I pounced upon my opportunity—that is on the first
volume of it—and paid scant attention to my friend's explanation of his appeal. What explanation could be more
to the point than my obvious fitness for the task? I had
written on Hugh Vereker, but never a word in *The Middle*,
where my dealings were mainly with the ladies and the

minor poets. This was his new novel, an advance copy, and whatever much or little it should do for his reputation I was clear on the spot as to what it should do for mine. Moreover if I always read him as soon as I could get hold of him I had a particular reason for wishing to read him now: I had accepted an invitation to Bridges for the following Sunday, and it had been mentioned in Lady Jane's note that Mr. Vereker was to be there. I was young enough for a flutter at meeting a man of his renown, and innocent enough to believe the occasion would demand the display of an acquaintance with his "last."

Corvick, who had promised a review of it, had not even had time to read it; he had gone to pieces in consequence of news requiring—as on precipitate reflexion he judged— that he should catch the night-mail to Paris. He had had a telegram from Gwendolen Erme in answer to his letter offering to fly to her aid. I knew already about Gwendolen Erme; I had never seen her, but I had my ideas, which were mainly to the effect that Corvick would marry her if her mother would only die. That lady seemed now in a fair way to oblige him; after some dreadful mistake about a climate or a "cure" she had suddenly collapsed on the return from abroad. Her daughter, unsupported and alarmed, desiring to make a rush for home but hesitating at the risk, had accepted our friend's assistance, and it was my secret belief that at sight of him Mrs. Erme would pull round. His own belief was scarcely to be called secret; it discernibly at any rate differed from mine. He had showed me Gwendolen's photograph with the remark that she wasn't pretty but was awfully interesting; she had published at the age of nineteen a novel in three volumes, "Deep Down," about which, in *The Middle*, he had been really splendid. He appreciated my present eagerness and undertook that the periodical in question should do no less; then at the last, with his hand on the door, he said to me: "Of course you'll be all right, you know." Seeing I was a trifle vague he added: "I mean you won't be silly."

"Silly—about Vereker! Why what do I ever find him but awfully clever?"

"Well, what's that but silly? What on earth does 'awfully

clever' mean? For God's sake try to get *at* him. Don't let
him suffer by our arrangement. Speak of him, you know, if
you can, as *I* should have spoken of him."

I wondered an instant. "You mean as far and away the
biggest of the lot—that sort of thing?"

Corvick almost groaned. "Oh you know, I don't put them
back to back that way; it's the infancy of art! But he gives
me a pleasure so rare; the sense of"—he mused a little—
"something or other."

I wondered again. "The sense, pray, of what?"

"My dear man, that's just what I want *you* to say!"

Even before he had banged the door I had begun, book
in hand, to prepare myself to say it. I sat up with Vereker
half the night; Corvick couldn't have done more than that.
He was awfully clever—I stuck to that, but he wasn't a bit
the biggest of the lot. I didn't allude to the lot, however;
I flattered myself that I emerged on this occasion from
the infancy of art. "It's all right," they declared vividly at
the office; and when the number appeared I felt there was
a basis on which I could meet the great man. It gave me
confidence for a day or two—then that confidence dropped.
I had fancied him reading it with relish, but if Corvick
wasn't satisfied how could Vereker himself be? I reflected
indeed that the heat of the admirer was sometimes grosser
even than the appetite of the scribe. Corvick at all events
wrote me from Paris a little ill-humouredly. Mrs. Erme was
pulling round, and I hadn't at all said what Vereker gave
him the sense of.

I I

The effect of my visit to Bridges was to turn me out for
more profundity. Hugh Vereker, as I saw him there, was
of a contact so void of angles that I blushed for the poverty
of imagination involved in my small precautions. If he was
in spirits it wasn't because he had read my review; in fact
on the Sunday morning I felt sure he hadn't read it, though
The Middle had been out three days and bloomed, I assured myself, in the stiff garden of periodicals which gave
one of the ormolu tables the air of a stand at a station. The

impression he made on me personally was such that I wished him to read it, and I corrected to this end with a surreptitious hand what might be wanting in the careless conspicuity of the sheet. I'm afraid I even watched the result of my manœuvre, but up to luncheon I watched in vain.

When afterwards, in the course of our gregarious walk, I found myself for half an hour, not perhaps without another manœuvre, at the great man's side, the result of his affability was a still livelier desire that he shouldn't remain in ignorance of the peculiar justice I had done him. It wasn't that he seemed to thirst for justice; on the contrary I hadn't yet caught in his talk the faintest grunt of a grudge—a note for which my young experience had already given me an ear. Of late he had had more recognition, and it was pleasant, as we used to say in *The Middle*, to see how it drew him out. He wasn't of course popular, but I judged one of the sources of his good humour to be precisely that his success was independent of that. He had none the less become in a manner the fashion; the critics at least had put on a spurt and caught up with him. We had found out at last how clever he was, and he had had to make the best of the loss of his mystery. I was strongly tempted, as I walked beside him, to let him know how much of that unveiling was my act; and there was a moment when I probably should have done so had not one of the ladies of our party, snatching a place at his other elbow, just then appealed to him in a spirit comparatively selfish. It was very discouraging: I almost felt the liberty had been taken with myself.

I had had on my tongue's end, for my own part, a phrase or two about the right word at the right time; but later on I was glad not to have spoken, for when on our return we clustered at tea I perceived Lady Jane, who had not been out with us, brandishing *The Middle* with her longest arm. She had taken it up at her leisure; she was delighted with what she had found, and I saw that, as a mistake in a man may often be a felicity in a woman, she would practically do for me what I hadn't been able to do for myself. "Some sweet little truths that needed to be spoken," I heard her declare, thrusting the paper at rather a bewildered couple by the fireplace. She grabbed it away from them again on the reappearance of Hugh Vereker, who after our walk had been upstairs to change something. "I know you don't in general look at this kind of thing, but it's an occasion really for doing so. You *haven't* seen it? Then you must. The man has actually got *at* you, at what *I* always feel, you know." Lady Jane threw into her eyes a look evidently intended to give an idea of what she always felt; but she added that she couldn't have expressed it. The man in the paper expressed it in a striking manner. "Just see there, and there, where I've dashed it, how he brings it out." She had literally marked for him the brightest patches of my prose, and if I was a little amused Vereker himself may well have been. He showed how much he was when before us all Lady Jane wanted to read something aloud. I liked at any rate the way he defeated her purpose by jerking the paper affectionately out of her clutch. He'd take it upstairs with him and look at it on going to dress. He did this half an hour later—I saw it in his hand when he repaired to his room. That was the moment at which, thinking to give her pleasure, I mentioned to Lady Jane that I was the author of the review. I did give her pleasure, I judged, but perhaps not quite so much as I had expected. If the author was "only me" the thing didn't seem quite so remarkable. Hadn't I had the effect rather of diminishing the lustre of the article than of adding to my own? Her ladyship was subject to the most extraordinary drops. It didn't matter; the only effect I cared about was the one it would have on Vereker up there by his bedroom fire.

At dinner I watched for the signs of this impression, tried to fancy some happier light in his eyes; but to my disappointment Lady Jane gave me no chance to make sure. I had hoped she'd call triumphantly down the table, publicly demand if she hadn't been right. The party was large—there were people from outside as well, but I had never seen a table long enough to deprive Lady Jane of a triumph. I was just reflecting in truth that this interminable board would deprive *me* of one when the guest next me, dear woman— she was Miss Poyle, the vicar's sister, a robust unmodulated person—had the happy inspiration and the unusual courage to address herself across it to Vereker, who was opposite, but not directly, so that when he replied they were both leaning forward. She inquired, artless body, what he thought of Lady Jane's "panegyric," which she had read—not connecting it however with her right-hand neighbour; and while I strained my ear for his reply I heard him, to my stupefaction, call back gaily, his mouth full of bread: "Oh it's all right—the usual twaddle!"

I had caught Vereker's glance as he spoke, but Miss Poyle's surprise was a fortunate cover for my own. "You mean he doesn't do you justice?" said the excellent woman.

Vereker laughed out, and I was happy to be able to do the same. "It's a charming article," he tossed us.

Miss Poyle thrust her chin half across the cloth. "Oh you're so deep!" she drove home.

"As deep as the ocean! All I pretend is that the author doesn't see—" But a dish was at this point passed over his shoulder, and we had to wait while he helped himself.

"Doesn't see what?" my neighbour continued.

"Doesn't see anything."

"Dear me—how very stupid!"

"Not a bit," Vereker laughed again. "Nobody does."

The lady on his further side appealed to him and Miss Poyle sank back to myself. "Nobody sees anything!" she cheerfully announced; to which I replied that I had often thought so too, but had somehow taken the thought for a proof on my own part of a tremendous eye. I didn't tell her the article was mine; and I observed that Lady Jane, occupied at the end of the table, had not caught Vereker's words.

I rather avoided him after dinner, for I confess he struck me as cruelly conceited, and the revelation was a pain. "The usual twaddle"—my acute little study! That one's admiration should have had a reserve or two could gall him to that point? I had thought him placid, and he was placid enough; such a surface was the hard polished glass that encased the bauble of his vanity. I was really ruffled, and the only comfort was that if nobody saw anything George Corvick was quite as much out of it as I. This comfort however was not sufficient, after the ladies had dispersed, to carry me in the proper manner—I mean in a spotted jacket and humming an air—into the smoking-room. I took my way in some dejection to bed; but in the passage I encountered Mr. Vereker, who had been up once more to change, coming out of his room. *He* was humming an air and had on a spotted jacket, and as soon as he saw me his gaiety gave a start.

"My dear young man," he exclaimed, "I'm so glad to lay hands on you! I'm afraid I most unwittingly wounded you by those words of mine at dinner to Miss Poyle. I learned but half an hour ago from Lady Jane that you're the author of the little notice in *The Middle*."

I protested that no bones were broken; but he moved with me to my own door, his hand, on my shoulder, kindly feeling for a fracture; and on hearing that I had come up to bed he asked leave to cross my threshold and just tell me in three words what his qualification of my remarks had represented. It was plain he really feared I was hurt, and the sense of his solicitude suddenly made all the difference to me. My cheap review fluttered off into space, and the best things I had said in it became flat enough beside the brilliancy of his being there. I can see him there still, on my rug, in the firelight and his spotted jacket, his fine clear face all bright with the desire to be tender to my youth. I don't know what he had at first meant to say, but I think the sight of my relief touched him, excited him, brought up words to his lips from far within. It was so these words presently conveyed to me something that, as I afterwards knew, he had never uttered to any one. I've always done justice to the generous impulse that made him speak; it was simply compunction for a snub unconsciously administered to a man of letters in a position inferior to his own, a man of letters moreover in the very act of praising him. To make the thing right he talked to me exactly as an equal and on the ground of what we both loved best. The hour, the place, the unexpectedness deepened the impression: he couldn't have done anything more intensely effective.

III

"I don't quite know how to explain it to you," he said, "but it was the very fact that your notice of my book had a spice of intelligence, it was just your exceptional sharpness, that produced the feeling—a very old story with me, I beg you to believe—under the momentary influence of which I used in speaking to that good lady the words you so naturally resent. I don't read the things in the newspapers unless they're thrust upon me as that one was—it's always one's best friend who does it! But I used to read them sometimes—ten years ago. I dare say they were in general rather stupider then; at any rate it always struck me they missed my little point with a perfection exactly as admirable when they patted me on the back as when they kicked me in the shins. Whenever since I've happened to have a glimpse of them they were still blazing away—still missing it, I mean, deliciously. *You* miss it, my dear fellow, with inimitable assurance; the fact of your being awfully clever and your article's being awfully nice doesn't make a hair's breadth of difference. It's quite with you rising young men," Vereker laughed, "that I feel most what a failure I am!"

I listened with keen interest; it grew keener as he talked. "*You* a failure—heavens! What then may your 'little point' happen to be?"

"Have I got to *tell* you, after all these years and labours?" There was something in the friendly reproach of this—jocosely exaggerated—that made me, as an ardent young seeker for truth, blush to the roots of my hair. I'm as much in the dark as ever, though I've grown used in a sense to my obtuseness; at that moment, however, Vereker's happy accent made me appear to myself, and probably to him, a rare dunce. I was on the point of exclaiming "Ah yes, don't tell me: for my honour, for that of the craft, don't!" when he went on in a manner that showed he had read my thought and had his own idea of the probability of our some day redeeming ourselves. "By my little point I mean—what shall I call it?—the particular thing I've written my books most *for*. Isn't there for every writer a particular thing of that sort, the thing that most makes him apply himself, the thing without the effort to achieve which he wouldn't write at all, the very passion of his passion, the part of the business in which, for him, the flame of art burns most intensely? Well, it's *that!*"

I considered a moment—that is I followed at a respectful distance, rather gasping. I was fascinated—easily, you'll say; but I wasn't going after all to be put off my guard. "Your description's certainly beautiful, but it doesn't make what you describe very distinct."

"I promise you it would be distinct if it should dawn on you at all." I saw that the charm of our topic overflowed for my companion into an emotion as lively as my own. "At any rate," he went on, "I can speak for myself: there's an idea in my work without which I wouldn't have given a straw for the whole job. It's the finest fullest intention of the lot, and the application of it has been, I think, a triumph of patience, of ingenuity. I ought to leave that to somebody else to say; but that nobody does say it is precisely what we're talking about. It stretches, this little trick of mine, from book to book, and everything else, comparatively, plays over the surface of it. The order, the form, the texture of my books will perhaps someday constitute for the initiated a complete representation of it. So it's naturally the thing for the critic to look for. It strikes me," my visitor added, smiling, "even as the thing for the critic to find."

This seemed a responsibility indeed. "You call it a little trick?"

"That's only my little modesty. It's really an exquisite scheme."

"And you hold that you've carried the scheme out?"

"The way I've carried it out is the thing in life I think a bit well of myself for."

I had a pause. "Don't you think you ought—just a trifle —to assist the critic?"

"Assist him? What else have I done with every stroke of my pen? I've shouted my intention in his great blank face!" At this, laughing out again, Vereker laid his hand on my shoulder to show the allusion wasn't to my personal appearance.

"But you talk about the initiated. There must therefore, you see, *be* initiation."

"What else in heaven's name is criticism supposed to be?" I'm afraid I coloured at this too; but I took refuge in repeating that his account of his silver lining was poor in something or other that a plain man knows things by. "That's only because you've never had a glimpse of it," he returned. "If you had had one the element in question would soon have become practically all you'd see. To me it's exactly as palpable as the marble of this chimney. Besides, the critic just *isn't* a plain man: if he were, pray, what would he be doing in his neighbour's garden? You're anything but a plain man yourself, and the very *raison d'être* of you all is that you're little demons of subtlety. If my great affair's a secret, that's only because it's a secret in spite of itself—the amazing event has made it one. I not only never took the smallest precaution to keep it so, but never dreamed of any such accident. If I had I shouldn't in advance have had the heart to go on. As it was, I only became aware little by little, and meanwhile I had done my work."

"And now you quite like it?" I risked.

"My work?"

"Your secret. It's the same thing."

"Your guessing that," Vereker replied, "is a proof that you're as clever as I say!" I was encouraged by this to remark that he would clearly be pained to part with it, and he confessed that it was indeed with him now the great amusement of life. "I live almost to see if it will ever be detected." He looked at me for a jesting challenge; something far within his eyes seemed to peep out. "But I needn't worry—it won't!"

"You fire me as I've never been fired," I declared; "you make me determined to do or die." Then I asked: "Is it a kind of esoteric message?"

His countenance fell at this—he put out his hand as if to bid me good-night. "Ah my dear fellow, it can't be described in cheap journalese!"

I knew of course he'd be awfully fastidious, but our talk had made me feel how much his nerves were exposed. I was unsatisfied—I kept hold of his hand. "I won't make use of the expression then," I said, "in the article in which I shall eventually announce my discovery, though I dare say I shall have hard work to do without it. But meanwhile, just to hasten that difficult birth, can't you give a fellow a clue?" I felt much more at my ease.

"My whole lucid effort gives him the clue—every page and line and letter. The thing's as concrete there as a bird in a cage, a bait on a hook, a piece of cheese in a mouse-trap. It's stuck into every volume as your foot is stuck into your shoe. It governs every line, it chooses every word, it dots every i, it places every comma."

I scratched my head. "Is it something in the style or something in the thought? An element of form or an element of feeling?"

He indulgently shook my hand again, and I felt my questions to be crude and my distinctions pitiful. "Good-night, my dear boy—don't bother about it. After all, you do like a fellow."

"And a little intelligence might spoil it?" I still detained him.

He hesitated. "Well, you've got a heart in your body. Is that an element of form or an element of feeling? What I contend that nobody has ever mentioned in my work is the organ of life."

"I see—it's some idea *about* life, some sort of philosophy. Unless it be," I added with the eagerness of a thought perhaps still happier, "some kind of game you're up to with your style, something you're after in the language. Perhaps it's a preference for the letter P!" I ventured profanely to break out. "Papa, potatoes, prunes—that sort of thing?" He was suitably indulgent: he only said I hadn't got the right letter. But his amusement was over; I could see he was bored. There was nevertheless something else I had absolutely to learn. "Should you be able, pen in hand, to state it clearly yourself—to name it, phrase it, formulate it?"

"Oh," he almost passionately sighed, "if I were only, pen in hand, one of *you* chaps!"

"That would be a great chance for you of course. But

why should you despise us chaps for not doing what you
can't do yourself?"

"Can't do?" He opened his eyes. "Haven't I done it in
twenty volumes? I do it in my way," he continued. "Go *you*
and do it in yours."

"Ours is so devilish difficult," I weakly observed.

"So's mine! We each choose our own. There's no com-
pulsion. You won't come down and smoke?"

"No. I want to think this thing out."

"You'll tell me then in the morning that you've laid me
bare?"

"I'll see what I can do; I'll sleep on it. But just one word
more," I added. We had left the room—I walked again with
him a few steps along the passage. "This extraordinary 'general intention,' as you call it—for that's the most vivid description I can induce you to make of it—is then, generally,
a sort of buried treasure?"

His face lighted. "Yes, call it that, though it's perhaps
not for me to do so."

"Nonsense!" I laughed. "You know you're hugely proud
of it."

"Well, I didn't propose to tell you so; but it *is* the joy
of my soul!"

"You mean it's a beauty so rare, so great?"

He waited a little again. "The loveliest thing in the
world!" We had stopped, and on these words he left me;
but at the end of the corridor, while I looked after him
rather yearningly, he turned and caught sight of my puzzled face. It made him earnestly, indeed I thought quite
anxiously, shake his head and wave his finger. "Give it up
—give it up!"

This wasn't a challenge—it was fatherly advice. If I had
had one of his books at hand I'd have repeated my recent
act of faith—I'd have spent half the night with him. At
three o'clock in the morning, not sleeping, remembering
moreover how indispensable he was to Lady Jane, I stole
down to the library with a candle. There wasn't, so far as
I could discover, a line of his writing in the house.

IV

Returning to town I feverishly collected them all; I picked out each in its order and held it up to the light. This gave me a maddening month, in the course of which several things took place. One of these, the last, I may as well immediately mention, was that I acted on Vereker's advice: I renounced my ridiculous attempt. I could really make nothing of the business; it proved a dead loss. After all I had always, as he had himself noted, liked him; and what now occurred was simply that my new intelligence and vain preoccupation damaged my liking. I not only failed to run a general intention to earth, I found myself missing the subordinate intentions I had formerly enjoyed. His books didn't even remain the charming things they had been for me; the exasperation of my search put me out of conceit of them. Instead of being a pleasure the more they became a resource the less; for from the moment I was unable to follow up the author's hint I of course felt it a point of honour not to make use professionally of my knowledge of them. I *had* no knowledge—nobody had any. It was humiliating, but I could bear it—they only annoyed me now. At last they even bored me, and I accounted for my confusion—perversely, I allow—by the idea that Vereker had made a fool of me. The buried treasure was a bad joke, the general intention a monstrous *pose*.

The great point of it all is, however, that I told George Corvick what had befallen me and that my information had an immense effect on him. He had at last come back, but so, unfortunately, had Mrs. Erme, and there was as yet, I could see, no question of his nuptials. He was immensely stirred up by the anecdote I had brought from Bridges; it fell in so completely with the sense he had had from the first that there was more in Vereker than met the eye. When I remarked that the eye seemed what the printed page had been expressly invented to meet he immediately accused me of being spiteful because I had been foiled. Our commerce had always that pleasant latitude. The thing Vereker had mentioned to me was exactly the thing he, Corvick, had wanted me to speak of in my review. On my suggesting at last that with the assistance I had now given him he would doubtless be prepared to speak of it himself he admitted freely that before doing this there was more he must understand. What he would have said, had he reviewed the new book, was that there was evidently in the writer's inmost art something to *be* understood. I hadn't so much as hinted at that: no wonder the writer hadn't been flattered! I asked Corvick what he really considered he meant by his own supersubtlety, and, unmistakably kindled, he replied: "It isn't for the vulgar—it isn't for the vulgar!" He had hold of the tail of something: he would pull hard, pull it right out. He pumped me dry on Vereker's strange confidence and, pronouncing me the luckiest of mortals, mentioned half-a-dozen questions he wished to goodness I had had the gumption to put. Yet on the other hand he didn't want to be told too much—it would spoil the fun of seeing what would come. The failure of *my* fun was at the moment of our meeting not complete, but I saw it ahead, and Corvick saw that I saw it. I, on my side, saw likewise that one of the first things he would do would be to rush off with my story to Gwendolen.

On the very day after my talk with him I was surprised by the receipt of a note from Hugh Vereker, to whom our encounter at Bridges had been recalled, as he mentioned, by his falling, in a magazine, on some article to which my signature was attached. "I read it with great pleasure," he wrote, "and remembered under its influence our lively conversation by your bedroom fire. The consequence of this has been that I begin to measure the temerity of my having saddled you with a knowledge that you may find something of a burden. Now that the fit's over I can't imagine how I came to be moved so much beyond my wont. I had never before mentioned, no matter in what state of expansion, the fact of my little secret, and I shall never speak of that mystery again. I was accidentally so much more explicit with you than it had ever entered into my game to be, that I find this game—I mean the pleasure of playing it —suffers considerably. In short, if you can understand it, I've rather spoiled my sport. I really don't want to give anybody what I believe you clever young men call the tip.

That's of course a selfish solicitude, and I name it to you for what it may be worth to you. If you're disposed to humour me don't repeat my revelation. Think me demented —it's your right; but don't tell anybody why."

The sequel to this communication was that as early on the morrow as I dared I drove straight to Mr. Vereker's door. He occupied in those years one of the honest old houses in Kensington Square. He received me immediately, and as soon as I came in I saw I hadn't lost my power to minister to his mirth. He laughed out at sight of my face, which doubtless expressed my perturbation. I had been indiscreet—my compunction was great. "I *have* told somebody," I panted, "and I'm sure that person will by this time have told somebody else! It's a woman, into the bargain."

"The person you've told?"

"No, the other person. I'm quite sure he must have told her."

"For all the good it will do her—or do *me!* A woman will never find out."

"No, but she'll talk all over the place: she'll do just what you don't want."

Vereker thought a moment, but wasn't so disconcerted as I had feared: he felt that if the harm was done it only served him right. "It doesn't matter—don't worry."

"I'll do my best, I promise you, that your talk with me shall go no further."

"Very good; do what you can."

"In the meantime," I pursued, "George Corvick's possession of the tip may, on his part, really lead to something."

"That will be a brave day."

I told him about Corvick's cleverness, his admiration, the intensity of his interest in my anecdote; and without making too much of the divergence of our respective estimates mentioned that my friend was already of opinion that he saw much further into a certain affair than most people. He was quite as fired as I had been at Bridges. He was moreover in love with the young lady: perhaps the two together would puzzle something out.

Vereker seemed struck with this. "Do you mean they're to be married?"

"I dare say that's what it will come to."

"That may help them," he conceded, "but we must give them time!"

I spoke of my own renewed assault and confessed my difficulties; whereupon he repeated his former advice: "Give it up, give it up!" He evidently didn't think me intellectually equipped for the adventure. I stayed half an hour, and he was most good-natured, but I couldn't help pronouncing him a man of unstable moods. He had been free with me in a mood, he had repented in a mood, and now in a mood he had turned indifferent. This general levity helped me to believe that, so far as the subject of the tip went, there wasn't much in it. I contrived however to make him answer a few more questions about it, though he did so with visible impatience. For himself, beyond doubt, the thing we were all so blank about was vividly there. It was something, I guessed, in the primal plan; something like a complex figure in a Persian carpet. He highly approved of this image when I used it, and he used another himself. "It's the very string," he said, "that my pearls are strung on!" The reason of his note to me had been that he really didn't want to give us a grain of succour—our density was a thing too perfect in its way to touch. He had formed the habit of depending on it, and if the spell was to break it must break by some force of its own. He comes back to me from that last occasion—for I was never to speak to him again—as a man with some safe preserve for sport. I wondered as I walked away where he had got *his* tip.

V

When I spoke to George Corvick of the caution I had received he made me feel that any doubt of his delicacy would be almost an insult. He had instantly told Gwendolen, but Gwendolen's ardent response was in itself a pledge of discretion. The question would now absorb them and would offer them a pastime too precious to be shared with the crowd. They appeared to have caught instinctively at Vereker's high idea of enjoyment. Their intellectual pride, however, was not such as to make them indifferent to any further light I might throw on the affair they had in hand. They were indeed of the "artistic temperament," and I was freshly struck with my colleague's power to excite himself over a question of art. He'd call it letters, he'd call it life, but it was all one thing. In what he said I now seemed to understand that he spoke equally for Gwendolen, to whom, as soon as Mrs. Erme was sufficiently better to allow her a little leisure, he made a point of introducing me. I remember our going together one Sunday in August to a huddled house in Chelsea, and my renewed envy of Corvick's possession of a friend who had some light to mingle with his own. He could say things to her that I could never say to him. She had indeed no sense of humour and, with her pretty way of holding her head on one side, was one of those persons whom you want, as the phrase is, to shake, but who have learnt Hungarian by themselves. She conversed perhaps in Hungarian with Corvick; she had remarkably little English for his friend. Corvick afterwards told me that I had chilled her by my apparent indisposition to oblige them with the detail of what Vereker had said to me. I allowed that I felt I had given thought enough to that indication: hadn't I even made up my mind that it was vain and would lead nowhere? The importance they attached to it was irritating and quite envenomed my doubts.

That statement looks unamiable, and what probably happened was that I felt humiliated at seeing other persons deeply beguiled by an experiment that had brought me only chagrin. I was out in the cold while, by the evening fire, under the lamp, they followed the chase for which I myself had sounded the horn. They did as I had done, only more deliberately and sociably—they went over their author from the beginning. There was no hurry, Corvick said —the future was before them and the fascination could only grow; they would take him page by page, as they would take one of the classics, inhale him in slow draughts and let him sink all the way in. They would scarce have got

so wound up, I think, if they hadn't been in love: poor
Vereker's inner meaning gave them endless occasion to put
and to keep their young heads together. None the less it
represented the kind of problem for which Corvick had a
special aptitude, drew out the particular pointed patience
of which, had he lived, he would have given more striking
and, it is to be hoped, more fruitful examples. He at least
was, in Vereker's words, a little demon of subtlety. We had
begun by disputing, but I soon saw that without my stirring a finger his infatuation would have its bad hours. He
would bound off on false scents as I had done—he would
clap his hands over new lights and see them blown out by
the wind of the turned page. He was like nothing, I told
him, but the maniacs who embrace some bedlamitical theory of the cryptic character of Shakespeare. To this he replied that if we had had Shakespeare's own word for his
being cryptic he would at once have accepted it. The case
there was altogether different—we had nothing but the
word of Mr. Snooks. I returned that I was stupefied to see
him attach such importance even to the word of Mr.
Vereker. He wanted thereupon to know if I treated Mr.
Vereker's word as a lie. I wasn't perhaps prepared, in my
unhappy rebound, to go so far as that, but I insisted that
till the contrary was proved I should view it as too fond an
imagination. I didn't, I confess, say—I didn't at that time
quite know—all I felt. Deep down, as Miss Erme would
have said, I was uneasy, I was expectant. At the core of
my disconcerted state—for my wonted curiosity lived in its
ashes—was the sharpness of a sense that Corvick would at
last probably come out somewhere. He made, in defence of
his credulity, a great point of the fact that from of old, in
his study of this genius, he had caught whiffs and hints of
he didn't know what, faint wandering notes of a hidden
music. That was just the rarity, that was the charm: it
fitted so perfectly into what I reported.

If I returned on several occasions to the little house in
Chelsea I dare say it was as much for news of Vereker as
for news of Miss Erme's ailing parent. The hours spent there
by Corvick were present to my fancy as those of a chess-
player bent with a silent scowl, all the lamplit winter, over

his board and his moves. As my imagination filled it out the picture held me fast. On the other side of the table was a ghostlier form, the faint figure of an antagonist good-humouredly but a little wearily secure—an antagonist who leaned back in his chair with his hands in his pockets and a smile on his fine clear face. Close to Corvick, behind him, was a girl who had begun to strike me as pale and wasted and even, on more familiar view, as rather handsome, and who rested on his shoulder and hung on his moves. He would take up a chessman and hold it poised a while over one of the little squares, and then would put it back in its place with a long sigh of disappointment. The young lady, at this, would slightly but uneasily shift her position and look across, very hard, very long, very strangely, at their dim participant. I had asked them at an early stage of the business if it mightn't contribute to their success to have some closer communication with him. The special circum-stances would surely be held to have given me a right to introduce them. Corvick immediately replied that he had no wish to approach the altar before he had prepared the sacrifice. He quite agreed with our friend both as to the delight and as to the honour of the chase—he would bring down the animal with his own rifle. When I asked him if Miss Erme were as keen a shot he said after thinking: "No, I'm ashamed to say she wants to set a trap. She'd give any-thing to see him; she says she requires another tip. She's really quite morbid about it. But she must play fair—she *shan't* see him!" he emphatically added. I wondered if they hadn't even quarrelled a little on the subject—a suspicion not corrected by the way he more than once exclaimed to me: "She's quite incredibly literary, you know—quite fan-tastically!" I remember his saying of her that she felt in italics and thought in capitals. "Oh when I've run him to earth," he also said, "then, you know, I shall knock at his door. Rather—I beg you to believe. I'll have it from his own lips: 'Right you are, my boy; you've done it this time!' He shall crown me victor—with the critical laurel."

Meanwhile he really avoided the chances London life might have given him of meeting the distinguished novelist; a danger, however, that disappeared with Vereker's leaving

England for an indefinite absence, as the newspapers announced—going to the south for motives connected with the
health of his wife, which had long kept her in retirement.
A year—more than a year—had elapsed since the incident
at Bridges, but I had had no further sight of him. I think
I was at bottom rather ashamed—I hated to remind him
that, though I had irremediably missed his point, a reputation for acuteness was rapidly overtaking me. This scruple
led me a dance; kept me out of Lady Jane's house, made
me even decline, when in spite of my bad manners she was
a second time so good as to make me a sign, an invitation
to her beautiful seat. I once became aware of her under
Vereker's escort at a concert, and was sure I was seen by
them, but I slipped out without being caught. I felt, as on
that occasion I splashed along in the rain, that I couldn't
have done anything else; and yet I remember saying to myself that it was hard, was even cruel. Not only had I lost
the books, but I had lost the man himself: they and their
author had been alike spoiled for me. I knew too which was
the loss I most regretted. I had taken to the man still more
than I had ever taken to the books.

VI

Six months after our friend had left England George
Corvick, who made his living by his pen, contracted for a
piece of work which imposed on him an absence of some
length and a journey of some difficulty, and his undertak-
ing of which was much of a surprise to me. His brother-in-
law had become editor of a great provincial paper, and the
great provincial paper, in a fine flight of fancy, had conceived the idea of sending a "special commissioner" to India. Special commissioners had begun, in the "metropolitan
press," to be the fashion, and the journal in question must
have felt it had passed too long for a mere country cousin.
Corvick had no hand, I knew, for the big brush of the correspondent, but that was his brother-in-law's affair, and the
fact that a particular task was not in his line was apt to be
with himself exactly a reason for accepting it. He was prepared to out-Herod the metropolitan press; he took solemn

precautions against priggishness, he exquisitely outraged taste. Nobody ever knew it—that offended principle was all his own. In addition to his expenses he was to be conveniently paid, and I found myself able to help him, for the usual fat book, to a plausible arrangement with the usual fat publisher. I naturally inferred that his obvious desire to make a little money was not unconnected with the prospect of a union with Gwendolen Erme. I was aware that her mother's opposition was largely addressed to his want of means and of lucrative abilities, but it so happened that, on my saying the last time I saw him something that bore on the question of his separation from our young lady, he brought out with an emphasis that startled me: "Ah I'm not a bit engaged to her, you know!

"Not overtly," I answered, "because her mother doesn't like you. But I've always taken for granted a private understanding."

"Well, there *was* one. But there isn't now." That was all he said save something about Mrs. Erme's having got on her feet again in the most extraordinary way—a remark pointing, as I supposed, the moral that private understandings were of little use when the doctor didn't share them. What I took the liberty of more closely inferring was that the girl might in some way have estranged him. Well, if he had taken the turn of jealousy, for instance, it could scarcely be jealousy of me. In that case—over and above the absurdity of it—he wouldn't have gone away just to leave us together. For some time before his going we had indulged in no allusion to the buried treasure, and from his silence, which my reserve simply emulated, I had drawn a sharp conclusion. His courage had dropped, his ardour had gone the way of mine—this appearance at least he left me to scan. More than that he couldn't do; he couldn't face the triumph with which I might have greeted an explicit admission. He needn't have been afraid, poor dear, for I had by this time lost all need to triumph. In fact I considered I showed magnanimity in not reproaching him with his collapse, for the sense of his having thrown up the game made me feel more than ever how much I at last depended on him. If Corvick had broken down I should never know; no

one would be of any use if *he* wasn't. It wasn't a bit true
I had ceased to care for knowledge; little by little my curiosity not only had begun to ache again, but had become
the familiar torment of my days and my nights. There are
doubtless people to whom torments of such an order appear hardly more natural than the contortions of disease;
but I don't after all know why I should in this connexion
so much as mention them. For the few persons, at any rate,
abnormal or not, with whom my anecdote is concerned,
literature was a game of skill, and skill meant courage, and
courage meant honour, and honour meant passion, meant
life. The stake on the table was a special substance and
our roulette the revolving mind, but we sat round the green
board as intently as the grim gamblers at Monte Carlo.
Gwendolen Erme, for that matter, with her white face and
her fixed eyes, was of the very type of the lean ladies one
had met in the temples of chance. I recognised in Corvick's
absence that she made this analogy vivid. It was extravagant, I admit, the way she lived for the art of the pen. Her
passion visibly preyed on her, and in her presence I felt
almost tepid. I got hold of "Deep Down" again: it was a
desert in which she had lost herself, but in which too she
had dug a wonderful hole in the sand—a cavity out of which
Corvick had still more remarkably pulled her.

Early in March I had a telegram from her, in consequence of which I repaired immediately to Chelsea, where
the first thing she said to me was: "He has got it, he has
got it!"

She was moved, as I could see, to such depths that she
must mean the great thing. "Vereker's idea?"

"His general intention. George has cabled from Bombay."

She had the missive open there; it was emphatic though
concise. "Eureka. Immense." That was all—he had saved
the cost of the signature. I shared her emotion, but I was
disappointed. "He doesn't say what it is."

"How could he—in a telegram? He'll write it."

"But how does he know?"

"Know it's the real thing? Oh I'm sure that when you see
it you do know. *Vera incessu patuit dea!*"

"It's you, Miss Erme, who are a 'dear' for bringing me such news!"—I went all lengths in my high spirits. "But fancy finding our goddess in the temple of Vishnu! How strange of George to have been able to go into the thing again in the midst of such different and such powerful solicitations!"

"He hasn't gone into it, I know; it's the thing itself, let severely alone for six months, that has simply sprung out at him like a tigress out of the jungle. He didn't take a book with him—on purpose; indeed he wouldn't have needed to —he knows every page, as I do, by heart. They all worked in him together, and some day somewhere, when he wasn't thinking, they fell, in all their superb intricacy, into the one right combination. The figure in the carpet came out. That's the way he knew it would come and the real reason —you didn't in the least understand, but I suppose I may tell you now—why he went and why I consented to his going. We knew the change would do it—that the difference of thought, of scene, would give the needed touch, the magic shake. We had perfectly, we had admirably calculated. The elements were all in his mind, and in the *secousse* of a new and intense experience they just struck light." She positively struck light herself—she was literally, facially luminous. I stammered something about unconscious cerebration, and she continued: "He'll come right home—this will bring him."

"To see Vereker, you mean?"

"To see Vereker—and to see *me*. Think what he'll have to tell me!"

I hesitated. "About India?"

"About fiddlesticks! About Vereker—about the figure in the carpet."

"But, as you say, we shall surely have that in a letter."

She thought like one inspired, and I remembered how Corvick had told me long before that her face was interesting. "Perhaps it can't be got into a letter if it's 'immense.'"

"Perhaps not if it's immense bosh. If he has hold of something that can't be got into a letter he hasn't hold of *the* thing. Vereker's own statement to me was exactly that the 'figure' *would* fit into a letter."

"Well, I cabled to George an hour ago—two words," said Gwendolen.

"Is it indiscreet of me to ask what they were?"

She hung fire, but at last brought them out. "'Angel, write.'"

"Good!" I cried. "I'll make it sure—I'll send him the same."

VII

My words however were not absolutely the same—I put something instead of "angel"; and in the sequel my epithet seemed the more apt, for when eventually we heard from our traveller it was merely, it was thoroughly to be tantalised. He was magnificent in his triumph, he described his discovery as stupendous; but his ecstasy only obscured it—there were to be no particulars till he should have submitted his conception to the supreme authority. He had thrown up his commission, he had thrown up his book, he had thrown up everything but the instant need to hurry to Rapallo, on the Genoese shore, where Vereker was making a stay. I wrote him a letter which was to await him at Aden—I besought him to relieve my suspense. That he had found my letter was indicated by a telegram which, reaching me after weary days and in the absence of any answer to my laconic dispatch to him at Bombay, was evidently intended as a reply to both communications. Those few words were in familiar French, the French of the day, which Corvick often made use of to show he wasn't a prig. It had for some persons the opposite effect, but his message may fairly be paraphrased. "Have patience; I want to see, as it breaks on you, the face you'll make!" "Tellement envie de voir ta tête!"—that was what I had to sit down with. I can certainly not be said to have sat down, for I seem to remember myself at this time as rattling constantly between the little house in Chelsea and my own. Our impatience, Gwendolen's and mine, was equal, but I kept hoping her light would be greater. We all spent during this episode, for people of our means, a great deal of money in telegrams and cabs, and I counted on the receipt of news from Rapallo immediately after the junction of the discoverer with the discovered. The interval seemed an age, but late one day I heard a hansom precipitated to my door with the crash engendered by a hint of liberality. I lived with my heart in my mouth and accordingly bounded to the window—a movement which gave me a view of a young lady erect on the footboard of the vehicle and eagerly looking up at my house. At sight of me she flourished a paper with a movement that brought me straight down, the movement with which, in melodramas, handkerchiefs and reprieves are flourished at the foot of the scaffold.

"Just seen Vereker—not a note wrong. Pressed me to bosom—keeps me a month." So much I read on her paper while the cabby dropped a grin from his perch. In my excitement I paid him profusely and in hers she suffered it; then as he drove away we started to walk about and talk. We had talked, heaven knows, enough before, but this was a wondrous lift. We pictured the whole scene at Rapallo, where he would have written, mentioning my name, for permission to call; that is *I* pictured it, having more material than my companion, whom I felt hang on my lips as we stopped on purpose before shop-windows we didn't look into. About one thing we were clear: if he was staying on for fuller communication we should at least have a letter from him that would help us through the dregs of delay. We understood his staying on, and yet each of us saw, I think, that the other hated it. The letter we were clear about arrived; it was for Gwendolen, and I called on her in time to save her the trouble of bringing it to me. She didn't read it out, as was natural enough; but she repeated to me what it chiefly embodied. This consisted of the remarkable statement that he'd tell her after they were married exactly what she wanted to know.

"Only *then*, when I'm his wife—not before," she explained. "It's tantamount to saying—isn't it?—that I must marry him straight off!" She smiled at me while I flushed with disappointment, a vision of fresh delay that made me at first unconscious of my surprise. It seemed more than a hint that on me as well he would impose some tiresome condition. Suddenly, while she reported several more things from his letter, I remembered what he had told me before going away. He had found Mr. Vereker deliriously interesting and his own possession of the secret a real intoxication. The buried treasure was all gold and gems. Now that it was there it seemed to grow and grow before him; it would have been, through all time and taking all tongues, one of the most wonderful flowers of literary art. Nothing, in especial, once you were face to face with it, could show for more consummately *done*. When once it came out it came out, was there with a splendour that made you ashamed; and there hadn't been, save in the bottomless vulgarity of the age, with every one tasteless and tainted, every sense stopped, the smallest reason why it should have been overlooked. It was great, yet so simple, was simple, yet so great, and the final knowledge of it was an experience quite apart. He intimated that the charm of such an experience, the desire to drain it, in its freshness, to the last drop, was what kept him there close to the source. Gwendolen, frankly radiant as she tossed me these fragments, showed the elation of a prospect more assured than my own. That brought me back to the question of her marriage, prompted me to ask if what she meant by what she had just surprised me with was that she was under an engagement.

"Of course I am!" she answered. "Didn't you know it?" She seemed astonished, but I was still more so, for Corvick had told me the exact contrary. I didn't mention this, however; I only reminded her how little I had been on that score in her confidence, or even in Corvick's, and that moreover I wasn't in ignorance of her mother's interdict. At bottom I was troubled by the disparity of the two accounts; but after a little I felt Corvick's to be the one I least doubted. This simply reduced me to asking myself if the girl had on the spot improvised an engagement—vamped up an old one or dashed off a new—in order to arrive at the satisfaction she desired. She must have had resources of which I was destitute, but she made her case slightly more intelligible by returning presently: "What the state of things has been is that we felt of course bound to do nothing in mamma's lifetime."

"But now you think you'll just dispense with mamma's consent?"

"Ah it mayn't come to that!" I wondered what it might come to, and she went on: "Poor dear, she may swallow the dose. In fact, you know," she added with a laugh, "she really *must!*"—a proposition of which, on behalf of every one concerned, I fully acknowledged the force.

VIII

Nothing more vexatious had ever happened to me than to become aware before Corvick's arrival in England that I shouldn't be there to put him through. I found myself abruptly called to Germany by the alarming illness of my younger brother, who, against my advice, had gone to Munich to study, at the feet indeed of a great master, the art of portraiture in oils. The near relative who made him an allowance had threatened to withdraw it if he should, under specious pretexts, turn for superior truth to Paris— Paris being somehow, for a Cheltenham aunt, the school of evil, the abyss. I deplored this prejudice at the time, and the deep injury of it was now visible—first in the fact that it hadn't saved the poor boy, who was clever frail and foolish, from congestion of the lungs, and second in the greater break with London to which the event condemned me. I'm afraid that what was uppermost in my mind during several anxious weeks was the sense that if we had only been in Paris I might have run over to see Corvick. This was actually out of the question from every point of view: my brother, whose recovery gave us both plenty to do, was ill for three months, during which I never left him and at the end of which we had to face the absolute prohibition of a return to England. The consideration of climate imposed itself, and he was in no state to meet it alone. I took him to Meran and there spent the summer with him, trying to show him by example how to get back to work and nursing a rage of another sort that I tried *not* to show him.

The whole business proved the first of a series of phenomena so strangely interlaced that, taken all together— which was how I had to take them—they form as good an illustration as I can recall of the manner in which, for the good of his soul doubtless, fate sometimes deals with a man's avidity. These incidents certainly had larger bearings than the comparatively meagre consequence we are here concerned with—though I feel that consequence also a thing to speak of with some respect. It's mainly in such a light, I confess, at any rate, that the ugly fruit of my exile is at this hour present to me. Even at first indeed the spirit in which my avidity, as I have called it, made me regard that term owed no element of ease to the fact that before coming back from Rapallo George Corvick addressed me in a way I objected to. His letter had none of the sedative action I must to-day profess myself sure he had wished to give it, and the march of occurrences was not so ordered as to make up for what it lacked. He had begun on the spot, for one of the quarterlies, a great last word on Vereker's writings, and this exhaustive study, the only one that would have counted, have existed, was to turn on the new light, to utter—oh so quietly!—the unimagined truth. It was in other words to trace the figure in the carpet through every convolution, to reproduce it in every tint. The result, according to my friend, would be the greatest literary portrait ever painted, and what he asked of me was just to be so good as not to trouble him with questions till he should hang up his masterpiece before me. He did me the honour to declare that, putting aside the great sitter himself, all aloft in his indifference, I was individually the connoisseur he was most working for. I was therefore to be a good boy and not try to peep under the curtain before the show was ready: I should enjoy it all the more if I sat very still.

I did my best to sit very still, but I couldn't help giving a jump on seeing in *The Times,* after I had been a week or two in Munich and before, as I knew, Corvick had reached London, the announcement of the sudden death of poor Mrs. Erme. I instantly, by letter, appealed to Gwendolen for particulars, and she wrote me that her mother had yielded to long-threatened failure of the heart. She didn't say, but I took the liberty of reading into her words, that from the point of view of her marriage and also of her eagerness, which was quite a match for mine, this was a solution more prompt than could have been expected and more radical than waiting for the old lady to swallow the dose. I candidly admit indeed that at the time—for I heard from her repeatedly—I read some singular things into Gwendolen's words and some still more extraordinary ones into her silences. Pen in hand, this way, I live the time over, and it brings back the oddest sense of my having been, both for months and in spite of myself a kind of coerced spectator. All my life had taken refuge in my eyes, which the procession of events appeared to have committed itself to keep astare. There were days when I thought of writing to Hugh Vereker and simply throwing myself on his charity. But I felt more deeply that I hadn't fallen quite so low—besides which, quite properly, he would send me about my business. Mrs. Erme's death brought Corvick straight home, and within the month he was united "very quietly"—as quietly, I seemed to make out, as he meant in his article to bring out his *trouvaille*—to the young lady he had loved and quitted. I use this last term, I may parenthetically say, because I subsequently grew sure that at the time he went to India, at the time of his great news from Bombay, there had been no positive pledge between them whatever. There had been none at the moment she was affirming to me the very opposite. On the other hand he had certainly become engaged the day he returned. The happy pair went down to Torquay for their honeymoon, and there, in a reckless hour, it occurred to poor Corvick to take his young bride a drive. He had no command of that business: this had been brought home to me of old in a little tour we had once made together in a dogcart. In a dogcart he perched his companion for a rattle over Devonshire hills, on one of the likeliest of which he brought his horse, who, it was true, had bolted, down with such violence that the occupants of the cart were hurled forward and that he fell horribly on his head. He was killed on the spot; Gwendolen escaped unhurt.

I pass rapidly over the question of this unmitigated tragedy, of what the loss of my best friend meant for me, and I complete my little history of my patience and my pain by the frank statement of my having, in a postscript to my very first letter to her after the receipt of the hideous news, asked Mrs. Corvick whether her husband mightn't at least have finished the great article on Vereker. Her answer was as prompt as my question: the article, which had been barely begun, was a mere heartbreaking scrap. She explained that our friend, abroad, had just settled down to it when interrupted by her mother's death, and that then, on his return, he had been kept from work by the engrossments into which that calamity was to plunge them. The opening pages were all that existed; they were striking, they were promising, but they didn't unveil the idol. That great intellectual feat was obviously to have formed his climax. She said nothing more, nothing to enlighten me as to the state of her own knowledge—the knowledge for the acquisition of which I had fancied her prodigiously acting. This was above all what I wanted to know: had *she* seen the idol unveiled? Had there been a private ceremony for a palpitating audience of one? For what else but that ceremony had the nuptials taken place? I didn't like as yet to press her, though when I thought of what had passed between us on the subject in Corvick's absence her reticence surprised me. It was therefore not till much later, from Meran, that I risked another appeal, risked it in some trepidation, for she continued to tell me nothing. "Did you hear in those few days of your blighted bliss," I wrote, "what we desired so to hear?" I said "we" as a little hint; and she showed me she could take a little hint. "I heard everything," she replied, "and I mean to keep it to myself!"

IX

It was impossible not to be moved with the strongest sympathy for her, and on my return to England I showed her every kindness in my power. Her mother's death had made her means sufficient, and she had gone to live in a more convenient quarter. But her loss had been great and her visitation cruel; it never would have occurred to me, moreover, to suppose she could come to feel the possession of a technical tip, of a piece of literary experience, a counterpoise to her grief. Strange to say, none the less, I couldn't help believing after I had seen her a few times that I caught a glimpse of some such oddity. I hasten to add that there had been other things I couldn't help believing, or at least imagining; and as I never felt I was really clear about these, so, as to the point I here touch on, I give her memory the benefit of the doubt. Stricken and solitary, highly accomplished and now, in her deep mourning, her maturer grace and her uncomplaining sorrow, incontestably handsome, she presented herself as leading a life of singular dignity and beauty. I had at first found a way to persuade myself that I should soon get the better of the reserve formulated, the week after the catastrophe, in her reply to an appeal as to which I was not unconscious that it might strike her as mistimed. Certainly that reserve was something of a shock to me—certainly it puzzled me the more I thought of it and even though I tried to explain it (with moments of success) by an imputation of exalted sentiments, of superstitious scruples, of a refinement of loyalty. Certainly it added at the same time hugely to the price of Vereker's secret, precious as this mystery already appeared. I may as well confess abjectly that Mrs. Corvick's unexpected attitude was the final tap on the nail that was to fix fast my luckless idea, convert it into the obsession of which I'm for ever conscious.

But this only helped me the more to be artful, to be adroit, to allow time to elapse before renewing my suit. There were plenty of speculations for the interval, and one of them was deeply absorbing. Corvick had kept his information from his young friend till after the removal of the last barrier to their intimacy—then only had he let the cat out of the bag. Was it Gwendolen's idea, taking a hint from him, to liberate this animal only on the basis of the renewal of such a relation? Was the figure in the carpet traceable or describable only for husbands and wives—for lovers supremely united? It came back to me in a mystifying manner that in Kensington Square, when I mentioned that Corvick would have told the girl he loved, some word had dropped from Vereker that gave colour to this possibility. There might be little in it, but there was enough to make me wonder if I should have to marry Mrs. Corvick to get

what I wanted. Was I prepared to offer her this price for
the blessing of her knowledge? Ah that way madness lay!
—so I at least said to myself in bewildered hours. I could
see meanwhile the torch she refused to pass on flame away
in her chamber of memory—pour through her eyes a light
that shone in her lonely house. At the end of six months
I was fully sure of what this warm presence made up to
her for. We had talked again and again of the man who
had brought us together—of his talent, his character, his
personal charm, his certain career, his dreadful doom, and
even of his clear purpose in that great study which was
to have been a supreme literary portrait, a kind of critical
Vandyke or Velasquez. She had conveyed to me in abundance that she was tongue-tied by her perversity, by her
piety, that she would never break the silence it had not
been given to the "right person," as she said, to break. The
hour, however, finally arrived. One evening when I had
been sitting with her longer than usual I laid my hand
firmly on her arm. "Now at last what *is* it?"

She had been expecting me and was ready. She gave a
long slow soundless headshake, merciful only in being inarticulate. This mercy didn't prevent its hurling at me the
largest finest coldest "Never!" I had yet, in the course of
a life that had known denials, had to take full in the face.
I took it and was aware that with the hard blow the tears
had come into my eyes. So for a while we sat and looked
at each other; after which I slowly rose. I was wondering
if some day she would accept me; but this was not what
I brought out. I said as I smoothed down my hat: "I know
what to think then. It's nothing!"

A remote disdainful pity for me gathered in her dim
smile; then she spoke in a voice that I hear at this hour.
"It's my *life!*" As I stood at the door she added: "You've
insulted him!"

"Do you mean Vereker?"

"I mean the Dead!"

I recognised when I reached the street the justice of her
charge. Yes, it was her life—I recognised that too; but her
life none the less made room with the lapse of time for another interest. A year and a half after Corvick's death she

published in a single volume her second novel, "Overmastered," which I pounced on in the hope of finding in it some tell-tale echo or some peeping face. All I found was a much better book than her younger performance, showing I thought the better company she had kept. As a tissue tolerably intricate it was a carpet with a figure of its own; but the figure was not the figure I was looking for. On sending a review of it to *The Middle* I was surprised to learn from the office that a notice was already in type. When the paper came out I had no hesitation in attributing this article, which I thought rather vulgarly overdone, to Drayton Deane, who in the old days had been something of a friend of Corvick's, yet had only within a few weeks made the acquaintance of his widow. I had had an early copy of the book, but Deane had evidently had an earlier. He lacked all the same the light hand with which Corvick had gilded the gingerbread—he laid on the tinsel in splotches.

X

Six months later appeared "The Right of Way," the last chance, though we didn't know it, that we were to have to redeem ourselves. Written wholly during Vereker's sojourn abroad, the book had been heralded, in a hundred paragraphs, by the usual ineptitudes. I carried it, as early a copy as any, I this time flattered myself, straightway to Mrs. Corvick. This was the only use I had for it; I left the inevitable tribute of *The Middle* to some more ingenious mind and some less irritated temper. "But I already have it," Gwendolen said. "Drayton Deane was so good as to bring it to me yesterday, and I've just finished it."

"Yesterday? How did he get it so soon?"

"He gets everything so soon! He's to review it in *The Middle*."

"He—Drayton Deane—review Vereker?" I couldn't believe my ears.

"Why not? One fine ignorance is as good as another."

I winced but I presently said: "You ought to review him yourself!"

"I don't 'review,' " she laughed. "I'm reviewed!"

Just then the door was thrown open. "Ah yes, here's your reviewer!" Drayton Deane was there with his long legs and his tall forehead: he had come to see what she thought of "The Right of Way," and to bring news that was singularly relevant. The evening papers were just out with a telegram on the author of that work, who, in Rome, had been ill for some days with an attack of malarial fever. It had at first not been thought grave, but had taken, in consequence of complications, a turn that might give rise to anxiety. Anxiety had indeed at the latest hour begun to be felt.

I was struck in the presence of these tidings with the fundamental detachment that Mrs. Corvick's overt concern quite failed to hide: it gave me the measure of her consummate independence. That independence rested on her knowledge, the knowledge which nothing now could destroy and which nothing could make different. The figure in the carpet might take on another twist or two, but the sentence had virtually been written. The writer might go down to his grave: she was the person in the world to whom —as if she had been his favoured heir—his continued existence was least of a need. This reminded me how I had observed at a particular moment—after Corvick's death—the drop of her desire to see him face to face. She had got what she wanted without that. I had been sure that if she hadn't got it she wouldn't have been restrained from the endeavour to sound him personally by those superior reflexions, more conceivable on a man's part than on a woman's, which in my case had served as a deterrent. It wasn't however, I hasten to add, that my case, in spite of this invidious comparison, wasn't ambiguous enough. At the thought that Vereker was perhaps at that moment dying there rolled over me a wave of anguish—a poignant sense of how inconsistently I still depended on him. A delicacy that it was my one compensation to suffer to rule me had left the Alps and the Apennines between us, but the sense of the waning occasion suggested that I might in my despair at last have gone to him. Of course I should really have done nothing of the sort. I remained five minutes, while my companions talked of the new book, and when Drayton Deane appealed to me for my opinion of it I made answer, getting up, that I detested Hugh Vereker and simply couldn't read him. I departed with the moral certainty that as the door closed behind me Deane would brand me for awfully superficial. His hostess wouldn't contradict *that* at least.

I continue to trace with a briefer touch our intensely odd successions. Three weeks after this came Vereker's death, and before the year was out the death of his wife. That poor lady I had never seen, but I had had a futile theory that, should she survive him long enough to be decorously accessible, I might approach her with the feeble flicker of my plea. Did she know and if she knew would she speak? It was much to be presumed that for more reasons than one she would have nothing to say; but when she passed out of all reach I felt renouncement indeed my appointed lot. I was shut up in my obsession for ever—my gaolers had gone off with the key. I find myself quite as vague as a captive in a dungeon about the time that further elapsed before Mrs. Corvick became the wife of Drayton Deane. I had foreseen, through my bars, this end of the business, though there was no indecent haste and our friendship had rather fallen off. They were both so "awfully intellectual" that it struck people as a suitable match, but I had measured better than any one the wealth of understanding the bride would contribute to the union. Never, for a marriage in literary circles—so the newspapers described the alliance —had a lady been so bravely dowered. I began with due promptness to look for the fruit of the affair—that fruit, I mean, of which the premonitory symptoms would be peculiarly visible in the husband. Taking for granted the splendour of the other party's nuptial gift, I expected to see him make a show commensurate with his increase of means. I knew what his means had been—his article on "The Right of Way" had distinctly given one the figure. As he was now exactly in the position in which still more exactly I was not I watched from month to month, in the likely periodicals, for the heavy message poor Corvick had been unable to deliver and the responsibility of which would have fallen on his successor. The widow and wife would have broken by the rekindled hearth the silence that only a widow and wife might break, and Deane would be as aflame with the knowledge as Corvick in his own hour, as Gwendolen in hers, had been. Well, he was aflame doubtless, but the fire was apparently not to become a public blaze. I scanned the periodicals in vain: Drayton Deane filled them with exuberant pages, but he withheld the page I most feverishly sought. He wrote on a thousand subjects, but never on the subject of Vereker. His special line was to tell truths that other people either "funked," as he said, or overlooked, but he never told the only truth that seemed to me in these days to signify. I met the couple in those literary circles referred to in the papers: I have sufficiently intimated that it was only in such circles we were all constructed to revolve. Gwendolen was more than ever committed to them by the publication of her third novel, and I myself definitely classed by holding the opinion that this work was inferior to its immediate predecessor. Was it worse because she had been keeping worse company? If her secret was, as she had told me, her life—a fact discernible in her increasing bloom, an air of conscious privilege that, cleverly corrected by pretty charities, gave distinction to her appearance—it had yet not a direct influence on her work. That only made one—everything only made one—yearn the more for it; only rounded it off with a mystery finer and subtler.

XI

It was therefore from her husband I could never remove my eyes: I beset him in a manner that might have made him uneasy. I went even so far as to engage him in conversation. *Didn't* he know, hadn't he come into it as a matter of course?—that question hummed in my brain. Of course he knew; otherwise he wouldn't return my stare so queerly. His wife had told him what I wanted and he was amiably amused at my impotence. He didn't laugh—he wasn't a laugher: his system was to present to my irritation, so that I should crudely expose myself, a conversational blank as vast as his big bare brow. It always happened that I turned away with a settled conviction from these unpeopled expanses, which seemed to complete each other geographically and to symbolise together Drayton Deane's want of voice, want of form. He simply hadn't the art to use what he knew; he literally was incompetent to take up the duty where Corvick had left it. I went still further—it was the only glimpse of happiness I had. I made up my mind that the duty didn't appeal to him. He wasn't interested, he didn't care. Yes, it quite comforted me to believe him too stupid to have joy of the thing I lacked. He was as stupid after as he had been before, and that deepened for me the golden glory in which the mystery was wrapped. I had of course none the less to recollect that his wife might have imposed her conditions and exactions. I had above all to remind myself that with Vereker's death the major incentive dropped. He was still there to be honoured by what might be done—he was no longer there to give it his sanction. Who alas but he had the authority?

Two children were born to the pair, but the second cost the mother her life. After this stroke I seemed to see another ghost of a chance. I jumped at it in thought, but I waited a certain time for manners, and at last my opportunity arrived in a remunerative way. His wife had been dead a year when I met Drayton Deane in the smoking-room of a small club of which we both were members, but where for months—perhaps because I rarely entered it—I hadn't seen him. The room was empty and the occasion propitious. I deliberately offered him, to have done with the matter for ever, that advantage for which I felt he had long been looking.

"As an older acquaintance of your late wife's than even you were," I began, "you must let me say to you something I have on my mind. I shall be glad to make any terms with you that you see fit to name for the information she must have had from George Corvick—the information, you know, that had come to *him*, poor chap, in one of the happiest hours of his life, straight from Hugh Vereker."

He looked at me like a dim phrenological bust. "The information—?"

"Vereker's secret, my dear man—the general intention of

his books: the string the pearls were strung on, the buried treasure, the figure in the carpet."

He began to flush—the numbers on his bumps to come out. "Vereker's books had a general intention?"

I stared in my turn. "You don't mean to say you don't know it?" I thought for a moment he was playing with me. "Mrs. Deane knew it; she had it, as I say, straight from Corvick, who had, after infinite search and to Vereker's own delight, found the very mouth of the cave. Where *is* the mouth? He told after their marriage—and told alone—the person who, when the circumstances were reproduced, must have told *you*. Have I been wrong in taking for granted that she admitted you, as one of the highest privileges of the relation in which you stood to her, to the knowledge of which she was after Corvick's death the sole depository? All *I* know is that that knowledge is infinitely precious, and what I want you to understand is that if you'll in your turn admit me to it you'll do me a kindness for which I shall be lastingly grateful."

He had turned at last very red; I dare say he had begun by thinking I had lost my wits. Little by little he followed me; on my own side I stared with a livelier surprise. Then he spoke. "I don't know what you're talking about."

He wasn't acting—it was the absurd truth. "She *didn't* tell you—?"

"Nothing about Hugh Vereker."

I was stupefied; the room went round. It had been too good even for that! "Upon your honour?"

"Upon my honour. What the devil's the matter with you?" he growled.

"I'm astounded—I'm disappointed. I wanted to get it out of you."

"It isn't *in* me!" he awkwardly laughed. "And even if it were—"

"If it were you'd let me have it—oh yes, in common humanity. But I believe you. I see—I see!" I went on, conscious, with the full turn of the wheel, of my great delusion, my false view of the poor man's attitude. What I saw, though I couldn't say it, was that his wife hadn't thought him worth enlightening. This struck me as strange for a woman who had thought him worth marrying. At last I explained it by the reflexion that she couldn't possibly have married him for his understanding. She had married him for something else.

He was to some extent enlightened now, but he was even more astonished, more disconcerted: he took a moment to compare my story with his quickened memories. The result of his meditation was his presently saying with a good deal of rather feeble form: "This is the first I hear of what you allude to. I think you must be mistaken as to Mrs. Drayton Deane's having had any unmentioned, and still less any unmentionable, knowledge of Hugh Vereker. She'd certainly have wished it—should it have borne on his literary character—to be used."

"It *was* used. She used it herself. She told me with her own lips that she 'lived' on it."

I had no sooner spoken than I repented of my words; he grew so pale that I felt as if I had struck him. "Ah 'lived'—!" he murmured, turning short away from me.

My compunction was real; I laid my hand on his shoulder. "I beg you to forgive me—I've made a mistake. You *don't* know what I thought you knew. You could, if I had been right, have rendered me a service; and I had my reasons for assuming that you'd be in a position to meet me."

"Your reasons?" he echoed. "What were your reasons?"

I looked at him well; I hesitated; I considered. "Come and sit down with me here and I'll tell you." I drew him to a sofa, I lighted another cigar and, beginning with the anecdote of Vereker's one descent from the clouds, I recited to him the extraordinary chain of accidents that had, in spite of the original gleam, kept me till that hour in the dark. I told him in a word just what I've written out here. He listened with deepening attention, and I became aware, to my surprise, by his ejaculations, by his questions, that he would have been after all not unworthy to be trusted by his wife. So abrupt an experience of her want of trust had now a disturbing effect on him; but I saw the immediate shock throb away little by little and then gather again into waves

of wonder and curiosity—waves that promised, I could perfectly judge, to break in the end with the fury of my own
highest tides. I may say that to-day as victims of unap-
peased desire there isn't a pin to choose between us. The
poor man's state is almost my consolation; there are really
moments when I feel it to be quite my revenge.

[1896]

IN THE CAGE

I

It had occurred to her early that in her position—that of a young person spending, in framed and wired confinement, the life of a guinea-pig or a magpie—she should know a great many persons without their recognising the acquaintance. That made it an emotion the more lively—though singularly rare and always, even then, with opportunity still very much smothered—to see any one come in whom she knew outside, as she called it, any one who could add anything to the meanness of her function. Her function was to sit there with two young men—the other telegraphist and the counter-clerk; to mind the "sounder," which was always going, to dole out stamps and postal-orders, weigh letters, answer stupid questions, give difficult change and, more than anything else, count words as numberless as the sands of the sea, the words of the telegrams thrust, from morning to night, through the gap left in the high lattice, across the encumbered shelf that her forearm ached with rubbing. This transparent screen fenced out or fenced in, according to the side of the narrow counter on which the human lot was cast, the duskiest corner of a shop pervaded not a little, in winter, by the poison of perpetual gas, and at all times by the presence of hams, cheese, dried fish, soap, varnish, paraffin and other solids and fluids that she came to know perfectly by their smells without consenting to know them by their names.

The barrier that divided the little post-and-telegraph-office from the grocery was a frail structure of wood and wire; but the social, the professional separation was a gulf that fortune, by a stroke quite remarkable, had spared her the necessity of contributing at all publicly to bridge. When Mr. Cocker's young men stepped over from behind the other counter to change a five-pound note—and Mr. Cocker's situation, with the cream of the "Court Guide" and the dearest furnished apartments, Simpkin's, Ladle's, Thrupp's, just round the corner, was so select that his place was quite pervaded by the crisp rustle of these emblems— she pushed out the sovereigns as if the applicant were no more to her than one of the momentary, the practically featureless, appearances in the great procession; and this perhaps all the more from the very fact of the connexion (only recognised outside indeed) to which she had lent herself with ridiculous inconsequence. She recognised the others the less because she had at last so unreservedly, so irredeemably, recognised Mr. Mudge. However that might be, she was a little ashamed of having to admit to herself that Mr. Mudge's removal to a higher sphere—to a more commanding position, that is, though to a much lower neighbourhood—would have been described still better as a luxury than as the mere simplification, the corrected awkwardness, that she contented herself with calling it. He had at any rate ceased to be all day long in her eyes, and this left something a little fresh for them to rest on of a Sunday. During the three months of his happy survival at Cocker's after her consent to their engagement she had often asked herself what it was marriage would be able to add to a familiarity that seemed already to have scraped the platter so clean. Opposite there, behind the counter of which his superior stature, his whiter apron, his more clustering curls and more present, too present, *h*'s had been for a couple of years the principal ornament, he had moved to and fro before her as on the small sanded floor of their contracted future. She was conscious now of the improvement of not having to take her present and her future at once. They were about as much as she could manage when taken separate.

She had, none the less, to give her mind steadily to what Mr. Mudge had again written her about, the idea of her applying for a transfer to an office quite similar—she couldn't yet hope for a place in a bigger—under the very roof where he was foreman, so that, dangled before her every minute of the day, he should see her, as he called it, "hourly," and in a part, the far N.W. district, where, with her mother, she would save on their two rooms alone nearly three shillings. It would be far from dazzling to exchange Mayfair for Chalk Farm, and it wore upon her much that he could never drop a subject; still, it didn't wear as things *had* worn, the worries of the early times of their great misery, her own, her mother's and her elder sister's—the last of whom had succumbed to all but absolute want when, as conscious and incredulous ladies, suddenly bereft, betrayed, overwhelmed, they had slipped faster and faster down the steep slope at the bottom of which she alone had rebounded. Her mother had never rebounded any more at the bottom than on the way; had only rumbled and grumbled down and down, making, in respect of caps, topics and "habits," no effort whatever—which simply meant smelling much of the time of whiskey.

II

It was always rather quiet at Cocker's while the contingent from Ladle's and Thrupp's and all the other great places were at luncheon, or, as the young men used vulgarly to say, while the animals were feeding. She had forty minutes in advance of this to go home for her own dinner; and when she came back and one of the young men took his turn there was often half an hour during which she could pull out a bit of work or a book—a book from the place where she borrowed novels, very greasy, in fine print and all about fine folks, at a ha'penny a day. This sacred pause was one of the numerous ways in which the establishment kept its finger on the pulse of fashion and fell into the rhythm of the larger life. It had something to do, one day,

with the particular flare of importance of an arriving customer, a lady whose meals were apparently irregular, yet
whom she was destined, she afterwards found, not to forget. The girl was *blasée;* nothing could belong more, as she
perfectly knew, to the intense publicity of her profession;
but she had a whimsical mind and wonderful nerves; she
was subject, in short, to sudden flickers of antipathy and
sympathy, red gleams in the grey, fitful needs to notice and
to "care," odd caprices of curiosity. She had a friend who
had invented a new career for women—that of being in and
out of people's houses to look after the flowers. Mrs. Jordan
had a manner of her own of sounding this allusion; "the
flowers," on her lips, were, in fantastic places, in happy
homes, as usual as the coals or the daily papers. She took
charge of them, at any rate, in all the rooms, at so much
a month, and people were quickly finding out what it was
to make over this strange burden of the pampered to the
widow of a clergyman. The widow, on her side, dilating
on the initiations thus opened up to her, had been splendid
to her young friend over the way she was made free of
the greatest houses—the way, especially when she did the
dinner-tables, set out so often for twenty, she felt that a
single step more would transform her whole social position.
On its being asked of her then if she circulated only in a
sort of tropical solitude, with the upper servants for picturesque natives, and on her having to assent to this glance
at her limitations, she had found a reply to the girl's invidious question. "You've no imagination, my dear!"—that was
because a door more than half open to the higher life
couldn't be called anything but a thin partition. Mrs. Jordan's imagination quite did away with the thickness.

Our young lady had not taken up the charge, had dealt
with it good-humouredly, just because she knew so well
what to think of it. It was at once one of her most cherished complaints and most secret supports that people
didn't understand her, and it was accordingly a matter of
indifference to her that Mrs. Jordan shouldn't; even though
Mrs. Jordan, handed down from their early twilight of gentility and also the victim of reverses, was the only member
of her circle in whom she recognised an equal. She was

perfectly aware that her imaginative life was the life in which she spent most of her time; and she would have been ready, had it been at all worth while, to contend that, since her outward occupation didn't kill it, it must be strong indeed. Combinations of flowers and greenstuff forsooth! What *she* could handle freely, she said to herself, was combinations of men and women. The only weakness in her faculty came from the positive abundance of her contact with the human herd; this was so constant, it had so the effect of cheapening her privilege, that there were long stretches in which inspiration, divination and interest quite dropped. The great thing was the flashes, the quick revivals, absolute accidents all, and neither to be counted on nor to be resisted. Some one had only sometimes to put in a penny for a stamp and the whole thing was upon her. She was so absurdly constructed that these were literally the moments that made up—made up for the long stiffness of sitting there in the stocks, made up for the cunning hostility of Mr. Buckton and the importunate sympathy of the counter-clerk, made up for the daily deadly flourishy letter from Mr. Mudge, made up even for the most haunting of her worries, the rage at moments of not knowing how her mother did "get it."

She had surrendered herself moreover of late to a certain expansion of her consciousness; something that seemed perhaps vulgarly accounted for by the fact that, as the blast of the season roared louder and the waves of fashion tossed their spray further over the counter, there were more impressions to be gathered and really—for it came to that—more life to be led. Definite at any rate it was that by the time May was well started the kind of company she kept at Cocker's had begun to strike her as a reason—a reason she might almost put forward for a policy of procrastination. It sounded silly, of course, as yet, to plead such a motive, especially as the fascination of the place was after all a sort of torment. But she liked her torment; it was a torment she should miss at Chalk Farm. She was ingenious and uncandid, therefore, about leaving the breadth of London a little longer between herself and that austerity. If she hadn't quite the courage in short to say to Mr. Mudge that her actual chance for a play of mind was worth any week the three shillings he desired to help her to save, she yet saw something happen in the course of the month that in her heart of hearts at least answered the subtle question. This was connected precisely with the appearance of the memorable lady.

III

She pushed in three bescribbled forms which the girl's hand was quick to appropriate, Mr. Buckton having so frequent a perverse instinct for catching first any eye that promised the sort of entertainment with which she had her peculiar affinity. The amusements of captives are full of a desperate contrivance, and one of our young friend's ha'pennyworths had been the charming tale of "Picciola." It was of course the law of the place that they were never to take no notice, as Mr. Buckton said, whom they served; but this also never prevented, certainly on the same gentleman's own part, what he was fond of describing as the underhand game. Both her companions, for that matter, made no secret of the number of favourites they had among the ladies; sweet familiarities in spite of which she had repeatedly caught each of them in stupidities and mistakes, confusions of identity and lapses of observation that never failed to remind her how the cleverness of men ends where the cleverness of women begins. "Marguerite, Regent Street. Try on at six. All Spanish lace. Pearls. The full length." That was the first; it had no signature. "Lady Agnes Orme, Hyde Park Place. Impossible to-night, dining Haddon. Opera to-morrow, promised Fritz, but could do play Wednesday. Will try Haddon for Savoy, and anything in the world you like, if you can get Gussy. Sunday Montenero. Sit Mason Monday, Tuesday. Marguerite awful. Cissy." That was the second. The third, the girl noted when she took it, was on a foreign form: "Everard, Hôtel Brighton, Paris. Only understand and believe. 22d to 26th, and certainly 8th and 9th. Perhaps others. Come. Mary."

Mary was very handsome, the handsomest woman, she felt in a moment, she had ever seen—or perhaps it was only

Cissy. Perhaps it was both, for she had seen stranger things
than that—ladies wiring to different persons under different
names. She had seen all sorts of things and pieced together
all sorts of mysteries. There had once been one—not long
before—who, without winking, sent off five over five different signatures. Perhaps these represented five different
friends who had asked her—all women, just as perhaps now
Mary and Cissy, or one or other of them, were wiring by
deputy. Sometimes she put in too much—too much of her
own sense; sometimes she put in too little; and in either
case this often came round to her afterwards, for she had
an extraordinary way of keeping clues. When she noticed
she noticed; that was what it came to. There were days
and days, there were weeks sometimes, of vacancy. This
arose often from Mr. Buckton's devilish and successful sub-
terfuges for keeping her at the sounder whenever it looked
as if anything might amuse; the sounder, which it was
equally his business to mind, being the innermost cell of
captivity, a cage within the cage, fenced off from the rest
by a frame of ground glass. The counter-clerk would have
played into her hands; but the counter-clerk was really reduced to idiocy by the effect of his passion for her. She flattered herself moreover, nobly, that with the unpleasant conspicuity of this passion she would never have consented to
be obliged to him. The most she would ever do would be
always to shove off on him whenever she could the regis-
tration of letters, a job she happened particularly to loathe.
After the long stupors, at all events, there almost always
suddenly would come a sharp taste of something; it was
in her mouth before she knew it; it was in her mouth now.

To Cissy, to Mary, whichever it was, she found her curiosity going out with a rush, a mute effusion that floated
back to her, like a returning tide, the living colour and
splendour of the beautiful head, the light of eyes that
seemed to reflect such utterly other things than the mean
things actually before them; and, above all, the high curt
consideration of a manner that even at bad moments was a
magnificent habit and of the very essence of the innumerable things—her beauty, her birth, her father and mother,
her cousins and all her ancestors—that its possessor couldn't

have got rid of even had she wished. How did our obscure little public servant know that for the lady of the telegrams this was a bad moment? How did she guess all sorts of impossible things, such as, almost on the very spot, the presence of drama at a critical stage and the nature of the tie with the gentleman at the Hôtel Brighton? More than ever before it floated to her through the bars of the cage that this at last was the high reality, the bristling truth that she had hitherto only patched up and eked out—one of the creatures, in fine, in whom all the conditions for happiness actually met, and who, in the air they made, bloomed with an unwitting insolence. What came home to the girl was the way the insolence was tempered by something that was equally a part of the distinguished life, the custom of a flower-like bend to the less fortunate—a dropped fragrance, a mere quick breath, but which in fact pervaded and lingered. The apparition was very young, but certainly married, and our fatigued friend had a sufficient store of mythological comparison to recognise the port of Juno. Marguerite might be "awful," but she knew how to dress a goddess.

Pearls and Spanish lace—she herself, with assurance, could see them, and the "full length" too, and also red velvet bows, which, disposed on the lace in a particular manner (she could have placed them with the turn of a hand) were of course to adorn the front of a black brocade that would be like a dress in a picture. However, neither Marguerite nor Lady Agnes nor Haddon nor Fritz nor Gussy was what the wearer of this garment had really come in for. She had come in for Everard—and that was doubtless not *his* true name either. If our young lady had never taken such jumps before it was simply that she had never before been so affected. She went all the way. Mary and Cissy had been round together, in their single superb person, to see him—he must live round the corner; they had found that, in consequence of something they had come, precisely, to make up for or to have another scene about, he had gone off—gone off just on purpose to make them feel it: on which they had come together to Cocker's as to the nearest place; where they had put in the three forms partly in order not

to put in the one alone. The two others in a manner covered it, muffled it, passed it off. Oh yes, she went all the
way, and this was a specimen of how she often went. She
would know the hand again any time. It was as handsome
and as everything else as the woman herself. The woman
herself had, on learning his flight, pushed past Everard's
servant and into his room; she had written her missive at
his table and with his pen. All this, every inch of it, came
in the waft that she blew through and left behind her, the
influence that, as I have said, lingered. And among the
things the girl was sure of, happily, was that she should
see her again.

IV

She saw her in fact, and only ten days later; but this
time not alone, and that was exactly a part of the luck of
it. Not unaware—as how could her observation have left
her so?—of the possibilities through which it could range,
our young lady had ever since had in her mind a dozen
conflicting theories about Everard's type; as to which, the
instant they came into the place, she felt the point settled
with a thump that seemed somehow addressed straight to
her heart. That organ literally beat faster at the approach
of the gentleman who was this time with Cissy, and who,
as seen from within the cage, became on the spot the happiest of the happy circumstances with which her mind had
invested the friend of Fritz and Gussy. He was a very happy
circumstance indeed as, with his cigarette in his lips and
his broken familiar talk caught by his companion, he put
down the half-dozen telegrams it would take them together
several minutes to dispatch. And here it occurred, oddly
enough, that if, shortly before, the girl's interest in his companion had sharpened her sense for the messages then transmitted, her immediate vision of himself had the effect, while
she counted his seventy words, of preventing intelligibility.
His words were mere numbers, they told her nothing whatever; and after he had gone she was in possession of no
name, of no address, of no meaning, of nothing but a vague
sweet sound and an immense impression. He had been

there but five minutes, he had smoked in her face, and, busy with his telegrams, with the tapping pencil and the conscious danger, the odious betrayal that would come from a mistake, she had had no wandering glances nor round-about arts to spare. Yet she had taken him in; she knew everything; she had made up her mind.

He had come back from Paris; everything was re-arranged; the pair were again shoulder to shoulder in their high encounter with life, their large and complicated game. The fine soundless pulse of this game was in the air for our young woman while they remained in the shop. While they remained? They remained all day; their presence continued and abode with her, was in everything she did till nightfall, in the thousands of other words she counted, she transmitted, in all the stamps she detached and the letters she weighed and the change she gave, equally unconscious and unerring in each of these particulars, and not, as the run on the little office thickened with the afternoon hours, looking up at a single ugly face in the long sequence, nor really hearing the stupid questions that she patiently and perfectly answered. All patience was possible now, all questions were stupid after his, all faces were ugly. She had been sure she should see the lady again; and even now she should perhaps, she should probably, see her often. But for him it was totally different; she should never never see him. She wanted it too much. There was a kind of wanting that helped—she had arrived, with her rich experience, at that generalisation; and there was another kind that was fatal. It was this time the fatal kind; it would prevent.

Well, she saw him the very next day, and on this second occasion it was quite different; the sense of every syllable he paid for was fiercely distinct; she indeed felt her progressive pencil, dabbing as if with a quick caress the marks of his own, put life into every stroke. He was there a long time—had not brought his forms filled out but worked them off in a nook on the counter; and there were other people as well—a changing pushing cluster, with every one to mind at once and endless right change to make and information to produce. But she kept hold of him throughout; she continued, for herself, in a relation with him as close as that in which, behind the hated ground glass, Mr. Buckton luckily continued with the sounder. This morning everything changed, but rather to dreariness; she had to swallow the rebuff to her theory about fatal desires, which she did without confusion and indeed with absolute levity; yet if it was now flagrant that he did live close at hand— at Park Chambers—and belonged supremely to the class that wired everything, even their expensive feelings (so that, as he evidently never wrote, his correspondence cost him weekly pounds and pounds and he might be in and out five times a day) there was, all the same, involved in the prospect, and by reason of its positive excess of light, a perverse melancholy, a gratuitous misery. This was at once to give it a place in an order of feelings on which I shall presently touch.

Meanwhile, for a month, he was very constant. Cissy, Mary, never re-appeared with him; he was always either alone or accompanied only by some gentleman who was lost in the blaze of his glory. There was another sense, how-ever—and indeed there was more than one—in which she mostly found herself counting in the splendid creature with whom she had originally connected him. He addressed this correspondent neither as Mary nor as Cissy; but the girl was sure of whom it was, in Eaton Square, that he was perpetually wiring to—and all so irreproachably!—as Lady Bradeen. Lady Bradeen was Cissy, Lady Bradeen was Mary, Lady Bradeen was the friend of Fritz and of Gussy, the customer of Marguerite and the close ally in short (as was ideally right, only the girl had not yet found a descrip-tive term that was) of the most magnificent of men. Noth-ing could equal the frequency and variety of his commu-nications to her ladyship but their extraordinary, their abysmal propriety. It was just the talk—so profuse some-times that she wondered what was left for their real meet-ings—of the very happiest people. Their real meetings must have been constant, for half of it was appointments and al-lusions, all swimming in a sea of other allusions still, tan-gled in a complexity of questions that gave a wondrous image of their life. If Lady Bradeen was Juno it was all certainly Olympian. If the girl, missing the answers, her ladyship's own outpourings, vainly reflected that Cocker's should have been one of the bigger offices where telegrams arrived as well as departed, there were yet ways in which, on the whole, she pressed the romance closer by reason of the very quantity of imagination it demanded and consumed. The days and hours of this new friend, as she came to account him, were at all events unrolled, and however much more she might have known she would still have wished to go beyond. In fact she did go beyond; she went quite far enough.

But she could none the less, even after a month, scarce have told if the gentlemen who came in with him recurred or changed; and this in spite of the fact that they too were always posting and wiring, smoking in her face and signing or not signing. The gentlemen who came in with him were nothing when he was there. They turned up alone at other times—then only perhaps with a dim richness of reference. He himself, absent as well as present, was all. He was very tall, very fair, and had, in spite of his thick preoccupations, a good humour that was exquisite, particularly as it so often had the effect of keeping him on. He could have reached over anybody, and anybody—no matter who—would have let him; but he was so extraordinarily kind that he quite pathetically waited, never waggling things at her out of his turn nor saying "Here!" with horrid sharpness. He waited for pottering old ladies, for gaping slaveys, for the perpetual Buttonses from Thrupp's; and the thing in all this that she would have liked most unspeakably to put to the test was the possibility of her having for him a personal identity that might in a particular way appeal. There were moments when he actually struck her as on her side, as arranging to help, to support, to spare her.

But such was the singular spirit of our young friend that she could remind herself with a pang that when people had awfully good manners—people of that class—you couldn't tell. These manners were for everybody, and it might be drearily unavailing for any poor particular body to be overworked and unusual. What he did take for granted was all sorts of facility; and his high pleasantness, his relighting of cigarettes while he waited, his unconscious bestowal of opportunities, of boons, of blessings, were all a part of his splendid security, the instinct that told him there was nothing such an existence as his could ever lose by. He was somehow all at once very bright and very grave, very young and immensely complete; and whatever he was at any moment it was always as much as all the rest the mere bloom of his beatitude. He was sometimes Everard, as he had been at the Hôtel Brighton, and he was sometimes Captain Everard. He was sometimes Philip with his surname and sometimes Philip without it. In some directions he was merely Phil, in others he was merely Captain. There were relations in which he was none of these things, but a quite different person—"the Count." There were several friends for whom he was William. There were several for whom, in allusion perhaps to his complexion, he was "the Pink 'Un." Once, once only by good luck, he had, coinciding comically, quite miraculously, with another person also near to her, been "Mudge." Yes, whatever he was, it was a part of his happiness—whatever he was and probably whatever he wasn't. And his happiness was a part—it became so little by little—of something that, almost from the first of her being at Cocker's, had been deeply with the girl.

V

This was neither more nor less than the queer extension of her experience, the double life that, in the cage, she grew at last to lead. As the weeks went on there she lived more and more into the world of whiffs and glimpses, she found her divinations work faster and stretch further. It was a prodigious view as the pressure heightened, a panorama fed with facts and figures, flushed with a torrent of colour and accompanied with wondrous world-music. What it mainly came to at this period was a picture of how London could amuse itself; and that, with the running commentary of a witness so exclusively a witness, turned for the most part to a hardening of the heart. The nose of this observer was brushed by the bouquet, yet she could never really pluck even a daisy. What could still remain fresh in her daily grind was the immense disparity, the difference and contrast, from class to class, of every instant and every motion. There were times when all the wires in the country seemed to start from the little hole-and-corner where she plied for a livelihood, and where, in the shuffle of feet, the flutter of "forms," the straying of stamps and the ring of change over the counter, the people she had fallen into the habit of remembering and fitting together with others, and of having her theories and interpretations of, kept up before her their long procession and rotation. What twisted the knife in her vitals was the way the profligate rich scattered about them, in extravagant chatter over their extravagant pleasures and sins, an amount of money that would have held the stricken household of her frightened childhood, her poor pinched mother and tormented father and lost brother and starved sister, together for a lifetime. During her first weeks she had often gasped at the sums people were willing to pay for the stuff they transmitted—the "much love"s, the "awful" regrets, the compliments and wonderments and vain vague gestures that cost the price of a new pair of boots. She had had a way then of glancing at the people's faces, but she had early learnt that if you became a telegraphist you soon ceased to be astonished. Her eye for types amounted nevertheless to genius, and there were those she liked and those she hated, her feeling for the latter of which grew to a positive possession, an instinct of observation and detection. There were the brazen women, as she called them, of the higher and the lower fashion, whose squanderings and graspings, whose struggles and secrets and love-affairs and lies, she tracked and stored up against them till she had at moments, in private, a triumphant vicious feeling of mastery and ease, a sense of carrying their silly guilty secrets in her pocket, her small retentive brain, and thereby knowing so much more about them than they suspected or would care to think. There were those she would have liked to betray, to trip up, to bring down with words altered and fatal; and all through a personal hostility provoked by the lightest signs, by their accidents of tone and manner, by the particular kind of relation she always happened instantly to feel.

There were impulses of various kinds, alternately soft and severe, to which she was constitutionally accessible and which were determined by the smallest accidents. She was rigid in general on the article of making the public itself affix its stamps, and found a special enjoyment in dealing to that end with some of the ladies who were too grand to touch them. She had thus a play of refinement and subtlety greater, she flattered herself, than any of which she could be made the subject; and though most people were too stupid to be conscious of this it brought her endless small consolations and revenges. She recognised quite as much those of her sex whom she would have liked to help, to warn, to rescue, to see more of; and that alternative as well operated exactly through the hazard of personal sympathy, her vision for silver threads and moonbeams and her gift for keeping the clues and finding her way in the tangle. The moonbeams and silver threads presented at moments all the vision of what poor *she* might have made of happiness. Blurred and blank as the whole thing often inevitably, or mercifully, became, she could still, through crevices and crannies, be stupefied, especially by what, in spite of all seasoning, touched the sorest place in her consciousness, the revelation of the golden shower flying about without a gleam of gold for herself. It remained prodigious to the end, the money her fine friends were able to spend to get still more, or even to complain to fine friends of their own that they were in want. The pleasures they proposed were equalled only by those they declined, and they made their appointments often so expensively that she was left wondering at the nature of the delights to which the mere approaches were so paved with shillings. She quivered on occasion into the perception of this and that one whom she would on the chance have just simply liked to *be*. Her conceit, her baffled vanity, was possibly monstrous; she certainly often threw herself into a defiant conviction that she would have done the whole thing much better. But her greatest comfort, mostly, was her comparative vision of the men; by whom I mean the unmistakeable gentlemen, for she had no interest in the spurious or the shabby and no mercy at all for the poor. She could have found a sixpence, outside, for an appearance of want; but her fancy, in some directions so alert, had never a throb of response for any sign of the sordid. The men she did track, moreover, she tracked mainly in one relation, the relation as to which the cage convinced her, she believed, more than anything else could have done, that it was quite the most diffused.

She found her ladies, in short, almost always in communication with her gentlemen, and her gentlemen with her ladies, and she read into the immensity of their intercourse stories and meanings without end. Incontestably she grew to think that the men cut the best figure; and in this particular, as in many others, she arrived at a philosophy of her own, all made up of her private notations and cynicisms. It was a striking part of the business, for example, that it was much more the women, on the whole, who were after the men than the men who were after the women: it was literally visible that the general attitude of the one sex was that of the object pursued and defensive, apologetic and attenuating, while the light of her own nature helped her more or less to conclude as to the attitude of the other. Perhaps she herself a little even fell into the custom of pursuit in occasionally deviating only for gentlemen from her high rigour about the stamps. She had early in the day made up her mind, in fine, that they had the best manners; and if there were none of them she noticed when Captain Everard was there, there were plenty she could place and trace and name at other times, plenty who, with their way of being "nice" to her and of handling, as if their pockets were private tills, loose mixed masses of silver and gold, were such pleasant appearances that she could envy them without dislike. *They* never had to give change— they only had to get it. They ranged through every suggestion, every shade of fortune, which evidently included indeed lots of bad luck as well as of good, declining even toward Mr. Mudge and his bland firm thrift, and ascending, in wild signals and rocket-flights, almost to within hail of her highest standard. So from month to month she went on with them all, through a thousand ups and downs and a thousand pangs and indifferences. What virtually hap-

pened was that in the shuffling herd that passed before her
by far the greater part only passed—a proportion but just
appreciable stayed. Most of the elements swam straight
away, lost themselves in the bottomless common, and by
so doing really kept the page clear. On the clearness therefore what she did retain stood sharply out; she nipped and
caught it, turned it over and interwove it.

VI

She met Mrs. Jordan when she could, and learned
from her more and more how the great people, under her
gentle shake and after going through everything with the
mere shops, were waking up to the gain of putting into
the hands of a person of real refinement the question that
the shop-people spoke of so vulgarly as that of the floral
decorations. The regular dealers in these decorations were
all very well; but there was a peculiar magic in the play
of taste of a lady who had only to remember, through whatever intervening dusk, all her own little tables, little bowls
and little jars and little other arrangements, and the wonderful thing she had made of the garden of the vicarage.
This small domain, which her young friend had never seen,
bloomed in Mrs. Jordan's discourse like a new Eden, and
she converted the past into a bank of violets by the tone
in which she said "Of course you always knew my one passion!" She obviously met now, at any rate, a big contemporary need, measured what it was rapidly becoming for
people to feel they could trust her without a tremor. It
brought them a peace that—during the quarter of an hour
before dinner in especial—was worth more to them than
mere payment could express. Mere payment, none the less,
was tolerably prompt; she engaged by the month, taking
over the whole thing; and there was an evening on which,
in respect to our heroine, she at last returned to the charge.
"It's growing and growing, and I see that I must really di-
vide the work. One wants an associate—of one's own kind,
don't you know? You know the look they want it all to have?
—of having come, not from a florist, but from one of themselves. Well, I'm sure *you* could give it—because you *are*

one. Then we *should* win. Therefore just come in with me."

"And leave the P. O.?"

"Let the P. O. simply bring you your letters. It would bring you lots, you'd see: orders, after a bit, by the score." It was on this, in due course, that the great advantage again came up: "One seems to live again with one's own people." It had taken some little time (after their having parted company in the tempest of their troubles and then, in the glimmering dawn, finally sighted each other again) for each to admit that the other was, in her private circle, her only equal; but the admission came, when it did come, with an honest groan; and since equality *was* named, each found much personal profit in exaggerating the other's original grandeur. Mrs. Jordan was ten years the older, but her young friend was struck with the smaller difference this now made: it had counted otherwise at the time when, much more as a friend of her mother's, the bereaved lady, without a penny of provision and with stopgaps, like their own, all gone, had, across the sordid landing on which the opposite doors of the pair of scared miseries opened and to which they were bewilderedly bolted, borrowed coals and umbrellas that were repaid in potatoes and postage-stamps. It had been a questionable help, at that time, to ladies submerged, floundering, panting, swimming for their lives, that they *were* ladies; but such an advantage could come up again in proportion as others vanished, and it had grown very great by the time it was the only ghost of one they possessed. They had literally watched it take to itself a portion of the substance of each that had departed; and it became prodigious now, when they could talk of it together, when they could look back at it across a desert of accepted derogation, and when, above all, they could together work up a credulity about it that neither could otherwise work up. Nothing was really so marked as that they felt the need to cultivate this legend much more after having found their feet and stayed their stomachs in the ultimate obscure than they had done in the upper air of mere frequent shocks. The thing they could now oftenest say to each other was that they knew what they meant; and the sentiment with which, all round, they knew it was known had well-nigh amounted to a promise not again to fall apart.

Mrs. Jordan was at present fairly dazzling on the subject of the way that, in the practice of her fairy art, as she called it, she more than peeped in—she penetrated. There was not a house of the great kind—and it was of course only a question of those, real homes of luxury—in which she was not, at the rate such people now had things, all over the place. The girl felt before the picture the cold breath of disinheritance as much as she had ever felt it in the cage; she knew moreover how much she betrayed this, for the experience of poverty had begun, in her life, too early, and her ignorance of the requirements of homes of luxury had grown, with other active knowledge, a depth of simplification. She had accordingly at first often found that in these colloquies she could only pretend she understood. Educated as she had rapidly been by her chances at Cocker's, there were still strange gaps in her learning—she could never, like Mrs. Jordan, have found her way about one of the "homes." Little by little, however, she had caught on, above all in the light of what Mrs. Jordan's redemption had materially made of that lady, giving her, though the years and the struggles had naturally not straightened a feature, an almost super-eminent air. There were women in and out of Cocker's who were quite nice and who yet didn't look well; whereas Mrs. Jordan looked well and yet, with her extraordinarily protrusive teeth, was by no means quite nice. It would seem, mystifyingly, that it might really come from all the greatness she could live with. It was fine to hear her talk so often of dinners of twenty and of her doing, as she said, exactly as she liked with them. She spoke as if, for that matter, she invited the company. "They simply *give* me the table—all the rest, all the other effects, come afterwards."

VII

"Then you *do* see them?" the girl again asked.

Mrs. Jordan hesitated, and indeed the point had been ambiguous before. "Do you mean the guests?"

Her young friend, cautious about an undue exposure of innocence, was not quite sure. "Well—the people who live there."

"Lady Ventnor? Mrs. Bubb? Lord Rye? Dear, yes. Why they *like* one."

"But does one personally *know* them?" our young lady went on, since that was the way to speak. "I mean socially, don't you know?—as you know *me*."

"They're not so nice as you!" Mrs. Jordan charmingly cried. "But I *shall* see more and more of them."

Ah this was the old story. "But how soon?"

"Why almost any day. Of course," Mrs. Jordan honestly added, "they're nearly always out."

"Then why do they want flowers all over?"

"Oh that doesn't make any difference." Mrs. Jordan was not philosophic; she was just evidently determined it *shouldn't* make any. "They're awfully interested in my ideas, and it's inevitable they should meet me over them."

Her interlocutress was sturdy enough. "What do you call your ideas?"

Mrs. Jordan's reply was fine. "If you were to see me some day with a thousand tulips you'd discover."

"A thousand?"—the girl gaped at such a revelation of the scale of it; she felt for the instant fairly planted out. "Well, but if in fact they never do meet you?" she none the less pessimistically insisted.

"Never? They *often* do—and evidently quite on purpose. We have grand long talks."

There was something in our young lady that could still stay her from asking for a personal description of these apparitions; that showed too starved a state. But while she considered she took in afresh the whole of the clergyman's widow. Mrs. Jordan couldn't help her teeth, and her sleeves were a distinct rise in the world. A thousand tulips at a shilling clearly took one further than a thousand words at a penny; and the betrothed of Mr. Mudge, in whom the sense of the race for life was always acute, found herself wondering, with a twinge of her easy jealousy, if it mightn't after all then, for *her* also, be better—better than where she was—to follow some such scent. Where she was was where

Mr. Buckton's elbow could freely enter her right side and the counter-clerk's breathing—he had something the matter with his nose—pervade her left ear. It was something to fill an office under Government, and she knew but too well there were places commoner still than Cocker's; but it needed no great range of taste to bring home to her the picture of servitude and promiscuity she couldn't but offer to the eye of comparative freedom. She was so boxed up with her young men, and anything like a margin so absent, that it needed more art than she should ever possess to pretend in the least to compass, with any one in the nature of an acquaintance—say with Mrs. Jordan herself, flying in, as it might happen, to wire sympathetically to Mrs. Bubb —an approach to a relation of elegant privacy. She remembered the day when Mrs. Jordan *had*, in fact, by the greatest chance, come in with fifty-three words for Lord Rye and a five-pound note to change. This had been the dramatic manner of their reunion—their mutual recognition was so great an event. The girl could at first only see her from the waist up, besides making but little of her long telegram to his lordship. It was a strange whirligig that had converted the clergyman's widow into such a specimen of the class that went beyond the sixpence.

Nothing of the occasion, all the more, had ever become dim; least of all the way that, as her recovered friend looked up from counting, Mrs. Jordan had just blown, in explanation, through her teeth and through the bars of the cage: "I *do* flowers, you know." Our young woman had always, with her little finger crooked out, a pretty movement for counting; and she had not forgotten the small secret advantage, a sharpness of triumph it might even have been called, that fell upon her at this moment and avenged her for the incoherence of the message, an unintelligible enumeration of numbers, colours, days, hours. The correspondence of people she didn't know was one thing; but the correspondence of people she did had an aspect of its own for her even when she couldn't understand it. The speech in which Mrs. Jordan had defined a position and announced a profession was like a tinkle of bluebells; but for herself her one idea about flowers was that people had them at funerals, and her present sole gleam of light was that lords probably had them most. When she watched, a minute later, through the cage, the swing of her visitor's departing petticoats, she saw the sight from the waist down; and when the counter-clerk, after a mere male glance, remarked, with an intention unmistakeably low, "Handsome woman!" she had for him the finest of her chills: "She's the widow of a bishop." She always felt, with the counter-clerk, that it was impossible sufficiently to put it on; for what she wished to express to him was the maximum of her contempt, and that element in her nature was confusedly stored. "A bishop" *was* putting it on, but the counter-clerk's approaches were vile. The night, after this, when, in the fulness of time, Mrs. Jordan mentioned the grand long talks, the girl at last brought out: "Should *I* see them?—I mean if I *were* to give up everything for you."

Mrs. Jordan at this became most arch. "I'd send you to all the bachelors!"

Our young lady could be reminded by such a remark that she usually struck her friend as pretty. "Do *they* have their flowers?"

"Oceans. And they're the most particular." Oh it was a wonderful world. "You should see Lord Rye's."

"His flowers?"

"Yes, and his letters. He writes me pages on pages—with the most adorable little drawings and plans. You should see his diagrams!"

VIII

The girl had in course of time every opportunity to inspect these documents, and they a little disappointed her; but in the mean while there had been more talk, and it had led to her saying, as if her friend's guarantee of a life of elegance were not quite definite: "Well, I see every one at *my* place."

"Every one?"

"Lots of swells. They flock. They live, you know, all round, and the place is filled with all the smart people, all the fast people, those whose names are in the papers—

mamma has still the *Morning Post*—and who come up for the season."

Mrs. Jordan took this in with complete intelligence. "Yes, and I dare say it's some of your people that *I* do."

Her companion assented, but discriminated. "I doubt if you 'do' them as much as I! Their affairs, their appointments and arrangements, their little games and secrets and vices—those things all pass before me."

This was a picture that could make a clergyman's widow not imperceptibly gasp; it was in intention moreover something of a retort to the thousand tulips. "Their vices? Have they got vices?"

Our young critic even more overtly stared; then with a touch of contempt in her amusement: "Haven't you found *that* out?" The homes of luxury then hadn't so much to give. "*I* find out everything."

Mrs. Jordan, at bottom a very meek person, was visibly struck. "I see. You do 'have' them."

"Oh I don't care! Much good it does me!"

Mrs. Jordan after an instant recovered her superiority. "No—it doesn't lead to much." Her own initiations so clearly did. Still—after all; and she was not jealous: "There must be a charm."

"In seeing them?" At this the girl suddenly let herself go. "I hate them. There's that charm!"

Mrs. Jordan gaped again. "The *real* 'smarts'?"

"Is that what you call Mrs. Bubb? Yes—it comes to me; I've had Mrs. Bubb. I don't think she has been in herself, but there are things her maid has brought. Well, my dear!" —and the young person from Cocker's, recalling these things and summing them up, seemed suddenly to have much to say. She didn't say it, however; she checked it; she only brought out: "Her maid, who's horrid—*she* must have her!" Then she went on with indifference: "They're *too* real! They're selfish brutes."

Mrs. Jordan, turning it over, adopted at last the plan of treating it with a smile. She wished to be liberal. "Well, of course, they do lay it out."

"They bore me to death," her companion pursued with slightly more temperance.

But this was going too far. "Ah that's because you've no sympathy!"

The girl gave an ironic laugh, only retorting that nobody could have any who had to count all day all the words in the dictionary; a contention Mrs. Jordan quite granted, the more that she shuddered at the notion of ever failing of the very gift to which she owed the vogue—the rage she might call it—that had caught her up. Without sympathy —or without imagination, for it came back again to that— how should she get, for big dinners, down the middle and toward the far corners at all? It wasn't the combinations, which were easily managed: the strain was over the ineffable simplicities, those that the bachelors above all, and Lord Rye perhaps most of any, threw off—just blew off like cigarette-puffs—such sketches of. The betrothed of Mr. Mudge at all events accepted the explanation, which had the effect, as almost any turn of their talk was now apt to have, of bringing her round to the terrific question of that gentleman. She was tormented with the desire to get out of Mrs. Jordan, on this subject, what she was sure was at the back of Mrs. Jordan's head; and to get it out of her, queerly enough, if only to vent a certain irritation at it. She knew that what her friend would already have risked if she hadn't been timid and tortuous was: "Give him up—yes, give him up: you'll see that with your sure chances you'll be able to do much better."

Our young woman had a sense that if that view could only be put before her with a particular sniff for poor Mr. Mudge she should hate it as much as she morally ought. She was conscious of not, as yet, hating it quite so much as that. But she saw that Mrs. Jordan was conscious of something too, and that there was a degree of confidence she was waiting little by little to arrive at. The day came when the girl caught a glimpse of what was still wanting to make her friend feel strong; which was nothing less than the prospect of being able to announce the climax of sundry private dreams. The associate of the aristocracy had personal calculations—matter for brooding and dreaming, even for peeping out not quite hopelessly from behind the window-curtains of lonely lodgings. If she did the flowers for

the bachelors, in short, didn't she expect that to have consequences very different from such an outlook at Cocker's
as she had pronounced wholly desperate? There seemed in
very truth something auspicious in the mixture of bachelors
and flowers, though, when looked hard in the eye, Mrs.
Jordan was not quite prepared to say she had expected a
positive proposal from Lord Rye to pop out of it. Our
young woman arrived at last, none the less, at a definite
vision of what was in her mind. This was a vivid fore-
knowledge that the betrothed of Mr. Mudge would, unless
conciliated in advance by a successful rescue, almost hate
her on the day she should break a particular piece of news.
How could that unfortunate otherwise endure to hear of
what, under the protection of Lady Ventnor, was after all
so possible?

IX

Meanwhile, since irritation sometimes relieved her, the
betrothed of Mr. Mudge found herself indebted to that admirer for amounts of it perfectly proportioned to her fidelity.
She always walked with him on Sundays, usually in the
Regent's Park, and quite often, once or twice a month, he
took her, in the Strand or thereabouts, to see a piece that
was having a run. The productions he always preferred
were the really good ones—Shakespeare, Thompson or some
funny American thing; which, as it also happened that she
hated vulgar plays, gave him ground for what was almost
the fondest of his approaches, the theory that their tastes
were, blissfully, just the same. He was for ever reminding
her of that, rejoicing over it and being affectionate and wise
about it. There were times when she wondered how in the
world she could "put up with" him, how she could put up
with any man so smugly unconscious of the immensity of
her difference. It was just for this difference that, if she
was to be liked at all, she wanted to be liked, and if that
was not the source of Mr. Mudge's admiration, she asked
herself, what on earth *could* be? She was not different only
at one point, she was different all round; unless perhaps
indeed in being practically human, which her mind just

barely recognised that he also was. She would have made tremendous concessions in other quarters: there was no limit for instance to those she would have made to Captain Everard; but what I have named was the most she was prepared to do for Mr. Mudge. It was because *he* was different that, in the oddest way, she liked as well as deplored him; which was after all a proof that the disparity, should they frankly recognise it, wouldn't necessarily be fatal. She felt that, oleaginous—too oleaginous—as he was, he was somehow comparatively primitive: she had once, during the portion of his time at Cocker's that had overlapped her own, seen him collar a drunken soldier, a big violent man who, having come in with a mate to get a postal-order cashed, had made a grab at the money before his friend could reach it and had so determined, among the hams and cheeses and the lodgers from Thrupp's, immediate and alarming reprisals, a scene of scandal and consternation. Mr. Buckton and the counter-clerk had crouched within the cage, but Mr. Mudge had, with a very quiet but very quick step round the counter, an air of masterful authority she shouldn't soon forget, triumphantly interposed in the scrimmage, parted the combatants and shaken the delinquent in his skin. She had been proud of him at that moment, and had felt that if their affair had not already been settled the neatness of his execution would have left her without resistance.

Their affair had been settled by other things: by the evident sincerity of his passion and by the sense that his high white apron resembled a front of many floors. It had gone a great way with her that he would build up a business to his chin, which he carried quite in the air. This could only be a question of time; he would have all Piccadilly in the pen behind his ear. That was a merit in itself for a girl who had known what she had known. There were hours at which she even found him good-looking, though frankly there could be no crown for her effort to imagine on the part of the tailor or the barber some such treatment of his appearance as would make him resemble even remotely a man of the world. His very beauty was the beauty of a grocer, and the finest future would offer it none too much

room consistently to develop. She had engaged herself in
short to the perfection of a type, and almost anything
square and smooth and whole had its weight for a person
still conscious herself of being a mere bruised fragment of
wreckage. But it contributed hugely at present to carry on
the two parallel lines of her experience in the cage and her
experience out of it. After keeping quiet for some time
about this opposition she suddenly—one Sunday afternoon
on a penny chair in the Regent's Park—broke, for him, ca-
priciously, bewilderingly, into an intimation of what it came
to. He had naturally pressed more and more on the point
of her again placing herself where he could see her hourly,
and for her to recognise that she had as yet given him no
sane reason for delay he had small need to describe himself
as unable to make out what she was up to. As if, with
her absurd bad reasons, she could have begun to tell him!
Sometimes she thought it would be amusing to let him have
them full in the face, for she felt she should die of him
unless she once in a while stupefied him; and sometimes
she thought it would be disgusting and perhaps even fatal.
She liked him, however, to think her silly, for that gave her
the margin which at the best she would always require;
and the only difficulty about this was that he hadn't enough
imagination to oblige her. It produced none the less something of the desired effect—to leave him simply wondering
why, over the matter of their reunion, she didn't yield to
his arguments. Then at last, simply as if by accident and
out of mere boredom on a day that was rather flat, she
preposterously produced her own. "Well, wait a bit. Where
I am I still see things." And she talked to him even worse, if
possible, than she had talked to Mrs. Jordan.

Little by little, to her own stupefaction, she caught that
he was trying to take it as she meant it and that he was
neither astonished nor angry. Oh the British tradesman—
this gave her an idea of his resources! Mr. Mudge would
be angry only with a person who, like the drunken soldier
in the shop, should have an unfavourable effect on business.
He seemed positively to enter, for the time and without the
faintest flash of irony or ripple of laughter, into the whimsical grounds of her enjoyment of Cocker's custom, and in-

stantly to be casting up whatever it might, as Mrs. Jordan
had said, lead to. What he had in mind was not of course
what Mrs. Jordan had had: it was obviously not a source
of speculation with him that his sweetheart might pick up
a husband. She could see perfectly that this was not for a
moment even what he supposed she herself dreamed of.
What she had done was simply to give his sensibility another push into the dim vast of trade. In that direction it
was all alert and she had whisked before it the mild fragrance of a "connexion." That was the most he could see
in any account of her keeping in, on whatever roundabout
lines, with the gentry; and when, getting to the bottom of
this, she quickly proceeded to show him the kind of eye
she turned on such people and to give him a sketch of
what that eye discovered, she reduced him to the particular
prostration in which he could still be amusing to her.

X

"They're the most awful wretches, I assure you—the
lot all about there."

"Then why do you want to stay among them?"

"My dear man, just because they *are*. It makes me hate
them so."

"Hate them? I thought you liked them."

"Don't be stupid. What I 'like' is just to loathe them.
You wouldn't believe what passes before my eyes."

"Then why have you never told me? You didn't mention
anything before I left."

"Oh I hadn't got round to it then. It's the sort of thing
you don't believe at first; you have to look round you a bit
and then you understand. You work into it more and
more. Besides," the girl went on, "this is the time of the
year when the worst lot come up. They're simply packed
together in those smart streets. Talk of the numbers of the
poor! What *I* can vouch for is the numbers of the rich!
There are new ones every day and they seem to get richer
and richer. Oh they do come up!" she cried, imitating for
her private recreation—she was sure it wouldn't reach Mr.
Mudge—the low intonation of the counter-clerk.

"And where do they come from?" her companion candidly enquired.

She had to think a moment; then she found something. "From the 'spring meetings.' They bet tremendously."

"Well, they bet enough at Chalk Farm, if that's all."

"It *isn't* all. It isn't a millionth part!" she replied with some sharpness. "It's immense fun"—she *had* to tantalise him. Then as she had heard Mrs. Jordan say, and as the ladies at Cocker's even sometimes wired, "It's quite too dreadful!" She could fully feel how it was Mr. Mudge's propriety, which was extreme—he had a horror of coarseness and attended a Wesleyan chapel—that prevented his asking for details. But she gave him some of the more innocuous in spite of himself, especially putting before him how, at Simpkin's and Ladle's, they all made the money fly. That was indeed what he liked to hear: the connexion was not direct, but one was somehow more in the right place where the money was flying than where it was simply and meagrely nesting. The air felt that stir, he had to acknowledge, much less at Chalk Farm than in the district in which his beloved so oddly enjoyed her footing. She gave him, she could see, a restless sense that these might be familiarities not to be sacrificed; germs, possibilities, faint foreshowings—heaven knew what—of the initiation it would prove profitable to have arrived at when in the fulness of time he should have his own shop in some such paradise. What really touched him—that was discernible—was that she could feed him with so much mere vividness of reminder, keep before him, as by the play of a fan, the very wind of the swift bank-notes and the charm of the existence of a class that Providence had raised up to be the blessing of grocers. He liked to think that the class was there, that it was always there, and that she contributed in her slight but appreciable degree to keep it up to the mark. He couldn't have formulated his theory of the matter, but the exuberance of the aristocracy was the advantage of trade, and everything was knit together in a richness of pattern that it was good to follow with one's finger-tips. It was a comfort to him to be thus assured that there were no symptoms of a drop. What did the sounder, as she called it, nimbly worked, do but keep the ball going?

What it came to therefore for Mr. Mudge was that all enjoyments were, as might be said, inter-related, and that the more people had the more they wanted to have. The more flirtations, as he might roughly express it, the more cheese and pickles. He had even in his own small way been dimly struck with the linked sweetness connecting the tender passion with cheap champagne, or perhaps the other way round. What he would have liked to say had he been able to work out his thought to the end was: "I see, I see. Lash them up then, lead them on, keep them going: some of it can't help, some time, coming *our* way." Yet he was troubled by the suspicion of subtleties on his companion's part that spoiled the straight view. He couldn't understand people's hating what they liked or liking what they hated; above all it hurt him somewhere—for he had his private delicacies—to see anything *but* money made out of his betters. To be too enquiring, or in any other way too free, at the expense of the gentry was vaguely wrong; the only thing that was distinctly right was to be prosperous at any price. Wasn't it just because they were up there aloft that they were lucrative? He concluded at any rate by saying to his young friend: "If it's improper for you to remain at Cocker's, then that falls in exactly with the other reasons I've put before you for your removal."

"Improper?"—her smile became a prolonged boldness. "My dear boy, there's no one like you!"

"I dare say," he laughed; "but that doesn't help the question."

"Well," she returned, "I can't give up my friends. I'm making even more than Mrs. Jordan."

Mr. Mudge considered. "How much is *she* making?"

"Oh you dear donkey!"—and, regardless of all the Regent's Park, she patted his cheek. This was the sort of moment at which she was absolutely tempted to tell him that she liked to be near Park Chambers. There was a fascination in the idea of seeing if, on a mention of Captain Everard, he wouldn't do what she thought he might; wouldn't weigh against the obvious objection the still more obvious advantage. The advantage of course could only strike him at the best as rather fantastic; but it was always to the good to keep hold when you *had* hold, and such an attitude would also after all involve a high tribute to her fidelity. Of one thing she absolutely never doubted: Mr. Mudge believed in her with a belief—! She believed in herself too, for that matter: if there was a thing in the world no one could charge her with it was being the kind of low barmaid person who rinsed tumblers and bandied slang. But she forbore as yet to speak; she had not spoken even to Mrs. Jordan; and the hush that on her lips surrounded the Captain's name maintained itself as a kind of symbol of the success that, up to this time, had attended something or other—she couldn't have said what—that she humoured herself with calling, without words, her relation with him.

XI

She would have admitted indeed that it consisted of little more than the fact that his absences, however frequent and however long, always ended with his turning up again. It was nobody's business in the world but her own if that fact continued to be enough for her. It was of course not enough just in itself; what it had taken on to make it so was the extraordinary possession of the elements of his life that memory and attention had at last given her. There came a day when this possession on the girl's part actually seemed to enjoy between them, while their eyes met, a tacit recognition that was half a joke and half a deep solemnity. He bade her good-morning always now; he often quite raised his hat to her. He passed a remark when there was time or room, and once she went so far as to say to him that she hadn't seen him for "ages." "Ages" was the word she consciously and carefully, though a trifle tremulously, used; "ages" was exactly what she meant. To this he replied in terms doubtless less anxiously selected, but perhaps on that account not the less remarkable, "Oh yes, hasn't it been awfully wet?" That was a specimen of their give and take; it fed her fancy that no form of intercourse so transcendent and distilled had ever been established on earth. Everything, so far as they chose to consider it so, might mean almost anything. The want of margin in the cage, when he peeped through the bars, wholly ceased to be appreciable. It was a drawback only in superficial commerce. With Captain Everard she had simply the margin of the universe. It may be imagined therefore how their unuttered reference to all she knew about him could in this immensity play at its ease. Every time he handed in a telegram it was an addition to her knowledge: what did his constant smile mean to mark if it didn't mean to mark that? He never came into the place without saying to her in this manner: "Oh yes, you have me by this time so completely at your mercy that it doesn't in the least matter what I give you now. You've become a comfort, I assure you!"

She had only two torments; the greatest of which was that she couldn't, not even once or twice, touch with him on any individual fact. She would have given anything to have been able to allude to one of his friends by name, to one of his engagements by date, to one of his difficulties by the solution. She would have given almost as much for just the right chance—it would have to be tremendously right—to show him in some sharp sweet way that she had perfectly penetrated the greatest of these last and now lived with it in a kind of heroism of sympathy. He was in love with a woman to whom, and to any view of whom, a lady-telegraphist, and especially one who passed a life among hams and cheeses, was as the sand on the floor; and what her dreams desired was the possibility of its somehow coming to him that her own interest in him could take a pure and noble account of such an infatuation and even of such an impropriety. As yet, however, she could only rub along with the hope that an accident, sooner or later, might give her a lift toward popping out with something that would surprise and perhaps even, some fine day, assist him. What could people mean moreover—cheaply sarcastic people—by not feeling all that could be got out of the weather? *She* felt it all, and seemed literally to feel it most when she went quite wrong, speaking of the stuffy days as cold, of the cold ones as stuffy, and betraying how little she knew, in her cage, of whether it was foul or fair. It was for that matter always stuffy at Cocker's, and she finally settled down to the safe proposition that the outside element was "changeable." Anything seemed true that made him so radiantly assent.

This indeed is a small specimen of her cultivation of insidious ways of making things easy for him—ways to which of course she couldn't be at all sure he did real justice. Real justice was not of this world: she had had too often to come back to that; yet, strangely, happiness was, and her traps had to be set for it in a manner to keep them unperceived by Mr. Buckton and the counter-clerk. The most she could hope for apart from the question, which constantly flickered up and died down, of the divine chance of his consciously liking her, would be that, without analysing it, he should arrive at a vague sense that Cocker's was—well, attractive: easier, smoother, sociably brighter, slightly more picturesque, in short more propitious in general to his little affairs, than any other establishment just thereabouts. She was quite aware that they couldn't be, in so huddled a hole, particularly quick; but she found her account in the slowness—she certainly could bear it if *he* could. The great pang was that just thereabouts post-offices were so awfully thick. She was always seeing him in imagination at other places and with other girls. But she would defy any other girl to follow him as she followed. And though they weren't, for so many reasons, quick at Cocker's, she could hurry for him when, through an intimation light as air, she gathered that he was pressed.

When hurry was, better still, impossible, it was because of the pleasantest thing of all, the particular element of their contact—she would have called it their friendship—that consisted of an almost humorous treatment of the look of some of his words. They would never perhaps have grown half so intimate if he had not, by the blessing of heaven, formed some of his letters with a queerness—! It was positive that the queerness could scarce have been greater if he had practised it for the very purpose of bringing their heads together over it as far as was possible to heads on different sides of a wire fence. It had taken her truly but once or twice to master these tricks, but, at the cost of striking him perhaps as stupid, she could still challenge them when circumstances favoured. The great circumstance that favoured was that she sometimes actually believed he knew she only feigned perplexity. If he knew it therefore he tolerated it; if he tolerated it he came back; and if he came back he liked her. This was her seventh heaven; and she didn't ask much of his liking—she only asked of it to reach the point of his not going away because of her own. He had at times to be away for weeks; he had to lead his life; he had to travel—there were places to which he was constantly wiring for "rooms": all this she granted him, forgave him; in fact, in the long run, literally blessed and thanked him for. If he had to lead his life, that precisely fostered his leading it so much by telegraph: therefore the benediction was to come in when he could. That was all she asked—that he shouldn't wholly deprive her.

Sometimes she almost felt that he couldn't have deprived her even had he been minded, by reason of the web of revelation that was woven between them. She quite thrilled herself with thinking what, with such a lot of material, a bad girl would do. It would be a scene better than many in her ha'penny novels, this going to him in the dusk of evening at Park Chambers and letting him at last have it. "I know too much about a certain person now not to put it to you—excuse my being so lurid—that it's quite worth your while to buy me off. Come therefore: buy me!" There was a point indeed at which such flights had to drop again —the point of an unreadiness to name, when it came to that, the purchasing medium. It wouldn't certainly be anything so gross as money, and the matter accordingly remained rather vague, all the more that *she* was not a bad girl. It wasn't for any such reason as might have aggravated a mere minx that she often hoped he would again bring Cissy. The difficulty of this, however, was constantly present to her, for the kind of communion to which Cocker's so richly ministered rested on the fact that Cissy and he were so often in different places. She knew by this time all the places—Suchbury, Monkhouse, Whiteroy, Finches—

and even how the parties on these occasions were composed; but her subtlety found ways to make her knowledge
fairly protect and promote their keeping, as she had heard
Mrs. Jordan say, in touch. So, when he actually sometimes
smiled as if he really felt the awkwardness of giving her
again one of the same old addresses, all her being went
out in the desire—which her face must have expressed—that
he should recognise her forbearance to criticise as one of
the finest tenderest sacrifices a woman had ever made for
love.

XII

She was occasionally worried, however this might be,
by the impression that these sacrifices, great as they were,
were nothing to those that his own passion had imposed;
if indeed it was not rather the passion of his confederate,
which had caught him up and was whirling him round like
a great steam-wheel. He was at any rate in the strong
grip of a splendid dizzy fate; the wild wind of his life blew
him straight before it. Didn't she catch in his face at
times, even through his smile and his happy habit, the
gleam of that pale glare with which a bewildered victim
appeals, as he passes, to some pair of pitying eyes? He perhaps didn't even himself know how scared he was; but
she knew. They were in danger, they were in danger,
Captain Everard and Lady Bradeen: it beat every novel in
the shop. She thought of Mr. Mudge and his safe sentiment; she thought of herself and blushed even more for
her tepid response to it. It was a comfort to her at such
moments to feel that in another relation—a relation supplying that affinity with her nature that Mr. Mudge, deluded
creature, would never supply—she should have been no
more tepid than her ladyship. Her deepest soundings were
on two or three occasions of finding herself almost sure
that, if she dared, her ladyship's lover would have gathered
relief from "speaking" to her. She literally fancied once or
twice that, projected as he was toward his doom, her own
eyes struck him, while the air roared in his ears, as the one
pitying pair in the crowd. But how could he speak to her

while she sat sandwiched there between the counter-clerk and the sounder?

She had long ago, in her comings and goings, made acquaintance with Park Chambers and reflected as she looked up at their luxurious front that *they* of course would supply the ideal setting for the ideal speech. There was not an object in London that, before the season was over, was more stamped upon her brain. She went roundabout to pass it, for it was not on the short way; she passed on the opposite side of the street and always looked up, though it had taken her a long time to be sure of the particular set of windows. She had made that out finally by an act of audacity that at the time had almost stopped her heart-beats and that in retrospect greatly quickened her blushes. One evening she had lingered late and watched—watched for some moment when the porter, who was in uniform and often on the steps, had gone in with a visitor. Then she followed boldly, on the calculation that he would have taken the visitor up and that the hall would be free. The hall *was* free, and the electric light played over the gilded and lettered board that showed the names and numbers of the occupants of the different floors. What she wanted looked straight at her—Captain Everard was on the third. It was as if, in the immense intimacy of this, they were, for the instant and the first time, face to face outside the cage. Alas! they were face to face but a second or two: she was whirled out on the wings of a panic fear that he might just then be entering or issuing. This fear was indeed, in her shameless deflexions, never very far from her, and was mixed in the oddest way with depressions and disappointments. It was dreadful, as she trembled by, to run the risk of looking to him as if she basely hung about; and yet it was dreadful to be obliged to pass only at such moments as put an encounter out of the question.

At the horrible hour of her first coming to Cocker's he was always—it was to be hoped—snug in bed; and at the hour of her final departure he was of course—she had such things all on her fingers'-ends—dressing for dinner. We may let it pass that if she couldn't bring herself to hover till he was dressed, this was simply because such a process for such a person could only be terribly prolonged. When she went in the middle of the day to her own dinner she had too little time to do anything but go straight, though it must be added that for a real certainty she would joyously have omitted the repast. She had made up her mind as to there being on the whole no decent pretext to justify her flitting casually past at three o'clock in the morning. That was the hour at which, if the ha'penny novels were not all wrong, he probably came home for the night. She was therefore reduced to the vainest figuration of the miraculous meeting toward which a hundred impossibilities would have to conspire. But if nothing was more impossible than the fact, nothing was more intense than the vision. What may not, we can only moralise, take place in the quickened muffled perception of a young person with an ardent soul? All our humble friend's native distinction, her refinement of personal grain, of heredity, of pride, took refuge in this small throbbing spot; for when she was most conscious of the abjection of her vanity and the pitifulness of her little flutters and manœuvres, then the consolation and the redemption were most sure to glow before her in some just discernible sign. He did like her!

XIII

He never brought Cissy back, but Cissy came one day without him, as fresh as before from the hands of Marguerite, or only, at the season's end, a trifle less fresh. She was, however, distinctly less serene. She had brought nothing with her and looked about with impatience for the forms and the place to write. The latter convenience, at Cocker's, was obscure and barely adequate, and her clear voice had the light note of disgust which her lover's never showed as she responded with a "There?" of surprise to the gesture made by the counter-clerk in answer to her sharp question. Our young friend was busy with half a dozen people, but she had dispatched them in her most business-like manner by the time her ladyship flung through the bars this light of re-appearance. Then the directness with which the girl managed to receive the accompanying missive was the result of the concentration that had caused her to make the stamps fly during the few minutes occupied by the production of it. This concentration, in turn, may be described as the effect of the apprehension of imminent relief. It was nineteen days, counted and checked off, since she had seen the object of her homage; and as, had he been in London, she should, with his habits, have been sure to see him often, she was now about to learn what other spot his presence might just then happen to sanctify. For she thought of them, the other spots, as ecstatically conscious of it, expressively happy in it.

But, gracious, how handsome *was* her ladyship, and what an added price it gave him that the air of intimacy he threw out should have flowed originally from such a source! The girl looked straight through the cage at the eyes and lips that must so often have been so near his own—looked at them with a strange passion that for an instant had the result of filling out some of the gaps, supplying the missing answers, in his correspondence. Then as she made out that the features she thus scanned and associated were totally unaware of it, that they glowed only with the colour of quite other and not at all guessable thoughts, this directly added to their splendour, gave the girl the sharpest impression she had yet received of the uplifted, the unattainable plains of heaven, and yet at the same time caused her to thrill with a sense of the high company she did somehow keep. She was with the absent through her ladyship and with her ladyship through the absent. The only pang—but it didn't matter—was the proof in the admirable face, in the sightless preoccupation of its possessor, that the latter hadn't a notion of her. Her folly had gone to the point of half-believing that the other party to the affair must sometimes mention in Eaton Square the extraordinary little person at the place from which he so often wired. Yet the perception of her visitor's blankness actually helped this extraordinary little person, the next instant, to take refuge in a reflexion that could be as proud as it liked. "How little she knows, how little she knows!" the girl cried to herself; for what did that show after all but that Captain Everard's telegraphic confidant was Captain Everard's charming se-

cret? Our young friend's perusal of her ladyship's telegram
was literally prolonged by a momentary daze: what swam
between her and the words, making her see them as
through rippled shallow sun-shot water, was the great, the
perpetual flood of "How much *I* know—how much *I* know!"
This produced a delay in her catching that, on the face,
these words didn't give her what she wanted, though she
was prompt enough with her remembrance that her grasp
was, half the time, just of what was *not* on the face. "Miss
Dolman, Parade Lodge, Parade Terrace, Dover. Let him
instantly know right one, Hôtel de France, Ostend. Make
it seven nine four nine six one. Wire me alternative Burfield's."

The girl slowly counted. Then he was at Ostend. This
hooked on with so sharp a click that, not to feel she was
as quickly letting it all slip from her, she had absolutely to
hold it a minute longer and to do something to that end.
Thus it was that she did on this occasion what she never
did—threw off a "Reply paid?" that sounded officious, but
that she partly made up for by deliberately affixing the
stamps and by waiting till she had done so to give change.
She had, for so much coolness, the strength that she considered she knew all about Miss Dolman.

"Yes—paid." She saw all sorts of things in this reply, even
to a small suppressed start of surprise at so correct an assumption; even to an attempt the next minute at a fresh
air of detachment. "How much, with the answer?" The
calculation was not abstruse, but our intense observer required a moment more to make it, and this gave her ladyship time for a second thought. "Oh just wait!" The white
begemmed hand bared to write rose in sudden nervousness
to the side of the wonderful face which, with eyes of anxiety for the paper on the counter, she brought closer to the
bars of the cage. "I think I must alter a word!" On this
she recovered her telegram and looked over it again; but
she had a new, an obvious trouble, and studied it without
deciding and with much of the effect of making our young
woman watch her.

This personage meanwhile, at the sight of her expression,
had decided on the spot. If she had always been sure they

were in danger her ladyship's expression was the best possible sign of it. There was a word wrong, but she had lost the right one, and much clearly depended on her finding it again. The girl therefore, sufficiently estimating the affluence of customers and the distraction of Mr. Buckton and the counter-clerk, took the jump and gave it. "Isn't it Cooper's?"

It was as if she had bodily leaped—cleared the top of the cage and alighted on her interlocutress. "Cooper's?"—the stare was heightened by a blush. Yes, she had made Juno blush.

This was all the greater reason for going on. "I mean instead of Burfield's."

Our young friend fairly pitied her; she had made her in an instant so helpless, and yet not a bit haughty nor outraged. She was only mystified and scared. "Oh you know—?"

"Yes, I know!" Our young friend smiled, meeting the other's eyes, and, having made Juno blush, proceeded to patronise her. "*I'll* do it"—she put out a competent hand. Her ladyship only submitted, confused and bewildered, all presence of mind quite gone; and the next moment the telegram was in the cage again and its author out of the shop. Then quickly, boldly, under all the eyes that might have witnessed her tampering, the extraordinary little person at Cocker's made the proper change. People were really too giddy, and if they *were*, in a certain case, to be caught, it shouldn't be the fault of her own grand memory. Hadn't it been settled weeks before?—for Miss Dolman it was always to be "Cooper's."

XIV

But the summer "holidays" brought a marked difference; they were holidays for almost every one but the animals in the cage. The August days were flat and dry, and, with so little to feed it, she was conscious of the ebb of her interest in the secrets of the refined. She was in a position to follow the refined to the extent of knowing—they had made so many of their arrangements with her aid—

exactly where they were; yet she felt quite as if the panorama had ceased unrolling and the band stopped playing.
A stray member of the latter occasionally turned up, but
the communications that passed before her bore now
largely on rooms at hotels, prices of furnished houses, hours
of trains, dates of sailings and arrangements for being
"met": she found them for the most part prosaic and coarse.
The only thing was that they brought into her stuffy corner
as straight a whiff of Alpine meadows and Scotch moors
as she might hope ever to inhale; there were moreover in
especial fat hot dull ladies who had out with her, to exasperation, the terms for seaside lodgings, which struck her
as huge, and the matter of the number of beds required,
which was not less portentous: this in reference to places
of which the names—Eastbourne, Folkestone, Cromer, Scar-
borough, Whitby—tormented her with something of the
sound of the plash of water that haunts the traveller in the
desert. She had not been out of London for a dozen years,
and the only thing to give a taste to the present dead weeks
was the spice of a chronic resentment. The sparse customers, the people she did see, were the people who were "just
off"—off on the decks of fluttered yachts, off to the uttermost
point of rocky headlands where the very breeze was then
playing for the want of which she said to herself that she
sickened.

There was accordingly a sense in which, at such a period,
the great differences of the human condition could press
upon her more than ever; a circumstance drawing fresh
force in truth from the very fact of the chance that at last,
for a change, did squarely meet her—the chance to be
"off," for a bit, almost as far as anybody. They took their
turns in the cage as they took them both in the shop and
at Chalk Farm; she had known these two months that time
was to be allowed in September—no less than eleven days—
for her personal private holiday. Much of her recent intercourse with Mr. Mudge had consisted of the hopes and
fears, expressed mainly by himself, involved in the question
of their getting the same dates—a question that, in proportion as the delight seemed assured, spread into a sea of
speculation over the choice of where and how. All through

July, on the Sunday evenings and at such other odd times as he could seize, he had flooded their talk with wild waves of calculation. It was practically settled that, with her mother, somewhere "on the south coast" (a phrase of which she liked the sound) they should put in their allowance together; but she already felt the prospect quite weary and worn with the way he went round and round on it. It had become his sole topic, the theme alike of his most solemn prudences and most placid jests, to which every opening led for return and revision and in which every little flower of a foretaste was pulled up as soon as planted. He had announced at the earliest day—characterising the whole business, from that moment, as their "plans," under which name he handled it as a Syndicate handles a Chinese or other Loan—he had promptly declared that the question must be thoroughly studied, and he produced, on the whole subject, from day to day, an amount of information that excited her wonder and even, not a little, as she frankly let him know, her disdain. When she thought of the danger in which another pair of lovers rapturously lived she enquired of him anew why he could leave nothing to chance. Then she got for answer that this profundity was just his pride, and he pitted Ramsgate against Bournemouth and even Boulogne against Jersey—for he had great ideas—with all the mastery of detail that was some day, professionally, to carry him far.

The longer the time since she had seen Captain Everard the more she was booked, as she called it, to pass Park Chambers; and this was the sole amusement that in the lingering August days and the twilights sadly drawn out it was left her to cultivate. She had long since learned to know it for a feeble one, though its feebleness was perhaps scarce the reason for her saying to herself each evening as her time for departure approached: "No, no—not to-night." She never failed of that silent remark, any more than she failed of feeling, in some deeper place than she had even yet fully sounded, that one's remarks were as weak as straws and that, however one might indulge in them at eight o'clock, one's fate infallibly declared itself in absolute indifference to them at about eight-fifteen. Remarks were remarks, and very well for that; but fate was fate, and this young lady's was to pass Park Chambers every night in the working week. Out of the immensity of her knowledge of the life of the world there bloomed on these occasions a specific remembrance that it was regarded in that region, in August and September, as rather pleasant just to be caught for something or other in passing through town. Somebody was always passing and somebody might catch somebody else. It was in full cognisance of this subtle law that she adhered to the most ridiculous circuit she could have made to get home. One warm dull featureless Friday, when an accident had made her start from Cocker's a little later than usual, she became aware that something of which the infinite possibilities had for so long peopled her dreams was at last prodigiously upon her, though the per-fection in which the conditions happened to present it was almost rich enough to be but the positive creation of a dream. She saw, straight before her, like a vista painted in a picture, the empty street and the lamps that burned pale in the dusk not yet established. It was into the convenience of this quiet twilight that a gentleman on the doorstep of the Chambers gazed with a vagueness that our young lady's little figure violently trembled, in the approach, with the measure of its power to dissipate. Everything indeed grew in a flash terrific and distinct; her old uncertainties fell away from her, and, since she was so familiar with fate, she felt as if the very nail that fixed it were driven in by the hard look with which, for a moment, Captain Everard awaited her.

The vestibule was open behind him and the porter as absent as on the day she had peeped in; he had just come out—was in town, in a tweed suit and a pot-hat, but be-tween two journeys—duly bored over his evening and at a loss what to do with it. Then it was that she was glad she had never met him in that way before: she reaped with such ecstasy the benefit of his not being able to think she passed often. She jumped in two seconds to the determina-tion that he should even suppose it to be the very first time and the very oddest chance: this was while she still won-dered if he would identify or notice her. His original attention had not, she instinctively knew, been for the young woman at Cocker's; it had only been for any young woman who might advance to the tune of her not troubling the quiet air, and in fact the poetic hour, with ugliness. Ah but then, and just as she had reached the door, came his second observation, a long light reach with which, visibly and quite amusedly, he recalled and placed her. They were on different sides, but the street, narrow and still, had only made more of a stage for the small momentary drama. It was not over, besides, it was far from over, even on his sending across the way, with the pleasantest laugh she had ever heard, a little lift of his hat and an "Oh good-evening!" It was still less over on their meeting, the next minute, though rather indirectly and awkwardly, in the middle of the road—a situation to which three or four steps of her own had unmistakeably contributed—and then passing not again to the side on which she had arrived, but back toward the portal of Park Chambers.

"I didn't know you at first. Are you taking a walk?"

"Ah I don't take walks at night! I'm going home after my work."

"Oh!"

That was practically what they had meanwhile smiled out, and his exclamation to which for a minute he appeared to have nothing to add, left them face to face and in just such an attitude as, for his part, he might have worn had he been wondering if he could properly ask her to come in. During this interval in fact she really felt his question to be just *"How* properly—?" It was simply a question of the degree of properness.

XV

She never knew afterwards quite what she had done to settle it, and at the time she only knew that they presently moved, with vagueness, yet with continuity, away from the picture of the lighted vestibule and the quiet stairs and well up the street together. This also must have been in the absence of a definite permission, of anything vulgarly articulate, for that matter, on the part of either; and it was

to be, later on, a thing of remembrance and reflexion for
her that the limit of what just here for a longish minute
passed between them was his taking in her thoroughly
successful deprecation, though conveyed without pride or
sound or touch, of the idea that she might be, out of the
cage, the very shopgirl at large that she hugged the theory
she wasn't. Yes, it was strange, she afterwards thought,
that so much could have come and gone and yet not disfigured the dear little intense crisis either with impertinence
or with resentment, with any of the horrid notes of that
kind of acquaintance. He had taken no liberty, as she would
have called it; and, through not having to betray the sense
of one, she herself had, still more charmingly, taken none.
On the spot, nevertheless, she could speculate as to what
it meant that, if his relation with Lady Bradeen continued
to be what her mind had built it up to, he should feel free
to proceed with marked independence. This was one of
the questions he was to leave her to deal with—the question
whether people of his sort still asked girls up to their rooms
when they were so awfully in love with other women.
Could people of his sort do that without what people of
her sort would call being "false to their love"? She had already a vision of how the true answer was that people of
her sort didn't, in such cases, matter—didn't count as infidelity, counted only as something else: she might have
been curious, since it came to that, to see exactly as what.

Strolling together slowly in their summer twilight and
their empty corner of Mayfair, they found themselves
emerge at last opposite to one of the smaller gates of the
Park; upon which, without àny particular word about it—
they were talking so of other things—they crossed the street
and went in and sat down on a bench. She had gathered
by this time one magnificent hope about him—the hope he
would say nothing vulgar. She knew thoroughly what she
meant by that; she meant something quite apart from any
matter of his being "false." Their bench was not far within;
it was near the Park Lane paling and the patchy lamplight
and the rumbling cabs and buses. A strange emotion had
come to her, and she felt indeed excitement within excitement; above all a conscious joy in testing him with chances

he didn't take. She had an intense desire he should know the type she really conformed to without her doing anything so low as tell him, and he had surely begun to know it from the moment he didn't seize the opportunities into which a common man would promptly have blundered. These were on the mere awkward surface, and *their* relation was beautiful behind and below them. She had questioned so little on the way what they might be doing that as soon as they were seated she took straight hold of it. Her hours, her confinement, the many conditions of service in the post-office, had—with a glance at his own postal resources and alternatives—formed, up to this stage, the subject of their talk. "Well, here we are, and it may be right enough; but this isn't the least, you know, where I was going."

"You were going home?"

"Yes, and I was already rather late. I was going to my supper."

"You haven't had it?"

"No indeed!"

"Then you haven't eaten—?"

He looked of a sudden so extravagantly concerned that she laughed out. "All day? Yes, we do feed once. But that was long ago. So I must presently say good-bye."

"Oh deary *me!*" he exclaimed with an intonation so droll and yet a touch so light and a distress so marked—a confession of helplessness for such a case, in short, so unrelieved—that she at once felt sure she had made the great difference plain. He looked at her with the kindest eyes and still without saying what she had known he wouldn't. She had known he wouldn't say "Then sup with *me!*" but the proof of it made her feel as if she had feasted.

"I'm not a bit hungry," she went on.

"Ah you *must* be, awfully!" he made answer, but settling himself on the bench as if, after all, that needn't interfere with his spending his evening. "I've always quite wanted the chance to thank you for the trouble you so often take for me."

"Yes, I know," she replied; uttering the words with a sense of the situation far deeper than any pretence of not fitting his allusion. She immediately felt him surprised and even a little puzzled at her frank assent; but for herself the trouble she had taken could only, in these fleeting minutes —they would probably never come back—be all there like a little hoard of gold in her lap. Certainly he might look at it, handle it, take up the pieces. Yet if he understood anything he must understand all. "I consider you've already immensely thanked me." The horror was back upon her of having seemed to hang about for some reward. "It's awfully odd you should have been there just the one time—!"

"The one time you've passed my place?"

"Yes; you can fancy I haven't many minutes to waste. There was a place to-night I had to stop at."

"I see, I see"—he knew already so much about her work. "It must be an awful grind—for a lady."

"It is, but I don't think I groan over it any more than my companions—and you've seen *they're* not ladies!" She mildly jested, but with an intention. "One gets used to things, and there are employments I should have hated much more." She had the finest conception of the beauty of not at least boring him. To whine, to count up her wrongs, was what a barmaid or a shopgirl would do, and it was quite enough to sit there like one of these.

"If you had had another employment," he remarked after a moment, "we might never have become acquainted."

"It's highly probable—and certainly not in the same way." Then, still with her heap of gold in her lap and something of the pride of it in her manner of holding her head, she continued not to move—she only smiled at him. The evening had thickened now; the scattered lamps were red; the Park, all before them, was full of obscure and ambiguous life; there were other couples on other benches whom it was impossible not to see, yet at whom it was impossible to look. "But I've walked so much out of my way with you only just to show you that—that"—with this she paused; it was not after all so easy to express—"that anything you may have thought is perfectly true."

"Oh I've thought a tremendous lot!" her companion laughed. "Do you mind my smoking?"

"Why should I? You always smoke *there*."

"At your place? Oh yes, but here it's different."

"No," she said as he lighted a cigarette, "that's just what it isn't. It's quite the same."

"Well then, that's because 'there' it's so wonderful!"

"Then you're conscious of how wonderful it is?" she returned.

He jerked his handsome head in literal protest at a doubt. "Why that's exactly what I mean by my gratitude for all your trouble. It has been just as if you took a particular interest." She only looked at him by way of answer in such sudden headlong embarrassment, as she was quite aware, that while she remained silent he showed himself checked by her expression. "You *have*—haven't you?—taken a particular interest?"

"Oh a particular interest!" she quavered out, feeling the whole thing—her headlong embarrassment—get terribly the better of her, and wishing, with a sudden scare, all the more to keep her emotion down. She maintained her fixed smile a moment and turned her eyes over the peopled darkness, unconfused now, because there was something much more confusing. This, with a fatal great rush, was simply the fact that they were thus together. They were near, near, and all she had imagined of that had only become more true, more dreadful and overwhelming. She stared straight away in silence till she felt she looked an idiot; then, to say something, to say nothing, she attempted a sound which ended in a flood of tears.

XVI

Her tears helped her really to dissimulate, for she had instantly, in so public a situation, to recover herself. They had come and gone in half a minute, and she immediately explained them. "It's only because I'm tired. It's that—it's that!" Then she added a trifle incoherently: "I shall never see you again."

"Ah but why not?" The mere tone in which her companion asked this satisfied her once for all as to the amount of imagination for which she could count on him. It was naturally not large: it had exhausted itself in having ar-

rived at what he had already touched upon—the sense of
an intention in her poor zeal at Cocker's. But any deficiency
of this kind was no fault in him: *he* wasn't obliged to have
an inferior cleverness—to have second-rate resources and
virtues. It had been as if he almost really believed she had
simply cried for fatigue, and he had accordingly put in
some kind confused plea—"You ought really to take something: won't you have something or other *somewhere?*"
—to which she had made no response but a headshake of
a sharpness that settled it. "Why shan't we all the more
keep meeting?"

"I mean meeting this way—only this way. At my place
there—*that* I've nothing to do with, and I hope of course
you'll turn up, with your correspondence, when it suits
you. Whether I stay or not, I mean; for I shall probably
not stay."

"You're going somewhere else?"—he put it with positive
anxiety.

"Yes, ever so far away—to the other end of London.
There are all sorts of reasons I can't tell you, and it's practically settled. It's better for me, much; and I've only kept
on at Cocker's for *you.*"

"For me?"

Making out in the dusk that he fairly blushed, she now
measured how far he had been from knowing too much.
Too much, she called it at present; and that was easy, since
it proved so abundantly enough for her that he should
simply be where he was. "As we shall never talk this way
but to-night—never, never again!—here it all is. I'll say it; I
don't care what you think; it doesn't matter; I only want to
help you. Besides, you're kind—you're kind. I've been thinking then of leaving for ever so long. But you've come so
often—at times—and you've had so much to do, and it has
been so pleasant and interesting, that I've remained, I've
kept putting off my change. More than once, when I had
nearly decided, you've turned up again and I've thought
'Oh no!' That's the simple fact!" She had by this time got
her confusion down so completely that she could laugh.
"This's what I meant when I said to you just now that I
'knew.' I've known perfectly that you knew I took trouble

for you; and that knowledge has been for me, and I seemed to see it was for you, as if there were something—I don't know what to call it!—between us. I mean something unusual and good and awfully nice—something not a bit horrid or vulgar."

She had by this time, she could see, produced a great effect on him; but she would have spoken the truth to herself had she at the same moment declared that she didn't in the least care: all the more that the effect must be one of extreme perplexity. What, in it all, was visibly clear for him, none the less, was that he was tremendously glad he had met her. She held him, and he was astonished at the force of it; he was intent, immensely considerate. His elbow was on the back of the seat, and his head, with the pot-hat pushed quite back, in a boyish way, so that she really saw almost for the first time his forehead and hair, rested on the hand into which he had crumpled his gloves. "Yes," he assented, "it's not a bit horrid or vulgar."

She just hung fire a moment, then she brought out the whole truth. "I'd do anything for you. I'd do anything for you." Never in her life had she known anything so high and fine as this, just letting him have it and bravely and magnificently leaving it. Didn't the place, the associations and circumstances, perfectly make it sound what it wasn't? and wasn't that exactly the beauty?

So she bravely and magnificently left it, and little by little she felt him take it up, take it down, as if they had been on a satin sofa in a boudoir. She had never seen a boudoir, but there had been lots of boudoirs in the telegrams. What she had said at all events sank into him, so that after a minute he simply made a movement that had the result of placing his hand on her own—presently indeed that of her feeling herself firmly enough grasped. There was no pressure she need return, there was none she need decline; she just sat admirably still, satisfied for the time with the surprise and bewilderment of the impression she made on him. His agitation was even greater on the whole than she had at first allowed for. "I say, you know, you mustn't think of leaving!" he at last broke out.

"Of leaving Cocker's, you mean?"

"Yes, you must stay on there, whatever happens, and help a fellow."

She was silent a little, partly because it was so strange and exquisite to feel him watch her as if it really mattered to him and he were almost in suspense. "Then you *have* quite recognised what I've tried to do?" she asked.

"Why, wasn't that exactly what I dashed over from my door just now to thank you for?"

"Yes; so you said."

"And don't you believe it?"

She looked down a moment at his hand, which continued to cover her own; whereupon he presently drew it back, rather restlessly folding his arms. Without answering his question she went on: "Have you ever spoken of me?"

"Spoken of you?"

"Of my being there—of my knowing, and that sort of thing."

"Oh never to a human creature!" he eagerly declared.

She had a small drop at this, which was expressed in another pause, and she then returned to what he had just asked her. "Oh yes, I quite believe you like it—my always being there and our taking things up so familiarly and successfully: if not exactly where we left them," she laughed, "almost always at least at an interesting point!" He was about to say something in reply to this, but her friendly gaiety was quicker. "You want a great many things in life, a great many comforts and helps and luxuries—you want everything as pleasant as possible. Therefore so far as it's in the power of any particular person to contribute to all that—" She had turned her face to him smiling, just thinking.

"Oh see here!" But he was highly amused. "Well, what then?" he enquired as if to humour her.

"Why the particular person must never fail. We must manage it for you somehow."

He threw back his head, laughing out; he was really exhilarated. "Oh yes, somehow!"

"Well, I think we each do—don't we?—in one little way and another and according to our limited lights. I'm pleased at any rate, for myself, that you are; for I assure you I've done my best."

"You do better than any one!" He had struck a match for another cigarette, and the flame lighted an instant his responsive finished face, magnifying into a pleasant grimace the kindness with which he paid her this tribute. "You're awfully clever, you know; cleverer, cleverer, cleverer—!" He had appeared on the point of making some tremendous statement; then suddenly, puffing his cigarette and shifting almost with violence on his seat, he let it altogether fall.

XVII

In spite of this drop, if not just by reason of it, she felt as if Lady Bradeen, all but named out, had popped straight up; and she practically betrayed her consciousness by waiting a little before she rejoined: "Cleverer than who?"

"Well, if I wasn't afraid you'd think I swagger I should say—than anybody! If you leave your place there, where shall you go?" he more gravely asked.

"Oh too far for you ever to find me!"

"I'd find you anywhere."

The tone of this was so still more serious that she had but her one acknowledgement. "I'd do anything for you— I'd do anything for you," she repeated. She had already, she felt, said it all; so what did anything more, anything less, matter? That was the very reason indeed why she could, with a lighter note, ease him generously of any awkwardness produced by solemnity, either his own or hers. "Of course it must be nice for you to be able to think there are people all about who feel in such a way."

In immediate appreciation of this, however, he only smoked without looking at her. "But you don't want to give up your present work?" he at last threw out. "I mean you *will* stay in the post-office?"

"Oh yes; I think I've a genius for that."

"Rather! No one can touch you." With this he turned more to her again. "But you can get, with a move, greater advantages?"

"I can get in the suburbs cheaper lodgings. I live with

my mother. We need some space. There's a particular place that has other inducements."

He just hesitated. "Where is it?"

"Oh quite out of *your* way. You'd never have time."

"But I tell you I'd go anywhere. Don't you believe it?"

"Yes, for once or twice. But you'd soon see it wouldn't do for you."

He smoked and considered; seemed to stretch himself a little and, with his legs out, surrender himself comfortably. "Well, well, well—I believe everything you say. I take it from you—anything you like—in the most extraordinary way." It struck her certainly—and almost without bitterness —that the way in which she was already, as if she had been an old friend, arranging for him and preparing the only magnificence she could muster, was quite the most extraordinary. "Don't, *don't* go!" he presently went on. "I shall miss you too horribly!"

"So that you just put it to me as a definite request?"— oh how she tried to divest this of all sound of the hardness of bargaining! That ought to have been easy enough, for what was she arranging to get? Before he could answer she had continued: "To be perfectly fair I should tell you I recognise at Cocker's certain strong attractions. All you people come. I like all the horrors."

"The horrors?"

"Those you all—you know the set I mean, *your* set—show me with as good a conscience as if I had no more feeling than a letter-box."

He looked quite excited at the way she put it. "Oh they don't know!"

"Don't know I'm not stupid? No, how should they?"

"Yes, how should they?" said the Captain sympathetically. "But isn't 'horrors' rather strong?"

"What you *do* is rather strong!" the girl promptly returned.

"What *I* do?"

"Your extravagance, your selfishness, your immorality, your crimes," she pursued without heeding his expression.

"I *say!*"—her companion showed the queerest stare.

"I like them, as I tell you—I revel in them. But we needn't

go into that," she quietly went on; "for all I get out of it is the harmless pleasure of knowing. I know, I know, I know!"—she breathed it ever so gently.

"Yes; that's what has been between us," he answered much more simply.

She could enjoy his simplicity in silence, and for a moment she did so. "If I do stay because you want it—and I'm rather capable of that—there are two or three things I think you ought to remember. One is, you know, that I'm there sometimes for days and weeks together without your ever coming."

"Oh I'll come every day!" he honestly cried.

She was on the point, at this, of imitating with her hand his movement of shortly before; but she checked herself, and there was no want of effect in her soothing substitute. "How can you? How can you?" He had, too manifestly, only to look at it there, in the vulgarly animated gloom, to see that he couldn't; and at this point, by the mere action of his silence, everything they had so definitely not named, the whole presence round which they had been circling, became part of their reference, settled in solidly between them. It was as if then for a minute they sat and saw it all in each other's eyes, saw so much that there was no need of a pretext for sounding it at last. "Your danger, your danger—!" Her voice indeed trembled with it, and she could only for the moment again leave it so.

During this moment he leaned back on the bench, meeting her in silence and with a face that grew more strange. It grew so strange that after a further instant she got straight up. She stood there as if their talk were now over, and he just sat and watched her. It was as if now—owing to the third person they had brought in—they must be more careful; so that the most he could finally say was: "That's where it is!"

"That's where it is!" the girl as guardedly replied. He sat still, and she added: "I won't give you up. Good-bye."

"Good-bye?"—he appealed, but without moving.

"I don't quite see my way, but I won't give you up," she repeated. "There. Good-bye."

It brought him with a jerk to his feet, tossing away his

cigarette. His poor face was flushed. "See here—see here!"

"No, I won't; but I must leave you now," she went on as if not hearing him.

"See here—see here!" He tried, from the bench, to take her hand again.

But that definitely settled it for her: this would, after all, be as bad as his asking her to supper. "You mustn't come with me—no, no!"

He sank back, quite blank, as if she had pushed him. "I mayn't see you home?"

"No, no; let me go." He looked almost as if she had struck him, but she didn't care; and the manner in which she spoke—it was literally as if she were angry—had the force of a command. "Stay where you are!"

"See here—see here!" he nevertheless pleaded.

"I won't give you up!" she cried once more—this time quite with passion; on which she got away from him as fast as she could and left him staring after her.

XVIII

Mr. Mudge had lately been so occupied with their famous "plans" that he had neglected for a while the question of her transfer; but down at Bournemouth, which had found itself selected as the field of their recreation by a process consisting, it seemed, exclusively of innumerable pages of the neatest arithmetic in a very greasy but most orderly little pocketbook, the distracting possible melted away—the fleeting absolute ruled the scene. The plans, hour by hour, were simply superseded, and it was much of a rest to the girl, as she sat on the pier and overlooked the sea and the company, to see them evaporate in rosy fumes and to feel that from moment to moment there was less left to cipher about. The week proved blissfully fine, and her mother, at their lodgings—partly to her embarrassment and partly to her relief—struck up with the landlady an alliance that left the younger couple a great deal of freedom. This relative took her pleasure of a week at Bournemouth in a stuffy back kitchen and endless talks; to that degree even that Mr. Mudge himself—habitually inclined indeed to a scrutiny of all mysteries and to seeing, as he sometimes admitted, too much in things—made remarks on it as he sat on the cliff with his betrothed, or on the decks of steamers that conveyed them, close-packed items in terrific totals of enjoyment, to the Isle of Wight and the Dorset coast.

He had a lodging in another house, where he had speedily learned the importance of keeping his eyes open, and he made no secret of his suspecting that sinister mutual connivances might spring, under the roof of his companions, from unnatural sociabilities. At the same time he fully recognised that as a source of anxiety, not to say of expense, his future mother-in-law would have weighted them more by accompanying their steps than by giving her hostess, in the interest of the tendency they considered that they never mentioned, equivalent pledges as to the tea-caddy and the jam-pot. These were the questions—these indeed the familiar commodities—that he had now to put into the scales; and his betrothed had in consequence, during her holiday, the odd and yet pleasant and almost languid sense of an anticlimax. She had become conscious of an extraordinary collapse, a surrender to stillness and to retrospect. She cared neither to walk nor to sail; it was enough for her to sit on benches and wonder at the sea and taste the air and not be at Cocker's and not see the counter-clerk. She still seemed to wait for something—something in the key of the immense discussions that had mapped out their little week of idleness on the scale of a world-atlas. Something came at last, but without perhaps appearing quite adequately to crown the monument.

Preparation and precaution were, however, the natural flowers of Mr. Mudge's mind, and in proportion as these things declined in one quarter they inevitably bloomed elsewhere. He could always, at the worst, have on Tuesday the project of their taking the Swanage boat on Thursday, and on Thursday that of their ordering minced kidneys on Saturday. He had moreover a constant gift of inexorable enquiry as to where and what they should have gone and have done if they hadn't been exactly as they were. He had in short his resources, and his mistress had never been so conscious of them; on the other hand they had never

interfered so little with her own. She liked to be as she was
—if it could only have lasted. She could accept even without bitterness a rigour of economy so great that the little
fee they paid for admission to the pier had to be bal-
anced against other delights. The people at Ladle's and at
Thrupp's had *their* ways of amusing themselves, whereas
she had to sit and hear Mr. Mudge talk of what he might
do if he didn't take a bath, or of the bath he might take if
he only hadn't taken something else. He was always with
her now, of course, always beside her; she saw him more
than "hourly," more than ever yet, more even than he had
planned she should do at Chalk Farm. She preferred to sit
at the far end, away from the band and the crowd; as to
which she had frequent differences with her friend, who
reminded her often that they could have only in the thick
of it the sense of the money they were getting back. That
had little effect on her, for she got back her money by seeing many things, the things of the past year, fall together
and connect themselves, undergo the happy relegation that
transforms melancholy and misery, passion and effort, into
experience and knowledge.

She liked having done with them, as she assured herself
she had practically done, and the strange thing was that
she neither missed the procession now nor wished to keep
her place for it. It had become there, in the sun and the
breeze and the sea-smell, a far-away story, a picture of another life. If Mr. Mudge himself liked processions, liked
them at Bournemouth and on the pier quite as much as at
Chalk Farm or anywhere, she learned after a little not to
be worried by his perpetual counting of the figures that
made them up. They were dreadful women in particular,
usually fat and in men's caps and white shoes, whom he
could never let alone—not that *she* cared; it was not
the great world, the world of Cocker's and Ladle's and
Thrupp's, but it offered an endless field to his faculties of
memory, philosophy and frolic. She had never accepted
him so much, never arranged so successfully for making
him chatter while she carried on secret conversations. This
separate commerce was with herself; and if they both
practised a great thrift she had quite mastered that of

merely spending words enough to keep him imperturbably and continuously going.

He was charmed with the panorama, not knowing—or at any rate not at all showing that he knew—what far other images peopled her mind than the women in the navy caps and the shopboys in the blazers. His observations on these types, his general interpretation of the show, brought home to her the prospect of Chalk Farm. She wondered sometimes that he should have derived so little illumination, during his period, from the society at Cocker's. But one evening while their holiday cloudlessly waned he gave her such a proof of his quality as might have made her ashamed of her many suppressions. He brought out something that, in all his overflow, he had been able to keep back till other matters were disposed of. It was the announcement that he was at last ready to marry—that he saw his way. A rise at Chalk Farm had been offered him; he was to be taken into the business, bringing with him a capital the estimation of which by other parties constituted the handsomest recognition yet made of the head on his shoulders. Therefore their waiting was over—it could be a question of a near date. They would settle this date before going back, and he meanwhile had his eye on a sweet little home. He would take her to see it on their first Sunday.

XIX

His having kept this great news for the last, having had such a card up his sleeve and not floated it out in the current of his chatter and the luxury of their leisure, was one of those incalculable strokes by which he could still affect her; the kind of thing that reminded her of the latent force that had ejected the drunken soldier—an example of the profundity of which his promotion was the proof. She listened a while in silence, on this occasion, to the wafted strains of the music; she took it in as she had not quite done before that her future was now constituted. Mr. Mudge was distinctly her fate; yet at this moment she turned her face quite away from him, showing him so long a mere quarter of her cheek that she at last again heard his voice. He

couldn't see a pair of tears that were partly the reason of
her delay to give him the assurance he required; but he
expressed at a venture the hope that she had had her fill
of Cocker's.

She was finally able to turn back. "Oh quite. There's
nothing going on. No one comes but the Americans at
Thrupp's, and *they* don't do much. They don't seem to have
a secret in the world."

"Then the extraordinary reason you've been giving me
for holding on there has ceased to work?"

She thought a moment. "Yes, that one. I've seen the thing
through—I've got them all in my pocket."

"So you're ready to come?"

For a little again she made no answer. "No, not yet, all
the same. I've still got a reason—a different one."

He looked her all over as if it might have been something she kept in her mouth or her glove or under her jacket
—something she was even sitting upon. "Well I'll have it,
please."

"I went out the other night and sat in the Park with a
gentleman," she said at last.

Nothing was ever seen like his confidence in her; and she
wondered a little now why it didn't irritate her. It only gave
her ease and space, as she felt, for telling him the whole
truth that no one knew. It had arrived at present at her
really wanting to do that, and yet to do it not in the least
for Mr. Mudge, but altogether and only for herself. This
truth filled out for her there the whole experience she was
about to relinquish, suffused and coloured it as a picture
that she should keep and that, describe it as she might, no
one but herself would ever really see. Moreover she had no
desire whatever to make Mr. Mudge jealous; there would
be no amusement in it, for the amusement she had lately
known had spoiled her for lower pleasures. There were even
no materials for it. The odd thing was how she never
doubted that, properly handled, his passion was poisonable;
what had happened was that he had cannily selected a
partner with no poison to distil. She read then and there
that she should never interest herself in anybody as to
whom some other sentiment, some superior view, wouldn't

be sure to interfere for him with jealousy. "And what did you get out of that?" he asked with a concern that was not in the least for his honour.

"Nothing but a good chance to promise him I wouldn't forsake him. He's one of my customers."

"Then it's for him not to forsake *you*."

"Well, he won't. It's all right. But I must just keep on as long as he may want me."

"Want you to sit with him in the Park?"

"He may want me for that—but I shan't. I rather liked it, but once, under the circumstances, is enough. I can do better for him in another manner."

"And what manner, pray?"

"Well, elsewhere."

"Elsewhere?—I *say!*"

This was an ejaculation used also by Captain Everard, but oh with what a different sound! "You needn't 'say'— there's nothing to be said. And yet you ought perhaps to know."

"Certainly I ought. But *what*—up to now?"

"Why exactly what I told him. That I'd do anything for him."

"What do you mean by 'anything'?"

"Everything."

Mr. Mudge's immediate comment on this statement was to draw from his pocket a crumpled paper containing the remains of half a pound of "sundries." These sundries had figured conspicuously in his prospective sketch of their tour, but it was only at the end of three days that they had defined themselves unmistakeably as chocolate-creams. "Have another?—*that* one," he said. She had another, but not the one he indicated, and then he continued: "What took place afterwards?"

"Afterwards?"

"What did you do when you had told him you'd do everything?"

"I simply came away."

"Out of the Park?"

"Yes, leaving him there. I didn't let him follow me."

"Then what did you let him do?"

"I didn't let him do anything."

Mr. Mudge considered an instant. "Then what did you go there for?" His tone was even slightly critical.

"I didn't quite know at the time. It was simply to be with him, I suppose—just once. He's in danger, and I wanted him to know I know it. It makes meeting him—at Cocker's, since it's that I want to stay on for—more interesting."

"It makes it mighty interesting for *me!*" Mr. Mudge freely declared. "Yet he didn't follow you?" he asked. "*I* would!"

"Yes, of course. That was the way you began, you know. You're awfully inferior to him."

"Well, my dear, you're not inferior to anybody. You've got a cheek! What's he in danger of?"

"Of being found out. He's in love with a lady—and it isn't right—and *I've* found him out."

"That'll be a lookout for *me!*" Mr. Mudge joked. "You mean she has a husband?"

"Never mind what she has! They're in awful danger, but his is the worst, because he's in danger from her too."

"Like me from you—the woman *I* love? If he's in the same funk as me—"

"He's in a worse one. He's not only afraid of the lady—he's afraid of other things."

Mr. Mudge selected another chocolate-cream. "Well, I'm only afraid of one! But how in the world can you help this party?"

"I don't know—perhaps not at all. But so long as there's a chance—!"

"You won't come away?"

"No, you've got to wait for me."

Mr. Mudge enjoyed what was in his mouth. "And what will he give you?"

"Give me?"

"If you do help him."

"Nothing. Nothing in all the wide world."

"Then what will he give *me?*" Mr. Mudge enquired. "I mean for waiting."

The girl thought a moment, then she got up to walk. "He never heard of you," she replied.

"You haven't mentioned me?"

"We never mention anything. What I've told you is just what I've found out."

Mr. Mudge, who had remained on the bench, looked up at her; she often preferred to be quiet when he proposed to walk, but now that he seemed to wish to sit she had a desire to move. "But you haven't told me what *he* has found out."

She considered her lover. "He'd never find *you*, my dear!"

Her lover, still on his seat, appealed to her in something of the attitude in which she had last left Captain Everard, but the impression was not the same. "Then where do I come in?"

"You don't come in at all. That's just the beauty of it!"— and with this she turned to mingle with the multitude collected round the band. Mr. Mudge presently overtook her and drew her arm into his own with a quiet force that expressed the serenity of possession; in consonance with which it was only when they parted for the night at her door that he referred again to what she had told him.

"Have you seen him since?"

"Since the night in the Park? No, not once."

"Oh what a cad!" said Mr. Mudge.

XX

It was not till the end of October that she saw Captain Everard again, and on that occasion—the only one of all the series on which hindrance had been so utter—no communication with him proved possible. She had made out even from the cage that it was a charming golden day: a patch of hazy autumn sunlight lay across the sanded floor and also, higher up, quickened into brightness a row of ruddy bottled syrups. Work was slack and the place in general empty; the town, as they said in the cage, had not waked up, and the feeling of the day likened itself to something that in happier conditions she would have thought of romantically as Saint Martin's summer. The counter-clerk had gone to his dinner; she herself was busy with arrears of postal jobs, in the midst of which she became aware that

Captain Everard had apparently been in the shop a minute and that Mr. Buckton had already seized him.

He had as usual half a dozen telegrams; and when he
saw that she saw him and their eyes met he gave, on bow-
ing to her, an exaggerated laugh in which she read a
new consciousness. It was a confession of awkwardness; it
seemed to tell her that of course he knew he ought better
to have kept his head, ought to have been clever enough
to wait, on some pretext, till he should have found her free.
Mr. Buckton was a long time with him, and her attention
was soon demanded by other visitors; so that nothing
passed between them but the fulness of their silence. The
look she took from him was his greeting, and the other one
a simple sign of the eyes sent her before going out. The only
token they exchanged therefore was his tacit assent to her
wish that since they couldn't attempt a certain frankness
they should attempt nothing at all. This was her intense
preference; she could be as still and cold as any one when
that was the sole solution.

Yet more than any contact hitherto achieved these
counted instants struck her as marking a step: they were
built so—just in the mere flash—on the recognition of his
now definitely knowing what it was she would do for him.
The "anything, anything" she had uttered in the Park went
to and fro between them and under the poked-out chins
that interposed. It had all at last even put on the air of their
not needing now clumsily to manœuvre to converse: their
former little postal make-believes, the intense implications
of questions and answers and change, had become in the
light of the personal fact, of their having had their moment,
a possibility comparatively poor. It was as if they had met
for all time—it exerted on their being in presence again an
influence so prodigious. When she watched herself, in the
memory of that night, walk away from him as if she were
making an end, she found something too pitiful in the prim-
ness of such a gait. Hadn't she precisely established on the
part of each a consciousness that could end only with death?

It must be admitted that in spite of this brave margin
an irritation, after he had gone, remained with her; a sense
that presently became one with a still sharper hatred of Mr.

Buckton, who, on her friend's withdrawal, had retired with
the telegrams to the sounder and left her the other work.
She knew indeed she should have a chance to see them,
when she would, on file; and she was divided, as the day
went on, between the two impressions of all that was lost
and all that was re-asserted. What beset her above all, and
as she had almost never known it before, was the desire to
bound straight out, to overtake the autumn afternoon before
it passed away for ever and hurry off to the Park and perhaps be with him there again on a bench. It became for
an hour a fantastic vision with her that he might just have
gone to sit and wait for her. She could almost hear him,
through the tick of the sounder, scatter with his stick, in
his impatience, the fallen leaves of October. Why should
such a vision seize her at this particular moment with such
a shake? There was a time—from four to five—when she
could have cried with happiness and rage.

Business quickened, it seemed, toward five, as if the town
did wake up; she had therefore more to do, and she went
through it with little sharp stampings and jerkings: she
made the crisp postal-orders fairly snap while she breathed
to herself "It's the last day—the last day!" The last day of
what? She couldn't have told. All she knew now was that
if she *were* out of the cage she wouldn't in the least have
minded, this time, its not yet being dark. She would have
gone straight toward Park Chambers and have hung about
there till no matter when. She would have waited, stayed,
rung, asked, have gone in, sat on the stairs. What the day
was the last of was probably, to her strained inner sense,
the group of golden ones, of any occasion for seeing the
hazy sunshine slant at that angle into the smelly shop, of
any range of chances for his wishing still to repeat to her
the two words she had in the Park scarcely let him bring
out. "See here—see here!"—the sound of these two words
had been with her perpetually; but it was in her ears to-
day without mercy, with a loudness that grew and grew.
What was it they then expressed? what was it he had
wanted her to see? She seemed, whatever it was, perfectly
to see it now—to see that if she should just chuck the whole
thing, should have a great and beautiful courage, he would

somehow make everything up to her. When the clock struck five she was on the very point of saying to Mr. Buckton that she was deadly ill and rapidly getting worse. This announcement was on her lips and she had quite composed the pale hard face she would offer him: "I can't stop—I must go home. If I feel better, later on, I'll come back. I'm very sorry, but I *must* go." At that instant Captain Everard once more stood there, producing in her agitated spirit, by his real presence, the strangest, quickest revolution. He stopped her off without knowing it, and by the time he had been a minute in the shop she felt herself saved.

That was from the first minute how she thought of it. There were again other persons with whom she was occupied, and again the situation could only be expressed by their silence. It was expressed, of a truth, in a larger phrase than ever yet, for her eyes now spoke to him with a kind of supplication. "Be quiet, be quiet!" they pleaded; and they saw his own reply: "I'll do whatever you say; I won't even look at you—see, see!" They kept conveying thus, with the friendliest liberality, that they wouldn't look, quite positively wouldn't. What she was to see was that he hovered at the other end of the counter, Mr. Buckton's end, and surrendered himself again to that frustration. It quickly proved so great indeed that what she was to see further was how he turned away before he was attended to, and hung off, waiting, smoking, looking about the shop; how he went over to Mr. Cocker's own counter and appeared to price things, gave in fact presently two or three orders and put down money, stood there a long time with his back to her, considerately abstaining from any glance round to see if she were free. It at last came to pass in this way that he had remained in the shop longer than she had ever yet known him to do, and that, nevertheless, when he did turn about she could see him time himself—she was freshly taken up—and cross straight to her postal subordinate, whom some one else had released. He had in his hand all this while neither letters nor telegrams, and now that he was close to her—for she was close to the counter-clerk— it brought her heart into her mouth merely to see him look at her neighbour and open his lips. She was too nervous to bear it. He asked for a Post-Office Guide, and the young man whipped out a new one; whereupon he said he wished not to purchase, but only to consult one a moment; with which, the copy kept on loan being produced, he once more wandered off.

What was he doing to her? What did he want of her? Well, it was just the aggravation of his "See here!" She felt at this moment strangely and portentously afraid of him—had in her ears the hum of a sense that, should it come to that kind of tension, she must fly on the spot to Chalk Farm. Mixed with her dread and with her reflexion was the idea that, if he wanted her so much as he seemed to show, it might be after all simply to do for him the "anything" she had promised, the "everything" she had thought it so fine to bring out to Mr. Mudge. He might want her to help him, might have some particular appeal; though indeed his manner didn't denote that—denoted on the contrary an embarrassment, an indecision, something of a desire not so much to be helped as to be treated rather more nicely than she had treated him the other time. Yes, he considered quite probably that he had help rather to offer than to ask for. Still, none the less, when he again saw her free he continued to keep away from her; when he came back with his thumbed "Guide" it was Mr. Buckton he caught —it was from Mr. Buckton he obtained half-a-crown's-worth of stamps.

After asking for the stamps he asked, quite as a second thought, for a postal-order for ten shillings. What did he want with so many stamps when he wrote so few letters? How could he enclose a postal-order in a telegram? She expected him, the next thing, to go into the corner and make up one of his telegrams—half a dozen of them—on purpose to prolong his presence. She had so completely stopped looking at him that she could only guess his movements—guess even where his eyes rested. Finally she saw him make a dash that might have been toward the nook where the forms were hung; and at this she suddenly felt that she couldn't keep it up. The counter-clerk had just taken a telegram from a slavey, and, to give herself something to cover her, she snatched it out of his hand. The gesture was so violent that he gave her in return an odd look, and she also perceived that Mr. Buckton noticed it. The latter personage, with a quick stare at her, appeared for an instant to wonder whether his snatching it in *his* turn mightn't be the thing she would least like, and she antici-pated this practical criticism by the frankest glare she had ever given him. It sufficed: this time it paralysed him, and she sought with her trophy the refuge of the sounder.

XXI

It was repeated the next day; it went on for three days; and at the end of that time she knew what to think. When, at the beginning, she had emerged from her temporary shelter Captain Everard had quitted the shop; and he had not come again that evening, as it had struck her he pos-sibly might—might all the more easily that there were num-berless persons who came, morning and afternoon, number-less times, so that he wouldn't necessarily have attracted attention. The second day it was different and yet on the whole worse. His access to her had become possible—she felt herself even reaping the fruit of her yesterday's glare at Mr. Buckton; but transacting his business with him didn't simplify—it could, in spite of the rigour of circum-stance, feed so her new conviction. The rigour was tremen-dous, and his telegrams—not now mere pretexts for getting at her—were apparently genuine; yet the conviction had taken but a night to develop. It could be simply enough expressed; she had had the glimmer of it the day before in her idea that he needed no more help than she had al-ready given; that it was help he himself was prepared to render. He had come up to town but for three or four days; he had been absolutely obliged to be absent after the other time; yet he would, now that he was face to face with her, stay on as much longer as she liked. Little by little it was thus clarified, though from the first flash of his re-appear-ance she had read into it the real essence.

That was what the night before, at eight o'clock, her hour to go, had made her hang back and dawdle. She did last things or pretended to do them; to be in the cage had suddenly become her safety, and she was literally afraid of the alternate self who might be waiting outside. *He* might be waiting; it was he who was her alternate self, and of him she was afraid. The most extraordinary change had taken place in her from the moment of her catching the impression he seemed to have returned on purpose to give her. Just before she had done so, on that bewitched afternoon, she had seen herself approach without a scruple the porter at Park Chambers; then as the effect of the rush of a consciousness quite altered she had, on at last quitting Cocker's, gone straight home for the first time since her return from Bournemouth. She had passed his door every night for weeks, but nothing would have induced her to pass it now. This change was the tribute of her fear—the result of a change in himself as to which she needed no more explanation than his mere face vividly gave her; strange though it was to find an element of deterrence in the object that she regarded as the most beautiful in the world. He had taken it from her in the Park that night that she wanted him not to propose to her to sup; but he had put away the lesson by this time—he practically proposed supper every time he looked at her. This was what, for that matter, mainly filled the three days. He came in twice on each of these, and it was as if he came in to give her a chance to relent. That was after all, she said to herself in the intervals, the most that he did. There were ways, she fully recognised, in which he spared her, and other particular ways as to which she meant that her silence should be full to him of exquisite pleading. The most particular of all was his not being outside, at the corner, when she quitted the place for the night. This he might so easily have been—so easily if he hadn't been so nice. She continued to recognise in his forbearance the fruit of her dumb supplication, and the only compensation he found for it was the harmless freedom of being able to appear to say: "Yes, I'm in town only for three or four days, but, you know, I *would* stay on." He struck her as calling attention each day, each hour, to the rapid ebb of time; he exaggerated to the point of putting it that there were only two days more, that there was at last, dreadfully, only one.

There were other things still that he struck her as doing with a special intention; as to the most marked of which—unless indeed it were the most obscure—she might well have marvelled that it didn't seem to her more horrid. It was either the frenzy of her imagination or the disorder of his baffled passion that gave her once or twice the vision of his putting down redundant money—sovereigns not concerned with the little payments he was perpetually making—so that she might give him some sign of helping him to slip them over to her. What was most extraordinary in this impression was the amount of excuse that, with some incoherence, she found for him. He wanted to pay her because there was nothing to pay her for. He wanted to offer her things he knew she wouldn't take. He wanted to show her how much he respected her by giving her the supreme chance to show *him* she was respectable. Over the dryest transactions, at any rate, their eyes had out these questions. On the third day he put in a telegram that had evidently something of the same point as the stray sovereigns—a message that was in the first place concocted and that on a second thought he took back from her before she had stamped it. He had given her time to read it and had only then bethought himself that he had better not send it. If it was not to Lady Bradeen at Twindle—where she knew her ladyship then to be—this was because an address to Doctor Buzzard at Brickwood was just as good, with the added merit of its not giving away quite so much a person whom he had still, after all, in a manner to consider. It was of course most complicated, only half-lighted; but there was, discernibly enough, a scheme of communication in which Lady Bradeen at Twindle and Dr. Buzzard at Brickwood were, within limits, one and the same person. The words he had shown her and then taken back consisted, at all events, of the brief but vivid phrase "Absolutely impossible." The point was not that she should transmit it; the point was just that she should see it. What was absolutely impossible was that before he had settled something at Cocker's he should go either to Twindle or to Brickwood.

The logic of this, in turn, for herself, was that she could lend herself to no settlement so long as she so intensely knew. What she knew was that he was, almost under peril of life, clenched in a situation: therefore how could she also know where a poor girl in the P. O. might really stand? It was more and more between them that if he might convey to her he was free, with all the impossible locked away into a closed chapter, her own case might become different for her, she might understand and meet him and listen. But he could convey nothing of the sort, and he only fidgeted and floundered in his want of power. The chapter wasn't in the least closed, not for the other party; and the other party had a pull, somehow and somewhere: this his whole attitude and expression confessed, at the same time that they entreated her not to remember and not to mind. So long as she did remember and did mind he could only circle about and go and come, doing futile things of which he was ashamed. He was ashamed of his two words to Dr. Buzzard; he went out of the shop as soon as he had crumpled up the paper again and thrust it into his pocket. It had been an abject little exposure of dreadful impossible passion. He appeared in fact to be too ashamed to come back. He had once more left town, and a first week elapsed, and a second. He had had naturally to return to the real mistress of his fate; she had insisted—she knew how to insist, and he couldn't put in another hour. There was always a day when she called time. It was known to our young friend moreover that he had now been dispatching telegrams from other offices. She knew at last so much that she had quite lost her earlier sense of merely guessing. There were no different shades of distinctness—it all bounced out.

XXII

Eighteen days elapsed, and she had begun to think it probable she should never see him again. He too then understood now: he had made out that she had secrets and reasons and impediments, that even a poor girl at the P. O. might have her complications. With the charm she had cast on him lightened by distance he had suffered a final delicacy to speak to him, had made up his mind that it would be only decent to let her alone. Never so much as during these latter days had she felt the precariousness of their relation—the happy beautiful untroubled original one, if it could only have been restored—in which the public servant and the casual public only were concerned. It hung at the best by the merest silken thread, which was at the mercy of any accident and might snap at any minute. She arrived by the end of the fortnight at the highest sense of actual fitness, never doubting that her decision was now complete. She would just give him a few days more to come back to her on a proper impersonal basis—for even to an embarrassing representative of the casual public a public servant with a conscience did owe something—and then would signify to Mr. Mudge that she was ready for the little home. It had been visited, in the further talk she had had with him at Bournemouth, from garret to cellar, and they had especially lingered, with their respectively darkened brows, before the niche into which it was to be broached to her mother that she must find means to fit.

He had put it to her more definitely than before that his calculations had allowed for that dingy presence, and he had thereby marked the greatest impression he had ever made on her. It was a stroke superior even again to his handling of the drunken soldier. What she considered that in the face of it she hung on at Cocker's for was something she could only have described as the common fairness of a last word. Her actual last word had been, till it should be superseded, that she wouldn't forsake her other friend, and it stuck to her through thick and thin that she was still at her post and on her honour. This other friend had shown so much beauty of conduct already that he would surely after all just re-appear long enough to relieve her, to give her something she could take away. She saw it, caught it, at times, his parting present; and there were moments when she felt herself sitting like a beggar with a hand held out to an almsgiver who only fumbled. She hadn't taken the sovereigns, but she *would* take the penny. She heard, in imagination, on the counter, the ring of the copper. "Don't put yourself out any longer," he would say, "for so bad a case. You've done all there is to be done. I thank and acquit and release you. Our lives take us. I don't know much—

though I've really been interested—about yours, but I suppose you've got one. Mine at any rate will take *me*—and where it will. Heigh-ho! Good-bye." And then once more, for the sweetest faintest flower of all: "Only I say—see here!" She had framed the whole picture with a squareness that included also the image of how again she would decline to "see there," decline, as she might say, to see anywhere, see anything. Yet it befell that just in the fury of this escape she saw more than ever.

He came back one night with a rush, near the moment of their closing, and showed her a face so different and new, so upset and anxious, that almost anything seemed to look out of it but clear recognition. He poked in a telegram very much as if the simple sense of pressure, the distress of extreme haste, had blurred the remembrance of where in particular he was. But as she met his eyes a light came; it broke indeed on the spot into a positive conscious glare. That made up for everything, since it was an instant proclamation of the celebrated "danger"; it seemed to pour things out in a flood. "Oh yes, here it is—it's upon me at last! Forget, for God's sake, my having worried or bored you, and just help me, just *save* me, by getting this off without the loss of a second!" Something grave had clearly occurred, a crisis declared itself. She recognised immediately the person to whom the telegram was addressed—the Miss Dolman of Parade Lodge to whom Lady Bradeen had wired, at Dover, on the last occasion, and whom she had then, with her recollection of previous arrangements, fitted into a particular setting. Miss Dolman had figured before and not figured since, but she was now the subject of an imperative appeal. "Absolutely necessary to see you. Take last train Victoria if you can catch it. If not, earliest morning, and answer me direct either way."

"Reply paid?" said the girl. Mr. Buckton had just departed and the counter-clerk was at the sounder. There was no other representative of the public, and she had never yet, as it seemed to her, not even in the street nor in the Park, been so alone with him.

"Oh yes, reply paid, and as sharp as possible, please."

She affixed the stamps in a flash. "She'll catch the train!"

she then declared to him breathlessly, as if she could absolutely guarantee it.

"I don't know—I hope so. It's awfully important. So kind of you. Awfully sharp, please." It was wonderfully innocent now, his oblivion of all but his danger. Anything else that had ever passed between them was utterly out of it. Well, she had wanted him to be impersonal!

There was less of the same need therefore, happily, for herself; yet she only took time, before she flew to the sounder, to gasp at him: "You're in trouble?"

"Horrid, horrid—there's a row!" But they parted, on it, in the next breath; and as she dashed at the sounder, almost pushing, in her violence, the counter-clerk off the stool, she caught the bang with which, at Cocker's door, in his further precipitation, he closed the apron of the cab into which he had leaped. As he rebounded to some other precaution suggested by his alarm, his appeal to Miss Dolman flashed straight away.

But she had not, on the morrow, been in the place five minutes before he was with her again, still more discomposed and quite, now, as she said to herself, like a frightened child coming to its mother. Her companions were there, and she felt it to be remarkable how, in the presence of his agitation, his mere scared exposed nature, she suddenly ceased to mind. It came to her as it had never come to her before that with absolute directness and assurance they might carry almost anything off. He had nothing to send—she was sure he had been wiring all over—and yet his business was evidently huge. There was nothing but that in his eyes—not a glimmer of reference or memory. He was almost haggard with anxiety and had clearly not slept a wink. Her pity for him would have given her any courage, and she seemed to know at last why she had been such a fool. "She didn't come?" she panted.

"Oh yes, she came; but there has been some mistake. We want a telegram."

"A telegram?"

"One that was sent from here ever so long ago. There was something in it that has to be recovered. Something very, *very* important, please—we want it immediately."

He really spoke to her as if she had been some strange young woman at Knightsbridge or Paddington; but it had no other effect on her than to give her the measure of his tremendous flurry. Then it was that, above all, she felt how much she had missed in the gaps and blanks and absent answers—how much she had had to dispense with: it was now black darkness save for this little wild red flare. So much as that she saw, so much her mind dealt with. One of the lovers was quaking somewhere out of town, and the other was quaking just where he stood. This was vivid enough, and after an instant she knew it was all she wanted. She wanted no detail, no fact—she wanted no nearer vision of discovery or shame. "When was your telegram? Do you mean you sent it from here?" She tried to do the young woman at Knightsbridge.

"Oh yes, from here—several weeks ago. Five, six, seven" —he was confused and impatient—"don't you remember?"

"Remember?" she could scarcely keep out of her face, at the word, the strangest of smiles.

But the way he didn't catch what it meant was perhaps even stranger still. "I mean don't you keep the old ones?"

"For a certain time."

"But how long?"

She thought; she *must* do the young woman, and she knew exactly what the young woman would say and, still more, wouldn't. "Can you give me the date?"

"Oh God, no! It was some time or other in August—toward the end. It was to the same address as the one I gave you last night."

"Oh!" said the girl, knowing at this the deepest thrill she had ever felt. It came to her there, with her eyes on his face, that she held the whole thing in her hand, held it as she held her pencil, which might have broken at that instant in her tightened grip. This made her feel like the very fountain of fate, but the emotion was such a flood that she had to press it back with all her force. That was positively the reason, again, of her flute-like Paddington tone. "You can't give us anything a little nearer?" Her "little" and her "us" came straight from Paddington. These things were no false note for him—his difficulty absorbed them all. The eyes with which he pressed her, and in the depths of which she read terror and rage and literal tears, were just the same he would have shown any other prim person.

"I don't know the date. I only know the thing went from here, and just about the time I speak of. It wasn't delivered, you see. We've got to recover it."

XXIII

She was as struck with the beauty of his plural pronoun as she had judged he might be with that of her own; but she knew now so well what she was about that she could almost play with him and with her new-born joy. "You say 'about the time you speak of.' But I don't think you speak of an exact time—*do* you?"

He looked splendidly helpless. "That's just what I want to find out. Don't you keep the old ones?—can't you look it up?"

Our young lady—still at Paddington—turned the question over. "It wasn't delivered?"

"Yes, it *was;* yet, at the same time, don't you know? it wasn't." He just hung back, but he brought it out. "I mean it was intercepted, don't you know? and there was something in it." He paused again and, as if to further his quest and woo and supplicate success and recovery, even smiled with an effort at the agreeable that was almost ghastly and that turned the knife in her tenderness. What must be the pain of it all, of the open gulf and the throbbing fever, when this was the mere hot breath? "We want to get what was in it—to know what it was."

"I see—I see." She managed just the accent they had at Paddington when they stared like dead fish. "And you have no clue?"

"Not at all—I've the clue I've just given you."

"Oh the last of August?" If she kept it up long enough she would make him really angry.

"Yes, and the address, as I've said."

"Oh the same as last night?"

He visibly quivered, as with a gleam of hope; but it only

poured oil on her quietude, and she was still deliberate. She ranged some papers. "Won't you look?" he went on.

"I remember your coming," she replied.

He blinked with a new uneasiness; it might have begun to come to him, through her difference, that he was somehow different himself. "You were much quicker then, you know!"

"So were you—you must do me that justice," she answered with a smile. "But let me see. Wasn't it Dover?"

"Yes, Miss Dolman—"

"Parade Lodge, Parade Terrace?"

"Exactly—thank you so awfully much!" He began to hope again. "Then you *have* it—the other one?"

She hesitated afresh; she quite dangled him. "It was brought by a lady?"

"Yes; and she put in by mistake something wrong. That's what we've got to get hold of!"

Heavens, what was he going to say?—flooding poor Paddington with wild betrayals! She couldn't too much, for her joy, dangle him, yet she couldn't either, for his dignity, warn or control or check him. What she found herself doing was just to treat herself to the middle way. "It was intercepted?"

"It fell into the wrong hands. But there's something in it," he continued to blurt out, "that *may* be all right. That is if it's wrong, don't you know? It's all right if it's wrong," he remarkably explained.

What *was* he, on earth, going to say? Mr. Buckton and the counter-clerk were already interested; no one *would* have the decency to come in; and she was divided between her particular terror for him and her general curiosity. Yet she already saw with what brilliancy she could add, to carry the thing off, a little false knowledge to all her real. "I quite understand," she said with benevolent, with almost patronising quickness. "The lady has forgotten what she did put."

"Forgotten most wretchedly, and it's an immense inconvenience. It has only just been found that it didn't get there; so that if we could immediately have it—"

"Immediately?"

"Every minute counts. You *have*," he pleaded, "surely got them on file?"

"So that you can see it on the spot?"

"Yes, please—this very minute." The counter rang with his knuckles, with the knob of his stick, with his panic of alarm. "Do, *do* hunt it up!" he repeated.

"I dare say we could get it for you," the girl sweetly returned.

"Get it?"—he looked aghast. "When?"

"Probably by to-morrow."

"Then it isn't here?"—his face was pitiful.

She caught only the uncovered gleams that peeped out of the blackness, and she wondered what complication, even among the most supposable, the very worst, could be bad enough to account for the degree of his terror. There were twists and turns, there were places where the screw drew blood, that she couldn't guess. She was more and more glad she didn't want to. "It has been sent on."

"But how do you know if you don't look?"

She gave him a smile that was meant to be, in the absolute irony of its propriety, quite divine. "It was August 23d, and we've nothing later here than August 27th."

Something leaped into his face. "27th—23d? Then you're sure? You know?"

She felt she scarce knew what—as if she might soon be pounced upon for some lurid connexion with a scandal. It was the queerest of all sensations, for she had heard, she had read, of these things, and the wealth of her intimacy with them at Cocker's might be supposed to have schooled and seasoned her. This particular one that she had really quite lived with was, after all, an old story; yet what it had been before was dim and distant beside the touch under which she now winced. Scandal?—it had never been but a silly word. Now it was a great tense surface, and the surface was somehow Captain Everard's wonderful face. Deep down in his eyes was a picture, a scene—a great place like a chamber of justice, where, before a watching crowd, a poor girl, exposed but heroic, swore with a quavering voice to a document, proved an *alibi*, supplied a link. In this picture she bravely took her place. "It was the twenty-third."

"Then can't you get it this morning—or some time to-day?"

She considered, still holding him with her look, which she then turned on her two companions, who were by this time unreservedly enlisted. She didn't care—not a scrap, and she glanced about for a piece of paper. With this she had to recognise the rigour of official thrift—a morsel of blackened blotter was the only loose paper to be seen. "Have you got a card?" she said to her visitor. He was quite away from Paddington now, and the next instant, pocketbook in hand, he had whipped a card out. She gave no glance at the name on it—only turned it to the other side. She continued to hold him, she felt at present, as she had never held him; and her command of her colleagues was for the moment not less marked. She wrote something on the back of the card and pushed it across to him.

He fairly glared at it. "Seven, nine, four—"

"Nine, six, one"—she obligingly completed the number. "Is it right?" she smiled.

He took the whole thing in with a flushed intensity; then there broke out in him a visibility of relief that was simply a tremendous exposure. He shone at them all like a tall lighthouse, embracing even, for sympathy, the blinking young men. "By all the powers—it's wrong!" And without another look, without a word of thanks, without time for anything or anybody, he turned on them the broad back of his great stature, straightened his triumphant shoulders and strode out of the place.

She was left confronted with her habitual critics. " 'If it's wrong it's all right!' " she extravagantly quoted to them.

The counter-clerk was really awestricken. "But how did you know, dear?"

"I remembered, love!"

Mr. Buckton, on the contrary, was rude. "And what game is that, miss?"

No happiness she had ever known came within miles of it, and some minutes elapsed before she could recall herself sufficiently to reply that it was none of his business.

XXIV

If life at Cocker's, with the dreadful drop of August, had lost something of its savour, she had not been slow to infer that a heavier blight had fallen on the graceful industry of Mrs. Jordan. With Lord Rye and Lady Ventnor and Mrs. Bubb all out of town, with the blinds down on all the homes of luxury, this ingenious woman might well have found her wonderful taste left quite on her hands. She bore up, however, in a way that began by exciting much of her young friend's esteem; they perhaps even more frequently met as the wine of life flowed less free from other sources, and each, in the lack of better diversion, carried on with more mystification for the other an intercourse that consisted not a little in peeping out and drawing back. Each waited for the other to commit herself, each profusely curtained for the other the limits of low horizons. Mrs. Jordan was indeed probably the more reckless skirmisher; nothing could exceed her frequent incoherence unless it was indeed her occasional bursts of confidence. Her account of her private affairs rose and fell like a flame in the wind—sometimes the bravest bonfire and sometimes a handful of ashes. This our young woman took to be an effect of the position, at one moment and another, of the famous door of the great world. She had been struck in one of her ha'penny volumes with the translation of a French proverb according to which such a door, any door, had to be either open or shut; and it seemed part of the precariousness of Mrs. Jordan's life that hers mostly managed to be neither. There had been occasions when it appeared to gape wide—fairly to woo her across its threshold; there had been others, of an order distinctly disconcerting, when it was all but banged in her face. On the whole, however, she had evidently not lost heart; these still belonged to the class of things in spite of which she looked well. She intimated that the profits of her trade had swollen so as to float her through any state of the tide, and she had, besides this, a hundred profundities and explanations.

She rose superior, above all, on the happy fact that there were always gentlemen in town and that gentlemen were

her greatest admirers; gentlemen from the City in especial
—as to whom she was full of information about the passion
and pride excited in such breasts by the elements of her
charming commerce. The City men *did* in short go in for
flowers. There was a certain type of awfully smart stock-
broker—Lord Rye called them Jews and bounders, but she
didn't care—whose extravagance, she more than once threw
out, had really, if one had any conscience, to be forcibly
restrained. It was not perhaps a pure love of beauty; it was
a matter of vanity and a sign of business; they wished to
crush their rivals, and that was one of their weapons. Mrs.
Jordan's shrewdness was extreme; she knew in any case her
customer—she dealt, as she said, with all sorts; and it was
at the worst a race for her—a race even in the dull months
—from one set of chambers to another. And then, after all,
there were also still the ladies; the ladies of stockbroking
circles were perpetually up and down. They were not quite
perhaps Mrs. Bubb or Lady Ventnor; but you couldn't tell
the difference unless you quarrelled with them, and then
you knew it only by their making-up sooner. These ladies
formed the branch of her subject on which she most
swayed in the breeze; to that degree that her confidant had
ended with an inference or two tending to banish regret for
opportunities not embraced. There were indeed tea-gowns
that Mrs. Jordan described—but tea-gowns were not the
whole of respectability, and it was odd that a clergyman's
widow should sometimes speak as if she almost thought so.
She came back, it was true, unfailingly to Lord Rye, never,
evidently, quite losing sight of him even on the longest ex-
cursions. That he was kindness itself had become in fact
the very moral it all pointed—pointed in strange flashes of
the poor woman's nearsighted eyes. She launched at her
young friend portentous looks, solemn heralds of some extraordinary communication. The communication itself, from
week to week, hung fire; but it was to the facts over which
it hovered that she owed her power of going on. "They *are*,
in one way *and* another," she often emphasised, "a tower
of strength"; and as the allusion was to the aristocracy the
girl could quite wonder why, if they were so in "one way,"
they should require to be so in two. She thoroughly knew,

however, how many ways Mrs. Jordan counted in. It all
meant simply that her fate was pressing her close. If that
fate was to be sealed at the matrimonial altar it was perhaps not remarkable that she shouldn't come all at once to
the scratch of overwhelming a mere telegraphist. It would
necessarily present to such a person a prospect of regretful
sacrifice. Lord Rye—if it *was* Lord Rye—wouldn't be "kind"
to a nonentity of that sort, even though people quite as
good had been.

One Sunday afternoon in November they went, by arrangement, to church together; after which—on the inspiration of the moment; the arrangement had not included it—
they proceeded to Mrs. Jordan's lodging in the region of
Maida Vale. She had raved to her friend about her service
of predilection; she was excessively "high" and had more
than once wished to introduce the girl to the same comfort
and privilege. There was a thick brown fog and Maida Vale
tasted of acrid smoke; but they had been sitting among
chants and incense and wonderful music, during which,
though the effect of such things on her mind was great,
our young lady had indulged in a series of reflexions but
indirectly related to them. One of these was the result of
Mrs. Jordan's having said to her on the way, and with a
certain fine significance, that Lord Rye had been for some
time in town. She had spoken as if it were a circumstance
to which little required to be added—as if the bearing of
such an item on her life might easily be grasped. Perhaps
it was the wonder of whether Lord Rye wished to marry
her that made her guest, with thoughts straying to that
quarter, quite determine that some other nuptials also
should take place at Saint Julian's. Mr. Mudge was still an
attendant at his Wesleyan chapel, but this was the least of
her worries—it had never even vexed her enough for her
to so much as name it to Mrs. Jordan. Mr. Mudge's form
of worship was one of several things—they made up in superiority and beauty for what they wanted in number—that
she had long ago settled he should take from her, and she
had now moreover for the first time definitely established
her own. Its principal feature was that it was to be the
same as that of Mrs. Jordan and Lord Rye; which was in-

deed very much what she said to her hostess as they sat together later on. The brown fog was in this hostess's little parlour, where it acted as a postponement of the question of there being, besides, anything else than the teacups and a pewter pot and a very black little fire and a paraffin lamp without a shade. There was at any rate no sign of a flower; it was not for herself Mrs. Jordan gathered sweets. The girl waited till they had had a cup of tea—waited for the announcement that she fairly believed her friend had, this time, possessed herself of her formally at last to make; but nothing came, after the interval, save a little poke at the fire, which was like the clearing of a throat for a speech.

XXV

"I think you must have heard me speak of Mr. Drake?" Mrs. Jordan had never looked so queer, nor her smile so suggestive of a large benevolent bite.

"Mr. Drake? Oh yes; isn't he a friend of Lord Rye?"

"A great and trusted friend. Almost—I may say—a loved friend."

Mrs. Jordan's "almost" had such an oddity that her companion was moved, rather flippantly perhaps, to take it up. "Don't people as good as love their friends when they 'trust' them?"

It pulled up a little the eulogist of Mr. Drake. "Well, my dear, I love *you*—"

"But you don't trust me?" the girl unmercifully asked.

Again Mrs. Jordan paused—still she looked queer. "Yes," she replied with a certain austerity; "that's exactly what I'm about to give you rather a remarkable proof of." The sense of its being remarkable was already so strong that, while she bridled a little, this held her auditor in a momentary muteness of submission. "Mr. Drake has rendered his lordship for several years services that his lordship has highly appreciated and that make it all the more—a—unexpected that they should, perhaps a little suddenly, separate."

"Separate?" Our young lady was mystified, but she tried to be interested; and she already saw that she had put the saddle on the wrong horse. She had heard something of Mr. Drake, who was a member of his lordship's circle—the member with whom, apparently, Mrs. Jordan's avocations had most happened to throw her. She was only a little puzzled at the "separation." "Well, at any rate," she smiled, "if they separate as friends—!"

"Oh his lordship takes the greatest interest in Mr. Drake's future. He'll do anything for him; he has in fact just done a great deal. There *must,* you know, be changes—!"

"No one knows it better than I," the girl said. She wished to draw her interlocutress out. "There will be changes enough for me."

"You're leaving Cocker's?"

The ornament of that establishment waited a moment to answer, and then it was indirect. "Tell me what *you're* doing."

"Well, what will you think of it?"

"Why that you've found the opening you were always so sure of."

Mrs. Jordan, on this, appeared to muse with embarrassed intensity. "I was always sure, yes—and yet I often wasn't!"

"Well, I hope you're sure now. Sure, I mean, of Mr. Drake."

"Yes, my dear, I think I may say I *am.* I kept him going till I was."

"Then he's yours?"

"My very own."

"How nice! And awfully rich?" our young woman went on.

Mrs. Jordan showed promptly enough that she loved for higher things. "Awfully handsome—six foot two. And he *has* put by."

"Quite like Mr. Mudge then!" that gentleman's friend rather desperately exclaimed.

"Oh not *quite!*" Mr. Drake's was ambiguous about it, but the name of Mr. Mudge had evidently given her some sort of stimulus. "He'll have more opportunity now, at any rate. He's going to Lady Bradeen."

"To Lady Bradeen?" This was bewilderment. " 'Going'—?"

The girl had seen, from the way Mrs. Jordan looked at

her, that the effect of the name had been to make her let something out. "Do you know her?"

She floundered, but she found her feet. "Well, you'll remember I've often told you that if you've grand clients I have them too."

"Yes," said Mrs. Jordan; "but the great difference is that you hate yours, whereas I really love mine. *Do* you know Lady Bradeen?" she pursued.

"Down to the ground! She's always in and out."

Mrs. Jordan's foolish eyes confessed, in fixing themselves on this sketch, to a degree of wonder and even of envy. But she bore up and, with a certain gaiety, "Do you hate *her?*" she demanded.

Her visitor's reply was prompt. "Dear no!—not nearly so much as some of them. She's too outrageously beautiful."

Mrs. Jordan continued to gaze. "Outrageously?"

"Well, yes; deliciously." What was really delicious was Mrs. Jordan's vagueness. "You don't know her? you've not seen her?" her guest lightly continued.

"No, but I've heard a great deal about her."

"So have I!" our young lady exclaimed.

Mrs. Jordan looked an instant as if she suspected her good faith, or at least her seriousness. "You know some friend—?"

"Of Lady Bradeen's? Oh yes—I know one."

"Only one?"

The girl laughed out. "Only one—but he's so intimate."

Mrs. Jordan just hesitated. "He's a gentleman?"

"Yes, he's not a lady."

Her interlocutress appeared to muse. "She's immensely surrounded."

"She *will* be—with Mr. Drake!"

Mrs. Jordan's gaze became strangely fixed. "Is she *very* good-looking?"

"The handsomest person I know."

Mrs. Jordan continued to brood. "Well, *I* know some beauties." Then with her odd jerkiness: "Do you think she looks *good?*"

"Because that's not always the case with the good-looking?"—the other took it up. "No indeed, it isn't: that's one thing Cocker's has taught me. Still, there are some people who have everything. Lady Bradeen, at any rate, has enough: eyes and a nose and a mouth, a complexion, a figure—"

"A figure?" Mrs. Jordan almost broke in.

"A figure, a head of hair!" The girl made a little conscious motion that seemed to let the hair all down, and her companion watched the wonderful show. "But Mr. Drake *is* another—?"

"Another?"—Mrs. Jordan's thoughts had to come back from a distance.

"Of her ladyship's admirers. He's 'going,' you say, to her?"

At this Mrs. Jordan really faltered. "She has engaged him."

"Engaged him?"—our young woman was quite at sea.

"In the same capacity as Lord Rye."

"And was Lord Rye engaged?"

XXVI

Mrs. Jordan looked away from her now—looked, she thought, rather injured and, as if trifled with, even a little angry. The mention of Lady Bradeen had frustrated for a while the convergence of our heroine's thoughts; but with this impression of her old friend's combined impatience and diffidence they began again to whirl round her, and continued it till one of them appeared to dart at her, out of the dance, as if with a sharp peck. It came to her with a lively shock, with a positive sting, that Mr. Drake was—could it be possible? With the idea she found herself afresh on the edge of laughter, of a sudden and strange perversity of mirth. Mr. Drake loomed, in a swift image, before her; such a figure as she had seen in open doorways of houses in Cocker's quarter—majestic, middle-aged, erect, flanked on either side by a footman and taking the name of a visitor. Mr. Drake then verily *was* a person who opened the door! Before she had time, however, to recover from the effect of her evocation, she was offered a vision which quite engulfed it. It was communicated to her somehow that the face with which she had seen it rise prompted Mrs. Jordan to dash, a bit wildly, at something, at anything, that might attenuate criticism. "Lady Bradeen's re-arranging—she's going to be married."

"Married?" The girl echoed it ever so softly, but there it was at last.

"Didn't you know it?"

She summoned all her sturdiness. "No, she hasn't told me."

"And her friends—haven't they?"

"I haven't seen any of them lately. I'm not so fortunate as *you*."

Mrs. Jordan gathered herself. "Then you haven't even heard of Lord Bradeen's death?"

Her comrade, unable for a moment to speak, gave a slow headshake. "You know it from Mr. Drake?" It was better surely not to learn things at all than to learn them by the butler.

"She tells him everything."

"And he tells *you*—I see." Our young lady got up; recovering her muff and her gloves she smiled. "Well, I haven't unfortunately any Mr. Drake. I congratulate you with all my heart. Even without your sort of assistance, however, there's a trifle here and there that I do pick up. I gather that if she's to marry any one it must quite necessarily be my friend."

Mrs. Jordan was now also on her feet. "Is Captain Everard your friend?"

The girl considered, drawing on a glove. "I saw, at one time, an immense deal of him."

Mrs. Jordan looked hard at the glove, but she hadn't after all waited for that to be sorry it wasn't cleaner. "What time was that?"

"It must have been the time you were seeing so much of Mr. Drake." She had now fairly taken it in: the distinguished person Mrs. Jordan was to marry would answer bells and put on coals and superintend, at least, the cleaning of boots for the other distinguished person whom *she* might—well, whom she might have had, if she had wished, so much more to say to. "Good-bye," she added; "good-bye."

Mrs. Jordan, however, again taking her muff from her, turned it over, brushed it off and thoughtfully peeped into it. "Tell me this before you go. You spoke just now of your own changes. Do you mean that Mr. Mudge—?"

"Mr. Mudge has had great patience with me—he has brought me at last to the point. We're to be married next month and have a nice little home. But he's only a grocer, you know"—the girl met her friend's intent eyes—"so that I'm afraid that, with the set you've got into, you won't see your way to keep up our friendship."

Mrs. Jordan for a moment made no answer to this; she only held the muff up to her face, after which she gave it back. "You don't like it. I see, I see."

To her guest's astonishment there were tears now in her eyes. "I don't like what?" the girl asked.

"Why my engagement. Only, with your great cleverness," the poor lady quavered out, "you put it in your own way. I mean that you'll cool off. You already *have*—!" And on this, the next instant, her tears began to flow. She succumbed to them and collapsed; she sank down again, burying her face and trying to smother her sobs.

Her young friend stood there, still in some rigour, but taken much by surprise even if not yet fully moved to pity. "I don't put anything in any 'way,' and I'm very glad you're suited. Only, you know, you did put to me so splendidly what, even for me, if I had listened to you, it might lead to."

Mrs. Jordan kept up a mild thin weak wail; then, drying her eyes, as feebly considered this reminder. "It has led to my not starving!" she faintly gasped.

Our young lady, at this, dropped into the place beside her, and now, in a rush, the small silly misery was clear. She took her hand as a sign of pitying it, then, after another instant, confirmed this expression with a consoling kiss. They sat there together; they looked out, hand in hand, into the damp dusky shabby little room and into the future, of no such very different complexion, at last accepted by each. There was no definite utterance, on either side, of Mr. Drake's position in the great world, but the temporary collapse of his prospective bride threw all further necessary light; and what our heroine saw and felt for in the whole business was the vivid reflexion of her own dreams and delusions and her own return to reality. Reality, for the poor things they both were, could only be ugliness and obscurity, could never be the escape, the rise. She pressed her friend—she had tact enough for that—with no other personal question, brought on no need of further revelations, only just continued to hold and comfort her and to acknowledge by stiff little forbearances the common element in their fate. She felt indeed magnanimous in such matters; since if it was very well, for condolence or reassurance, to suppress just then invidious shrinkings, she yet by no means saw herself sitting down, as she might say, to the same table with Mr. Drake. There would luckily, to all appearance, be little question of tables; and the circumstance that, on their peculiar lines, her friend's interests would still attach themselves to Mayfair flung over Chalk Farm the first radiance it had shown. Where was one's pride and one's passion when the real way to judge of one's luck was by making not the wrong but the right comparison? Before she had again gathered herself to go she felt very small and cautious and thankful. "We shall have our own house," she said, "and you must come very soon and let me show it you."

"*We* shall have our own too," Mrs. Jordan replied; "for, don't you know? he makes it a condition that he sleeps out."

"A condition?"—the girl felt out of it.

"For any new position. It was on that he parted with Lord Rye. His lordship can't meet it. So Mr. Drake has given him up."

"And all for you?"—our young woman put it as cheerfully as possible.

"For me and Lady Bradeen. Her ladyship's too glad to get him at any price. Lord Rye, out of interest in us, has in fact quite *made* her take him. So, as I tell you, he will have his own establishment."

Mrs. Jordan, in the elation of it, had begun to revive; but there was nevertheless between them rather a conscious pause—a pause in which neither visitor nor hostess brought out a hope or an invitation. It expressed in the last resort that, in spite of submission and sympathy, they could now after all only look at each other across the social gulf. They remained together as if it would be indeed their last chance, still sitting, though awkwardly, quite close, and feeling also —and this most unmistakeably—that there was one thing more to go into. By the time it came to the surface, moreover, our young friend had recognised the whole of the main truth, from which she even drew again a slight irritation. It was not the main truth perhaps that most signified; but after her momentary effort, her embarrassment and her tears Mrs. Jordan had begun to sound afresh—and even without speaking—the note of a social connexion. She hadn't really let go of it that she was marrying into society. Well, it was a harmless compensation, and it was all the prospective bride of Mr. Mudge had to leave with her.

XXVII

This young lady at last rose again, but she lingered before going. "And has Captain Everard nothing to say to it?"

"To what, dear?"

"Why, to such questions—the domestic arrangements, things in the house."

"How *can* he, with any authority, when nothing in the house is his?"

"Not his?" The girl wondered, perfectly conscious of the appearance she thus conferred on Mrs. Jordan of knowing, in comparison with herself, so tremendously much about it. Well, there were things she wanted so to get at that she was willing at last, though it hurt her, to pay for them with humiliation. "Why are they not his?"

"Don't you know, dear, that he has nothing?"

"Nothing?" It was hard to see him in such a light, but Mrs. Jordan's power to answer for it had a superiority that began, on the spot, to grow. "Isn't he rich?"

Mrs. Jordan looked immensely, looked both generally and particularly, informed. "It depends upon what you call—! Not at any rate in the least as *she* is. What does he bring? Think what she has. And then, love, his debts."

"His debts?" His young friend was fairly betrayed into

helpless innocence. She could struggle a little, but she had to let herself go; and if she had spoken frankly she would have said: "Do tell me, for I don't know so much about him as *that!*" As she didn't speak frankly she only said: "His debts are nothing—when she so adores him."

Mrs. Jordan began to fix her again, and now she saw that she must only take it all. That was what it had come to: his having sat with her there on the bench and under the trees in the summer darkness and put his hand on her, making her know what he would have said if permitted; his having returned to her afterwards, repeatedly, with supplicating eyes and a fever in his blood; and her having on her side, hard and pedantic, helped by some miracle and with her impossible condition, only answered him, yet supplicating back, through the bars of the cage—all simply that she might hear of him, now for ever lost, only through Mrs. Jordan, who touched him through Mr. Drake, who reached him through Lady Bradeen. "She adores him—but of course that wasn't all there was about it."

The girl met her eyes a minute, then quite surrendered. "What was there else about it?"

"Why, don't you know?"—Mrs. Jordan was almost compassionate.

Her interlocutress had, in the cage, sounded depths, but there was a suggestion here somehow of an abyss quite measureless. "Of course I know she would never let him alone."

"How *could* she—fancy!—when he had so compromised her?"

The most artless cry they had ever uttered broke, at this, from the younger pair of lips. "*Had* he so—?"

"Why, don't you know the scandal?"

Our heroine thought, recollected; there was something, whatever it was, that she knew after all much more of than Mrs. Jordan. She saw him again as she had seen him come that morning to recover the telegram—she saw him as she had seen him leave the shop. She perched herself a moment on this. "Oh there was nothing public."

"Not exactly public—no. But there was an awful scare

and an awful row. It was all on the very point of coming out. Something was lost—something was found."

"Ah yes," the girl replied, smiling as if with the revival of a blurred memory; "something was found."

"It all got about—and there was a point at which Lord Bradeen had to act."

"Had to—yes. But he didn't."

Mrs. Jordan was obliged to admit it. "No, he didn't. And then, luckily for them, he died."

"I didn't know about his death," her companion said.

"It was nine weeks ago, and most sudden. It has given them a prompt chance."

"To get married"—this was a wonder—"within nine weeks?"

"Oh not immediately, but—in all the circumstances—very quietly and, I assure you, very soon. Every preparation's made. Above all she holds him."

"Oh yes, she holds him!" our young friend threw off. She had this before her again a minute; then she continued: "You mean through his having made her talked about?"

"Yes, but not only that. She has still another pull."

"Another?"

Mrs. Jordan hesitated. "Why, he was *in* something."

Her comrade wondered. "In what?"

"I don't know. Something bad. As I tell you, something was found."

The girl stared. "Well?"

"It would have been very bad for him. But she helped him some way—she recovered it, got hold of it. It's even said she stole it!"

Our young woman considered afresh. "Why it was what was found that precisely saved him."

Mrs. Jordan, however, was positive. "I beg your pardon. I happen to know."

Her disciple faltered but an instant. "Do you mean through Mr. Drake? Do they tell *him* these things?"

"A good servant," said Mrs. Jordan, now thoroughly superior and proportionately sententious, "doesn't need to be told! Her ladyship saved—as a woman so often saves!—the man she loves."

This time our heroine took longer to recover herself, but she found a voice at last. "Ah well—of course I don't know! The great thing was that he got off. They seem then, in a manner," she added, "to have done a great deal for each other."

"Well, it's she that has done most. She has him tight."

"I see, I see. Good-bye." The women had already embraced, and this was not repeated; but Mrs. Jordan went down with her guest to the door of the house. Here again the younger lingered, reverting, though three or four other remarks had on the way passed between them, to Captain Everard and Lady Bradeen. "Did you mean just now that if she hadn't saved him, as you call it, she wouldn't hold him so tight?"

"Well, I dare say." Mrs. Jordan, on the doorstep, smiled with a reflexion that had come to her; she took one of her big bites of the brown gloom. "Men always dislike one when they've done one an injury."

"But what injury had he done her?"

"The one I've mentioned. He *must* marry her, you know."

"And didn't he want to?"

"Not before."

"Not before she recovered the telegram?"

Mrs. Jordan was pulled up a little. "Was it a telegram?"

The girl hesitated. "I thought you said so. I mean whatever it was."

"Yes, whatever it was, I don't think she saw *that*."

"So she just nailed him?"

"She just nailed him." The departing friend was now at the bottom of the little flight of steps; the other was at the top, with a certain thickness of fog. "And when am I to think of you in your little home?—next month?" asked the voice from the top.

"At the very latest. And when am I to think of you in yours?"

"Oh even sooner. I feel, after so much talk with you about it, as if I were already there!" Then "*Good*-bye!" came out of the fog.

"Good-*bye!*" went into it. Our young lady went into it also, in the opposed quarter, and presently, after a few sight-

less turns, came out on the Paddington canal. Distinguishing vaguely what the low parapet enclosed she stopped
close to it and stood a while very intently, but perhaps still
sightlessly, looking down on it. A policeman, while she remained, strolled past her; then, going his way a little further and half lost in the atmosphere, paused and watched
her. But she was quite unaware—she was full of her
thoughts. They were too numerous to find a place just here,
but two of the number may at least be mentioned. One of
these was that, decidedly, her little home must be not for
next month, but for next week; the other, which came indeed as she resumed her walk and went her way, was that
it was strange such a matter should be at last settled for
her by Mr. Drake.

[1898]

BROKEN WINGS

I

Conscious as he was of what was between them, though
perhaps less conscious than ever of why there should at that
time of day be anything, he would yet scarce have supposed they could be so long in a house together without
some word or some look. It had been since the Saturday
afternoon, and that made twenty-four hours. The party—
five-and-thirty people and some of them great—was one in
which words and looks might more or less have gone astray.
The effect, none the less, he judged, would have been, for
her quite as for himself, that no sound and no sign from
the other had been picked up by either. They had happened both at dinner and at luncheon to be so placed as
not to have to glare—or to grin—across; and for the rest they
could each, in such a crowd, as freely help the general ease
to keep them apart as assist it to bring them together. One
chance there was, of course, that might be beyond their
control. He had been the night before half-surprised at not
finding her his "fate" when the long procession to the
dining-room solemnly hooked itself together. He would
have said in advance—recognising it as one of the sharp
"notes" of Mundham—that, should the gathering contain a
literary lady, the literary lady would, for congruity, be ap-
portioned to the arm, when there was a question of arms,
of the gentleman present who represented the nearest thing

to literature. Poor Straith represented "art," and that, no doubt, would have been near enough had not the party offered for choice a slight excess of men. The representative of art had been of the two or three who went in alone, whereas Mrs. Harvey had gone in with one of the representatives of banking.

It was certain, however, that she wouldn't again be consigned to Lord Belgrove, and it was just possible that he himself should not be again alone. She would be on the whole the most probable remedy to that state, on his part, of disgrace; and this precisely was the great interest of their situation—they were the only persons present without some advantage over somebody else. They hadn't a single advantage; they could be named for nothing but their cleverness; they were at the bottom of the social ladder. The social ladder had even at Mundham—as they might properly have been told, as indeed practically they *were* told —to end somewhere; which is no more than to say that as he strolled about and thought of many things Stuart Straith had after all a good deal the sense of helping to hold it up. Another of the things he thought of was the special oddity —for it was nothing else—of his being there at all, being there in particular so out of his order and turn. He couldn't answer for Mrs. Harvey's turn and order. It might well be that she was *in* hers; but these Saturday-to-Monday occasions had hitherto mostly struck him as great gilded cages as to which care was taken that the birds should be birds of a feather.

There had been a wonderful walk in the afternoon, within the limits of the place, to a far-away tea-house; and in spite of the combinations and changes of this episode he had still escaped the necessity of putting either his old friend or himself to the test. Also it had been all, he flattered himself, without the pusillanimity of his avoiding her. Life was indeed well understood in these great conditions; the conditions constituted in their greatness a kind of fundamental facility, provided a general exemption, bathed the hour, whatever it was, in a universal blandness, that were all a happy solvent for awkward relations. It was for instance beautiful that if their failure to meet amid so much meeting had been of Mrs. Harvey's own contrivance he couldn't be in the least vulgarly sure of it. There were places in which he would have had no doubt, places different enough from Mundham. He felt all the same and without anguish that these were much more *his* places—even if she didn't feel that they were much more hers. The day had been warm and splendid, and this moment of its wane—with dinner in sight, but as across a field of polished pink marble which seemed to say that wherever in such a house there was space there was also, benignantly, time—formed, of the whole procession of the hours, the one dearest to our friend, who on such occasions interposed it, whenever he could, between the set of impressions that ended and the set that began with "dressing." The great terraces and gardens were almost void; people had scattered, though not altogether even yet to dress. The air of the place, with the immense house all seated aloft in strength, robed with summer and crowned with success, was such as to contribute something of its own to the poetry of early evening. This visitor at any rate saw and felt it all through one of those fine hazes of August that remind you —at least they reminded *him*—of the artful gauze stretched across the stage of a theatre when an effect of mystery or some particular pantomimic ravishment is desired.

Should he in fact have to pair with Mrs. Harvey for dinner it would be a shame to him not to have addressed her sooner; and should she on the contrary be put with some one else the loss of so much of the time would have but the greater ugliness. Didn't he meanwhile make out that there were ladies in the lower garden, from which the sound of voices, faint but, as always in the upper air of Mundham, exceedingly sweet, was just now borne to him? She might be among them, and if he should find her he'd let her know he had sought her. He'd treat it frankly as an occasion for declaring that what had happened between them—or rather what had *not* happened—was too absurd. What at present occurred, however, was that in his quest of her he suddenly, at the turn of an alley, perceived her, not far off, seated in a sort of bower with the Ambassador. With this he pulled up, going another way and pretending not to see

them. Three times already that afternoon he had observed
her in different situations with the Ambassador. He was the
more struck accordingly when, upwards of an hour later,
again alone and with his state unremedied, he saw her
placed for dinner next his Excellency. It wasn't at all what
would have been at Mundham her right seat, so that it
could only be explained by his Excellency's direct request.
She *was* a success! This time Straith was well in her view
and could see that in the candle-light of the wonderful
room, where the lustres were, like the table, all crystal and
silver, she was as handsome as any one, taking the women
of her age, and also as "smart" as the evening before, and
as true as any of the others to the law of a marked difference in her smartness. If the beautiful way she held herself
—for decidedly it *was* beautiful—came in a great measure
from the good thing she professionally made of it all, our
observer could reflect that the poor thing *he* professionally
made of it probably affected his attitude in just the opposite
way; but they communicated neither in the glare nor in the
grin he had dreaded. Still, their eyes did now meet, and
then it struck him her own were strange.

II

She, on her side, had her private consciousness, and
quite as full a one, doubtless, as he, but with the advantage
that when the company separated for the night she was not,
like her friend, reduced to a vigil unalloyed. Lady Claude,
at the top of the stairs, had said "May I look in—in five
minutes—if you don't mind?" and then had arrived in due
course and in a wonderful new beribboned gown, the thing
just launched for such occasions. Lady Claude was young
and earnest and delightfully bewildered and bewildering,
and however interesting she might, through certain elements in her situation, have seemed to a literary lady, her
own admirations and curiosities were such as from the first
promised to rule the hour. She had already expressed to
Mrs. Harvey a really informed enthusiasm. She not only
delighted in her numerous books, which was a tribute the
author had not infrequently met, but she even appeared to

have read them—an appearance with which our authoress was much less acquainted. The great thing was that she also yearned to write, and that she had turned up in her fresh furbelows not only to reveal this secret and to ask for direction and comfort, but literally to make a stranger confidence, for which the mystery of midnight seemed propitious. Midnight was indeed, as the situation developed, well over before her confidence was spent, for it had ended by gathering such a current as floated forth, with everything in Lady Claude's own life, many things more in that of her adviser. Mrs. Harvey was at all events amused, touched and effectually kept awake; so by the end of half an hour they had quite got what might have been called their second wind of frankness and were using it for a discussion of the people in the house. Their primary communion had been simply on the question of the pecuniary profits of literature as the producer of so many admired volumes was prepared to present them to an aspirant. Lady Claude was in financial difficulties and desired the literary issue. This was the breathless revelation she had rustled over a mile of crimson velvet corridor to make.

"Nothing?" she had three minutes later incredulously gasped. "I can make nothing at all?" But the gasp was slight compared with the stupefaction communicated by a brief further parley, in the course of which Mrs. Harvey had, after an hesitation, taken her own plunge. "*You* make so little—wonderful *you?*" And then as the producer of the admired volumes simply sat there in her dressing-gown, with the saddest of slow headshakes, looking suddenly too wan even to care that it was at last all out: "What in that case is the use of success and celebrity and genius? You *have* no success?" She had looked almost awestruck at this further confession of her friend. They were face to face in a poor human crudity, which transformed itself quickly into an effusive embrace. "You've had it and lost it? Then when it has been as great as yours one *can* lose it?"

"More easily than one can get it."

Lady Claude continued to marvel. "But you do so much —and it's so beautiful!" On which Mrs. Harvey simply smiled again in her handsome despair, and after a moment found herself again in the arms of her visitor. The younger woman had remained for a time a good deal arrested and hushed, and had at any rate, sensitive and charming, immediately dropped, in the presence of this almost august unveiling, the question of her own thin troubles. But there are short cuts at that hour of night that morning scarce knows, and it took but little more of the breath of the real to suggest to Lady Claude more questions in such a connexion than she could answer for herself. "How then, if you haven't private means, do you get on?"

"Ah I don't get on!"

Lady Claude looked about. There were objects scattered in the fine old French room. "You've lovely things."

"Two."

"Two?"

"Two frocks. I couldn't stay another day."

"Ah what's *that?* I couldn't either," said Lady Claude soothingly. "And you have," she continued, in the same spirit, "your nice maid—"

"Who's indeed a charming woman, but my cook in disguise!" Mrs. Harvey dropped.

"Ah you *are* clever!" her friend cried with a laugh that was as a climax of reassurance.

"Extraordinarily. But don't think," Mrs. Harvey hastened to add, "that I mean that that's why I'm here."

Her companion candidly thought. "Then why are you?"

"I haven't the least idea. I've been wondering all the while, as I've wondered so often before on such occasions, and without arriving at any other reason than that London's so wild."

Lady Claude wondered. "Wild?"

"Wild!" said her friend with some impatience. "That's the way London strikes."

"But do you call such an invitation a blow?"

"Yes—crushing. No one else, at all events, either," Mrs. Harvey added, "could tell you why I'm here."

Lady Claude's power to drink in (and it was perhaps her most attaching quality) was greater still, when she felt strongly, than her power to reject. "Why how can you say that when you've only to see how every one likes and admires you? Just look at the Ambassador," she had earnestly insisted. And this was what had precisely, as I have mentioned, carried the stream of their talk a good deal away from its source. It had therefore not much further to go before setting in motion the name of Stuart Straith, as to whom Lady Claude confessed to an interest—good-looking, distinguished, "sympathetic" as he was—that she could really almost hate him for having done nothing whatever to encourage. He hadn't spoken to her once.

"But, my dear, if he hasn't spoken to *me*—!"

Lady Claude appeared to regret this not too much for a hint that after all there might be a difference. "Oh but *could* he?"

"Without my having spoken to him first?" Mrs. Harvey turned it over. "Perhaps not; but I couldn't have done that." Then to explain, and not only because Lady Claude was naturally vague, but because what was still visibly most vivid to her was her independent right to have been "made up" to: "And yet not because we're not acquainted."

"You know him then?"

"But too well."

"You mean you don't like him?"

"On the contrary I like him to distraction."

"Then what's the matter?" Lady Claude asked with some impatience.

Her friend hung fire but a moment. "Well, he wouldn't have me."

" 'Have' you?"

"Ten years ago, after Mr. Harvey's death, when if he had lifted a finger I'd have married him."

"But he didn't lift it?"

"He was too grand. I was too small—by *his* measure. He wanted to keep himself. He saw his future."

Lady Claude earnestly followed. "His present position?"

"Yes—everything that was to come to him; his steady rise in value."

"Has it been so great?"

"Surely—his situation and name. Don't you know his lovely work and what's thought of it?"

"Oh yes, I know. That's why—" But Lady Claude stopped. After which: "But if he's still keeping himself?"

"Oh it's not for me," said Mrs. Harvey.

"And evidently not for *me*. Whom then," her visitor asked, "does he think good enough?"

"Oh these great people!" Mrs. Harvey smiled.

"But *we're* great people—you and I!" And Lady Claude kissed her good-night.

"You mustn't, all the same," the elder woman said, "betray the secret of *my* greatness, which I've told you, please remember, only in the deepest confidence."

Her tone had a quiet purity of bitterness that for a moment longer held her friend, after which Lady Claude had the happy inspiration of meeting it with graceful gaiety. "It's quite for the best, I'm sure, that Mr. Straith wouldn't have you. You've kept yourself too; you'll marry yet—an ambassador!" And with another good-night she reached the door. "You say you don't get on, but you do."

"Ah!" said Mrs. Harvey with vague attenuation.

"Oh yes, you do," Lady Claude insisted, while the door emphasised it with a little clap that sounded through the still house.

III

The first night of "The New Girl" occurred, as every one remembers, three years ago, and the play is running yet, a fact that may render strange the failure to be deeply conscious of which two persons in the audience were guilty. It was not till afterwards present either to Mrs. Harvey or to Stuart Straith that "The New Girl" was one of the greatest successes of modern times. Indeed if the question had been put to them on the spot they might have appeared much at sea. But this, I may as well immediately say, was the result of their having found themselves side by side in the stalls and thereby given most of their attention to their own predicament. Straith showed he felt the importance of meeting it promptly, for he turned to his neighbour, who was already in her place, as soon as her identity had flushed well through his own arrival and subsidence. "I don't quite see how you can help speaking to me now."

Her face could only show him how long she had been aware of his approach. "The sound of your voice, coming to me straight, makes it indeed as easy for me as I could possibly desire."

He looked about at the serried rows, the loaded galleries and the stuffed boxes, with recognitions and nods; and this made between them another pause, during which, while the music seemed perfunctory and the bustle that in a London audience represents concentration increased, they felt how effectually, in the thick preoccupied medium, how extraordinarily, they were together.

"Well, that second afternoon at Mundham, just before dinner, I was very near forcing your hand. But something put me off. You're really too grand."

"Oh!" she murmured.

"Ambassadors," said Stuart Straith.

"Oh!" she again sounded. And before anything more could pass the curtain was up. It came down in due course and achieved, after various intervals, the rest of its motions without interrupting for our friends the sense of an evening of talk. They said when it was down almost nothing about the play, and when one of them toward the end put to the other, vaguely, "Is—a—this thing going?" the question had scarce the effect of being even relevant. What was clearest to them was that the people about were somehow enough taken up to leave them at their ease—but what taken up with they but half made out. Mrs. Harvey had none the less mentioned early that her presence had a reason and that she ought to attend, and her companion had asked her what she thought of a certain picture made at a given moment by the stage, in the reception of which he was so interested that it was really what had brought him. These were glances, however, that quickly strayed—strayed, for instance (as this could carry them far), in its coming to one of them to say that, whatever the piece might be, the real thing, as they had seen it at Mundham, was more than a match for any piece. For Mundham *was*, theatrically, the real thing; better for scenery, dresses, music, pretty

women, bare shoulders, everything—even coherent dialogue; a much bigger and braver show, and got up, as it
were, infinitely more "regardless." By Mundham they were
held long enough to find themselves, though with an equal
surprise, quite at one as to the special oddity of their having caught each other in such a plight. Straith said that
he supposed what his friend meant was that it was odd *he*
should have been there; to which she returned that she had
been imputing to him exactly that judgement of her own
presence.

"But why shouldn't *you* be?" he asked. "Isn't that just
what you *are*? Aren't you in your way—like those people—
a child of fortune and fashion?"

He got no more answer to this for some time than if he
had fairly wounded her. He indeed that evening got no answer at all that was direct. But in the next interval she
brought out with abruptness, taking no account of some
other matter he had just touched: "Don't you really
know—?"

She had paused. "Know what?"

Again she went on without heeding. "A place like Mundham is, for me, a survival, though poor Mundham in particular won't, for me, have survived that visit—on which
it's to be pitied, isn't it? It was a glittering ghost—since
laid!—of my old time."

Straith, at this, almost gave a start. "Have *you* got a new
time?"

"Do you mean you yourself have?"

"Well," said Straith, "mine may now be called middle-
aged. It seems so long, I mean, since I set my watch to it."

"Oh I haven't even a watch!" she returned with a laugh.
"I'm beyond watches." After which she added: "We *might*
have met more—or, I should say perhaps, have got more
out of it when we *have* met."

"Yes, it has been too little. But I've always explained it
by our living in such different worlds."

Mrs. Harvey could risk an abruptness. "Are you unhappy?"

He gave her a mild glare. "You said just now that you're
beyond watches. I'm beyond unhappiness."

She turned from him and presently brought out: "I ought absolutely to take away *something* of the play."

"By all means. There's certainly something *I* shall take."

"Ah then you must help me—give it me."

"With all my heart," said Straith, "if it *can* help you. It's my feeling of our renewal."

She had one of the sad slow headshakes that at Mundham had been impressive to Lady Claude. "That won't help me."

"Then you must let me put to you now what I should have tried to get near enough to you there to put if I hadn't been so afraid of the Ambassador. What has it been so long—our impossibility?"

"Well, I can only answer for my own vision of it, which is—which always was—that you were sorry for me, but felt a sort of scruple of showing me you had nothing better than pity to give."

"May I come to see you?" Straith asked some minutes after this.

Her words, for which he had also a while to wait, had in truth as little as his own the appearance of a reply. "*Are* you unhappy—really? Haven't you everything?"

"You're beautiful!" he said for all answer. "Mayn't I come?"

She demurred. "Where's your studio?"

"Oh not too far for me to go to places. Don't be anxious; I can walk, or even take the bus."

Mrs. Harvey once more delayed. Then she said: "Mayn't I rather come there?"

"I shall be but too delighted."

It was spoken promptly, even eagerly; yet the understanding appeared shortly after to have left between them a certain awkwardness, and it was almost as if to change the subject and relieve them equally that she suddenly reminded him of something he had spoken earlier. "You were to tell me why in particular you had to be here."

"Oh yes. To see my dresses."

"Yours!" She wondered.

"The second act. I made them out for them—designed them."

Before she could check it her tone escaped. "You?"

"I." He looked straight before him. "For the fee. And we didn't even notice them."

"*I* didn't," she confessed. But it offered the fact as a sign of her kindness for him, and this kindness was traceably what inspired something she said in the draughty porch, after the performance, while the footman of the friend, a fat rich immensely pleased lady who had given her a lift and then rejoined her from a seat in the balcony, went off to make sure of the brougham. "May I do something about your things?"

" 'Do something'?"

"When I've paid you my visit. Write something—about your pictures. I do a correspondence," said Mrs. Harvey.

He wondered as she had done in the stalls. "For a paper?"

"*The Blackport Banner.* A 'London Letter.' The new books, the new plays, the new twaddle of any sort—a little music, a little gossip, a little 'art.' You'll help me—I need it awfully—with the art. I do three a month."

"*You*—wonderful you?" He spoke as Lady Claude had done, and could no more help it again than Mrs. Harvey had been able to help it in the stalls.

"Oh as you say, for the fee!" On which, as the footman signalled, her old lady began to plunge through the crowd.

IV

At the studio, where she came to him within the week, her first movement had been to exclaim on the splendid abundance of his work. She had looked round charmed—so struck as to be, as she called it, crushed. "You've such a wonderful lot to show."

"Indeed I have!" said Stuart Straith.

"That's where you beat *us*."

"I think it may very well be," he went on, "where I beat almost every one."

"And is much of it new?"

He looked about with her. "Some of it's pretty old. But my things have a way, I admit, of growing old extraordinarily fast. They seem to me in fact nowadays quite 'born old.'"

She had after a little the manner of coming back to something. "You *are* unhappy. You're *not* beyond it. You're just nicely, just fairly and squarely, in the middle of it."

"Well," said Straith, "if it surrounds me like a desert, so that I'm lost in it, that comes to the same thing. But I want you to tell me about yourself."

She had continued at first to move about and had taken out a pocketbook, which she held up at him. "This time I shall insist on notes. You made my mind a blank about that play, which is the sort of thing we can't afford. If it hadn't been for my fat old lady and the next day's papers!" She kept looking, going up to things, saying "How wonderful!" and "oh your *way!*" and then stopping for a general impression, something in the whole charm. The place, high handsome neat, with two or three pale tapestries and several rare old pieces of furniture, showed a perfection of order, an absence of loose objects, as if it had been swept and squared for the occasion and made almost too immaculate. It was polished and cold—rather cold for the season and the weather; and Stuart Straith himself, buttoned and brushed, as fine and as clean as his room, might at her arrival have reminded her of the master of a neat bare ship on his deck and awaiting a cargo. "May I see everything? May I 'use' everything?"

"Oh no; you mayn't by any means use everything. You mayn't use half. *Did* I spoil your 'London Letter'?" he continued after a moment.

"No one can spoil them as I spoil them myself. I can't do them—I don't know how, and don't want to. I do them wrong, and the people want such trash. Of course they'll 'sack' me."

She was in the centre, and he had the effect of going round her, restless and vague, in large slow circles. "Have you done them long?"

"Two or three months—this lot. But I've done others and I know what happens. Oh, my dear, I've done strange things!"

"And is it a good job?"

She hesitated, then puffed prettily enough an indifferent

sigh. "Three and ninepence. Is that good?" He had stopped
before her, looking at her up and down. "What do you get?"
she went on, "for what you do for a play?"

"A little more, it would seem, than you. Four and sixpence. But I've only done as yet that one. Nothing else has
offered."

"I see. But something *will*, eh?"

Poor Straith took a turn again. "Did you like them—for
colour?" But again he pulled up. "Oh I forgot; we didn't
notice them!"

For a moment they could laugh about it. "I noticed them,
I assure you, in the *Banner*. 'The costumes in the second
act are of the most marvellous beauty.' That's what I said."

"Oh that'll fetch the managers!" But before her again he
seemed to take her in from head to foot. "You speak of
'using' things. If you'd only use yourself—for my enlighten-
ment. Tell me all."

"You look at me," said Mrs. Harvey, "as with the wonder
of who designs *my* costumes. How I dress on it, how I do
even what I still do on it—on the three and ninepence—is
that what you want to know?"

"What has happened to you?" Straith asked.

"How do I keep it up?" she continued as if she hadn't
heard him. "But I *don't* keep it up. *You* do," she declared
as she again looked round her.

Once more it set him off, but for a pause again almost
as quick. "How long have you been—?"

"Been what?" she asked as he faltered.

"Unhappy."

She smiled at him from a depth of indulgence. "As long
as you've been ignorant—that what I've been *wanting* is
your pity. Ah to have to know, as I believed I did, that you
supposed it would wound me, and not to have been able to
make you see it was the one thing left to me that would
help me! Give me your pity now. It's all I want. I don't
care for anything else. But give me that."

He had, as it happened at the moment, to do a smaller
and a usual thing before he could do one so great and so
strange. The youth whom he kept for service arrived with
a tea-tray, in arranging a place for which, with the sequel

of serving Mrs. Harvey, seating her and seeing the youth again out of the room, some minutes passed. "What pity could I dream of for you," he demanded as he at last dropped near her, "when I was myself so miserably sore?"

"Sore?" she wondered. "But you were happy—then."

"Happy not to have struck you as good enough? For I didn't, you know," he insisted. "You had your success, which was so immense. You had your high value, your future, your big possibilities; and I perfectly understood that, given those things, and given also my very much smaller situation, you should wish to keep yourself."

"Oh, oh!" She gasped as if hurt.

"I understand it; but how could it really make me 'happy'?" he asked.

She turned at him as with her hand on the old scar she could now carry. "You mean that all these years you've really not known—?"

"But not known what?"

His voice was so blank that at the sound of it, and at something that looked out from him, she only found another "Oh, oh!" which became the next instant a burst of tears.

V

She had appeared at first unwilling to receive him at home; but he understood it after she had left him, turning over more and more everything their meeting had shaken to the surface and piecing together memories that at last, however darkly, made a sense. He was to call on her, it was finally agreed, but not till the end of the week, when she should have finished "moving"—she had but just changed quarters; and meanwhile, as he came and went, mainly in the cold chamber of his own past endeavour, which looked even to himself as studios look when artists are dead and the public, in the arranged place, are admitted to stare, he had plenty to think about. What had come out—he could see it now—was that each, ten years before, had miserably misunderstood and then had turned for relief from pain to a perversity of pride. But it was himself above all he now

sharply judged, since women, he felt, have to get on as they
can, and for the mistake of this woman there were reasons
he had to acknowledge with a sore heart. She had really
found in the pomp of his early success, at the time they
used to meet, and to care to, exactly the ground for her
sense of failure with him that he had found in the vision
of her gross popularity for his conviction that she judged
him as comparatively small. Each had blundered, as sensitive souls of the "artistic temperament" blunder, into a
conception not only of the other's attitude, but of the other's
material situation at the moment, that had thrown them
back on stupid secrecy, where their estrangement had
grown like an evil plant in the shade. He had positively
believed her to have gone on all the while making the five
thousand a year that the first eight or ten of her so supremely happy novels had brought her in, just as she on
her side had read into the felicity of his first new hits, his
pictures "of the year" at three or four Academies, the ab-
surdest theory of the sort of career that, thanks to big
dealers and intelligent buyers, his gains would have built
up for him. It looked vulgar enough now, but it had been
grave enough then. His long detached delusion about her
"prices," at any rate, appeared to have been more than
matched by the strange stories occasionally floated to her
—and all to make her but draw more closely in—on the
subject of his own.

It was with each equally that everything had changed—
everything but the stiff consciousness in either of the need
to conceal changes from the other. If she had cherished for
long years the soreness of her not being "good" enough, so
this was what had counted most in her sustained effort to
appear at least as good as he. London meanwhile was big,
London was blind and benighted; and nothing had ever
occurred to undermine for him the fiction of her prosperity.
Before his eyes there while she sat with him she had pulled
off one by one those vain coverings of her state that she
confessed she had hitherto done her best—and so always
with an eye on himself—deceptively to draw about it. He
had felt frozen, as he listened, by such likenesses to things
he knew. He recognised as she talked, he groaned as he

understood. He understood—oh at last, whatever he hadn't done before! And yet he could well have smiled, out of their common abyss, at such odd identities and recurrences. Truly the arts were sisters, as was so often said; for what apparently could be more like the experience of one than the experience of another? And she spared him things with it all. He felt this too, just as, even while showing her how he followed, he had bethought himself of closing his lips for the hour, none too soon, on his own stale story. There had been a beautiful intelligence for that matter in her having asked him nothing more. She had overflowed because shaken by not finding him happy, and her surrender had somehow offered itself to him as her way—the first that sprang up—of considering his trouble. She had left him at all events in full possession of all the phases through which in "literary circles" acclaimed states may pass on their regular march to eclipse and extinction. One had but one's hour, and if one had it soon—it was really almost a case of choice —one didn't have it late. It might also never even remotely have approached, at its best, things ridiculously rumoured. Straith felt on the whole how little he had known of literary circles, or of any mystery but his own indeed; on which, up to actual impending collapse, he had mounted such anxious guard.

It was when he went on the Friday to see her that he took in the latest of the phases in question, which might very well be almost the final one; there was at least that comfort in it. She had just settled in a small flat, where he recognised in the steady disposal, for the best, of various objects she had not yet parted with, her reason for having made him wait. Here they had together—these two worn and baffled workers—a wonderful hour of gladness in their lost battle and of freshness in their lost youth; for it was not till Stuart Straith had also raised the heavy mask and laid it beside her own on the table that they began really to feel themselves recover something of that possibility of each other they had so wearily wasted. Only she couldn't get over it that he was like herself and that what she had shrunken to in her three or four simplified rooms had its perfect image in the specious show of his ordered studio and his accumulated work. He told everything now, kept no more back than she had kept at their previous meeting, while she repeated over and over "You—wonderful you?" as if the knowledge made a deeper darkness of fate, as if the pain of his having come down at all almost quenched the joy of his having come so much nearer. When she learned that he hadn't for three years sold a picture—"You, beautiful you?"—it seemed a new cold breath out of the dusk of her own outlook. Disappointment and despair were in such relations contagious, and there was clearly as much less again left to her as the little that was left to him. He showed her, laughing at the long queerness of it, how awfully little, as they called it, this was. He let it all come, but with more mirth than misery, and with a final abandonment of pride that was like changing at the end of a dreadful day from tight shoes to loose ones. There were moments when they might have resembled a couple united by some misdeed and meeting to decide on some desperate course; they gave themselves so to the great irony—the vision of the comic in contrasts—that precedes surrenders and extinctions.

They went over the whole thing, remounted the dwindling stream, reconstructed, explained, understood—recognised in short the particular example they gave and how without mutual suspicion they had been giving it side by side. "We're simply the case," Straith familiarly put it, "of having been had enough of. No case is perhaps more common, save that for you and for me, each in our line, it did look in the good time—didn't it?—as if nobody *could* have enough." With which they counted backward, gruesome as it was, the symptoms of satiety up to the first dawn, and lived again together the unforgettable hours—distant now —out of which it had begun to glimmer that the truth had to be faced and the right names given to the wrong facts. They laughed at their original explanations and the minor scale even of their early fears; compared notes on the fallibility of remedies and hopes and, more and more united in the identity of their lesson, made out perfectly that, though there appeared to be many kinds of success, there was only one kind of failure. And yet what had been hardest had not been to have to shrink, but in the long game of bluff as Straith called it, to have to keep up. It fairly swept them away at present, however, the hugeness of the relief of no longer keeping up as against each other. This gave them all the measure of the motive their courage, on either side, in silence and gloom, had forced into its service.

"Only what shall we do now for a motive?" Straith went on.

She thought. "A motive for courage?"

"Yes—to keep up."

"And go again for instance, do you mean, to Mundham? We shall, thank heaven, never go again to Mundham. The Mundhams are over."

> "Nous n'irons plus au bois;
> Les lauriers sont coupés,"

sang Straith. "It does cost."

"As everything costs that one does for the rich. It's not our poor relations who make us pay."

"No; one must have means to acknowledge the others. We can't afford the opulent. But it isn't only the money they take."

"It's the imagination," said Mrs. Harvey. "As they have none themselves—"

"It's an article we have to supply? We've certainly to use a lot to protect ourselves," Straith agreed. "And the strange thing is they like us."

She thought again. "That's what makes it easy to cut them. They forgive."

"Yes," her companion laughed; "once they really don't know you enough—!"

"They treat you as old friends. But what do we want now of courage?" she went on.

He wondered. "Yes, after all, what?"

"To keep up, I mean. Why *should* we keep up?"

It seemed to strike him. "I see. After all, why? The courage *not* to keep up—!"

"We have *that* at least," she declared, "haven't we?" United there at her little high-perched window overhanging grey house-tops they let the consideration of this pass between them in a deep look as well as in a hush of which the intensity had something commensurate. "If we're beaten—!" she then continued.

"Let us at least be beaten together!" He took her in his arms, she let herself go, and he held her long and close for the compact. But when they had recovered themselves enough to handle their agreement more responsibly the words in which they confirmed it broke in sweetness as well as sadness from both together: "And now to work!"

[1900]

THE GREAT
GOOD PLACE

I

George Dane had opened his eyes to a bright new day, the
face of nature well washed by last night's downpour and
shining as with high spirits, good resolutions, lively intentions—the great glare of recommencement in short fixed in
his patch of sky. He had sat up late to finish work—arrears
overwhelming, then at last had gone to bed with the pile
but little reduced. He was now to return to it after the
pause of the night; but he could only look at it, for the
time, over the bristling hedge of letters planted by the early
postman an hour before and already, on the customary
table by the chimney-piece, formally rounded and squared
by his systematic servant. It was something too merciless,
the domestic perfection of Brown. There were newspapers
on another table, ranged with the same rigour of custom,
newspapers too many—what could any creature want of so
much news?—and each with its hand on the neck of the
other, so that the row of their bodiless heads was like a
series of decapitations. Other journals, other periodicals of
every sort, folded and in wrappers, made a huddled mound
that had been growing for several days and of which he
had been wearily, helplessly aware. There were new books,

also in wrappers as well as disenveloped and dropped again
—books from publishers, books from authors, books from
friends, books from enemies, books from his own bookseller,
who took, it sometimes struck him, inconceivable things for
granted. He touched nothing, approached nothing, only
turned a heavy eye over the work, as it were, of the night
—the fact, in his high wide-windowed room, where duty
shed its hard light into every corner, of the still unashamed
admonitions. It was the old rising tide, and it rose and rose
even under a minute's watching. It had been up to his
shoulders last night—it was up to his chin now.

Nothing had *gone*, had passed on while he slept—everything had stayed; nothing, that he could yet feel, had died
—so naturally, one would have thought; many things on
the contrary had been born. To let them alone, these things,
the new things, let them utterly alone and see if that, by
chance, wouldn't somehow prove the best way to deal with
them: this fancy brushed his face for a moment as a possible solution, just giving it, as so often before, a cool wave
of air. Then he knew again as well as ever that leaving was
difficult, leaving impossible—that the only remedy, the true
soft effacing sponge, would be to *be* left, to be forgotten.
There was no footing on which a man who had ever liked
life—liked it at any rate as *he* had—could now escape it.
He must reap as he had sown. It was a thing of meshes;
he had simply gone to sleep under the net and had simply
waked up there. The net was too fine; the cords crossed
each other at spots too near together, making at each a
little tight hard knot that tired fingers were this morning
too limp and too tender to touch. Our poor friend's touched
nothing—only stole significantly into his pockets as he wandered over to the window and faintly gasped at the energy
of nature. What was most overwhelming was that she herself was so ready. She had soothed him rather, the night
before, in the small hours by the lamp. From behind the
drawn curtain of his study the rain had been audible and
in a manner merciful; washing the window in a steady
flood, it had seemed the right thing, the retarding interrupting thing, the thing that, if it would only last, might
clear the ground by floating out to a boundless sea the

innumerable objects among which his feet stumbled and strayed. He had positively laid down his pen as on a sense of friendly pressure from it. The kind full swish had been on the glass when he turned out his lamp; he had left his phrase unfinished and his papers lying quite as for the flood to bear them away in its rush. But there still on the table were the bare bones of the sentence—and not all of those; the single thing borne away and that he could never recover was the missing half that might have paired with it and begotten a figure.

Yet he could at last only turn back from the window; the world was everywhere, without and within, and the great staring egotism of its health and strength wasn't to be trusted for tact or delicacy. He faced about precisely to meet his servant and the absurd solemnity of two telegrams on a tray. Brown ought to have kicked them into the room —then he himself might have kicked them out.

"And you told me to remind you, sir—"

George Dane was at last angry. "Remind me of nothing!"

"But you insisted, sir, that I was to insist!"

He turned away in despair, using a pathetic quaver at absurd variance with his words: "If you insist, Brown, I'll kill you!" He found himself anew at the window, whence, looking down from his fourth floor, he could see the vast neighbourhood, under the trumpet-blare of the sky, beginning to rush about. There was a silence, but he knew Brown hadn't left him—knew exactly how straight and serious and stupid and faithful he stood there. After a minute he heard him again.

"It's only because, sir, you know, sir, you can't remember—"

At this Dane did flash round; it was more than at such a moment he could bear. "Can't remember, Brown? I can't forget. That's what's the matter with me."

Brown looked at him with the advantage of eighteen years of consistency. "I'm afraid you're not well, sir."

Brown's master thought. "It's a shocking thing to say, but I wish to heaven I weren't! It would be perhaps an excuse."

Brown's blankness spread like the desert. "To put them off?"

"Ah!" The sound was a groan; the plural pronoun, *any* pronoun, so mistimed. "Who is it?"

"Those ladies you spoke of—to luncheon."

"Oh!" The poor man dropped into the nearest chair and stared a while at the carpet. It was very complicated.

"How many will there be, sir?" Brown asked.

"Fifty!"

"Fifty, sir?"

Our friend, from his chair, looked vaguely about; under his hand were the telegrams, still unopened, one of which he now tore asunder. "'Do hope you sweetly won't mind, today, 1.30, my bringing poor dear Lady Mullet, who's so awfully bent,'" he read to his companion.

His companion weighed it. "How many does *she* make, sir?"

"Poor dear Lady Mullet? I haven't the least idea."

"Is she—a—deformed, sir?" Brown enquired, as if in this case she might make more.

His master wondered, then saw he figured some personal curvature. "No; she's only bent on coming!" Dane opened the other telegram and again read out: "'So sorry it's at eleventh hour impossible, and count on you here, as very greatest favour, at two sharp instead.'"

"How many does *that* make?" Brown imperturbably continued.

Dane crumpled up the two missives and walked with them to the waste-paper basket, into which he thoughtfully dropped them. "I can't say. You must do it all yourself. I shan't be there."

It was only on this that Brown showed an expression. "You'll go instead—"

"I'll go instead!" Dane raved.

Brown, however, had had occasion to show before that *he* would never desert their post. "Isn't that rather sacrificing the three?" Between respect and reproach he paused.

"*Are* there three?"

"I lay for four in all."

His master had at any rate caught his thought. "Sacrificing the three to the one, you mean? Oh I'm not going to *her!*"

Brown's famous "thoroughness"—his great virtue—had never been so dreadful. "Then where *are* you going?"

Dane sat down to his table and stared at his ragged phrase. "'*There* is a happy land—far far away!'" He chanted it like a sick child and knew that for a minute Brown never moved. During this minute he felt between his shoulders the gimlet of criticism.

"Are you quite sure you're all right?"

"It's my certainty that overwhelms me, Brown. Look about you and judge. Could anything be more 'right,' in the view of the envious world, than everything that surrounds us here: that immense array of letters, notes, circulars; that pile of printers' proofs, magazines and books; these perpetual telegrams, these impending guests, this retarded, unfinished and interminable work? What could a man want more?"

"Do you mean there's too much, sir?"—Brown had sometimes these flashes.

"There's too much. There's too much. But *you* can't help it, Brown."

"No, sir," Brown assented. "Can't *you?*"

"I'm thinking—I must see. There are hours—!" Yes, there were hours, and this was one of them: he jerked himself up for another turn in his labyrinth, but still not touching, not even again meeting, his admonisher's eye. If he was a genius for any one he was a genius for Brown; but it was terrible what that meant, being a genius for Brown. There had been times when he had done full justice to the way it kept him up; now, however, it was almost the worst of the avalanche. "Don't trouble about me," he went on insincerely and looking askance through his window again at the bright and beautiful world. "Perhaps it will rain—that *may* not be over. I do love the rain," he weakly pursued. "Perhaps, better still, it will snow."

Brown now had indeed a perceptible expression, and the expression was of fear. "Snow, sir—the end of May?" Without pressing this point he looked at his watch. "You'll feel better when you've had breakfast."

"I dare say," said Dane, whom breakfast struck in fact as a pleasant alternative to opening letters. "I'll come in immediately."

"But without waiting—?"

"Waiting for what?"

Brown at last, under his apprehension, had his first lapse from logic, which he betrayed by hesitating in the evident hope his companion might by a flash of remembrance relieve him of an invidious duty. But the only flashes now were the good man's own. "You say you can't forget, sir; but you do forget—"

"Is it anything very horrible?" Dane broke in.

Brown hung fire. "Only the gentleman you told me you had asked—"

Dane again took him up; horrible or not it came back—indeed its mere coming back classed it. "To breakfast to-day? It *was* today; I see." It came back, yes, came back; the appointment with the young man—he supposed him young—whose letter, the letter about—what was it?—had struck him. "Yes, yes; wait, wait."

"Perhaps he'll do you good, sir," Brown suggested.

"Sure to—sure to. All right!" Whatever he might do he would at least prevent some other doing: that was present to our friend as, on the vibration of the electric bell at the door of the flat, Brown moved away. Two things in the short interval that followed were present to Dane: his having utterly forgotten the connexion, the whence, whither and why of his guest; and his continued disposition not to touch—no, not with the finger. Ah if he might *never* again touch! All the unbroken seals and neglected appeals lay there while, for a pause he couldn't measure, he stood before the chimney-piece with his hands still in his pockets. He heard a brief exchange of words in the hall, but never afterwards recovered the time taken by Brown to reappear, to precede and announce another person—a person whose name somehow failed to reach Dane's ear. Brown went off again to serve breakfast, leaving host and guest confronted. The duration of this first stage also, later on, defied measurement; but that little mattered, for in the train of what happened came promptly the second, the third, the fourth, the rich succession of the others. Yet what happened was but that Dane took his hand from his pocket, held it straight out and felt it taken. Thus indeed, if he had wanted never again to touch, it was already done.

II

He might have been a week in the place—the scene of his new consciousness—before he spoke at all. The occasion of it then was that one of the quiet figures he had been idly watching drew at last nearer and showed him a face that was the highest expression—to his pleased but as yet slightly confused perception—of the general charm. What *was* the general charm? He couldn't, for that matter, easily have phrased it; it was such an abyss of negatives, such an absence of positives and of everything. The oddity was that after a minute he was struck as by the reflexion of his own very image in this first converser seated with him, on the easy bench, under the high clear portico and above the wide far-reaching garden, where the things that most showed in the greenness were the surface of still water and the white note of old statues. The absence of everything was, in the aspect of the Brother who had thus informally joined him—a man of his own age, tired distinguished modest kind—really, as he could soon see, but the absence of what he didn't want. He didn't want, for the time, anything but just to *be* there, to steep in the bath. He was in the bath yet, the broad deep bath of stillness. They sat in it together now with the water up to their chins. He hadn't had to talk, he hadn't had to think, he had scarce even had to feel. He had been sunk that way before, sunk—when and where?—in another flood; only a flood of rushing waters in which bumping and gasping were all. *This* was a current so slow and so tepid that one floated practically without motion and without chill. The break of silence was not immediate, though Dane seemed indeed to feel it begin before a sound passed. It could pass quite sufficiently without words that he and his mate were Brothers, and what that meant.

He wondered, but with no want of ease—for want of ease

was impossible—if his friend found in *him* the same likeness, the proof of peace, the gage of what the place could do. The long afternoon crept to its end; the shadows fell further and the sky glowed deeper; but nothing changed—nothing *could* change—in the element itself. It was a conscious security. It was wonderful! Dane had lived into it, but he was still immensely aware. He would have been sorry to lose that, for just this fact as yet, the blest fact of consciousness, seemed the greatest thing of all. Its only fault was that, being in itself such an occupation, so fine an unrest in the heart of gratitude, the life of the day all went to it. But what even then was the harm? He had come only to come, to take what he found. This was the part where the great cloister, enclosed externally on three sides and probably the largest lightest fairest effect, to his charmed sense, that human hands could ever have expressed in dimensions of length and breadth, opened to the south its splendid fourth quarter, turned to the great view an outer gallery that combined with the rest of the portico to form a high dry loggia, such as he a little pretended to himself he had, in the Italy of old days, seen in old cities, old convents, old villas. This recalled disposition of some great abode of an Order, some mild Monte Cassino, some Grande Chartreuse more accessible, was his main term of comparison; but he knew he had really never anywhere beheld anything at once so calculated and so generous.

Three impressions in particular had been with him all the week, and he could but recognise in silence their happy effect on his nerves. How it was all managed he couldn't have told—he had been content moreover till now with his ignorance of cause and pretext; but whenever he chose to listen with a certain intentness he made out as from a distance the sound of slow sweet bells. How could they be so far and yet so audible? How could they be so near and yet so faint? How above all could they, in such an arrest of life, be, to *time* things, so frequent? The very essence of the bliss of Dane's whole change had been precisely that there was nothing now to time. It was the same with the slow footsteps that, always within earshot to the vague attention, marked the space and the leisure, seemed, in long cool arcades, lightly to fall and perpetually to recede. This was the second impression, and it melted into the third, as, for that matter, every form of softness, in the great good place, was but a further turn, without jerk or gap, of the endless roll of serenity. The quiet footsteps were quiet figures; the quiet figures that, to the eye, kept the picture human and brought its perfection within reach. This perfection, he felt on the bench by his friend, was now more within reach than ever. His friend at last turned to him a look different from the looks of friends in London clubs.

"The thing was to find it out!"

It was extraordinary how this remark fitted into his thought. "Ah wasn't it? And when I think," said Dane, "of all the people who haven't and who never will!" He sighed over these unfortunates with a tenderness that, in its degree, was practically new to him, feeling too how well his companion would know the people he meant. He only meant some, but they were all who'd want it; though of these, no doubt—well, for reasons, for things that, in the world, he had observed—there would never be too many. Not all perhaps who wanted would really find; but none at least would find who didn't really want. And then what the need would have to have been first! What it at first had had to be for himself! He felt afresh, in the light of his companion's face, what it might still be even when deeply satisfied, as well as what communication was established by the mere common knowledge of it.

"Every man must arrive by himself and on his own feet—isn't that so? We're Brothers here for the time, as in a great monastery, and we immediately think of each other and recognise each other as such; but we must have first got here as we can, and we meet after long journeys by complicated ways. Moreover we meet—don't we?—with closed eyes."

"Ah don't speak as if we were dead!" Dane laughed.

"I shan't mind death if it's like this," his friend replied.

It was too obvious, as Dane gazed before him, that one wouldn't; but after a moment he asked with the first articulation as yet of his most elementary wonder: "Where is it?"

"I shouldn't be surprised if it were much nearer than one ever suspected."

"Nearer 'town,' do you mean?"

"Nearer everything—nearer every one."

George Dane thought. "Would it be somewhere for instance down in Surrey?"

His Brother met him on this with a shade of reluctance. "Why should we call it names? It must have a climate, you see."

"Yes," Dane happily mused; "without that—!" All it so securely did have overwhelmed him again, and he couldn't help breaking out: "*What* is it?"

"Oh it's positively a part of our ease and our rest and our change, I think, that we don't at all know and that we may really call it, for that matter, anything in the world we like —the thing for instance we love it most for being."

"I know what *I* call it," said Dane after a moment. Then as his friend listened with interest: "Just simply 'The Great Good Place.' "

"I see—what can you say more? I've put it to myself perhaps a little differently." They sat there as innocently as small boys confiding to each other the names of toy animals. " 'The Great Want Met.' "

"Ah yes—that's it!"

"Isn't it enough for us that it's a place carried on for our benefit so admirably that we strain our ears in vain for a creak of the machinery? Isn't it enough for us that it's simply a thorough hit?"

"Ah a hit!" Dane benignantly murmured.

"It does for us what it pretends to do," his companion went on; "the mystery isn't deeper than that. The thing's probably simple enough in fact, and on a thoroughly practical basis; only it has had its origin in a splendid thought, in a real stroke of genius."

"Yes," Dane returned, "in a sense—on somebody or other's part—so exquisitely personal!"

"Precisely—it rests, like all good things, on experience. The 'great want' comes home—that's the great thing it does! On the day it came home to the right mind this dear place was constituted. It always moreover in the long run *has* been met—it always must be. How can it not require to be, more and more, as pressure of every sort grows?"

Dane, with his hands folded in his lap, took in these words of wisdom. "Pressure of every sort *is* growing!" he placidly observed.

"I see well enough what that fact has done to *you*," his Brother declared.

Dane smiled. "I couldn't have borne it longer. I don't know what would have become of me."

"I know what would have become of *me*."

"Well, it's the same thing."

"Yes," said Dane's companion, "it's doubtless the same thing." On which they sat in silence a little, seeming pleasantly to follow, in the view of the green garden, the vague movements of the monster—madness, surrender, collapse—they had escaped. Their bench was like a box at the opera. "And I may perfectly, you know," the Brother pursued, "have seen you before. I may even have known you well. We don't know."

They looked at each other again serenely enough, and at last Dane said: "No, we don't know."

"That's what I meant by our coming with our eyes closed. Yes—there's something out. There's a gap, a link missing, the great hiatus!" the Brother laughed. "It's as simple a story as the old, old rupture—the break that lucky Catholics have always been able to make, that they're still, with their innumerable religious houses, able to make, by going into 'retreat.' I don't speak of the pious exercises—I speak only of the material simplification. I don't speak of the putting off of one's self; I speak only—if one has a self worth sixpence—of the getting it back. The place, the time, the way were, for those of the old persuasion, always there —are indeed practically there for them as much as ever. They can always get off—the blessed houses receive. So it was high time that we—we of the great Protestant peoples, still more, if possible, in the sensitive individual case, over-scored and overwhelmed, still more congested with mere quantity and prostituted, through our 'enterprise,' to mere profanity—should learn how to get off, should find somewhere *our* retreat and remedy. There was such a huge chance for it!"

Dane laid his hand on his companion's arm. "It's charming how when we speak for ourselves we speak for each other. That was exactly what I said!" He had fallen to recalling from over the gulf the last occasion.

The Brother, as if it would do them both good, only desired to draw him out. "What you 'said'—?"

"To *him*—that morning." Dane caught a far bell again and heard a slow footstep. A quiet presence passed somewhere—neither of them turned to look. What was little by little more present to him was the perfect taste. It was supreme—it was everywhere. "I just dropped my burden—and he received it."

"And was it very great?"

"Oh such a load!" Dane said with gaiety.

"Trouble, sorrow, doubt?"

"Oh no—worse than that!"

"Worse?"

"'Success'—the vulgarest kind!" He mentioned it now as with amusement.

"Ah I know that too! No one in future, as things are going, will be able to face success."

"Without something of this sort—never. The better it is the worse—the greater the deadlier. But my one pain here," Dane continued, "is in thinking of my poor friend."

"The person to whom you've already alluded?"

He tenderly assented. "My substitute in the world. Such an unutterable benefactor. He turned up that morning when everything had somehow got on my nerves, when the whole great globe indeed, nerves or no nerves, seemed to have appallingly squeezed itself into my study and to be bent on simply swelling there. It wasn't a question of nerves, it was a mere question of the dislodgement and derangement of everything—of a general submersion by our eternal too much. I didn't know *où donner de la tête*—I couldn't have gone a step further."

The intelligence with which the Brother listened kept them as children feeding from the same bowl. "And then you got the tip?"

"I got the tip!" Dane happily sighed.

"Well, we all get it. But I dare say differently."

"Then how did *you*—?"

The Brother hesitated, smiling. "You tell me first."

III

"Well," said George Dane, "it was a young man I had never seen—a man at any rate much younger than myself —who had written to me and sent me some article, some book. I read the stuff, was much struck with it, told him so and thanked him—on which of course I heard from him again. Ah *that*—!" Dane comically sighed. "He asked me things—his questions were interesting; but to save time and writing I said to him: 'Come to see me—we can talk a little; but all I can give you is half an hour at breakfast.' He arrived to the minute on a day when more than ever in my life before I seemed, as it happened, in the endless press and stress, to have lost possession of my soul and to be surrounded only with the affairs of other people, smothered in mere irrelevant importunity. It made me literally ill—made me feel as I had never felt that should I once really for an hour lose hold of the thing itself, the thing that did matter and that I was trying for, I should never recover it again. The wild waters would close over me and I should drop straight to the dark depths where the vanquished dead lie."

"I follow you every step of your way," said the friendly Brother. "The wild waters, you mean, of our horrible time."

"Of our horrible time precisely. Not of course—as we sometimes dream—of any other."

"Yes, any other's only a dream. We really know none but our own."

"No, thank God—that's enough," Dane contentedly smiled. "Well, my young man turned up, and I hadn't been a minute in his presence before making out that practically it would be in him somehow or other to help me. He came to me with envy, envy extravagant—really passionate. I was, heaven save us, the great 'success' for him; he himself was starved and broken and beaten. How can I say what passed between us?—it was so strange, so swift, so much a matter, from one to the other, of instant perception and agreement. He was so clever and haggard and hungry!"

"Hungry?" the Brother asked.

"I don't mean for bread, though he had none too much, I think, even of that. I mean for—well, what *I* had and what I was a monument of to him as I stood there up to my neck in preposterous evidence. He, poor chap, had been for ten years serenading closed windows and had never yet caused a shutter to show that it stirred. *My* dim blind was the first raised to him an inch; my reading of his book, my impression of it, my note and my invitation, formed literally the only response ever dropped into his dark alley. He saw in my littered room, my shattered day, my bored face and spoiled temper—it's embarrassing, but I must tell you—the very proof of my pudding, the very blaze of my glory. And he saw in my repletion and my 'renown'—deluded innocent! —what he had yearned for in vain."

"What he had yearned for was to *be* you," said the Brother. Then he added: "I see where you're coming out."

"At my saying to him by the end of five minutes: 'My dear fellow, I wish you'd just try it—wish you'd for a while just *be* me!' You go straight to the mark, good Brother, and that was exactly what occurred—extraordinary though it was that we should both have understood. I saw what he could give, and he did too. He saw moreover what I could take; in fact what he saw was wonderful."

"He must be very remarkable!" Dane's converser laughed.

"There's no doubt of it whatever—far more remarkable than I. That's just the reason why what I put to him in joke—with a fantastic desperate irony—became, in his hands, with his vision of his chance, the blessed means and measure of my sitting on this spot in your company. 'Oh if I could just *shift* it all—make it straight over for an hour to other shoulders! If there only *were* a pair!'—that's the way I put it to him. And then at something in his face, 'Would *you*, by a miracle, undertake it?' I asked. I let him know all it meant—how it meant that he should at that very moment step in. It meant that he should finish my work and open my letters and keep my engagements and be subject, for better or worse, to my contacts and complications. It meant that he should live with my life and think with my brain and write with my hand and speak with my voice. It meant above all that I should get off. He accepted with greatness—rose to it like a hero. Only he said: 'What will become of *you?*'"

"There was the rub!" the Brother admitted.

"Ah but only for a minute. He came to my help again," Dane pursued, "when he saw I couldn't quite meet that, could at least only say that I wanted to think, wanted to cease, wanted to do the thing itself—the thing that mattered and that I was trying for, miserable me, and that thing only —and therefore wanted first of all really to *see* it again, planted out, crowded out, frozen out as it now so long had been. 'I know what you want,' he after a moment quietly remarked to me. 'Ah what I want doesn't exist!' 'I know what you want,' he repeated. At that I began to believe him."

"Had you any idea yourself?" the Brother's attention breathed.

"Oh yes," said Dane, "and it was just my idea that made me despair. There it was as sharp as possible in my imagination and my longing—there it was so utterly *not* in the fact. We were sitting together on my sofa as we waited for breakfast. He presently laid his hand on my knee—showed me a face that the sudden great light in it had made, for me, indescribably beautiful. 'It exists—it exists,' he at last said. And so I remember we sat a while and looked at each other, with the final effect of my finding that I absolutely believed him. I remember we weren't at all solemn—we smiled with the joy of discoverers. He was as glad as I—he was tremendously glad. That came out in the whole manner of his reply to the appeal that broke from me: 'Where is it then in God's name? Tell me without delay where it is!'"

The Brother had bent such a sympathy! "He gave you the address?"

"He was thinking it out—feeling for it, catching it. He has a wonderful head of his own and must be making of the whole thing, while we sit here patching and gossiping, something much better than ever *I* did. The mere sight of his face, the sense of his hand on my knee, made me, after a little, feel that he not only knew what I wanted but was getting nearer to it than I could have got in ten years. He suddenly sprang up and went over to my study-table—sat straight down there as if to write me my prescription or my passport. Then it was—at the mere sight of his back, which was turned to me—that I felt the spell work. I simply sat and watched him with the queerest deepest sweetest sense in the world—the sense of an ache that had stopped. All life was lifted; I myself at least was somehow off the ground. He was already where I had been."

"And where were you?" the Brother amusedly asked.

"Just on the sofa always, leaning back on the cushion and feeling a delicious ease. He was already me."

"And who were *you?*" the Brother continued.

"Nobody. That was the fun."

"That *is* the fun," said the Brother with a sigh like soft music.

Dane echoed the sigh, and, as nobody talking with nobody, they sat there together still and watched the sweet wide picture darken into tepid night.

I V

At the end of three weeks—so far as time was distinct —Dane began to feel there was something he had recovered. It was the thing they never named—partly for want of the need and partly for lack of the word; for what indeed was the description that would cover it all? The only real need was to know it, to see it in silence. Dane had a private practical sign for it, which, however, he had appropriated by theft—"the vision and the faculty divine." That doubtless was a flattering phrase for his idea of his genius; the genius was at all events what he had been in danger of losing and had at last held by a thread that might at any moment have broken. The change was that little by little his hold had grown firmer, so that he drew in the line—more and more each day—with a pull he was delighted to find it would bear. The mere dream-sweetness of the place was superseded; it was more and more a world of reason and order, of sensible visible arrangement. It ceased to be strange—it was high triumphant clearness. He cultivated, however, but vaguely the question of where he was, finding it near enough the mark to be almost sure that if he wasn't in Kent he was then probably in Hampshire. He paid for everything but that—that wasn't one of the items. Payment, he had soon learned, was definite; it consisted of sovereigns and shillings—just like those of the world he had left, only parted with more ecstatically—that he committed, in his room, to a fixed receptacle and that were removed in his absence by one of the unobtrusive effaced agents (shadows projected on the hours like the noiseless march of the sun-dial) that were always at work. The scene had whole sides that reminded and resembled, and a pleased resigned perception of these things was at once the effect and the cause of its grace.

Dane picked out of his dim past a dozen halting similes. The sacred silent convent was one; another was the bright country-house. He did the place no outrage to liken it to an hotel; he permitted himself on occasion to feel it suggest a club. Such images, however, but flickered and went out— they lasted only long enough to light up the difference. An hotel without noise, a club without newspapers—when he turned his face to what it was "without" the view opened wide. The only approach to a real analogy was in himself and his companions. They were brothers, guests, members; they were even, if one liked—and they didn't in the least mind what they were called—"regular boarders." It wasn't they who made the conditions, it was the conditions that made them. These conditions found themselves accepted, clearly, with an appreciation, with a rapture, it was rather to be called, that proceeded, as the very air that pervaded them and the force that sustained, from their quiet and noble assurance. They combined to form the large simple idea of a general refuge—an image of embracing arms, of liberal accommodation. What was the effect really but the poetisation by perfect taste of a type common enough? There was no daily miracle; the perfect taste, with the aid of space, did the trick. What underlay and overhung it all, better yet, Dane mused, was some original inspiration, but

confirmed, unquenched, some happy thought of an individual breast. It had been born somehow and somewhere—it
had had to insist on being—the blest conception. The author
might remain in the obscure for that was part of the perfection: personal service so hushed and regulated that you
scarce caught it in the act and only knew it by its results.
Yet the wise mind was everywhere—the whole thing infallibly centred at the core in a consciousness. And what a
consciousness it had been, Dane thought, a consciousness
how like his own! The wise mind had felt, the wise mind
had suffered; then, for all the worried company of minds,
the wise mind had seen a chance. Of the creation thus arrived at you could none the less never have said if it were
the last echo of the old or the sharpest note of the modern.

Dane again and again, among the far bells and the soft
footfalls, in cool cloister and warm garden, found himself
wanting not to know more and yet liking not to know less.
It was part of the high style and the grand manner that
there was no personal publicity, much less any personal
reference. Those things were in the world—in what he had
left; there was no vulgarity here of credit or claim or fame.
The real exquisite was to be without the complication of
an identity, and the greatest boon of all, doubtless, the solid
security, the clear confidence one could feel in the keeping
of the contract. That was what had been most in the wise
mind—the importance of the absolute sense, on the part
of its beneficiaries, that what was offered was guaranteed.
They had no concern but to pay—the wise mind knew what
they paid for. It was present to Dane each hour that he
could never be overcharged. Oh the deep deep bath, the
soft cool plash in the stillness!—this, time after time, as if
under regular treatment, a sublimated German "cure," was
the vivid name for his luxury. The inner life woke up again,
and it was the inner life, for people of his generation, victims
of the modern madness, mere maniacal extension and motion, that was returning health. He had talked of independence and written of it, but what a cold flat word it had
been! This was the wordless fact itself—the uncontested
possession of the long sweet stupid day. The fragrance of
flowers just wandered through the void, and the quiet re-

currence of delicate plain fare in a high, clean refectory where the soundless simple service was a triumph of art. That, as he analysed, remained the constant explanation: all the sweetness and serenity were created calculated things. He analysed, however, but in a desultory way and with a positive delight in the residuum of mystery that made for the great agent in the background the innermost shrine of the idol of a temple; there were odd moments for it, mild meditations when, in the broad cloister of peace or some garden-nook where the air was light, a special glimpse of beauty or reminder of felicity seemed, in passing, to hover and linger. In the mere ecstasy of change that had at first possessed him he hadn't discriminated—had only let himself sink, as I have mentioned, down to hushed depths. Then had come the slow soft stages of intelligence and notation, more marked and more fruitful perhaps after that long talk with his mild mate in the twilight, and seeming to wind up the process by putting the key into his hand. This key, pure gold, was simply the cancelled list. Slowly and blissfully he read into the general wealth of his comfort all the particular absences of which it was composed. One by one he touched, as it were, all the things it was such rapture to be without.

It was the paradise of his own room that was most in-debted to them—a great square fair chamber, all beautified with omissions, from which, high up, he looked over a long valley to a far horizon, and in which he was vaguely and pleasantly reminded of some old Italian picture, some Carpaccio or some early Tuscan, the representation of a world without newspapers and letters, without telegrams and photographs, without the dreadful fatal too much. There, for a blessing, he *could* read and write; there above all he could do nothing—he could live. And there were all sorts of freedoms—always, for the occasion, the particular right one. He could bring a book from the library—he could bring two, he could bring three. An effect produced by the charming place was that for some reason he never wanted to bring more. The library was a benediction—high and clear and plain like everything else, but with something, in all its arched amplitude, unconfused and brave and gay. He should never forget, he knew, the throb of immediate perception with which he first stood there, a single glance round sufficing so to show him that it would give him what for years he had desired. He had not had detachment, but there was detachment here—the sense of a great silver bowl from which he could ladle up the melted hours. He strolled about from wall to wall, too pleasantly in tune on that occasion to sit down punctually or to choose; only recognising from shelf to shelf every dear old book that he had had to put off or never returned to; every deep distinct voice of another time that in the hubbub of the world, he had had to take for lost and unheard. He came back of course soon, came back every day; enjoyed there, of all the rare strange moments, those that were at once most quickened and most caught—moments in which every apprehension counted double and every act of the mind was a lover's embrace. It was the quarter he perhaps, as the days went on, liked best; though indeed it only shared with the rest of the place, with every aspect to which his face happened to be turned, the power to remind him of the masterly general care.

There were times when he looked up from his book to lose himself in the mere tone of the picture that never failed at any moment or at any angle. The picture was always there, yet was made up of things common enough. It was in the way an open window in a broad recess let in the pleasant morning; in the way the dry air pricked into faint freshness the gilt of old bindings; in the way an empty chair beside a table unlittered showed a volume just laid down; in the way a happy Brother—as detached as one's self and with his innocent back presented—lingered before a shelf with the slow sound of turned pages. It was a part of the whole impression that, by some extraordinary law, one's vision seemed less from the facts than the facts from one's vision; that the elements were determined at the moment by the moment's need or the moment's sympathy. What most prompted this reflexion was the degree in which Dane had after a while a consciousness of company. After that talk with the good Brother on the bench there were other good Brothers in other places—always in cloister or garden some figure that stopped if he himself stopped and with which a greeting became, in the easiest way in the

world, a sign of the diffused amenity and the consecrating
ignorance. For always, always, in all contacts, was the balm
of a happy blank. What he had felt the first time recurred:
the friend was always new and yet at the same time—it was
amusing, not disturbing—suggested the possibility that he
might be but an old one altered. That was only delightful
—as positively delightful in the particular, the actual conditions as it might have been the reverse in the conditions
abolished. These others, the abolished, came back to Dane
at last so easily that he could exactly measure each difference, but with what he had finally been hustled on to hate
in them robbed of its terror in consequence of something
that had happened. What had happened was that in tran-
quil walks and talks the deep spell had worked and he had
got his soul again. He had drawn in by this time, with his
lightened hand, the whole of the long line, and that fact
just dangled at the end. He could put his other hand on it,
he could unhook it, he was once more in possession. This,
as it befell, was exactly what he supposed he must have
said to a comrade beside whom, one afternoon in the
cloister, he found himself measuring steps.

"Oh it comes—comes of itself, doesn't it, thank goodness?
—just by the simple fact of finding room and time!"

The comrade was possibly a novice or in a different stage
from his own; there was at any rate a vague envy in the
recognition that shone out of the fatigued yet freshened
face. "It has come to *you* then?—you've got what you
wanted?" That was the gossip and interchange that could
pass to and fro. Dane, years before, had gone in for three
months of hydropathy, and there was a droll echo, in this
scene, of the old questions of the water-cure, the questions
asked in the periodical pursuit of the "reaction"—the ail-
ment, the progress of each, the action of the skin and the
state of the appetite. Such memories worked in now—all
familiar reference, all easy play of mind; and among them
our friends, round and round, fraternised ever so softly till,
suddenly stopping short, Dane, with a hand on his companion's arm, broke into the happiest laugh he had yet
sounded.

V

"Why it's raining!" And he stood and looked at the splash of the shower and the shine of the wet leaves. It was one of the summer sprinkles that bring out sweet smells.

"Yes—but why not?" his mate demanded.

"Well—because it's so charming. It's so exactly right."

"But everything *is*. Isn't that just why we're here?"

"Just exactly," Dane said; "only I've been living in the beguiled supposition that we've somehow or other a climate."

"So have I, so I dare say has every one. Isn't that the blest moral?—that we live in beguiled suppositions. They come so easily here, where nothing contradicts them." The good Brother looked placidly forth—Dane could identify his phase. "A climate doesn't consist in its never raining, does it?"

"No, I dare say not. But somehow the good I've got has been half the great easy absence of all that friction of which the question of weather mostly forms a part—has been indeed largely the great easy perpetual air-bath."

"Ah yes—that's not a delusion; but perhaps the sense comes a little from our breathing an emptier medium. There are fewer things *in* it! Leave people alone, at all events, and the air's what they take to. Into the closed and the stuffy they have to be driven. I've had too—I think we must all have—a fond sense of the south."

"But imagine it," said Dane, laughing, "in the beloved British islands and so near as we are to Bradford!"

His friend was ready enough to imagine. "To Bradford?" he asked, quite unperturbed. "How near?"

Dane's gaiety grew. "Oh it doesn't matter!"

His friend, quite unmystified, accepted it. "There are things to puzzle out—otherwise it would be dull. It seems to me one can puzzle them."

"It's because we're so well disposed," Dane said.

"Precisely—we find good in everything."

"In everything," Dane went on. "The conditions settle that—they determine us."

They resumed their stroll, which evidently represented on the good Brother's part infinite agreement. "Aren't they probably in fact very simple?" he presently enquired. "Isn't simplification the secret?"

"Yes, but applied with a tact!"

"There it is. The thing's so perfect that it's open to as many interpretations as any other great work—a poem of Goethe, a dialogue of Plato, a symphony of Beethoven."

"It simply stands quiet, you mean," said Dane, "and lets us call it names?"

"Yes, but all such loving ones. We're 'staying' with some one—some delicious host or hostess who never shows."

"It's liberty-hall—absolutely," Dane assented.

"Yes—or a convalescent home."

To this, however, Dane demurred. "Ah that, it seems to me, scarcely puts it. You weren't *ill*—were you? I'm very sure *I* really wasn't. I was only, as the world goes, too 'beastly well'!"

The good Brother wondered. "But if we couldn't keep it up—?"

"We couldn't keep it *down*—that was all the matter!"

"I see—I see." The good Brother sighed contentedly; after which he brought out again with kindly humour: "It's a sort of kindergarten!"

"The next thing you'll be saying that we're babes at the breast!"

"Of some great mild invisible mother who stretches away into space and whose lap's the whole valley—?"

"And her bosom"—Dane completed the figure—"the noble eminence of our hill? That will do; anything will do that covers the essential fact."

"And what do you call the essential fact?"

"Why that—as in old days on Swiss lakesides—we're *en pension*."

The good Brother took this gently up. "I remember—I remember: seven francs a day without wine! But alas it's more than seven francs here."

"Yes, it's considerably more," Dane had to confess. "Perhaps it isn't particularly cheap."

"Yet should you call it particularly dear?" his friend after a moment enquired.

George Dane had to think. "How do I know, after all?

What practice has one ever had in estimating the inestima-
ble? Particular cheapness certainly isn't the note we feel
struck all round; but don't we fall naturally into the view
that there *must* be a price to anything so awfully sane?"

The good Brother in his turn reflected. "We fall into the
view that it must pay—that it does pay."

"Oh yes; it does pay!" Dane eagerly echoed. "If it didn't
it wouldn't last. It has *got* to last of course!" he declared.

"So that we can come back?"

"Yes—think of knowing that we shall be able to!"

They pulled up again at this and, facing each other,
thought of it, or at any rate pretended to; for what was
really in their eyes was the dread of a loss of the clue.
"Oh when we want it again we shall find it," said the good
Brother. "If the place really pays it will keep on."

"Yes, that's the beauty; that it isn't, thank goodness, carried on only for love."

"No doubt, no doubt; and yet, thank goodness, there's
love in it too." They had lingered as if, in the mild moist
air, they were charmed with the patter of the rain and the
way the garden drank it. After a little, however, it did look
rather as if they were trying to talk each other out of a
faint small fear. They saw the increasing rage of life and
the recurrent need, and they wondered proportionately
whether to return to the front when their hour should
sharply strike would be the end of the dream. Was this
a threshold perhaps, after all, that could only be crossed
one way? They must return to the front sooner or later—
that was certain: for each his hour would strike. The flower
would have been gathered and the trick played—the sands
would in short have run.

There, in its place, *was* life—with all its rage; the vague
unrest of the need for action knew it again, the stir of the
faculty that had been refreshed and reconsecrated. They
seemed each, thus confronted, to close their eyes a moment
for dizziness; then they were again at peace and the Brother's confidence rang out. "Oh we shall meet!"

"Here, do you mean?"

"Yes—and I dare say in the world too."

"But we shan't recognise or know," said Dane.

"In the world, do you mean?"

"Neither in the world nor here."

"Not a bit—not the least little bit, you think?"

Dane turned it over. "Well, so is it that it seems to me all best to hang together. But we shall see."

His friend happily concurred. "We shall see." And at this, for farewell, the Brother held out his hand.

"You're going?" Dane asked.

"No, but I thought *you* were."

It was odd, but at this Dane's hour seemed to strike—his consciousness to crystallise. "Well, I am. I've got it. You stay?" he went on.

"A little longer."

Dane hesitated. "You haven't yet got it?"

"Not altogether—but I think it's coming."

"Good!" Dane kept his hand, giving it a final shake, and at that moment the sun glimmered again through the shower, but with the rain still falling on the hither side of it and seeming to patter even more in the brightness. "Hallo —how charming!"

The Brother looked a moment from under the high arch —then again turned his face to our friend. He gave this time his longest happiest sigh. "Oh it's all right!"

But why was it, Dane after a moment found himself wondering, that in the act of separation his own hand was so long retained? Why but through a queer phenomenon of change, on the spot, in his companion's face—change that gave it another, but an increasing and above all a much more familiar identity, an identity not beautiful, but more and more distinct, an identity with that of his servant, with the most conspicuous, the physiognomic seat of the public propriety of Brown? To this anomaly his eyes slowly opened; it was not his good Brother, it was verily Brown who possessed his hand. If his eyes had to open it was because they had been closed and because Brown appeared to think he had better wake up. So much as this Dane took in, but the effect of his taking it was a relapse into darkness, a recontraction of the lids just prolonged enough to give Brown time, on a second thought, to withdraw his touch and move softly away. Dane's next consciousness was that of the desire to make sure he *was* away, and this desire had somehow the result of dissipating the obscurity. The obscurity was completely gone by the time he had made out that the back of a person writing at his study-table was presented to him. He recognised a portion of a figure that he had somewhere described to somebody —the intent shoulders of the unsuccessful young man who had come that bad morning to breakfast. It was strange, he at last mused, but the young man was still there. How long had he stayed—days, weeks, months? He was exactly in the position in which Dane had last seen him. Every-thing—stranger still—was exactly in that position; every-thing at least but the light of the window, which came in from another quarter and showed a different hour. It wasn't after breakfast now; it was after—well, what? He suppressed a gasp—it was after everything. And yet—quite literally—there were but two other differences. One of these was that if he was still on the sofa he was now lying down; the other was the patter on the glass that showed him how the rain —the great rain of the night—had come back. It was the rain of the night, yet when had he last heard it? But two minutes before? Then how many were there before the young man at the table, who seemed intensely occupied, found a moment to look round at him and, on meeting his open eyes, get up and draw near?

"You've slept all day," said the young man.

"All day?"

The young man looked at his watch. "From ten to six. You were extraordinarily tired. I just after a bit let you alone, and you were soon off." Yes, that was it; he had been "off"—off, off, off. He began to fit it together: while he had been off the young man had been on. But there were still some few confusions; Dane lay looking up. "Ev-erything's done," the young man continued.

"Everything?"

"Everything."

Dane tried to take it all in, but was embarrassed and could only say weakly and quite apart from the matter: "I've been so happy!"

"So have I," said the young man. He positively looked

so; seeing which George Dane wondered afresh, and then in his wonder read it indeed quite as another face, quite, in a puzzling way, as another person's. Every one was a little some one else. While he asked himself who else then the young man was, this benefactor, struck by his appealing stare, broke again into perfect cheer. "It's all right!" That answered Dane's question; the face was the face turned to him by the good Brother there in the portico while they listened together to the rustle of the shower. It was all queer, but all pleasant and all distinct, so distinct that the last words in his ear—the same from both quarters—appeared the effect of a single voice. Dane rose and looked about his room, which seemed disencumbered, different, twice as large. It *was* all right.

[1900]

THE JOLLY CORNER

I

"Every one asks me what I 'think' of everything," said
Spencer Brydon; "and I make answer as I can—begging or
dodging the question, putting them off with any nonsense.
It wouldn't matter to any of them really," he went on, "for,
even were it possible to meet in that stand-and-deliver way
so silly a demand on so big a subject, my 'thoughts' would
still be almost altogether about something that concerns
only myself." He was talking to Miss Staverton, with whom
for a couple of months now he had availed himself of every
possible occasion to talk; this disposition and this resource,
this comfort and support, as the situation in fact presented
itself, having promptly enough taken the first place in the
considerable array of rather unattenuated surprises attending his so strangely belated return to America. Everything
was somehow a surprise; and that might be natural when
one had so long and so consistently neglected everything,
taken pains to give surprises so much margin for play. He
had given them more than thirty years—thirty-three, to be
exact; and they now seemed to him to have organised their
performance quite on the scale of that licence. He had been
twenty-three on leaving New York—he was fifty-six today:
unless indeed he were to reckon as he had sometimes, since
his repatriation, found himself feeling; in which case he

would have lived longer than is often allotted to man. It would have taken a century, he repeatedly said to himself, and said also to Alice Staverton, it would have taken a longer absence and a more averted mind than those even of which he had been guilty, to pile up the differences, the newnesses, the queernesses, above all the bignesses, for the better or the worse, that at present assaulted his vision wherever he looked.

The great fact all the while however had been the incalculability; since he *had* supposed himself, from decade to decade, to be allowing, and in the most liberal and intelligent manner, for brilliancy of change. He actually saw that he had allowed for nothing; he missed what he would have been sure of finding, he found what he would never have imagined. Proportions and values were upside-down; the ugly things he had expected, the ugly things of his faraway youth, when he had too promptly waked up to a sense of the ugly—these uncanny phenomena placed him rather, as it happened, under the charm; whereas the "swagger" things, the modern, the monstrous, the famous things, those he had more particularly, like thousands of ingenuous enquirers every year, come over to see, were exactly his sources of dismay. They were as so many set traps for displeasure, above all for reaction, of which his restless tread was constantly pressing the spring. It was interesting, doubtless, the whole show, but it would have been too disconcerting hadn't a certain finer truth saved the situation. He had distinctly not, in this steadier light, come over *all* for the monstrosities; he had come, not only in the last analysis but quite on the face of the act, under an impulse with which they had nothing to do. He had come—putting the thing pompously—to look at his "property," which he had thus for a third of a century not been within four thousand miles of; or, expressing it less sordidly, he had yielded to the humour of seeing again his house on the jolly corner, as he usually, and quite fondly, described it—the one in which he had first seen the light, in which various members of his family had lived and had died, in which the holidays of his overschooled boyhood had been passed and the few social flowers of his chilled adolescence gathered, and which, alienated then for so long a period, had, through the successive deaths of his two brothers and the termination of old arrangements, come wholly into his hands. He was the owner of another, not quite so "good"—the jolly corner having been, from far back, superlatively extended and consecrated; and the value of the pair represented his main capital, with an income consisting, in these later years, of their respective rents which (thanks precisely to their original excellent type) had never been depressingly low. He could live in "Europe," as he had been in the habit of living, on the product of these flourishing New York leases, and all the better since, that of the second structure, the mere number in its long row, having within a twelvemonth fallen in, renovation at a high advance had proved beautifully possible.

These were items of property indeed, but he had found himself since his arrival distinguishing more than ever between them. The house within the street, two bristling blocks westward, was already in course of reconstruction as a tall mass of flats; he had acceded, some time before, to overtures for this conversion—in which, now that it was going forward, it had been not the least of his astonishments to find himself able, on the spot, and though without a previous ounce of such experience, to participate with a certain intelligence, almost with a certain authority. He had lived his life with his back so turned to such concerns and his face addressed to those of so different an order that he scarce knew what to make of this lively stir, in a compartment of his mind never yet penetrated, of a capacity for business and a sense for construction. These virtues, so common all round him now, had been dormant in his own organism—where it might be said of them perhaps that they had slept the sleep of the just. At present, in the splendid autumn weather—the autumn at least was a pure boon in the terrible place—he loafed about his "work" undeterred, secretly agitated; not in the least "minding" that the whole proposition, as they said, was vulgar and sordid, and ready to climb ladders, to walk the plank, to handle materials and look wise about them, to ask questions, in fine, and challenge explanations and really "go into" figures.

It amused, it verily quite charmed him; and, by the same stroke, it amused, and even more, Alice Staverton, though perhaps charming her perceptibly less. She wasn't however going to be better off for it, as *he* was—and so astonishingly much: nothing was now likely, he knew, ever to make her better off than she found herself, in the afternoon of life, as the delicately frugal possessor and tenant of the small house in Irving Place to which she had subtly managed to cling through her almost unbroken New York career. If he knew the way to it now better than to any other address among the dreadful multiplied numberings which seemed to him to reduce the whole place to some vast ledger-page, overgrown, fantastic, of ruled and criss-crossed lines and figures—if he had formed, for his consolation, that habit, it was really not a little because of the charm of his having encountered and recognised, in the vast wilderness of the wholesale, breaking through the mere gross generalisation of wealth and force and success, a small still scene where items and shades, all delicate things, kept the sharpness of the notes of a high voice perfectly trained, and where economy hung about like the scent of a garden. His old friend lived with one maid and herself dusted her relics and trimmed her lamps and polished her silver; she stood off, in the awful modern crush, when she could, but she sallied forth and did battle when the challenge was really to "spirit," the spirit she after all confessed to, proudly and a little shyly, as to that of the better time, that of *their* common, their quite far-away and antediluvian social period and order. She made use of the street-cars when need be, the terrible things that people scrambled for as the panic-stricken at sea scramble for the boats; she affronted, inscrutably, under stress, all the public concussions and ordeals; and yet, with that slim mystifying grace of her appearance, which defied you to say if she were a fair young woman who looked older through trouble, or a fine smooth older one who looked young through successful indifference; with her precious reference, above all, to memories and histories into which he could enter, she was as exquisite for him as some pale pressed flower (a rarity to begin with), and, failing other sweetnesses, she was a sufficient reward of his effort. They had communities of knowledge, "their" knowledge (this discriminating possessive was always on her lips) of presences of the other age, presences all overlaid, in his case, by the experience of a man and the freedom of a wanderer, overlaid by pleasure, by infidelity, by passages of life that were strange and dim to her, just by "Europe" in short, but still unobscured, still exposed and cherished, under that pious visitation of the spirit from which she had never been diverted.

She had come with him one day to see how his "apartment-house" was rising; he had helped her over gaps and explained to her plans, and while they were there had happened to have, before her, a brief but lively discussion with the man in charge, the representative of the building-firm that had undertaken his work. He had found himself quite "standing-up" to this personage over a failure on the latter's part to observe some detail of one of their noted conditions, and had so lucidly urged his case that, besides ever so prettily flushing, at the time, for sympathy in his triumph, she had afterwards said to him (though to a slightly greater effect of irony) that he had clearly for too many years neglected a real gift. If he had but stayed at home he would have anticipated the inventor of the sky-scraper. If he had but stayed at home he would have discovered his genius in time really to start some new variety of awful architectural hare and run it till it burrowed in a gold-mine. He was to remember these words, while the weeks elapsed, for the small silver ring they had sounded over the queerest and deepest of his own lately most disguised and most muffled vibrations.

It had begun to be present to him after the first fortnight, it had broken out with the oddest abruptness, this particular wanton wonderment: it met him there—and this was the image under which he himself judged the matter, or at least, not a little, thrilled and flushed with it—very much as he might have been met by some strange figure, some unexpected occupant, at a turn of one of the dim passages of an empty house. The quaint analogy quite hauntingly remained with him, when he didn't indeed rather improve it by a still intenser form: that of his opening a door

behind which he would have made sure of finding nothing, a door into a room shuttered and void, and yet so coming, with a great suppressed start, on some quite erect con-
fronting presence, something planted in the middle of the
place and facing him through the dusk. After that visit to
the house in construction he walked with his companion
to see the other and always so much the better one, which
in the eastward direction formed one of the corners, the
"jolly" one precisely, of the street now so generally dishon-
oured and disfigured in its westward reaches, and of the
comparatively conservative Avenue. The Avenue still had
pretensions, as Miss Staverton said, to decency; the old people had mostly gone, the old names were unknown, and
here and there an old association seemed to stray, all
vaguely, like some very aged person, out too late, whom
you might meet and feel the impulse to watch or follow,
in kindness, for safe restoration to shelter.

They went in together, our friends; he admitted himself
with his key, as he kept no one there, he explained, pre-
ferring, for his reasons, to leave the place empty, under
a simple arrangement with a good woman living in the
neighbourhood and who came for a daily hour to open windows and dust and sweep. Spencer Brydon had his reasons
and was growingly aware of them; they seemed to him better each time he was there, though he didn't name them
all to his companion, any more than he told her as yet how
often, how quite absurdly often, he himself came. He only
let her see for the present, while they walked through the
great blank rooms, that absolute vacancy reigned and that,
from top to bottom, there was nothing but Mrs. Muldoon's
broomstick, in a corner, to tempt the burglar. Mrs. Muldoon
was then on the premises, and she loquaciously attended
the visitors, preceding them from room to room and pushing back shutters and throwing up sashes—all to show them,
as she remarked, how little there was to see. There was
little indeed to see in the great gaunt shell where the main
dispositions and the general apportionment of space, the
style of an age of ampler allowances, had nevertheless for
its master their honest pleading message, affecting him as
some good old servant's, some lifelong retainer's appeal for

a character, or even for a retiring-pension; yet it was also a remark of Mrs. Muldoon's that, glad as she was to oblige him by her noonday round, there was a request she greatly hoped he would never make of her. If he should wish her for any reason to come in after dark she would just tell him, if he "plased," that he must ask it of somebody else.

The fact that there was nothing to see didn't militate for the worthy woman against what one *might* see, and she put it frankly to Miss Staverton that no lady could be expected to like, could she? "craping up to thim top storeys in the ayvil hours." The gas and the electric light were off the house, and she fairly evoked a gruesome vision of her march through the great grey rooms—so many of them as there were too!—with her glimmering taper. Miss Staverton met her honest glare with a smile and the profession that she herself certainly would recoil from such an adventure. Spencer Brydon meanwhile held his peace—for the moment; the question of the "evil" hours in his old home had already become too grave for him. He had begun some time since to "crape," and he knew just why a packet of candles addressed to that pursuit had been stowed by his own hand, three weeks before, at the back of a drawer of the fine old sideboard that occupied, as a "fixture," the deep recess in the dining-room. Just now he laughed at his companions—quickly however changing the subject; for the reason that, in the first place, his laugh struck him even at that moment as starting the odd echo, the conscious human resonance (he scarce knew how to qualify it) that sounds made while he was there alone sent back to his ear or his fancy; and that, in the second, he imagined Alice Staverton for the instant on the point of asking him, with a divination, if he ever so prowled. There were divinations he was unprepared for, and he had at all events averted enquiry by the time Mrs. Muldoon had left them, passing on to other parts.

There was happily enough to say, on so consecrated a spot, that could be said freely and fairly; so that a whole train of declarations was precipitated by his friend's having herself broken out, after a yearning look round: "But I hope you don't mean they want you to pull *this* to pieces!" His answer came, promptly, with his re-awakened wrath: it was of course exactly what they wanted, and what they were "at" him for, daily, with the iteration of people who couldn't for their life understand a man's liability to decent feelings. He had found the place, just as it stood and beyond what he could express, an interest and a joy. There were values other than the beastly rent-values, and in short, in short—! But it was thus Miss Staverton took him up. "In short you're to make so good a thing of your sky-scraper that, living in luxury on *those* ill-gotten gains, you can afford for a while to be sentimental here!" Her smile had for him, with the words, the particular mild irony with which he found half her talk suffused; an irony without bitterness and that came, exactly, from her having so much imagination—not, like the cheap sarcasms with which one heard most people, about the world of "society," bid for the reputation of cleverness, from nobody's really having any. It was agreeable to him at this very moment to be sure that when he had answered, after a brief demur, "Well yes: so, precisely, you may put it!" her imagination would still do him justice. He explained that even if never a dollar were to come to him from the other house he would nevertheless cherish this one; and he dwelt, further, while they lingered and wandered, on the fact of the stupefaction he was already exciting, the positive mystification he felt himself create.

He spoke of the value of all he read into it, into the mere sight of the walls, mere shapes of the rooms, mere sound of the floors, mere feel, in his hand, of the old silver-plated knobs of the several mahogany doors, which suggested the pressure of the palms of the dead; the seventy years of the past in fine that these things represented, the annals of nearly three generations, counting his grandfather's, the one that had ended there, and the impalpable ashes of his long-extinct youth, afloat in the very air like microscopic motes. She listened to everything; she was a woman who answered intimately but who utterly didn't chatter. She scattered abroad therefore no cloud of words; she could assent, she could agree, above all she could encourage, without doing that. Only at the last she went a little further than he had done himself. "And then how do you know? You may still, after all, want to live here." It rather indeed pulled him up, for it wasn't what he had been thinking, at least in her sense of the words. "You mean I may decide to stay on for the sake of it?"

"Well, *with* such a home—!" But, quite beautifully, she had too much tact to dot so monstrous an *i*, and it was precisely an illustration of the way she didn't rattle. How could any one—of any wit—insist on any one else's "wanting" to live in New York?

"Oh," he said, "I *might* have lived here (since I had my opportunity early in life); I might have put in here all these years. Then everything would have been different enough —and, I dare say, 'funny' enough. But that's another matter. And then the beauty of it—I mean of my perversity, of my refusal to agree to a 'deal'—is just in the total absence of a reason. Don't you see that if I had a reason about the matter at all it would *have* to be the other way, and would then be inevitably a reason of dollars? There are no reasons here *but* of dollars. Let us therefore have none whatever —not the ghost of one."

They were back in the hall then for departure, but from where they stood the vista was large, through an open door, into the great square main saloon, with its almost antique felicity of brave spaces between windows. Her eyes came back from that reach and met his own a moment. "Are you very sure the 'ghost' of one doesn't, much rather, serve—?"

He had a positive sense of turning pale. But it was as near as they were then to come. For he made answer, he believed, between a glare and a grin: "Oh ghosts—of course the place must swarm with them! I should be ashamed of it if it didn't. Poor Mrs. Muldoon's right, and it's why I haven't asked her to do more than look in."

Miss Staverton's gaze again lost itself, and things she didn't utter, it was clear, came and went in her mind. She might even for the minute, off there in the fine room, have imagined some element dimly gathering. Simplified like the death-mask of a handsome face, it perhaps produced for her just then an effect akin to the stir of an expression in the "set" commemorative plaster. Yet whatever her impression may have been she produced instead a vague platitude. "Well, if it were only furnished and lived in—!"

She appeared to imply that in case of its being still furnished he might have been a little less opposed to the idea of a return. But she passed straight into the vestibule, as if to leave her words behind her, and the next moment he had opened the house-door and was standing with her on the steps. He closed the door and, while he re-pocketed his key, looking up and down, they took in the comparatively harsh actuality of the Avenue, which reminded him of the assault of the outer light of the Desert on the traveller emerging from an Egyptian tomb. But he risked before they stepped into the street his gathered answer to her speech. "For me it *is* lived in. For me it *is* furnished." At which it was easy for her to sigh "Ah yes—!" all vaguely and discreetly; since his parents and his favourite sister, to say nothing of other kin, in numbers, had run their course and met their end there. That represented, within the walls, ineffaceable life.

It was a few days after this that, during an hour passed with her again, he had expressed his impatience of the too flattering curiosity—among the people he met—about his appreciation of New York. He had arrived at none at all that was socially producible, and as for that matter of his "thinking" (thinking the better or the worse of anything there) he was wholly taken up with one subject of thought. It was mere vain egoism, and it was moreover, if she liked, a morbid obsession. He found all things come back to the question of what he personally might have been, how he might have led his life and "turned out," if he had not so, at the outset, given it up. And confessing for the first time to the intensity within him of this absurd speculation—which but proved also, no doubt, the habit of too selfishly thinking— he affirmed the impotence there of any other source of interest, any other native appeal. "What would it have made of me, what would it have made of me? I keep for ever wondering, all idiotically; as if I could possibly know! I see what it has made of dozens of others, those I meet, and it positively aches within me, to the point of exasperation, that it would have made something of me as well. Only I can't make out *what,* and the worry of it, the small rage of curiosity never to be satisfied, brings back what I remember to have felt, once or twice, after judging best, for reasons, to burn some important letter unopened. I've been sorry, I've hated it—I've never known what was in the letter. You may of course say it's a trifle—!"

"I don't say it's a trifle," Miss Staverton gravely interrupted.

She was seated by her fire, and before her, on his feet and restless, he turned to and fro between this intensity of his idea and a fitful and unseeing inspection, through his single eye-glass, of the dear little old objects on her chimney-piece. Her interruption made him for an instant look at her harder. "I shouldn't care if you did!" he laughed, however; "and it's only a figure, at any rate, for the way I now feel. *Not* to have followed my perverse young course —and almost in the teeth of my father's curse, as I may say; not to have kept it up, so, 'over there,' from that day to this, without a doubt or a pang; not, above all, to have liked it, to have loved it, so much, loved it, no doubt, with such an abysmal conceit of my own preference: some variation from *that,* I say, must have produced some different effect for my life and for my 'form.' I should have stuck here—if it had been possible; and I was too young, at twenty-three, to judge, *pour deux sous,* whether it *were* possible. If I had waited I might have seen it was, and then I might have been, by staying here, something nearer to one of these types who have been hammered so hard and made so keen by their conditions. It isn't that I admire them so much—the question of any charm in them, or of any charm, beyond that of the rank money-passion, exerted by their conditions *for* them, has nothing to do with the matter: it's only a question of what fantastic, yet perfectly possible, development of my own nature I mayn't have missed. It comes over me that I had then a strange *alter ego* deep down somewhere within me, as the full-blown flower is in the small tight bud, and that I just took the course, I just transferred him to the climate, that blighted him for once and for ever."

"And you wonder about the flower," Miss Staverton said.

"So do I, if you want to know; and so I've been wondering these several weeks. I believe in the flower," she continued, "I feel it would have been quite splendid, quite huge and monstrous."

"Monstrous above all!" her visitor echoed; "and I imagine, by the same stroke, quite hideous and offensive."

"You don't believe that," she returned; "if you did you wouldn't wonder. You'd know, and that would be enough for you. What you feel—and what I feel *for* you—is that you'd have had power."

"You'd have liked me that way?" he asked.

She barely hung fire. "How should I not have liked you?"

"I see. You'd have liked me, have preferred me, a billionaire!"

"How should I not have liked you?" she simply again asked.

He stood before her still—her question kept him motionless. He took it in, so much there was of it; and indeed his not otherwise meeting it testified to that. "I know at least what I am," he simply went on; "the other side of the medal's clear enough. I've not been edifying—I believe I'm thought in a hundred quarters to have been barely decent. I've followed strange paths and worshipped strange gods; it must have come to you again and again—in fact you've admitted to me as much—that I was leading, at any time these thirty years, a selfish frivolous scandalous life. And you see what it has made of me."

She just waited, smiling at him. "You see what it has made of *me*."

"Oh you're a person whom nothing can have altered. You were born to be what you are, anywhere, anyway: you've the perfection nothing else could have blighted. And don't you see how, without my exile, I shouldn't have been waiting till now—?" But he pulled up for the strange pang.

"The great thing to see," she presently said, "seems to me to be that it has spoiled nothing. It hasn't spoiled your being here at last. It hasn't spoiled this. It hasn't spoiled your speaking—" She also however faltered.

He wondered at everything her controlled emotion might

mean. "Do you believe then—too dreadfully!—that I *am* as good as I might ever have been?"

"Oh no! Far from it!" With which she got up from her chair and was nearer to him. "But I don't care," she smiled.

"You mean I'm good enough?"

She considered a little. "Will you believe it if I say so? I mean will you let that settle your question for you?" And then as if making out in his face that he drew back from this, that he had some idea which, however absurd, he couldn't yet bargain away: "Oh you don't care either—but very differently: you don't care for anything but yourself."

Spencer Brydon recognised it—it was in fact what he had absolutely professed. Yet he importantly qualified. "*He* isn't myself. He's the just so totally other person. But I do want to see him," he added. "And I can. And I shall."

Their eyes met for a minute while he guessed from something in hers that she divined his strange sense. But neither of them otherwise expressed it, and her apparent understanding, with no protesting shock, no easy derision, touched him more deeply than anything yet, constituting for his stifled perversity, on the spot, an element that was like breatheable air. What she said however was unexpected. "Well, *I've* seen him."

"You—?"

"I've seen him in a dream."

"Oh a 'dream'—!" It let him down.

"But twice over," she continued. "I saw him as I see you now."

"You've dreamed the same dream—?"

"Twice over," she repeated. "The very same."

This did somehow a little speak to him, as it also gratified him. "You dream about me at that rate?"

"Ah about *him!*" she smiled.

His eyes again sounded her. "Then you know all about him." And as she said nothing more: "What's the wretch like?"

She hesitated, and it was as if he were pressing her so hard that, resisting for reasons of her own, she had to turn away. "I'll tell you some other time!"

II

It was after this that there was most of a virtue for
him, most of a cultivated charm, most of a preposterous
secret thrill, in the particular form of surrender to his obsession and of address to what he more and more believed
to be his privilege. It was what in these weeks he was living for—since he really felt life to begin but after Mrs. Muldoon had retired from the scene and, visiting the ample
house from attic to cellar, making sure he was alone, he
knew himself in safe possession and, as he tacitly expressed
it, let himself go. He sometimes came twice in the twenty-
four hours; the moments he liked best were those of gathering dusk, of the short autumn twilight; this was the time
of which, again and again, he found himself hoping most.
Then he could, as seemed to him, most intimately wander
and wait, linger and listen, feel his fine attention, never in
his life before so fine, on the pulse of the great vague place:
he preferred the lampless hour and only wished he might
have prolonged each day the deep crepuscular spell. Later
—rarely much before midnight, but then for a considerable
vigil—he watched with his glimmering light; moving slowly,
holding it high, playing it far, rejoicing above all, as much
as he might, in open vistas, reaches of communication between rooms and by passages; the long straight chance or
show, as he would have called it, for the revelation he pretended to invite. It was practice he found he could perfectly "work" without exciting remark; no one was in the
least the wiser for it; even Alice Staverton, who was moreover a well of discretion, didn't quite fully imagine.

He let himself in and let himself out with the assurance
of calm proprietorship; and accident so far favoured him
that, if a fat Avenue "officer" had happened on occasion to
see him entering at eleven-thirty, he had never yet, to the
best of his belief, been noticed as emerging at two. He
walked there on the crisp November nights, arrived regu-
larly at the evening's end; it was as easy to do this after
dining out as to take his way to a club or to his hotel.
When he left his club, if he hadn't been dining out, it was
ostensibly to go to his hotel; and when he left his hotel, if

he had spent a part of the evening there, it was ostensibly to go to his club. Everything was easy in fine; everything conspired and promoted: there was truly even in the strain of his experience something that glossed over, something that salved and simplified, all the rest of consciousness. He circulated, talked, renewed, loosely and pleasantly, old relations—met indeed, so far as he could, new expectations and seemed to make out on the whole that in spite of the career, of such different contacts, which he had spoken of to Miss Staverton as ministering so little, for those who might have watched it, to edification, he was positively rather liked than not. He was a dim secondary social success—and all with people who had truly not an idea of him. It was all mere surface sound, this murmur of their welcome, this popping of their corks—just as his gestures of response were the extravagant shadows, emphatic in proportion as they meant little, of some game of *ombres chinoises.* He projected himself all day, in thought, straight over the bristling line of hard unconscious heads and into the other, the real, the waiting life; the life that, as soon as he had heard behind him the click of his great house-door, began for him, on the jolly corner, as beguilingly as the slow opening bars of some rich music follows the tap of the conductor's wand.

He always caught the first effect of the steel point of his stick on the old marble of the hall pavement, large black-and-white squares that he remembered as the admiration of his childhood and that had then made in him, as he now saw, for the growth of an early conception of style. This effect was the dim reverberating tinkle as of some far-off bell hung who should say where?—in the depths of the house, of the past, of that mystical other world that might have flourished for him had he not, for weal or woe, abandoned it. On this impression he did ever the same thing; he put his stick noiselessly away in a corner—feeling the place once more in the likeness of some great glass bowl, all precious concave crystal, set delicately humming by the play of a moist finger round its edge. The concave crystal held, as it were, this mystical other world, and the indescribably fine murmur of its rim was the sigh there, the

scarce audible pathetic wail to his strained ear, of all the
old baffled forsworn possibilities. What he did therefore by
this appeal of his hushed presence was to wake them into
such measure of ghostly life as they might still enjoy. They
were shy, all but unappeasably shy, but they weren't really
sinister; at least they weren't as he had hitherto felt them
—before they had taken the Form he so yearned to make
them take, the Form he at moments saw himself in the light
of fairly hunting on tiptoe, the points of his evening-shoes,
from room to room and from storey to storey.

That was the essence of his vision—which was all rank
folly, if one would, while he was out of the house and
otherwise occupied, but which took on the last verisimili-
tude as soon as he was placed and posted. He knew what
he meant and what he wanted; it was as clear as the figure on a cheque presented in demand for cash. His *alter
ego* "walked"—that was the note of his image of him, while
his image of his motive for his own odd pastime was the
desire to waylay him and meet him. He roamed, slowly,
warily, but all restlessly, he himself did—Mrs. Muldoon
had been right, absolutely, with her figure of their "craping"; and the presence he watched for would roam restlessly too. But it would be as cautious and as shifty; the
conviction of its probable, in fact its already quite sensible, quite audible evasion of pursuit grew for him from
night to night, laying on him finally a rigour to which nothing in his life had been comparable. It had been the theory
of many superficially-judging persons, he knew, that he
was wasting that life in a surrender to sensations, but he
had tasted of no pleasure so fine as his actual tension, had
been introduced to no sport that demanded at once the patience and the nerve of this stalking of a creature more subtle, yet at bay perhaps more formidable, than any beast of
the forest. The terms, the comparisons, the very practices
of the chase positively came again into play; there were
even moments when passages of his occasional experience
as a sportsman, stirred memories, from his younger time,
of moor and mountain and desert, revived for him—and to
the increase of his keenness—by the tremendous force of
analogy. He found himself at moments—once he had placed

his single light on some mantel-shelf or in some recess—
stepping back into shelter or shade, effacing himself behind a door or in an embrasure, as he had sought of old
the vantage of rock and tree; he found himself holding his
breath and living in the joy of the instant, the supreme suspense created by big game alone.

He wasn't afraid (though putting himself the question
as he believed gentlemen on Bengal tiger-shoots or in close
quarters with the great bear of the Rockies had been
known to confess to having put it); and this indeed—since
here at least he might be frank!—because of the impression, so intimate and so strange, that he himself produced
as yet a dread, produced certainly a strain, beyond the live-
liest he was likely to feel. They fell for him into categories,
they fairly became familiar, the signs, for his own perception, of the alarm his presence and his vigilance created;
though leaving him always to remark, portentously, on his
probably having formed a relation, his probably enjoying
a consciousness, unique in the experience of man. People
enough, first and last, had been in terror of apparitions,
but who had ever before so turned the tables and become
himself, in the apparitional world, an incalculable terror?
He might have found this sublime had he quite dared to
think of it; but he didn't too much insist, truly, on that side
of his privilege. With habit and repetition he gained to
an extraordinary degree the power to penetrate the dusk
of distances and the darkness of corners, to resolve back
into their innocence the treacheries of uncertain light, the
evil-looking forms taken in the gloom by mere shadows, by
accidents of the air, by shifting effects of perspective; putting down his dim luminary he could still wander on without it, pass into other rooms and, only knowing it was there
behind him in case of need, see his way about, visually
project for his purpose a comparative clearness. It made
him feel, this acquired faculty, like some monstrous stealthy
cat; he wondered if he would have glared at these moments
with large shining yellow eyes, and what it mightn't verily
be, for the poor hard-pressed *alter ego,* to be confronted
with such a type.

He liked however the open shutters; he opened every-

where those Mrs. Muldoon had closed, closing them as
carefully afterwards, so that she shouldn't notice: he liked
—oh this he did like, and above all in the upper rooms!—
the sense of the hard silver of the autumn stars through
the window-panes, and scarcely less the flare of the street-
lamps below, the white electric lustre which it would have
taken curtains to keep out. This was human actual social;
this was of the world he had lived in, and he was more at
his ease certainly for the countenance, coldly general and
impersonal, that all the while and in spite of his detachment it seemed to give him. He had support of course
mostly in the rooms at the wide front and the prolonged
side; it failed him considerably in the central shades and
the parts at the back. But if he sometimes, on his rounds,
was glad of his optical reach, so none the less often the
rear of the house affected him as the very jungle of his
prey. The place was there more subdivided; a large "extension" in particular, where small rooms for servants had
been multiplied, abounded in nooks and corners, in closets
and passages, in the ramifications especially of an ample
back staircase over which he leaned, many a time, to look
far down—not deterred from his gravity even while aware
that he might, for a spectator, have figured some solemn
simpleton playing at hide-and-seek. Outside in fact he
might himself make that ironic *rapprochement;* but within
the walls, and in spite of the clear windows, his consistency
was proof against the cynical light of New York.

It had belonged to that idea of the exasperated consciousness of his victim to become a real test for him; since
he had quite put it to himself from the first that, oh distinctly! he could "cultivate" his whole perception. He had
felt it as above all open to cultivation—which indeed was
but another name for his manner of spending his time. He
was bringing it on, bringing it to perfection, by practice;
in consequence of which it had grown so fine that he was
now aware of impressions, attestations of his general pos-
tulate, that couldn't have broken upon him at once. This
was the case more specifically with a phenomenon at last
quite frequent for him in the upper rooms, the recognition
—absolutely unmistakeable, and by a turn dating from a

particular hour, his resumption of his campaign after a diplomatic drop, a calculated absence of three nights—of his
being definitely followed, tracked at a distance carefully
taken and to the express end that he should the less con-
fidently, less arrogantly, appear to himself merely to pur-
sue. It worried, it finally quite broke him up, for it proved,
of all the conceivable impressions, the one least suited to
his book. He was kept in sight while remaining himself—
as regards the essence of his position—sightless, and his
only recourse then was in abrupt turns, rapid recoveries of
ground. He wheeled about, retracing his steps, as if he
might so catch in his face at least the stirred air of some
other quick revolution. It was indeed true that his fully
dislocalised thought of these manœuvres recalled to him
Pantaloon, at the Christmas farce, buffeted and tricked
from behind by ubiquitous Harlequin; but it left intact the
influence of the conditions themselves each time he was re-
exposed to them, so that in fact this association, had he
suffered it to become constant, would on a certain side have
but ministered to his intenser gravity. He had made, as I
have said, to create on the premises the baseless sense of
a reprieve, his three absences; and the result of the third
was to confirm the after-effect of the second.

On his return, that night—the night succeeding his last
intermission—he stood in the hall and looked up the staircase with a certainty more intimate than any he had yet
known. "He's *there*, at the top, and waiting—not, as in
general, falling back for disappearance. He's holding his
ground, and it's the first time—which is a proof, isn't it?
that something has happened for him." So Brydon argued
with his hand on the banister and his foot on the lowest
stair; in which position he felt as never before the air chilled
by his logic. He himself turned cold in it, for he seemed
of a sudden to know what now was involved. "Harder
pressed?—yes, he takes it in, with its thus making clear to
him that I've come, as they say, 'to stay.' He finally doesn't
like and can't bear it, in the sense, I mean, that his wrath,
his menaced interest, now balances with his dread. I've
hunted him till he has 'turned': that, up there, is what has
happened—he's the fanged or the antlered animal brought

at last to bay." There came to him, as I say—but determined by an influence beyond my notation!—the acuteness
of this certainty; under which however the next moment
he had broken into a sweat that he would as little have
consented to attribute to fear as he would have dared immediately to act upon it for enterprise. It marked none the
less a prodigious thrill, a thrill that represented sudden dismay, no doubt, but also represented, and with the selfsame
throb, the strangest, the most joyous, possibly the next minute almost the proudest, duplication of consciousness.

"He has been dodging, retreating, hiding, but now,
worked up to anger, he'll fight!"—this intense impression
made a single mouthful, as it were, of terror and applause.
But what was wondrous was that the applause, for the felt
fact, was so eager, since, if it was his other self he was running to earth, this ineffable identity was thus in the last
resort not unworthy of him. It bristled there—somewhere
near at hand, however unseen still—as the hunted thing,
even as the trodden worm of the adage *must* at last bristle;
and Brydon at this instant tasted probably of a sensation
more complex than had ever before found itself consistent
with sanity. It was as if it would have shamed him that a
character so associated with his own should triumphantly
succeed in just skulking, should to the end not risk the open,
so that the drop of this danger was, on the spot, a great
lift of the whole situation. Yet with another rare shift of
the same subtlety he was already trying to measure by how
much more he himself might now be in peril of fear; so
rejoicing that he could, in another form, actively inspire
that fear, and simultaneously quaking for the form in which
he might passively know it.

The apprehension of knowing it must after a little have
grown in him, and the strangest moment of his adventure
perhaps, the most memorable or really most interesting,
afterwares, of his crisis, was the lapse of certain instants of
concentrated conscious *combat*, the sense of a need to hold
on to something, even after the manner of a man slipping
and slipping on some awful incline; the vivid impulse,
above all, to move, to act, to charge, somehow and upon
something—to show himself, in a word, that he wasn't

afraid. The state of "holding-on" was thus the state to which
he was momentarily reduced; if there had been anything,
in the great vacancy, to seize, he would presently have
been aware of having clutched it as he might under a shock
at home have clutched the nearest chair-back. He had
been surprised at any rate—of this he *was* aware—into something unprecedented since his original appropriation of the
place; he had closed his eyes, held them tight, for a long
minute, as with that instinct of dismay and that terror of
vision. When he opened them the room, the other contigu-
ous rooms, extraordinarily, seemed lighter—so light, almost,
that at first he took the change for day. He stood firm, however that might be, just where he had paused; his resistance
had helped him—it was as if there were something he had
tided over. He knew after a little what this was—it had been
in the imminent danger of flight. He had stiffened his will
against going; without this he would have made for the
stairs, and it seemed to him that, still with his eyes closed,
he would have descended them, would have known how,
straight and swiftly, to the bottom.

Well, as he had held out, here he was—still at the top,
among the more intricate upper rooms and with the gaunt-
let of the others, of all the rest of the house, still to run
when it should be his time to go. He would go at his time
—only at his time: didn't he go every night very much at
the same hour? He took out his watch—there was light for
that: it was scarcely a quarter past one, and he had never
withdrawn so soon. He reached his lodgings for the most
part at two—with his walk of a quarter of an hour. He
would wait for the last quarter—he wouldn't stir till then;
and he kept his watch there with his eyes on it, reflecting
while he held it that this deliberate wait, a wait with an
effort, which he recognised, would serve perfectly for the
attestation he desired to make. It would prove his courage
—unless indeed the latter might most be proved by his
budging at last from his place. What he mainly felt now
was that, since he hadn't originally scuttled, he had his dignities—which had never in his life seemed so many—all to
preserve and to carry aloft. This was before him in truth
as a physical image, an image almost worthy of an age of

greater romance. That remark indeed glimmered for him
only to glow the next instant with a finer light; since what
age of romance, after all, could have matched either the
state of his mind or, "objectively," as they said, the wonder of his situation? The only difference would have been
that, brandishing his dignities over his head as in a parch-
ment scroll, he might then—that is in the heroic time—have
proceeded downstairs with a drawn sword in his other
grasp.

At present, really, the light he had set down on the man-
tel of the next room would have to figure his sword; which
utensil, in the course of a minute, he had taken the requi-
site number of steps to possess himself of. The door between the rooms was open, and from the second another
door opened to a third. These rooms, as he remembered,
gave all three upon a common corridor as well, but there
was a fourth, beyond them, without issue save through the
preceding. To have moved, to have heard his step again,
was appreciably a help; though even in recognising this he
lingered once more a little by the chimney-piece on which
his light had rested. When he next moved, just hesitating
where to turn, he found himself considering a circumstance
that, after his first and comparatively vague apprehension
of it, produced in him the start that often attends some pang
of recollection, the violent shock of having ceased happily
to forget. He had come into sight of the door in which the
brief chain of communication ended and which he now surveyed from the nearer threshold, the one not directly facing
it. Placed at some distance to the left of this point, it would
have admitted him to the last room of the four, the room
without other approach or egress, had it not, to his intimate
conviction, been closed *since* his former visitation, the matter probably of a quarter of an hour before. He stared with
all his eyes at the wonder of the fact, arrested again where
he stood and again holding his breath while he sounded its
sense. Surely it had been *subsequently* closed—that is it had
been on his previous passage indubitably open!

He took it full in the face that something had happened
between—that he couldn't not have noticed before (by
which he meant on his original tour of all the rooms that

evening) that such a barrier had exceptionally presented itself. He had indeed since that moment undergone an agitation so extraordinary that it might have muddled for him any earlier view; and he tried to convince himself that he might perhaps then have gone into the room and, inadvertently, automatically, on coming out, have drawn the door after him. The difficulty was that this exactly was what he never did; it was against his whole policy, as he might have said, the essence of which was to keep vistas clear. He had them from the first, as he was well aware, quite on the brain: the strange apparition, at the far end of one of them, of his baffled "prey" (which had become by so sharp an irony so little the term now to apply!) was the form of success his imagination had most cherished, projecting into it always a refinement of beauty. He had known fifty times the start of perception that had afterwards dropped; had fifty times gasped to himself "There!" under some fond brief hallucination. The house, as the case stood, admirably lent itself; he might wonder at the taste, the native architecture of the particular time, which could rejoice so in the multiplication of doors—the opposite extreme to the modern, the actual almost complete proscription of them; but it had fairly contributed to provoke this obsession of the presence encountered telescopically, as he might say, focussed and studied in diminishing perspective and as by a rest for the elbow.

It was with these considerations that his present attention was charged—they perfectly availed to make what he saw portentous. He *couldn't*, by any lapse, have blocked that aperture; and if he hadn't, if it was unthinkable, why what else was clear but that there had been another agent? Another agent?—he had been catching, as he felt, a moment back, the very breath of him; but when had he been so close as in this simple, this logical, this completely personal act? It was so logical, that is, that one might have *taken* it for personal; yet for what did Brydon take it, he asked himself, while, softly panting, he felt his eyes almost leave their sockets. Ah this time at last they *were*, the two, the opposed projections of him, in presence; and this time, as much as one would, the question of danger loomed. With it rose, as not before, the question of courage—for what he knew the blank face of the door to say to him was "Show us how much you have!" It stared, it glared back at him with that challenge; it put to him the two alternatives: should he just push it open or not? Oh to have this consciousness was to *think*—and to think, Brydon knew, as he stood there, was, with the lapsing moments, not to have acted! Not to have acted—that was the misery and the pang —was even still not to act; was in fact *all* to feel the thing in another, in a new and terrible way. How long did he pause and how long did he debate? There was presently nothing to measure it; for his vibration had already changed —as just by the effect of its intensity. Shut up there, at bay, defiant, and with the prodigy of the thing palpably proveably *done,* thus giving notice like some stark signboard—under that accession of accent the situation itself had turned; and Brydon at last remarkably made up his mind on what it had turned to.

It had turned altogether to a different admonition; to a supreme hint, for him, of the value of Discretion! This slowly dawned, no doubt—for it could take its time; so perfectly, on his threshold, had he been stayed, so little as yet had he either advanced or retreated. It was the strangest of all things that now when, by his taking ten steps and applying his hand to a latch, or even his shoulder and his knee, if necessary, to a panel, all the hunger of his prime need might have been met, his high curiosity crowned, his unrest assuaged—it was amazing, but it was also exquisite and rare, that insistence should have, at a touch, quite dropped from him. Discretion—he jumped at that; and yet not, verily, at such a pitch, because it saved his nerves or his skin, but because, much more valuably, it saved the situation. When I say he "jumped" at it I feel the consonance of this term with the fact that—at the end indeed of I know not how long—he did move again, he crossed straight to the door. He wouldn't touch it—it seemed now that he might *if* he would: he would only just wait there a little, to show, to prove, that he wouldn't. He had thus another station, close to the thin partition by which revelation was denied him; but with his eyes bent and his hands held off in a mere intensity of stillness. He listened as if there had been something to hear, but this attitude, while it lasted, was his own communication. "If you won't then —good: I spare you and I give up. You affect me as by the appeal positively for pity: you convince me that for reasons rigid and sublime—what do I know?—we both of us should have suffered. I respect them then, and, though moved and privileged as, I believe, it has never been given to man, I retire, I renounce—never, on my honour, to try again. So rest for ever—and let *me!*"

That, for Brydon was the deep sense of this last demonstration—solemn, measured, directed, as he felt it to be. He brought it to a close, he turned away; and now verily he knew how deeply he had been stirred. He retraced his steps, taking up his candle, burnt, he observed, well-nigh to the socket, and marking again, lighten it as he would, the distinctness of his footfall; after which, in a moment, he knew himself at the other side of the house. He did here what he had not yet done at these hours—he opened half a casement, one of those in the front, and let in the air of the night; a thing he would have taken at any time previous for a sharp rupture of his spell. His spell was broken now, and it didn't matter—broken by his concession and his surrender, which made it idle henceforth that he should ever come back. The empty street—its other life so marked even by the great lamplit vacancy—was within call, within touch; he stayed there as to be in it again, high above it though he was still perched; he watched as for some comforting common fact, some vulgar human note, the passage of a scavenger or a thief, some night-bird however base. He would have blessed that sign of life; he would have welcomed positively the slow approach of his friend the policeman, whom he had hitherto only sought to avoid, and was not sure that if the patrol had come into sight he mightn't have felt the impulse to get into relation with it, to hail it, on some pretext, from his fourth floor.

The pretext that wouldn't have been too silly or too compromising, the explanation that would have saved his dignity and kept his name, in such a case, out of the papers, was not definite to him: he was so occupied with the

thought of recording his Discretion—as an effect of the vow
he had just uttered to his intimate adversary—that the importance of this loomed large and something had overtaken
all ironically his sense of proportion. If there had been a
ladder applied to the front of the house, even one of the
vertiginous perpendiculars employed by painters and roof-
ers and sometimes left standing overnight, he would have
managed somehow, astride of the window-sill, to compass
by outstretched leg and arm that mode of descent. If there
had been some such uncanny thing as he had found in
his room at hotels, a workable fire-escape in the form of
notched cable or a canvas shoot, he would have availed
himself of it as a proof—well, of his present delicacy. He
nursed that sentiment, as the question stood, a little in vain,
and even—at the end of he scarce knew, once more, how
long—found it, as by the action on his mind of the failure
of response of the outer world, sinking back to vague anguish. It seemed to him he had waited an age for some
stir of the great grim hush; the life of the town was itself
under a spell—so unnaturally, up and down the whole prospect of known and rather ugly objects, the blankness and
the silence lasted. Had they ever, he asked himself, the
hard-faced houses, which had begun to look livid in the
dim dawn, had they ever spoken so little to any need of
his spirit? Great builded voids, great crowded stillnesses
put on, often, in the heart of cities, for the small hours, a
sort of sinister mask, and it was of this large collective negation that Brydon presently became conscious—all the more
that the break of day was, almost incredibly, now at hand,
proving to him what a night he had made of it.

He looked again at his watch, saw what had become
of his time-values (he had taken hours for minutes—not,
as in other tense situations, minutes for hours) and the
strange air of the streets was but the weak, the sullen flush
of a dawn in which everything was still locked up. His
choked appeal from his own open window had been the
sole note of life, and he could but break off at last as for
a worse despair. Yet while so deeply demoralised he was
capable again of an impulse denoting—at least by his present measure—extraordinary resolution; of retracing his steps

to the spot where he had turned cold with the extinction of his last pulse of doubt as to there being in the place another presence than his own. This required an effort strong enough to sicken him; but he had his reason, which overmastered for the moment everything else. There was the whole of the rest of the house to traverse, and how should he screw himself to that if the door he had seen closed were at present open? He could hold to the idea that the closing had practically been for him an act of mercy, a chance offered him to descend, depart, get off the ground and never again profane it. This conception held together, it worked; but what it meant for him depended now clearly on the amount of forbearance his recent action, or rather his recent inaction, had engendered. The image of the "presence," whatever it was, waiting there for him to go—this image had not yet been so concrete for his nerves as when he stopped short of the point at which certainty would have come to him. For, with all his resolution, or more exactly with all his dread, he did stop short—he hung back from really seeing. The risk was too great and his fear too definite: it took at this moment an awful specific form.

He knew—yes, as he had never known anything—that, *should* he see the door open, it would all too abjectly be the end of him. It would mean that the agent of his shame —for his shame was the deep abjection—was once more at large and in general possession; and what glared him thus in the face was the act that this would determine for him. It would send him straight about to the window he had left open, and by that window, be long ladder and dangling rope as absent as they would, he saw himself uncontrollably insanely fatally take his way to the street. The hideous chance of this he at least could avert; but he could only avert it by recoiling in time from assurance. He had the whole house to deal with, this fact was still there; only he now knew that uncertainty alone could start him. He stole back from where he had checked himself—merely to do so was suddenly like safety—and, making blindly for the greater staircase, left gaping rooms and sounding passages behind. Here was the top of the stairs, with a fine large dim descent and three spacious landings to mark off. His instinct was all for mildness, but his feet were harsh on the floors, and, strangely, when he had in a couple of minutes become aware of this, it counted somehow for help. He couldn't have spoken, the tone of his voice would have scared him, and the common conceit or resource of "whistling in the dark" (whether literally or figuratively) have appeared basely vulgar; yet he liked none the less to hear himself go, and when he had reached his first landing—taking it all with no rush, but quite steadily—that stage of success drew from him a gasp of relief.

The house, withal, seemed immense, the scale of space again inordinate; the open rooms to no one of which his eyes deflected, gloomed in their shuttered state like mouths of caverns; only the high skylight that formed the crown of the deep well created for him a medium in which he could advance, but which might have been, for queerness of colour, some watery under-world. He tried to think of something noble, as that his property was really grand, a splendid possession; but this nobleness took the form too of the clear delight with which he was finally to sacrifice it. They might come in now, the builders, the destroyers —they might come as soon as they would. At the end of two flights he had dropped to another zone, and from the middle of the third, with only one more left, he recognised the influence of the lower windows, of half-drawn blinds, of the occasional gleam of street-lamps, of the glazed spaces of the vestibule. This was the bottom of the sea, which showed an illumination of its own and which he even saw paved—when at a given moment he drew up to sink a long look over the banisters—with the marble squares of his childhood. By that time indubitably he felt, as he might have said in a commoner cause, better; it had allowed him to stop and draw breath, and the ease increased with the sight of the old black-and-white slabs. But what he most felt was that now surely, with the element of impunity pulling him as by hard firm hands, the case was settled for what he might have seen above had he dared that last look. The closed door, blessedly remote now, was still closed— and he had only in short to reach that of the house.

He came down further, he crossed the passage forming

the access to the last flight; and if here again he stopped an
instant it was almost for the sharpness of the thrill of assured escape. It made him shut his eyes—which opened
again to the straight slope of the remainder of the stairs.
Here was impunity still, but impunity almost excessive; in-
asmuch as the side-lights and the high fan-tracery of the
entrance were glimmering straight into the hall; an appearance produced, he the next instant saw, by the fact that
the vestibule gaped wide, that the hinged halves of the
inner door had been thrown far back. Out of that again the
question sprang at him, making his eyes, as he felt, half-
start from his head, as they had done, at the top of the
house, before the sign of the other door. If he had left that
one open, hadn't he left this one closed, and wasn't he now
in *most* immediate presence of some inconceivable occult
activity? It was as sharp, the question, as a knife in his
side, but the answer hung fire still and seemed to lose itself
in the vague darkness to which the thin admitted dawn,
glimmering archwise over the whole outer door, made a
semicircular margin, a cold silvery nimbus that seemed to
play a little as he looked—to shift and expand and contract.

It was as if there had been something within it, protected
by indistinctness and corresponding in extent with the
opaque surface behind, the painted panels of the last barrier to his escape, of which the key was in his pocket. The
indistinctness mocked him even while he stared, affected
him as somehow shrouding or challenging certitude, so that
after faltering an instant on his step he let himself go with
the sense that here *was* at last something to meet, to touch,
to take, to know—something all unnatural and dreadful, but
to advance upon which was the condition for him either of
liberation or of supreme defeat. The penumbra, dense and
dark, was the virtual screen of a figure which stood in it as
still as some image erect in a niche or as some black-
vizored sentinel guarding a treasure. Brydon was to know
afterwards, was to recall and make out, the particular thing
he had believed during the rest of his descent. He saw, in
its great grey glimmering margin, the central vagueness
diminish, and he felt it to be taking the very form toward
which, for so many days, the passion of his curiosity had

yearned. It gloomed, it loomed, it was something, it was somebody, the prodigy of a personal presence.

Rigid and conscious, spectral yet human, a man of his own substance and stature waited there to measure himself with his power to dismay. This only could it be—this only till he recognised, with his advance, that what made the face dim was the pair of raised hands that covered it and in which, so far from being offered in defiance, it was buried as for dark deprecation. So Brydon, before him, took him in; with every fact of him now, in the higher light, hard and acute—his planted stillness, his vivid truth, his grizzled bent head and white masking hands, his queer actuality of evening-dress, of dangling double eye-glass, of gleaming silk lappet and white linen, of pearl button and gold watch-guard and polished shoe. No portrait by a great modern master could have presented him with more intensity, thrust him out of his frame with more art, as if there had been "treatment," of the consummate sort, in his every shade and salience. The revulsion, for our friend, had become, before he knew it, immense—this drop, in the act of apprehension, to the sense of his adversary's inscrutable manœuvre. That meaning at least, while he gaped, it offered him; for he could but gape at his other self in this other anguish, gape as a proof that *he*, standing there for the achieved, the enjoyed, the triumphant life, couldn't be faced in his triumph. Wasn't the proof in the splendid covering hands, strong and completely spread?—so spread and so intentional that, in spite of a special verity that surpassed every other, the fact that one of these hands had lost two fingers, which were reduced to stumps, as if accidentally shot away, the face was effectually guarded and saved.

"Saved," though, *would* it be?—Brydon breathed his wonder till the very impunity of his attitude and the very insistence of his eyes produced, as he felt, a sudden stir which showed the next instant as a deeper portent, while the head raised itself, the betrayal of a braver purpose. The hands, as he looked, began to move, to open; then, as if deciding in a flash, dropped from the face and left it uncovered and presented. Horror, with the sight, had leaped into Brydon's throat, gasping there in a sound he couldn't

utter; for the bared identity was too hideous as *his,* and his
glare was the passion of his protest. The face, *that* face,
Spencer Brydon's?—he searched it still, but looking away
from it in dismay and denial, falling straight from his height
of sublimity. It was unknown, inconceivable, awful, disconnected from any possibility—! He had been "sold," he in-
wardly moaned, stalking such game as this: the presence
before him was a presence, the horror within him a horror,
but the waste of his nights had been only grotesque and
the success of his adventure an irony. Such an identity fitted
his at *no* point, made its alternative monstrous. A thousand
times yes, as it came upon him nearer now—the face was
the face of a stranger. It came upon him nearer now, quite
as one of those expanding fantastic images projected by the
magic lantern of childhood; for the stranger, whoever he
might be, evil, odious, blatant, vulgar, had advanced as for
aggression, and he knew himself give ground. Then harder
pressed still, sick with the force of his shock, and falling
back as under the hot breath and the roused passion of a
life larger than his own, a rage of personality before which
his own collapsed, he felt the whole vision turn to darkness
and his very feet give way. His head went round; he was
going; he had gone.

III

What had next brought him back, clearly—though
after how long?—was Mrs. Muldoon's voice, coming to him
from quite near, from so near that he seemed presently to
see her as kneeling on the ground before him while he lay
looking up at her; himself not wholly on the ground, but
half-raised and upheld—conscious, yes, of tenderness of
support and, more particularly, of a head pillowed in extraordinary softness and faintly refreshing fragrance. He
considered, he wondered, his wit but half at his service;
then another face intervened, bending more directly over
him, and he finally knew that Alice Staverton had made
her lap an ample and perfect cushion to him, and that she
had to this end seated herself on the lowest degree of the
staircase, the rest of his long person remaining stretched on

his old black-and-white slabs. They were cold, these marble squares of his youth; but *he* somehow was not, in this rich return of consciousness—the most wonderful hour, little by little, that he had ever known, leaving him, as it did, so gratefully, so abysmally passive, and yet as with a treasure of intelligence waiting all round him for quiet appropriation; dissolved, he might call it, in the air of the place and producing the golden glow of a late autumn afternoon. He had come back, yes—come back from further away than any man but himself had ever travelled; but it was strange how with this sense what he had come back *to* seemed really the great thing, and as if his prodigious journey had been all for the sake of it. Slowly but surely his consciousness grew, his vision of his state thus completing itself: he had been miraculously *carried* back—lifted and carefully borne as from where he had been picked up, the uttermost end of an interminable grey passage. Even with this he was suffered to rest, and what had now brought him to knowledge was the break in the long mild motion.

It had brought him to knowledge, to knowledge—yes, this was the beauty of his state; which came to resemble more and more that of a man who has gone to sleep on some news of a great inheritance, and then, after dreaming it away, after profaning it with matters strange to it, has waked up again to serenity of certitude and has only to lie and watch it grow. This was the drift of his patience—that he had only to let it shine on him. He must moreover, with intermissions, still have been lifted and borne; since why and how else should he have known himself, later on, with the afternoon glow intenser, no longer at the foot of his stairs —situated as these now seemed at that dark other end of his tunnel—but on a deep window-bench of his high saloon, over which had been spread, couch-fashion, a mantle of soft stuff lined with grey fur that was familiar to his eyes and that one of his hands kept fondly feeling as for its pledge of truth. Mrs. Muldoon's face had gone, but the other, the second he had recognised, hung over him in a way that showed how he was still propped and pillowed. He took it all in, and the more he took it the more it seemed to suffice: he was as much at peace as if he had had food and drink. It was the two women who had found him, on Mrs. Muldoon's having plied, at her usual hour, her latch-key—and on her having above all arrived while Miss Staverton still lingered near the house. She had been turning away, all anxiety, from worrying the vain bell-handle—her calculation having been of the hour of the good woman's visit; but the latter, blessedly, had come up while she was still there, and they had entered together. He had then lain, beyond the vestibule, very much as he was lying now—quite, that is, as he appeared to have fallen, but all so wondrously without bruise or gash; only in a depth of stupor. What he most took in, however, at present, with the steadier clearance, was that Alice Staverton had for a long unspeakable moment not doubted he was dead.

"It must have been that I *was*." He made it out as she held him. "Yes—I can only have died. You brought me literally to life. Only," he wondered, his eyes rising to her, "only, in the name of all the benedictions, how?"

It took her but an instant to bend her face and kiss him, and something in the manner of it, and in the way her hands clasped and locked his head while he felt the cool charity and virtue of her lips, something in all this beatitude somehow answered everything. "And now I keep you," she said.

"Oh keep me, keep me!" he pleaded while her face still hung over him: in response to which it dropped again and stayed close, clingingly close. It was the seal of their situation—of which he tasted the impress for a long blissful moment in silence. But he came back. "Yet how did you know—?"

"I was uneasy. You were to have come, you remember —and you had sent no word."

"Yes, I remember—I was to have gone to you at one to-day." It caught on to their "old" life and relation—which were so near and so far. "I was still out there in my strange darkness—where was it, what was it? I must have stayed there so long." He could but wonder at the depth and the duration of his swoon.

"Since last night?" she asked with a shade of fear for her possible indiscretion.

"Since this morning—it must have been: the cold dim dawn of today. Where have I been," he vaguely wailed, "where have I been?" He felt her hold him close, and it was as if this helped him now to make in all security his mild moan. "What a long dark day!"

All in her tenderness she had waited a moment. "In the cold dim dawn?" she quavered.

But he had already gone on piecing together the parts of the whole prodigy. "As I didn't turn up you came straight—?"

She barely cast about. "I went first to your hotel—where they told me of your absence. You had dined out last evening and hadn't been back since. But they appeared to know you had been at your club."

"So you had the idea of *this*—?"

"Of what?" she asked in a moment.

"Well—of what has happened."

"I believed at least you'd have been here. I've known, all along," she said, "that you've been coming."

" 'Known' it—?"

"Well, I've believed it. I said nothing to you after that talk we had a month ago—but I felt sure. I knew you *would*," she declared.

"That I'd persist, you mean?"

"That you'd see him."

"Ah but I didn't!" cried Brydon with his long wail. "There's somebody—an awful beast; whom I brought, too horribly, to bay. But it's not me."

At this she bent over him again, and her eyes were in his eyes. "No—it's not you." And it was as if, while her face hovered, he might have made out in it, hadn't it been so near, some particular meaning blurred by a smile. "No, thank heaven," she repeated—"it's not you! Of course it wasn't to have been."

"Ah but it *was*," he gently insisted. And he stared before him now as he had been staring for so many weeks. "I was to have known myself."

"You couldn't!" she returned consolingly. And then reverting, and as if to account further for what she had herself done, "But it wasn't only *that*, that you hadn't been at home," she went on. "I waited till the hour at which we had found Mrs. Muldoon that day of my going with you; and she arrived, as I've told you, while, failing to bring any one to the door, I lingered in my despair on the steps. After a little, if she hadn't come, by such a mercy, I should have found means to hunt her up. But it wasn't," said Alice Staverton, as if once more with her fine intention—"it wasn't only that."

His eyes, as he lay, turned back to her. "What more then?"

She met it, the wonder she had stirred. "In the cold dim dawn, you say? Well, in the cold dim dawn of this morning I too saw you."

"Saw *me*—?"

"Saw *him*," said Alice Staverton. "It must have been at the same moment."

He lay an instant taking it in—as if he wished to be quite reasonable. "At the same moment?"

"Yes—in my dream again, the same one I've named to you. He came back to me. Then I knew it for a sign. He had come to you."

At this Brydon raised himself; he had to see her better. She helped him when she understood his movement, and he sat up, steadying himself beside her there on the window-bench and with his right hand grasping her left. "*He* didn't come to me."

"You came to yourself," she beautifully smiled.

"Ah I've come to myself now—thanks to you, dearest. But this brute, with his awful face—this brute's a black stranger. He's none of *me*, even as I *might* have been," Brydon sturdily declared.

But she kept the clearness that was like the breath of infallibility. "Isn't the whole point that you'd have been different?"

He almost scowled for it. "As different as *that*—?"

Her look again was more beautiful to him than the things of this world. "Haven't you exactly wanted to know *how* different? So this morning," she said, "you appeared to me."

"Like *him*?"

"A black stranger!"

"Then how did you know it was I?"

"Because, as I told you weeks ago, my mind, my imagination, had worked so over what you might, what you mightn't have been—to show you, you see, how I've thought of you. In the midst of that you came to me—that my wonder might be answered. So I knew," she went on; "and believed that, since the question held you too so fast, as you told me that day, you too would see for yourself. And when this morning I again saw I knew it would be because you had—and also then, from the first moment, because you somehow wanted me. *He* seemed to tell me of that. So why," she strangely smiled, "shouldn't I like him?"

It brought Spencer Brydon to his feet. "You 'like' that horror—?"

"I *could* have liked him. And to me," she said, "he was no horror. I had accepted him."

" 'Accepted'—?" Brydon oddly sounded.

"Before, for the interest of his difference—yes. And as *I* didn't disown him, as *I* knew him—which you at last, confronted with him in his difference, so cruelly didn't, my dear—well, he must have been, you see, less dreadful to me. And it may have pleased him that I pitied him."

She was beside him on her feet, but still holding his hand—still with her arm supporting him. But though it all brought for him thus a dim light, "You 'pitied' him?" he grudgingly, resentfully asked.

"He has been unhappy; he has been ravaged," she said.

"And haven't I been unhappy? Am not I—you've only to look at me!—ravaged?"

"Ah I don't say I like him *better*," she granted after a thought. "But he's grim, he's worn—and things have happened to him. He doesn't make shift, for sight, with your charming monocle."

"No"—it struck Brydon: "I couldn't have sported mine 'downtown.' They'd have guyed me there."

"His great convex pince-nez—I saw it, I recognised the kind—is for his poor ruined sight. And his poor right hand—!"

"Ah!" Brydon winced—whether for his proved identity or for his lost fingers. Then, "He has a million a year," he lucidly added. "But he hasn't you."

"And he isn't—no, he isn't—*you!*" she murmured as he drew her to his breast.

[1908]

BIBLIOGRAPHICAL NOTE

The details of publication given here for each story in the present volume are: (1) its serialization in case it first appeared in a periodical; (2) the book or books by Henry James in which it was first published; (3) the volume of the New York Edition of James's *Novels and Tales* (New York: Charles Scribner's Sons; London: Macmillan and Co., 1907–9) in which the tale was collected by James in the revised text here printed; and (4) the passages in James's prefaces for that edition, as now collected in *The Art of the Novel,* edited by Richard P. Blackmur [here indicated as *Prefaces*] (New York: Charles Scribner's Sons, 1934), and in *The Notebooks of Henry James,* edited by F. O. Matthiessen and Kenneth B. Murdock (New York: Oxford University Press, 1947), in which James discusses the story. The authorities on the facts of publication are *A Bibliography of the Writings of Henry James* by LeRoy Phillips (New York: Coward, McCann, second edition, 1930) and the new work, *A Bibliography of Henry James* by Leon Edel and Dan H. Laurence, in the Soho Bibliographies series (London: Rupert Hart-Davis, 1957).

"The Author of Beltraffio":

> (1) Serialized in *The English Illustrated Magazine* (London), June–July, 1884. (2) Included in *Stories Revived* by Henry James, Vol. I (London: Macmillan and Co., 1885) and in *The Author of Beltraffio* [and other tales] by Henry James (Boston: James R. Osgood and Co., 1885). (3) In the New York Edition, Vol. XVI: *The Author of Beltraffio,* etc. (4) *Prefaces,* pp. 235–36; *Notebooks,* pp. 57–59.

"Brooksmith":

> (1) First printed in *Harper's Weekly* (New York), May 2, 1891. (2) Included in *The Lesson of the Master* [and other tales] by Henry James (London and New York: Macmillan and Co., 1892). (3) In the New York Edition, Vol. XVIII: *Daisy Miller,* etc. (4) *Prefaces,* pp. 282–83; *Notebooks,* pp. 64–65, 104.

"The Altar of the Dead":

(1) Not serialized. (2) First published in *Terminations* by Henry James (New York: Harper and Bros.; London: William Heinemann, 1895). (3) In the New York Edition, Vol. XVII: *The Altar of the Dead*, etc. (4) *Prefaces*, pp. 241–47; *Notebooks*, pp. 164–67.

"The Figure in the Carpet":

(1) Serialized in *Cosmopolis* (London), January–February, 1896. (2) Included in *Embarrassments* by Henry James (London: William Heinemann; New York: Macmillan Co., 1896). (3) In the New York Edition, Vol. XV: *The Lesson of the Master*, etc. (4) *Prefaces*, pp. 227–29; *Notebooks*, pp. 220–24, 229–30.

"In the Cage":

(1) Not serialized. (2) Published as *In the Cage* by Henry James (London: Duckworth and Co.; Chicago and New York: Herbert S. Stone and Co., 1898). (3) In the New York Edition, Vol. XI: *What Maisie Knew*, etc. (4) *Prefaces*, pp. 154–58.

"Broken Wings":

(1) First printed in *The Century Magazine* (New York), December, 1900. (2) Included in *The Better Sort* by Henry James (London: Methuen and Co.; New York: Charles Scribner's Sons, 1903). (3) In the New York Edition, Vol. XVI: *The Author of Beltraffio*, etc. (4) *Prefaces*, pp. 236–37; *Notebooks*, p. 282.

"The Great Good Place":

(1) First printed in *Scribner's Magazine* (New York), January, 1900. (2) Included in *The Soft Side* by Henry James (London: Methuen and Co.; New York: Macmillan Co., 1900). (3) In the New York Edition, Vol. XVI: *The Author of Beltraffio*, etc. (4) *Prefaces*, p. 237; *Notebooks*, pp. 122–23, with no detailed discussion in either place.

"The Jolly Corner":

(1) First printed in *The English Review* (London), December, 1908. (2) First included in book form in Vol. XVII of the New York Edition: *The Altar of the Dead*, etc. (New York: Charles Scribner's Sons; London: Macmillan and Co., 1909.) (3) *Prefaces*, pp. 252–58; *Notebooks*, pp. 364,

367 (but see the general preliminary plan of *The Sense of the Past* in the *Notebooks,* pp. 361–69).

All the tales in this book follow the revised texts of the New York Edition. The orthography and punctuation used by James in that edition are also followed.